CW00957373

BROTHERS
AT ARMS

JEMIMA BRIGGES

Copyright © 2015 Jemima Brigges

The moral right of the author has been asserted.

Apart from any fair dealing for the purposes of research or private study,
or criticism or review, as permitted under the Copyright, Designs and Patents
Act 1988, this publication may only be reproduced, stored or transmitted, in
any form or by any means, with the prior permission in writing of the
publishers, or in the case of reprographic reproduction in accordance with
the terms of licences issued by the Copyright Licensing Agency. Enquiries
concerning reproduction outside those terms should be sent to the publishers.

This is a work of fiction. Any references to historical events, real people or places
are used fictitiously. Other names, characters, places and events are products
of the author's imagination and any resemblance to actual persons or
places is entirely coincidental.

Matador
9 Priory Business Park,
Wistow Road, Kibworth Beauchamp,
Leicestershire. LE8 0RX
Tel: 0116 279 2299
Email: books@troubador.co.uk
Web: www.troubador.co.uk/matador
Twitter: @matadorbooks

ISBN 978 1784624 453

British Library Cataloguing in Publication Data.
A catalogue record for this book is available from the British Library.

Typeset in 11pt Aldine by Troubador Publishing Ltd, Leicester, UK

Matador is an imprint of Troubador Publishing Ltd

To my late father, George Ernest Bradley, the youngest great-grandson

of the real Jemima Brigges (1753 – 1814)

Author's note

Whilst the historical figures are set in the context of fiction, the reputation of Thomas William Coke, as one of the significant personalities of the Agricultural Revolution is fact. Everyone knows of the Napoleonic Wars, but few remember the farmers who kept the people of England fed in those difficult times.

I have no idea whether such an innovative thinker as 'Mr Coke of Norfolk' had students of agriculture on his Norfolk estate, but the notion fitted the section of my story to which it relates so well, that I hope historians will forgive my literary fantasy.

PART 1

BROTHERS AT ARMS

(1794 -1801)

CHAPTER 1

Whereas most people who approached the porticoed entrance of No 20 Cavendish Square had to wait for admittance, it was evident from the speed in which the glossy black door opened that the tall gentleman who stepped out of the hackney carriage was expected.

"Is Mrs Pontesbury in, Brockley?" he said to the butler, his tone curt.

"Yes, sir," the man replied, as he handed the gentleman's hat, coat and gloves to the first footman. "She is in the drawing room, and asked that you join her."

Tom Norbery nodded and made his way up the long sweep of the elegant marble staircase of his sister's town house. Not so quickly as to imply a hurry, but brisk enough to be business-like. That was his intention. The servants would all know of the letter that arrived a few hours ago, which his sister immediately dispatched to his office in the hallowed portals of the House of Commons. Tom had read the contents and returned home as soon as his commitments allowed.

Now Winifred would want to know the contents, and no doubt, Brockley would bring refreshments, hopeful of gleaning news. Well, he would know soon enough.

At the top of the stairs, a footman opened the door for Tom to enter. His sister stood by the sash window, looking down into the street, but turned at his approach and waited until the servant had closed the door before speaking.

In that moment the family likeness was particularly marked. Mrs Pontesbury was a tall woman with the same aquiline profile and fair hair as her brother, expensively dressed in the latest fashion, as befitting one of the leaders of polite society.

"Tom, the letter from Linmore…" she said. "Is it about Kate?"

That was everyone's assumption. Kate; the wife he had never brought to London, whose very existence was shrouded in secrecy – but better that than have people know the truth. The society in which he lived loved a scandal, but his marriage was so bizarre as to beggar belief.

"No, not this time," he said, "but it means that I have to go home tonight. I'll take the night mail to Hereford."

She looked at him in disbelief, but was prevented from answering by a discreet knock on the door, which heralded the butler's appearance, followed by his minions carrying a tea tray. Tom would have preferred something stronger, but the tradition of afternoon tea could not be overborne.

As soon as it was poured, Winifred imperiously waved the servants aside, and the butler left the room in his unhurried way. No doubt to stand outside the door, to be ready for his mistress's next command and ensure that his minions did not listen at keyholes.

"If it is not about Kate, what did Jane say to provoke such a response? It is ridiculous. You simply cannot go."

Tom could understand his sister's incredulity, but it made no difference.

"She told me about a letter that she had received from a family connection of her cousin in Ireland. I only know as much of it as she related to me."

He took a folded sheet of paper from an inner pocket and showed her the contents. Although the letter was sent in haste, Jane's tone was calm.

I don't know what is happening in Dublin, but Charlotte's children have need of me. They have no one else. Don't worry, Tom; I will be quite safe.

Tom Norbery's first reaction was to forbid it. He could not allow Jane to travel alone, for she held his home together. If anyone went to Ireland, it should be him.

Never had he felt the distance from home more than now. With Parliament in session, he was in London, while Jane was at Linmore Hall, in Shropshire – one hundred and thirty miles away, according to the old country saying *as the crow flies*.

Birds might fly in a straight line, but not even the Romans built roads so direct.

The knowledge that Jane needed him made the acrimony and petty squabbles between politicians debating the Poor Laws and the war in Europe seem insignificant. Politics could wait, for his voice and others on the Whig benches made little impression while his Majesty favoured the Tories.

4

For a man slow to anger, and who never acted on impulse, Tom did just that, and had broached the subject of leave with Mr Fox, the Whig Party leader.

"A problem at home, Norbery?" his colleague said, in a voice of concern. "Something relating to your wife's health, I presume? Of course, you must go."

Before Tom could utter a word of thanks, Fox continued in a cynical tone, "I daresay the aftermath of today's debate will rumble on without agreement until the summer recess. It is, after all, only a couple of weeks away, and neither our honourable friend, Pitt nor his colleagues are likely to agree to the amendments we suggested. If anyone should remark your absence, I will simply pose another question for them to answer. That should keep them busy."

They laughed together, for everyone knew Charles Fox was the most brilliant orator on the Whig benches, and a permanent thorn in the Prime Minister's side.

Tom did not elaborate. Few people knew the truth about Kate's health problems, and the melancholia that followed her last delivery covered many things. It served him now. He was free to leave London.

Winifred refolded the paper, a troubled frown on her face.

"But how can you take leave when the House is in session?" she said.

"Charles Fox was with me when I received the letter," he said. "I wouldn't have told anyone else, but when I mentioned a problem at home, he assumed it related to Kate. I did not disabuse him of the notion."

"Why the mail coach, Tom?" She grumbled. "It is ridiculous. If you must go, then take our coach and travel in comfort. Pontesbury will insist on it."

Tom knew that she spoke the truth about her husband's kindly nature. It wasn't every gentleman who would house his brother-in-law without complaint, for months on end every year, thus rendering the need for separate accommodation unnecessary. Living with them was the only thing that made London bearable.

"Because this is one occasion when I need speed, not comfort, Winifred. Can you imagine me urging your coachman to *spring the horses, or to put 'em along?*"

"No, of course not, for Pontesbury never allows him to do any such thing, but you must know that living in Town is different to the country,"

5

she said with a sigh. "I used to love to drive fast. Do you remember the wild curricle races we had with Jack in the park at Linmore? They were such fun…" Her voice broke. "I do so miss him… even now."

Tom felt similarly choked, as he provided her with a clean handkerchief from his pocket. "Yes," he said. "We were young and life was different. That is why I have to go home, Winifred. Our brother's daughters are all that we have left of him. Now, two more children need help, but this time they are Jane's kindred."

"I suppose that you are right." Winifred sniffed indecorously, as she struggled to compose herself. "But it would not do for Lord Cardington to hear that Kate is supposedly ill, and for his wife not to be told. The first person he will harass is me."

Tom had forgotten Jane's second sister, Clarissa.

"I think that you are well able to deal with Humphrey Cardington," he said.

"He is dreadfully arrogant, and I have often wished to give him a set down," Winifred said in the tone of one relishing the prospect. "Now, there is much to be done before this evening. I will ask Foxton to procure your ticket, and then speak with the chef. You must dine early, for I am sure you will not have more than a few minutes to obtain food whilst in transit. I must also warn the stables that the Tilbury will be needed to take you wherever it is that you board the coach."

She bustled away, calling for her husband's secretary.

At seven o'clock, Tom was in Holborn, waiting to board the mail coach. Harnessed behind a team of four thoroughbred horses, its distinctive maroon door and lower panels contrasted effectively with its black upper panels, to create a mobile badge of office on four red wheels.

Undoubtedly the fastest means of transport in the country, the mail coach had priority over other vehicles on the road, but unlike the common stage, there was room only for four passengers who paid a premium rate for the privilege.

Standing slightly apart from the folk milling around, Tom Norbery looked what he was: a man of means, quiet and unassuming, gentle in the true sense. A tall man, not yet forty years of age, the excellence of his tailor did justice to a well-made form that showed no sign of stoutness. Even in repose, his aquiline profile gave him a natural hauteur, until his crooked smile came into play – but his grey eyes were sad, as if life had not been fair to him.

Had he sought rank and position, he could have acquired it by crossing the floor of the Commons to the Government benches. Things might have been different if he had the right wife by his side and the right son to inherit his country estate. Until that far off day, he would keep his integrity intact and remain Mr Norbery of Linmore.

Having placed his valise on the rack, Tom settled in a corner seat, knowing that it would be many hours before he reached his destination. He was glad of a reason to leave London before the summer heat and the smells made it untenable. At times like that, he wondered why he ever left Linmore.

As the coach set off, he raised a hand in farewell to the Pontesbury groom waiting at the roadside, and the man touched his hat in response. He had checked his gold timepiece before he left Winifred's carriage, and secured it in an inner pocket, not wishing to advertise it in his possession. One could not be too careful.

There were three other male passengers of varying ages and walks of life – all similarly anonymous. They said little and for that Tom was grateful.

While others dozed around him, he remained awake until the coach had safely crossed Hampstead Heath, and then let the swaying vehicle lull him to sleep. When daybreak came, he saw the Cotswold countryside through a mizzling rain that gradually cleared the further west they travelled.

Conditions were cramped and the only stops permitted were for essential needs. A regular change of horses was achieved in minutes, and likewise the dropping off of mail at postal collecting houses in Oxford and Gloucester, where relief drivers took their turn at holding the reins. Then they were on their way again, thundering along the toll roads, with the guard blowing the horn to warn tollhouse keepers of their approach. Obtaining food was of secondary consideration.

Tom was the only one of the original passengers to step down from the coach in Hereford the following evening. He felt bone tired, hungry and in dire need of a wash. But the knowledge that he was still thirty miles away from Linmore made him offer twice the normal charges to the postillions of a light travelling coach. Three teams of fresh horses later, the distant view of Linmore Hill in the glow of the setting sun brought tears to his eyes. He was almost home.

The clock over the stables was chiming the hour of eleven when the hired coach, drawn by a team of four sweating horses, galloped up the long drive to Linmore Hall and came to a halt in front of the entrance. The groom climbed down from the box to lower the steps for his passenger to alight, and then reached into the interior for the gentleman's valise, which he placed on the floor at his feet. A coin changed hands and within minutes, the coach had gone.

Tom Norbery looked thankfully towards the welcoming glow of light in the reception hall as one of the footmen opened the front door to peer outside.

"Good evening, Hayton," he said. "Is Miss Littlemore still downstairs?"

"Oh my goodness, it's Mr Norbery," the man said to someone unseen over his shoulder, and then turned back. "We didn't expect to see you tonight, sir."

Having thoroughly confused the footman by his appearance, Tom was removing his travelling coat when his sister-in-law emerged from the library.

At the sight of him, she looked astonished. "Tom," she said. "How can you be here so quickly, when you must only just have received my letter?"

He smiled, delighted by Jane's surprise. Surely she must know he would come when she needed his help. "It arrived early yesterday afternoon; but rather than send a reply, I caught the overnight mail coach to Hereford."

"Oh, Tom, you should not," she said, her eyes moist. "There was no need for such haste."

He caught her hand and raised it to his lips in greeting.

"There was every need," he said. "I was afraid you would set off without me."

"Yes," she said, gripping his fingers. "The thought did occur to me, but then I realised how foolish it would be to write, and not wait for your response. I didn't expect you to rush home." She shook her head in disbelief. "Have you eaten, or would you like supper? The fire is still lit in the library."

He gave a yawn and stretched his aching limbs.

"I forget what time we stopped to eat, but I think I could manage some bread, cheese and ham, or something similar." In fact, he was ravenous.

"Cuthbert," she called to the footman. "Please bring a tray to the library for Mr Norbery."

"Yes, Miss Littlemore. I'll be as quick as I can," the young man said, eager to oblige.

"Don't rush, Hayton," said Tom. "I need to wash my hands and face first."

Ten minutes later, he entered the library to find a side table, ready prepared with food, set on one side of the fire, next to his chair. Jane waved away the servants who would have stopped to assist, and when the door closed, she moved forward to receive the greeting that Tom saved for the privacy of his favourite room.

"I'm glad you're home," she said, returning his embrace. "I didn't know what else to do but send for you when I received the letter."

"Who else has the right and the duty to help you?"

"No one," she said with a special smile she reserved for him. Then she filled his plate with a selection of foods. Cold ham, freshly sliced from the bone, a portion of homemade Shropshire cheese, and a crust of bread liberally spread with creamy butter.

"Thank you, my dear," he said. "That looks delicious, and more so because you prepared it. Now, I can see you are bursting to tell me the news, so if you wish to unburden yourself whilst I eat, I am happy to listen."

Instead, Jane poured a tankard of ale and set it at his right hand, before returning to her seat opposite him by the fire.

Between mouthfuls, Tom watched as she picked up a folded sheet of parchment. He knew she would not interrupt while he was eating, unless he spoke first. "Is that the letter of which you spoke? Why don't you tell me the contents?"

She gave a sigh, nodded and began to speak.

"It's from Lucius Cobarne, who was brother-in-law to my cousin, Charlotte Littlemore. He tells me that his brother, Fergus, died in action three years ago, but it seems that the gentleman has had the care of the children since then. Now, for some reason he demands that I take charge of them. He does not say why, or for how long. Just, come and collect them from Ireland with all urgency."

Tom remembered Jane's excitement when her cousin and dearest childhood friend married the young army officer; and of her joy when they asked her to be godmother to their firstborn, a son named Charlie. In the event, heavy winter weather prevented her visit, so an Irish sister-in-law stood proxy for her.

"Didn't you tell me that Charlotte died in childbirth?"

It was not an uncommon occurrence.

"Yes, five or six years ago," she said in a whisper. "From her letters, she seemed to be in a permanent state of pregnancy, but only two babies survived."

When Tom finished eating, he dabbed his lips with the table napkin, and set it aside. Then he stood and walked to a chaise longue.

"Come, Jane, and sit by me. We can talk better here."

Irrespective of his public persona as Squire Norbery of Linmore Hall, and an elected member of parliament for South Shropshire, this was the part to which Tom looked forward, and the reason for which he had come home. Jane was his wife in all but name, whereas Kate, her older stepsister, was the woman with whom he had gone through a form of marriage, which gave her a title and rights for the two children to which she subsequently gave birth. Both favoured their mother in dark looks, but neither belonged to Tom, even though Matthew, the eldest, was assumed to be the heir to Linmore estate – a fact that irked him.

Joshua, the third child of the household was undoubtedly a Norbery. Bidding fair to be tall, he had the same golden curls that Tom had at his age; the distinctive aquiline profile, combined with smoky grey eyes and a crooked smile.

Therein was the reason why Tom could only publicly acknowledge Jane as his sister-in-law; but in his absence from Linmore, she had his full authority to run his home, while Kate lived in a separate wing of Linmore Hall. It was not an estrangement, so much as a marriage that had no legal standing, the details of which were too complicated for public knowledge.

"Mmm, that's nice," Jane said, resting her head against his shoulder.

"How old are the children?" he asked.

"Charlie is a few months older than Joshua, and Sophie, a year or two younger."

"Ten years old, and the man is casting out his own brother's son?" Tom said in disgust, knowing that he had legally adopted his late brother's daughters. The thought of children about to be abandoned justified his departure from London.

"How did you obtain leave of absence?" she said.

"Not knowing the true situation, I did not correct their assumption that Kate had another seizure. Winifred knows the truth, but no one will extract anything from her without being bitten. She is the most intimidating person of my acquaintance, and I thank God she is my sister."

Jane laughed at his comment. "I know, but for all her ferocity, Winifred has a heart of gold, and it still belongs to Linmore."

They were smiling at the thought, when a gentle click of metal caught their attention. Tom turned to the door and saw the shadowy figure of a child sidle into the room and wait hesitantly for permission to approach.

"Come in, Joshua." He stood up and opened his arms to welcome his son. The fair-haired boy ran straight into his embrace, and Tom drew him to sit down between them.

"I heard a coach coming up the drive, and wanted to see who had arrived," he said, clutching his father's hand. "I thought that I was dreaming when I heard your voice, Papa. Are you going to stay this time?"

Tom tried to lessen the disappointment he knew his son would feel.

"I have to go away again in a few days, over the sea to Ireland. When I return, I will bring two children, a boy and his sister, who are related to Aunt Jane, and I want you to help look after them."

Joshua frowned, looking from one to the other. "How old are they?" he asked, his tone wary.

"We think the boy is about your age, and his sister is younger."

He thought about it for a minute before saying, "So I will have a friend, and she can be friends with Lucy and Julia." The idea seemed to please him.

Tom knew that Joshua did not have any friends. Matthew, Kate's son, was his sworn enemy, and did everything he could to hurt the little lad, especially in their father's absence.

"Please, can I come with you to meet them, Papa?"

Seeing the look of entreaty, Tom wanted to grant his son's wish, but he could not. His intention was to travel in his phaeton with a groom, and there would not be room for anyone else, other than the children.

"I'm sorry, Joshua. Aunt Jane would love to come as well, but it's not possible." He saw the look of disappointment Joshua tried to hide.

"Never mind, Joshua," his aunt said. "I need your help to get the rooms ready for when our visitors arrive, and I'm relying on you to plan their welcome."

He looked at her and nodded a sleepy agreement. It was obvious, if Aunt Jane needed him, then he could not possibly go away and leave her.

While Jane led the way holding a lighted candlestick, Tom carried his son upstairs to the nursery corridor where Joshua slept. He was tired, and there were many plans to make before he set off to Ireland, but they could wait until tomorrow.

It was three days later before Tom was ready to embark on his errand of mercy. The first thing he did was to send a letter to inform Lucius Cobarne of his impending visit. Then he revised his intended mode of transport when Jane pointed out the difficulties of travelling with children.

"It would be impossible to drive a phaeton, and take charge of the children, with just a groom in attendance. You must take the travelling coach, and I will find someone to look after them. Apart from anything else, you are a stranger to them. Can you imagine how frightened they would be? Would you want Joshua to be in that situation?

After his recent journey home, Tom admitted that Jane's assessment of the situation was right. The Linmore coach was eminently more comfortable for travelling, and with a female along, he could relinquish care of the children to her.

"Miss Jane says we're taking Jack Kilcot's sister as nursemaid, so he'd better come along as an extra pair of hands," Dan Salter, the coachman said.

"He can come if he is prepared to look after her." Tom knew the lad was reliable from his training as a groom, and hoped the girl would be suitably adept.

In discussing the best route to take, Salter gave his opinion.

"Chester's the best place to head for, sir. From there, we can go to Liverpool, or take the mail coach route west to Bangor, and by ferry to Anglesey. The packet sails from Holyhead, when the weather allows."

Irrespective of the route, that would be the deciding factor.

"Which is the shortest distance?"

"I reckon we'd make better time to Liverpool," the coachman said. "We'll need to change horses, but if you are agreeable, sir, we can stop at a livery stable I know of just out of Chester, and collect the Linmore team on the return journey."

The following day they headed north in a travelling coach, drawn by a team of four, Linmore-bred chestnut horses. Three figures sat on the box; Dan Salter took the reins, with Hanwood the groom by his side and Jack Kilcot, in his newly appointed role as overseer to his sister's care of the children.

Mary Kilcot was already sitting in the coach when Tom climbed inside. Her brother introduced her as he closed the door.

"This is our Mary, sir. She's a good lass, and will do whatever you tell her."

Tom acknowledged the girl with a nod, and received a shy smile in response. Sensing that she might stand up to bob her knees, he waved her back to her seat.

"Now, just you remember, our wench," said her brother. "Don't you go chattering and being a nuisance to Squire Norbery, or I'll send you home again."

The girl's willingness was not in doubt. The unknown factor was her ability to travel any distance. If she could not do that, she would be a liability.

For the first few miles, Mary Kilcot huddled in the opposite corner of the coach to where Tom sat, too nervous to speak. Gradually, she relaxed and looked out of the windows, her face lit by a beatific smile. Eventually, her cheery nature got the better of her, and she could not resist exclaiming, "Ooh, this be lovely and comfy. I ain't ever been in one of these coaches before. I'm not surprised you likes travelling so much, sir. Our Jack tells me all about his travels to London."

The girl's simple assessment made Tom feel humble. She was overawed by her surroundings, whereas he was a jaded traveller who, until recently, had forgotten the simple pleasures derived from sitting in comfort. It was a salutary lesson.

In his position, he expected such things, but rarely gave it a thought. The trouble with political life was that he met too few ordinary people. Instead of being bored, this could be an interesting journey.

He lapsed into his thoughts and let the girl chatter away to herself. It was clear everything she saw fascinated her. He knew excitement could turn an inexperienced traveller's stomach. Apprehension was even worse, particularly when aggravated by the swaying of a coach and four at full gallop.

The coachman followed his normal practice when travelling, and made regular breaks to water the horses. After three hours, the party stopped for refreshments.

Mary sat down to enjoy her plate of crusty bread, cheese and pickles. "This travelling is thirsty work," the girl exclaimed, as she drained a tankard of ale.

Tom heard her comment, and smiled. He had cause to remember it again when she returned to her seat. He expected her to settle down to sleep, but instead, she started to moan. Recognising the portent, he hammered on the roof of the coach with his cane. The groom peered inside almost before the vehicle stopped.

"Kilcot," he said. "Your sister needs fresh air. Take her outside."

Hardly had the girl left the coach when he heard sounds outside as she gained relief. It was not a minute too soon.

When they returned, Kilcot said, "I'm sorry about that, sir. I'll take our Mary up on the box for a while."

Tom felt sorry for the girl, but knew she would learn more from her dietary indiscretion than any amount of telling in advance. It was better it happened now, and with any luck, she would be all right for the rest of the journey.

At the next stop to water the horses, Mary Kilcot returned to the coach looking windswept and flushed. "Oh, that was nice, sir. I felt better once I could see where we was going." Then she confided, "It wasn't the cheese what upset me, sir, it was the pickled onions. I parted company with them, so my innards will be all right now."

"Splendid," he said, cutting short any other confidences about the inner workings of her system, and signalled to the coachman to resume the journey.

They stayed the first night at a hostelry called the Cheshire Arms, and set off the following day with fresh horses, heading for Liverpool, intending to collect the Linmore team on their return.

When they resumed the journey, Mary Kilcot said, "An ordinary bed would have done for me and Jack, sir. I came here to work, sir, not sleep in luxury. Do you know, the chambermaid told me they changed the sheets only last week?"

Tom hoped the landlady had replaced his bed linen more recently.

He closed his eyes, and thought about the differences between the two half-sisters who occupied his home. Each had a different mother and father. The merest chance made them related, when James Littlemore married a widow with a young daughter. Jane's mother was the man's second wife.

Even as a young man, Tom had known his own mind. Jane was the only woman he had ever loved. He had never wished to marry a bad-tempered woman five years older than he, but circumstances at the time forced him to comply.

Later, his father claimed not to know of the bad blood in the Strettons of Norcott Abbey, but he should have. It was something for which Tom never forgave him – not even on his deathbed.

Tom knew that the next phase of the journey depended on whether fortune and a prevailing wind were with them. If all went well, and the sea crossings were favourable, he might complete his business within five days. They were lucky. On reaching Liverpool, he learned the squally weather in the Irish Sea had moderated sufficiently to enable the packet to Dublin to sail on the morning tide.

To his relief, sufficient berths were available and there were few delays with embarkation. Soon, he was standing on deck, with his entourage by his side, all suitably clad against the elements. The long hooded cloak was the latest thing to meet with Mary Kilcot's approval.

A brisk wind filled the sails as the craft slipped its moorings and moved out into the main shipping lane. Tom felt the swell of the waves beneath the boat, and braced himself to steady his balance.

For a time, he watched the wake of the boat as the port of Liverpool receded into the mist. He revelled in the smell of seawater in the wind as he drew the collar of his greatcoat under his chin, and lowered his hat against the lash of the freshening breeze. He hoped Mary Kilcot would not suffer mal de mer, but there was no alternative now. She would have to be capable of looking after the children when the time came.

Feeling the need to rest, Tom retired to his berth. Having taken an early breakfast, he needed little sustenance during the crossing. He was glad he had reserved two cabins. The young woman's presence complicated the matter, but she was happy to share with her brother, while Dan Salter, the coachman acted as valet, and rested in a chair in the corner of his room. Hanwood, the groom, was left in Liverpool with the Linmore coach to await their return.

His first view of the Irish coast was marred by a thick bank of fog, which slowed their approaches to land. By the time, the clouds cleared, and the quay at Poolbeg came into sight, they were standing on deck waiting to disembark.

From there, Tom and his servants travelled to the lodgings in Great George's Street, where Philip Penn his secretary had reserved rooms with a private parlour. Normally, he would have stayed at Gresham's Hotel, but considered a smaller establishment more discreet for the family business he wished to conduct. Fewer people would see him.

It was too late in the day to set out for the Cobarne household, so he sent word of his arrival, announcing his intention to visit Blackrock the following morning. Then he requested a bath be prepared, changed his travelling clothes and dined alone with his servants waiting at table. After which, he retired to bed.

Morning could not come soon enough. He wanted to collect the children and be on his way again. He was not looking forward to the forthcoming meeting with the adults.

CHAPTER 2

The following day was quiet, with little traffic on the roads. The fresh winds had eased and left a dry spell with an almost cloudless sky.

As they left Dublin behind, Tom sat back against the worn squabs of the hired coach and surveyed the surrounding landscape. It was a pretty land, yet the contrasts were stark. When he looked out towards the Dublin Mountains, he saw several fine mansions built on the hillsides for the Protestant landowners, but poverty was all too apparent in the dreary villages through which he passed.

The road to the coast was surprisingly good, an indication of the rise in Blackrock's seaside popularity, but the surrounding countryside belonged to another era. It was evident from the strips of common land that the agricultural changes prevalent in England had not reached these parts. There was not an enclosure in sight.

By half-past eleven, Tom was within sight of his destination. His mood should have been benign, but it was not, any more than the directions he obtained in the hotel were foolproof. They might have been to someone familiar with the locality, but not to a stranger.

He did not blame Salter for taking a wrong turning, which led to an isolated farm. By the time they realised the error, there was nowhere to turn the coach until they reached the farmyard.

Then they had difficulty communicating with a farmer's boy who spoke an unfamiliar language. Neither one understood the other until the coachman mentioned the lawyer's name. From the boy's willing demeanour, Tom deduced that Lucius Cobarne was well known in the district, and made sure the lad knew he would be rewarded for his help.

Probably a shilling would have sufficed, but half-a-crown got a better response and a ready smile when the boy walked back along the farm track to show them the road they should take – a hundred yards further on towards Blackrock. It was worth it to be on his way again.

In truth, he would have paid twice the amount for the extra knowledge he gained. For the first time, he realised travelling might not be the greatest problem the children would have to overcome. He had never considered the possibility they might not speak the same language.

At the outskirts to Blackrock village, Jack Kilcot came to the window, and pointed down the road. "Mr Salter said he thought the house up ahead set back from the road should be the one, sir."

When Tom stepped down from the coach, he looked beyond the house to where the road stopped and the seashore began. He saw the crests of the waves, a hint of aquamarine stretching out to the horizon, and could smell salt in the wind.

He took a deep breath in, and slowly exhaled. It was wonderful. Joshua would have loved to be here. Why, oh why, was Cobarne sending two children away from this place? Did they go down to the sea to paddle? It could not be more than half a mile at most.

"Thank you, Daniel, I enjoyed that," Tom said as he returned to his seat "Now we had better go on our way."

Within minutes, the coach passed through a pair of black-painted ornamental gates, along a sweeping gravelled driveway towards a three-storey, stone-built house, with white-painted sash windows, and came to a halt before a black-panelled door with curved fanlight over.

Kilcot let down the steps, and Tom approached the door to beat a tattoo on the highly polished brass doorknocker. Several minutes passed before he heard the sound of shuffling footsteps. Then the door opened a few inches, and a reedy male voice quavered, "Yes, what d'you want?"

Tom stepped forward, expecting the door to open further, but it refused to yield.

"My name is Norbery," he said, proffering his calling card through the crack in the door. "I have an appointment to see Mr Lucius Cobarne."

It was difficult to communicate with a person hidden behind a block of wood. Apart from the wheezy breath, there was little to indicate the age of the servant. The man's voice sounded old, much as the wizened brown hand appeared to be.

"The master's not here now," the owner of the rasping voice said as he started to close the door.

Anticipating the move, Tom leaned on the door, forcing it to remain ajar. The surly reception did not augur well for the meeting ahead if the servants looked askance when a gentleman presented on the doorstep.

"I would be obliged if you would tell Mrs Cobarne that Squire Norbery of Linmore has come from England to see her husband, in response to his letter to Miss Jane Littlemore," Tom said in his crispest tone. It was not his habit to puff off his position, but if there was a time, this was it.

"Who is it, Patrick?" a snappy female voice came from beyond the hallway.

Tom looked in the direction of the sound. "Thomas Norbery, Mrs Cobarne. I apologise for my late arrival, but the directions I was given were unclear and I had difficulty in finding your location."

"My husband is not in the house at present," the woman said. "Can you come back later?"

"Regrettably no, madam," he said. "I have come at his behest. If he is not here, I would be obliged if you could tell me where I can find him?"

There was a brief silence. Then she said in an ungracious tone, "He is in his office in the village. I will have to send the servant to tell him of your arrival. You'd better come in and wait."

He turned back towards the coach, and addressed Salter. "It looks as if I may be some little time. Apparently the gentleman was called to his office."

There was nothing for it, but to wait until Cobarne deigned to appear. As he turned back towards the door, Tom sensed he was being watched, and looked up to a little window high on the upper floor. There were two dark heads huddled together, looking in his direction, but they passed from view as he entered the hallway.

His first impression was of a well-ordered household, the scent of lavender polish with beeswax, and the absence of dust – clearly, a sign of conscientious workers.

The rich mahogany staircase and door surrounds drew his attention. There were many fine examples in England, but he had not expected to see them here. Mr Cobarne was evidently a man of means. His house might look deceptively plain on the outside, but the interior had quality fittings.

Having been obliged to admit him, the manservant led Tom past the open door of what he presumed was a drawing room, with an inlaid marble fire surround, and on to a sparsely furnished parlour, where the mistress of the house awaited him.

When he saw Mrs Cobarne, he understood why she did not receive him in the formal reception rooms. He had seen too many housekeepers not to know the parlour was her milieu.

Maybe that was what she had once been. She was disapproval personified in a shell of puffed-up self-importance. Her black silk gown, white cap and a fichu of the finest lace spoke of wealth, but her demeanour screamed of an upper servant worshipping on the altar of respectability.

If only Jane could have been with him. She would have known what to say to a miserable-looking woman, clad in silk, instead of the bombazine he assumed she had worn before. It was difficult to know if her dyspeptic expression denoted pain, or whether her tightly braided pepper-grey hair was responsible; and every so often, she un-pinched her mouth, giving the impression of ill-fitting teeth.

Normally, he could talk to anyone, but Mrs Cobarne made the simplest statement hard work as their conversation limped between the state of the weather and his sea crossing. Then there was a lull.

Conversing with her was almost as bad as trying to talk with his wife. When he spoke, Kate invariably responded in monosyllables, if he was lucky. More often than not, she ignored him.

Before he could ask if he could see the children, the servant shuffled into the room to announce that the master would return directly, and disappeared to the back of the house.

Mrs Cobarne's courtesy extended to offering him a seat, but she did not provide refreshment. Fortunately, her husband entered the room before Tom was obliged to seek a new topic of conversation.

Lucius Cobarne's appearance came as a surprise. With the precise letter to Jane in mind, Tom expected to see a dapper little man with a spare frame. Instead, the lawyer was of medium height and solid build.

Despite his air of pomposity, the man looked ill at ease. He was meticulously dressed for business in formal black tailcoat and breeches, with a dark grey waistcoat and crisp white neckcloth, tied in the plainest style. Even his bushy black hair, streaked with grey at the temples, echoed his sombre attire, as did his faded dark eyes peering myopically through wire spectacles.

Tom stood up at his entrance. "Good day to you, sir," he said. "The name is Norbery, and I have come in response to your letter about the children."

Cobarne cast an anxious glance towards his wife before replying in a ponderous tone, "I presume you refer to the letter I sent to my late sister-in-law's cousin, Mr Norbery."

Tom supposed it was natural for a lawyer to be pedantic about details, but this was ridiculous. "Indeed," he said. "To Miss Jane Littlemore, my… sister-in-law." Frustration made him hesitate. "I am here as her representative to collect the children."

"Of course, Mr Norbery, but you must understand my concern. I could not reconcile it with my conscience if I did not assure myself that I was letting my late brother's children go to a good home."

The hypocrisy was more than Norbery of Linmore could tolerate. He looked down from his superior height and said, "If you expected Miss Littlemore to supply references, sir, you should have made it clear when you instigated this matter."

He had not intended saying anything about his political connections, but this was too much. "I trust my word as a gentleman and member of the English Parliament will be sufficient to convince you that I have the means to provide for their comfort. They will become part of my family, and be educated with my children."

The woman sat rigid in her seat, but the man was clearly labouring under some deep emotion. Maybe it was guilt.

"Mr Norbery," he said. "When my brother, Fergus, was killed three years ago, we took his children into our home. We do not have any family of our own, but my wife and I tried to give them the care they required. I think we succeeded with the boy. Charlie is intelligent and obedient. Sophie, his sister, is wilful, and does not take kindly to instruction. We were forced to send her to a convent several miles away to be educated by the nuns, but I regret to say she caused considerable disruption."

Tom waited to hear the magnitude of the little girl's crime.

"She ran away, repeatedly. Climbed over the garden walls and disappeared for weeks at a time." The man's face was puce with the effort of containing his agitation. "They found her up in the hills, living with gypsies – not once, but several times."

So that was the reason for the abandonment. Sophie caused embarrassment.

Mrs Cobarne interrupted in a voice trembling with indignation.

"We were mortified when the nuns said she must leave. It meant everyone in the district knew my husband's niece was possessed of a devil."

"A devil, ma'am…?" Tom turned his attention to the woman. He had never favoured the use of a quizzing glass to imply disdain, but was sorely tempted now. "Surely, she is but a child, of… how many years?"

"Eight years," Cobarne said, almost in tears. "My wife mistakes the matter, sir. My late brother was full of devilment as a boy, but he learned discipline in the army. The girl has some of his nature in her."

Tom viewed the man with disbelief.

"As his daughter, it would be surprising if she did not. Maybe she needs the company of other children. She will have the opportunity at Linmore. I have three of my own and the two daughters of my late brother in my care. Joshua, my younger son, is Charlie's age, and the little girls are of a similar age to Sophie."

The man nodded. "If you would care to come to my book room, Mr Norbery, I would like to discuss the business arrangements of the transfer."

Obviously, that meant financial matters.

When the library door closed, Lucius Cobarne said, "I am loath to admit this to a stranger, Mr Norbery, but my brother, Fergus, was improvident with money. I do not know how he and his wife managed their finances whilst they were alive, but when she passed away, I believe my brother went mad with grief. He doted on the children, but made no provision for their future. In truth, they have nothing to look forward to, other than what I choose to leave them."

He shuffled some papers on his desk. "Business is difficult at present, but in the future, I hope there may be some small amount left for them."

It was clear the man was more concerned with having to pay for their keep.

"Mr Cobarne," said Tom. "Irrespective of what you do, or do not give them, you have my word that I will provide for their future. They will lack for nothing."

A look of abject relief spread across the troubled face before him.

"Good," the man said. "Would you be prepared to sign a document to that effect? I have one here, if you care to peruse it before you meet the children."

Of course, he might have expected a lawyer to think of that. Tom's antipathy was increasing by the minute. He glanced at the document, but was not prepared to put his signature to anything at such short notice.

"I think it only fair to meet the children first. No doubt this… piece of paper will be in order, but I would like to study it in detail."

The lawyer had no choice but to agree.

Charlie entered the room first, tightly clutching his sister's hand. He was clean, tidy and undoubtedly terrified. It was obvious from his dark brooding eyes, and the way his lower lip jutted beneath his gritted teeth. He was so tense, even his wavy hair occasionally seemed to ripple as he trembled.

Sophie was everything her prissy aunt was not, and for a moment, Tom wanted to laugh, because she reminded him of a gypsy girl he once saw at a Norcott horse fair. Someone had obviously tried to control her appearance, but no amount of scraping her hair into tight braids would change the picture. The weeks she lived with the gypsies had left their mark, but only time would tell whether the nuns had similarly influenced her.

Dressed entirely in black from neck to ankles, her podgy little frame and lank dark hair presented an almost repellent picture. Then he thought about the female company to which she was accustomed, and understood why her mouth was sullen.

He noticed her shifty black eyes flickering from face to face. When her fierce gaze alighted on her uncle, he recoiled. The man's reaction made Tom pity this strange little girl. Having heard the complaints about Sophie, he could understand Charlie's anxiety.

This then, was the little girl who discomfited the family, and harassed the nuns. Without doubt, she was as different to the dainty little girls at Linmore as it was possible to be. He could imagine she might be a rebel, but hardly the devil they accused her of being.

"Charlie," his uncle said, "this gentleman is Mr Norbery. He has come from England."

The boy's expression intensified as he extended a rigid hand. "I'm honoured to meet you, sir," he said, and promptly turned aside as his sister tugged at his sleeve.

Tom felt the scrutiny of those dark eyes as the little girl stepped forward. She looked from him to her uncle and back again. Then she shrugged her shoulders and nodded. He wondered if it meant he met with her approval.

Having made her assessment, Sophie wandered over to the window, climbed on a chair and surveyed the waiting coach. Her brother did not take his eyes off her until she returned to his side.

23

The girl glanced at her uncle and yawned. She did not say a word, but Charlie seemed to understand her meaning.

"Sophie wants to know if we are going with you today, sir."

"That is yet to be decided," Tom said. "There are matters I have to discuss with your uncle first."

"We'll be ready when you are, sir. Come on, Sophie, you'll have to get your coat." The boy's eagerness to leave surprised him.

The children did not wait for permission. They dashed from the room and Tom heard their footsteps clattering up the staircase. He looked from Lucius Cobarne to the pathetic piece of paper in his hand. It was in legalese, but he understood enough to know it held no surprises.

One thing was evident. The financial responsibility was his, and on his acceptance, the children would likewise be in his care, subject only to the addition of Jane's name on the document.

He felt an overwhelming sense of disgust against Cobarne for abdicating his duty to his dead brother's children. Cold logic told him that he should make the man wait for his signature – but in his heart, Tom knew he was committed, irrespective of the repercussions.

Selecting a quill from the desk, he dipped it in the inkwell and scribed his name with a flourish, *Thomas Norbery, Esquire.* Then he added, *Representing Miss Jane Littlemore, Linmore Hall, England.*

The lawyer looked bemused as he received the paper.

"I presume that was what you intended, Cobarne?" Tom felt he had regained the moral high ground. He did not want to stay with these parsimonious people. "I trust you will send a copy of this paper to my man of business. I will give you his directions."

"May I offer you refreshment, sir?" Cobarne belatedly remembered his manners.

"Thank you, no," Tom said. "It would appear the children have decided to come with me today. In which case, I think we should return to Dublin and make reservations for the morning crossing to Liverpool. To save time, I will instruct my grooms to assist with carrying the cases."

Within half an hour, the children stood waiting in the hallway to make their farewells. The moment Charlie shook his uncle's hand almost proved his undoing. If the boy had not been clutching his sister's arm, he would have broken down in tears, and the uncle was scarcely less controlled.

Tom did not particularly like Lucius Cobarne, but he could see the man felt some affection for the boy. The woman showed no trace of emotion. Neither did the little girl.

He was glad it was time to leave. He did not know how he would get on with the children, but so far, they seemed to have accepted him. Now he must take them home to Linmore.

CHAPTER 3

"Please, sir, will we soon be at Linmore? Sophie is tired."

It was obvious she was not the only one, but nothing would persuade Charlie to admit to such weakness. Squire Norbery looked at the boy's determined face, almost grey with fatigue, and thought of the courageous way he had supported his sister from the time they entered the coach. He had not moved his arm once from around her shoulders or loosened his grip on her hand.

Each one coped differently with the sea crossing. While Charlie was deeply engrossed in his responsibilities, Sophie became animated. It was the first time Tom had seen her smile. She clapped her hands and laughed at the waves lashing against the sides of the boat, as if daring them to do their worst. Her eyes shone as the wind blew back the hood of her cape and splashed her hair with spray, but she uttered not a word to him.

When they went below to their berths, Charlie accepted Jack Kilcot's offer of assistance, but Sophie ignored the girl who came to help her. She was still wearing the same clothes in which she left Blackrock, and when they sat down on their bunk, curled up alongside her brother.

She was still asleep when they reached Liverpool. With no way of judging her reaction on waking, Tom carried her from the ship to the waiting coach. Fortunately, she did not stir.

Once away from the port, they headed through the countryside towards the Cheshire inn and livery stables where they had left the Linmore coach horses. So far, caring for the children presented few problems. Charlie informed Mary Kilcot of his sister's needs and the maid complied with his requests.

The first time Charlie asked the distance, Tom said, "All being well, we should be home within a couple of days."

He could not blame the boy for wanting to know, but it was easier to say that, and let them be surprised if they arrived earlier. It was important for them to know they could trust his word.

Charlie accepted what he said. Tom thought it was better to let them grow accustomed to his presence than overwhelm them with talking. He was glad of the chance to rest, and relieved to be going home. Luckily, the children slept most of the way to the inn and then awoke, ready to eat.

He was right in thinking Sophie was not like other girls. She had no notion of decorum, table manners, or being clean. She refused to use cutlery to eat. Fingers came first and last with holding meat, dipping bread in gravy, and wiping the drips from her chin.

Mary Kilcot tutted with disapproval, but Tom shook his head and reached for a finger bowl. Charlie did likewise, drawing Sophie's attention as he rinsed his hands in the water and dried them on a cotton cloth. He bent his head close to his sister, and then requested, "Clean water, if you please, Mary, for Sophie."

While the rain beat down outside, Tom Norbery waited with his charges and servants under the wooden veranda covering the back door to the inn. Sophie was engrossed, watching Salter bring out the team of Linmore horses harnessed to the coach. Suddenly, she dashed forward onto the damp cobblestones of the courtyard amongst the bustle of shouting ostlers, travellers and conveyances.

Charlie leapt forward and pulled her back. "No, Sophie," he said. "You can look at the horses later."

She made no demur when he propelled her towards the waiting coach, but once inside, peered through the rain-splattered window and started to make a strange warbling sound.

"Is she all right?" Tom wondered what was happening.

Charlie sighed contentedly, and nodded. "Yes, sir," he said. "Sophie only sings when she is happy. It does not happen often, but it is a good sign. It was seeing the horses."

The thought brought a lump to Tom's throat. "In that case, I hope she will be happy at Linmore. We have many horses there."

It was not his only hope. He wanted them to find peace and the security of knowing they were wanted. He still felt anger on the children's behalf for the way their uncle discharged his obligations, but it was something to which Lucius Cobarne would have to come to terms.

If truth be told, Tom did not know how best to prepare the children for what lay ahead. If he advertised the size of Linmore Hall, with the servants, it sounded like a boast, and yet they needed to know what to expect. He had his suspicions about their uncle's establishment, but that was all they were – his assumptions; how to discover the truth, though, he did not know.

In the event, Mary Kilcot was instrumental in his discovery, when she clambered into the coach after a break in their journey.

"Come over here, young Sophie," the nursemaid said. "Let us girls sit together."

He knew the girl intended to be friendly, but instead of complying, Sophie scowled and edged closer to her brother, leaving Charlie to explain.

"I'm afraid she isn't used to girls. Uncle Lucius only employed older women as domestic servants. Aunt Barleycorn said the young ones were lazy."

"Aunt…Barleycorn? I thought your uncle's wife was Matilda." That was what Jane told him.

"Yes, sir." Charlie flushed with embarrassment. "Aunt Tilda was his wife. She was there when we first went to live with them, but after she died, the year before last, he married the housekeeper."

"I see," said Tom, and he did understand. Unless the woman was the lawyer's mistress, he probably did it to save paying wages.

"The trouble is, sir, although Barleycorn dresses in new clothes, she hasn't the way to be a real lady, like Aunt Tilda."

"Did you call her by that name?"

"Only between us, sir," said Charlie. "I tried to be polite, but Sophie didn't call her anything, because Barl… they… sent her away to the nuns for her schooling."

Tom nodded. He had heard the outcome of that from the adults.

"How should we address you, sir?"

"I'd be happy if you called me Uncle Tom."

Charlie looked puzzled. "But you're not a real uncle, like my father's brother, are you?"

"Your mother was a cousin to Aunt Jane, so it seems appropriate to me."

"Is that what we call Aunt Norbery?"

Tom wondered how best to explain the family relationships.

"No," he said. "Aunt Jane is my wife's sister. I doubt if you will see much of Mrs Norbery – she is an invalid."

Charlie turned to his sister. "Did you hear that, Sophie? Aunt Jane belongs to us."

The girl chewed it over and nodded her understanding.

"I don't wish to be rude, sir," Charlie said, "but will there be enough room for us at your home? I mean… my uncle's house was quite large."

"Lor bless me, young sir," Mary Kilcot interrupted. "Your uncle's house was nothing compared to Linmore Hall. It's a real mansion and no mistake, with acres and acres of gardens and parkland."

Tom was glad Mary explained. He could not have worded it better.

Charlie looked on with awe. "Is it really that big, sir? Do you have hundreds of servants as well?"

"Not hundreds," Tom said with a smile, "it's more like a few dozen, counting the ones who work in the gardens and stables."

"Don't forget the farm labourers, sir." Mary Kilcot added her mite.

Tom had not accounted for the many folk who owed their living to him. There were probably several hundred around the estate, if he included the servants in the agent's house as well.

After that, the children settled down to rest. Charlie asked a question or two along the way, but Tom sensed he was waiting to see the outcome of the story. That was only half the truth about life at Linmore. The rest would have to wait until they arrived.

Halfway through the third day, when Charlie posed the question again, Tom took his gold timepiece from his pocket, looked out through the window and said, "We should be there within a couple of hours, Charlie. The groom will tell us as soon as we are within sight of Linmore Hill."

At his words, Mary Kilcot started to fidget. She craned her neck to peer through the window on one side of the coach. Charlie did the same on the other, while Sophie dozed on, oblivious of her surroundings. Minutes later, the big girl grinned broadly and pointed.

"There it is, young sir. Linmore is the big hill in the middle distance. Give us half an hour and I reckon we'll be in the village."

Tom smiled at the maid's confident assertion. Travelling had broadened her horizons. He caught Charlie's eye and nodded agreement to the boy's unspoken question.

The nursemaid was almost right. The terrain became more familiar once they passed over the bridge from the eastern side of the River Linmore, near to Norcott. Half a mile further on, they joined the post road to Westbridge, but they still had six miles to travel before reaching the turn to Middlebrook, and Linmore village was a mile and a half beyond.

A few minutes later, the driver stopped the coach and the groom appeared to announce the same message.

"I saw it first," Mary said, grinning at her brother.

Tom chuckled at her enthusiasm, and guessed she would be glad to be home. They all would. Then he realised Sophie was watching him. He beckoned, and she unexpectedly slid off the seat to stand at his side.

"That's the hill that overlooks Linmore Estate, Sophie," he said, pointing through the window. "It won't be long until we're home."

"You needn't think you can escape me, brat." A voice rasped through the half-open door of the morning room. "I know you're there… somewhere."

Even before he heard the sound, Joshua recognised the ominous clicking of raised heels on his brother's Hessian boots, crossing from the marble tiled hallway to oak floorboards in the corridor, which meant he had a few seconds of freedom before his brother found him. Just long enough to hide in the full folds of the curtains lining the bay window.

Having gone there to avoid confrontation, Joshua froze, not daring to breathe. He closed his eyes; hoping the curtains of the enclosure would shield him from discovery.

"Mama said you're to take your daily punishment," Matthew Norbery's voice taunted, and then added with malice, "you might as well get it over. Father won't be back for hours yet."

Joshua gritted his teeth, promising himself that one day he'd take revenge on his brother for all the insults he endured. Yet knowing he was too small to make a difference. Somewhere in the background, he heard a door opening, a swish of skirts and a soft tread approaching.

"Matthew," Aunt Jane called from the corridor. Her tone was not quite a reproof, more a question. "What are you doing in the morning room? I asked you to tell your mother I am awaiting your father's return with Cousin Charlotte's children."

Caught out in his mischief, Matthew Norbery had no option but to obey.

Although he heard, Joshua did not move until the sound of his brother's clicking footsteps retreated along the corridor towards the main staircase, which led to his mother's apartments.

"It's all right, Joshua," Aunt Jane said. "You can come out now, he's gone."

He felt a comforting hand on his shoulder, and blinked back tears of relief. Aunt Jane always seemed to know when he needed her, which showed she cared, as his mother did not. He supposed it was due to the depression she suffered after his birth. It was lucky Aunt Jane was there to look after him. How he wished she really were his mother.

"Why don't you come into the drawing room with us, Joshua?" she said. "The view of the front drive is better from there."

He should have known she would guess the reason he was standing behind the curtains. Not hiding, that was for babies. He wanted to be first to see his father's coach returning from Ireland.

"Let me have a look at you," she said, smoothing aside the lock of fair hair draped across his brow. "Mm, yes, the bruise has almost gone; a few more days at the most."

That was a relief. The skin was still tender, but not as sore as when it was new. Aunt Jane applied salves to the abrasions, caused by the hard stone of his brother's signet ring, turned inside the hand to inflict the most damage. Then she fixed a pad on the wound, and brushed his hair forward, so it did not show.

By the time Matthew returned to the drawing room, Joshua was looking through the bay window, in full view of the other occupants of the room. He felt comforted by the quick smile of welcome his twin cousins, Lucy and Julia, gave when he entered the room with Aunt Jane, and safe in the knowledge his brother could not hurt him.

From his new position, Joshua could see the wide sweep of the drive as it approached the front door. He had not moved since he saw a coach appear around the curve of the birch coppice that screened Linmore Hall from the lower part of the drive and the village. He hugged the news of his father's imminent return to himself.

In one way, he was eager to know what the newcomers would be like, yet was half-dreading the moment. Suddenly, his mind filled with doubts, wondering what he would do if the new friend he expected was a bully like his brother? Could life be any worse? He did not think so. He was not bothered about the boy's sister. She would be like Caroline, and his cousins. Clean and tidy in her dress, and well behaved.

The sound of coach wheels on gravel broke through his reverie. A fluttering sense of excitement took hold as he heard the front door open, and a gruff voice bid his father welcome, then footsteps on the staircase. Joshua was waiting to move as the drawing room door opened. He hurtled across the room, anxious to be first to speak.

"Papa," he burst out, his voice filled with joy. "You're home."

That said everything he felt. He did not care if his brother belittled his actions, because life could be normal for a while.

Everyone looked up in anticipation as the door opened. Aunt Jane was the next to speak.

"Welcome home, Tom." She stepped forward and took her brother-in-law's hands. "I'm afraid Kate is indisposed."

Again, thought Joshua. His mother never made an effort to be polite if she could avoid it. Not that he minded. It kept him out of her way. He thought about it a lot, and felt even more, but long ago learned to say nothing.

He heard his father talking with Aunt Jane, but he was looking at the people standing behind them. A boy of about his age, with black, tousled hair and crumpled clothes moved forward and extended his hand.

"Hello," he said, sounding weary. "You must be Joshua. I'm Charlie Cobarne, and this is my sister, Sophie. We've come to live with you at Linmore."

Joshua gave thanks for what he saw when he looked at the boy. Then he saw the bedraggled little figure beside him, unlike any girl he had seen before. She looked like a smudgy-eyed black cat with a thumb stuffed in her mouth and was almost asleep. He supposed he should make allowances because she had travelled from Ireland. No doubt, she would look less dishevelled when she had a bath and changed her clothes.

He glanced across the room to where his sister, Caroline, sat straight-backed on the chaise longue, with his two cousins next to her. His brother lounged by the fireplace, looking decidedly overdressed for country life in his pale lemon pantaloons and white-topped Hessian boots.

"Good God – more stray brats," Matthew Norbery brayed. "Where the devil did he find this lot?"

Joshua cringed at his brother's ignorant behaviour. To show off in front of the family was bad, but when they had visitors was worse.

Determined not to embarrass his father, he smiled and grasped Charlie's hand. "I'm pleased to see you," he said.

"Sophie, come and meet Joshua," the boy said, with a soft lilt in his voice. "And remember to wipe your hands first."

The little girl gave a weary sigh as she dragged the thumb from her mouth, rubbed her fist across her nose and wiped it against her pelisse before extending a grubby little paw in his direction.

Joshua knew it would be a sticky handshake, but he could not refuse. Charlie was everything he hoped, but he supposed he could not expect too much of a girl.

"How old are you?" he asked, for something to say.

"I'll be eleven years old at Christmas," Charlie said, "and Sophie is eight, going on nine. Uncle Tom tells me that I'm older than you."

Like everyone else, but only by a few months.

While the grown-ups continued to talk in the background, Charlie peered at his face and said in an awestruck voice, "Wow, what a shiner. How did you get that, Josh?"

Out of habit, Joshua pushed back his hair from his forehead. Before he could cover the bruise, his brother barged in and boasted, "I gave him a thrashing."

Charlie turned around and seemed to notice Matthew Norbery for the first time. "What'd you be doing that for?" he asked, the Irish lilt sounding decidedly pronounced.

"I don't need a reason to kick him into shape. He'll never amount to anything." The dandified fop dismissed them with a supercilious sniff.

"You'd better not lay a finger on him whilst I'm here," Charlie growled. "I'll give you a dose of home brewed."

Matthew Norbery stepped back and raised his ornate gold quizzing glass.

"By Jove," he tittered. "We have a pugilist in our midst – how frightfully bourgeois."

Joshua could not believe a stranger would speak in his defence.

"Matthew," their father warned. "Kindly behave yourself."

When they were called into the salon, Joshua moved forward to lead the way, and felt a cuff across the back of his head.

"Get in line, brat. I go before you, because I'm the heir to Linmore," Matthew Norbery said and minced ahead of them.

Charlie waved his hands around to mimic the posturing.

"Don't worry, Josh," he said, "we'll get his measure. Come on, Sophie, you don't want to miss your tea, do you?"

Joshua waited because Charlie did, and took the expectant little hand in his. He looked at Sophie, and she almost grinned. At least, he thought it was a smile. It was the nearest thing to a grimace he could imagine.

"Oh, she likes you, Josh," said Charlie. "I'm so glad."

Joshua managed to contain his enthusiasm as best he could. He must be thankful for small things… he supposed.

CHAPTER 4

"I'm sorry if it offends you, Josh, but I don't like your brother."

Joshua was showing Charlie the bedroom next door to his. Sophie would sleep on the opposite side of the nursery corridor, near the other girls. For now, she was sitting on the floor openly listening to their conversation.

At first, he was anxious in case they thought the rooms were too plain, but Charlie immediately bounced on the bed and declared it met with his approval. That was a relief.

"Don't worry, Charlie. I don't think anyone likes him." It was a strange thing for Joshua to admit. Usually, he had to hide his feelings. "What did you mean about giving him some home-brewed? Do you know boxing cant?"

"That I do," said Charlie. "I used to do a bit of bare-knuckle practice with the stable lad back home in Ireland – but only when Uncle Lucius wasn't around. He is my pa's brother. We used to live with him and Aunt Barleycorn, but they didn't want Sophie and I couldn't forgive them. My uncle wanted me to stay, but I promised pa that I would always look after her, and a man must honour his promises. That was when they gave up on me and wrote to Uncle Tom, telling him to come and collect us."

Never before had Joshua had cause to view his family through the eyes of other people. Whilst Aunt Jane and his father were at pains to make the visitors welcome, his siblings set them apart. His younger cousins did not know what to do, so they copied his sister's manner. Caroline's demeanour was so prim that she scarcely turned her head to acknowledge the newcomers.

He felt ashamed of her reception, and determined to compensate for the lack of good manners. He could accept her remote attitude to him, but he resented it for Charlie and Sophie.

It was obvious his sister overawed Lucy and Julia, with her superior notions of etiquette. Most likely, she would deem it her bounden duty to correct any deficiencies in Sophie's character. He dreaded to think what his brother might do.

When they took tea, he noticed his sister's manner mellowed, and she went so far as to offer Sophie a seat beside her on the chaise longue. Instead, the girl sat on the floor, talking to the gundogs lying by the fire.

It was evident from Charlie's polite manner that he knew how to behave in company, whilst Sophie assured herself of a canine welcome by alternating every bite she took from the slice of fruitcake with a token piece for the dogs. Then she went back for a second and third slice.

After she swallowed the last crumb and licked her fingers, she walked around the room running her hands over the polished furniture while her brother looked anxiously on. Then she sat on the hearthrug, facing the heir to Linmore.

It was difficult to know what she would do next. As far as Joshua was concerned, his brother was the most repellent creature in existence – a parasite that would do anything to attract attention.

Usually, Matthew Norbery liked nothing better than for the servants to gape at his latest fashionable attire. He feigned to deplore such reverence, coming as it did from half-witted yokels, but it fed his insatiable vanity.

It was a new experience for Joshua to see his brother disconcerted by an eight-year-old girl, who fixed her gaze on him for quite ten minutes, with the intensity of a gundog watching its master.

There was only one thing worse than not being of interest to anyone. That was for a newcomer to make Matthew the sole object of her curiosity. His agitation increased by the minute. Eventually, he jumped to his feet and flounced around the room, while Sophie lay on the floor, waiting for him to return to his seat. Then she yawned to show her boredom, which astounded the other girls. Seeing his sister's look of horror, Joshua could imagine the scolding Sophie had in store.

Eventually, Charlie nudged Joshua in the ribs. "I know what she's doing, Josh," he whispered. "Sophie has a habit of collecting things. She never takes anything of real value – just enough to cause annoyance. It was the same when Aunt Barleycorn was nasty to her. Sophie hid her spectacles in a flowerpot, and it took days to find them."

It was hard to imagine what his brother possessed that would be of interest. Well, there was the ornate gold fob he wore at his waist, or the huge quizzing glass he waved about and through which he peered at people with a hideously magnified eye. It had frightened Joshua when he was a little lad, and he still had nightmares.

Then he realised if Sophie went for things of little monetary value, she might have designs on the exquisite trim around the top of his brother's brand new hessian boots, crafted by Mr Hoby.

She must have guessed the mirror shine, which Matthew truly believed was the best his valet could achieve, came second only to the gold tassels that adorned them.

They intrigued her so much that she often moved her head from side to side in time with the swaying tassels as Matthew paraded around the room. Eventually, he minced his way back, giving Sophie a wide berth, before sinking onto a seat with the foppish grace of a mannequin.

The minute he settled, she sidled up to him and crouched down to take a closer look. Then she looked him in the face, and smiled.

Immediately, he raised his open hand ready to strike, thinking to intimidate her.

"Ugh, get away from me, you dirty little wretch," he squawked. "Don't you dare touch my boots…"

His feeble demand was to no avail. Sophie was transfixed. It was as if she was waiting for something – and it came right on cue.

"Leave my sister alone," Charlie roared, hurtling forward with fists bunched.

Matthew Norbery recoiled in horror, but his lack of attention gave Sophie the opportunity she needed to snatch one of the tassels from a boot, and toss it amongst the retriever gundogs in front of the fire. The largest black one, of solid build, gobbled it up and promptly spat it out again, drenched with spittle.

While others in the room looked on in astonishment, Sophie darted back to Charlie's side in triumph. She had made her point.

Joshua started to giggle. He could not help himself. He had never seen his brother so enraged, or impotent. It was a joy to watch.

Snatching up his cane, Matthew leapt from the chair and turned menacingly on him. "What are you smirking at, Norbery?" he snarled. "I'll give you something else to think about."

"Matthew," their father admonished, "if you cannot behave better than a spoiled child, then leave the room."

Caught out in his abuse, the bully dissolved. "It's not fair," he blubbered. "Look what that… that… beastly creature did to my boots. She's ruined them."

"It does not excuse your behaviour. Stop the theatricals at once, and at least try to behave like a man."

His father's icy tone sent Matthew scuttling off in a huff to complain to his mother, and leaving Joshua to hope the inevitable backlash would not rebound on him, as it usually did.

Before he left the salon, Joshua looked for the missing tassel, but there was no sign of it anywhere. Then something caught his eye. He noticed Sophie slip her clenched fist into her coat pocket, and knew with a certainty Charlie was right about his sister. She did have magpie tendencies.

After he dined, Tom retired to the library and sat at his desk. He was tired from travelling and wanted to sleep, but the firm chair helped to keep him awake as he leaned forward, propping his elbows on the desk and chin in his hands.

He needed to think, and decide what to do about Matthew. No one could deny the provocation, but what shocked Tom was his eldest son's lack of control, so reminiscent of Kate.

He should not be surprised, because Jane told him about Matthew's aggressive behaviour to Joshua. Now he had seen it for himself, and it was clear that the older boy had been unchecked for too long. He needed occupation.

Kate was his next problem, for whatever decision he made, she would never agree. Irrespective of that, Tom knew it was better to wean them now with a year or two at university than wait for the extended period of a Grand Tour.

Goodness knows how long that would last, or what the cost would be; he would have to accept it.

It was doubtful if Matthew would derive any educational benefits from university, but his absence from Linmore would be a desirable outcome.

The sound of the door opening disturbed his reverie, although Tom sensed Jane's presence, even before she crossed the threshold. He stood up and moved towards the couch.

"Come and sit down, Jane," he said. "I haven't held a sensible conversation since I left home."

She glided forward and found a comfortable space beside him.

"I know," she said with a laugh. "I've just heard Mary Kilcot telling everyone about her travels. It seems she had a wonderful time, and I imagine she will still be talking at midnight."

Although the recollections amused him, Tom wanted to discuss other things.

"What am I going to do about Mathew? I know he is grossly overindulged, but I have never before seen him lose control over something as petty as an expensive pair of boots. For a moment, I thought he would have harmed her."

"No, he wouldn't have attacked Sophie," said Jane. "She did not show any fear, which is what he wants his victims to feel. He thrives on that. I've seen how terrified Joshua is when he is on the receiving end of Matthew's tantrums."

"I cannot let this go on any longer. He needs some kind of occupation, and company other than his mother. Kate's influence is destroying any sense he might have. He is becoming more like her every day. What do you think she would say if I send him to Oxford? It is, after all, a legitimate place for him to go."

"It might help, but I'm afraid Matthew already has other company – drinking friends, with whom he meets in Norcott, at least twice a week."

"William Rufus told me Matthew is frequently inebriated. Do you think his mood changes are alcohol induced?"

"Possibly, but I suspect there is more to it than that. There is something odd about him," said Jane. "If you look at his eyes, his pupils are fixed. He looks almost distant, and there is an aromatic smell on Kate's side of the house. I know Matthew smokes, but this is not like the cigars you use. I hate to say this, but it reminds me of…"

Tom interrupted. "Are you sure his friends come from Norcott?"

"Yes," said Jane, "and if the name Kate mentioned was correct, they have the most appalling reputation."

He looked at her, his face tense. "You mean types like his maternal uncle?"

"Yes," she said, "and knowing the Stretton family history, I don't know where it will end, but it won't be anywhere good."

At Jane's words, Tom felt a chill sense of unreality creeping over him.

"I hope you are wrong," he said, "but if that is the case, we must assume they are supplying Matthew with opium. That is the last thing we need."

"What will you do?"

"Consult with the physician, and find some way to separate Matthew from his local associates. Maybe he could visit some of the family – possibly at Rushmore. It might help distract him, and give me time to organise something more permanent for the future. I only hope we can persuade him to go."

"Don't worry, Tom. If there is anything Matthew likes more than low company, it is elevated – the higher up the social scale the better." Jane's dry tone expressed her feelings about her nephew. "With your agreement, I will write to my sister Clarissa in London, to invite the Cardington family to make a detour here when they return home. The timing is ideal, because the parliamentary session will soon be over. I have a feeling it will take little more to achieve an invitation for Matthew to go to Rushmore. If Kate can go as well, that is all to the good. A month, spent in the company of his cousin, Atcherly, would help eliminate the influence of the low life with whom he presently consorts."

"Bless you, Jane. Of course you may invite them."

"This is expediency," she said. "My concern is that Matthew will use the tassel incident as an excuse to punish Joshua. He was beside himself with rage."

"Yes, I know, but Sophie could not have chosen a more effective way to discomfit him. One minute he was bullying Joshua, the next a blubbering child. It won't be easy for you to be here with Kate if he goes to university."

"Don't worry about that," she said. "We must deal with the short term first. I doubt Matthew will cause problems at Rushmore. He's too much in awe of Lord Cardington, but just in case, I will suggest Martha takes one of her sons as support with Kate's care."

Tom nodded agreement. "Sidney, the eldest, has the right temperament, William Rufus, his brother, must stay here with the boys. When I am next in London, I will make enquiries about support at university, and a bear-leader for Matthew's tour." He yawned, and stretched out his long legs.

"D'you know, Jane," he said, "I'm looking forward to the next few weeks. I want to take the lads out driving, and renew my acquaintance with the estate. It is long overdue."

CHAPTER 5

When Joshua awoke the next morning, he could not wait to tell Charlie his plans for the day. A quick knock and he was through the door of the adjoining bedchamber. He stopped, perplexed as two tousled heads rose from the pillows.

"Oh, sorry," he said, backing out in confusion, wondering why Sophie was sleeping in Charlie's bed when she had a room of her own.

"It's all right, Josh," said Charlie. "You can come in. Sophie doesn't mind."

Cautiously, he peered round the door, and sure enough, she was sitting up in bed, rubbing her sleepy eyes. He could not imagine entering his sister's bedroom for any reason. That sort of thing just was not done.

He stood, uncertain what to do until Charlie said, by way of explanation,

"Sophie didn't want to be alone. We shared a room back in Ireland to save on the linen."

Anxious to avoid looking at Sophie in her nightclothes, Joshua turned instead to the framed sketch of a dragoon officer in regimental dress, which stood on the bedside table by Charlie's bed.

"Who's this?" he asked.

"It's our pa." Charlie's voice filled with pride. "He was a real hero, and that's why I want to be a soldier."

"So do I," said Joshua. "My father's brother was an officer in the East India Company Regiment. When he died, Lucy and Julia came to live here."

"Then we will be soldiers together," said Charlie, with a grin.

It was Joshua's dream come true. All he ever wanted was to be a soldier, and to have a friend.

"What about Sophie?"

Charlie was in no doubt about the answer. "She'll come with us and follow the drum."

That was not quite what Joshua had in mind.

41

Breakfast seemed to take forever. Joshua finished his repast easily enough, but the selection of food filling the heated trays in the dining room proved too tempting for Charlie to resist.

"Can we choose whatever we like?" he said, awestruck.

Receiving a nod of agreement from the attendant footman, he set to with a will, lifting one lid after another to inspect the contents.

When her brother finished making his choice, Sophie followed behind and pointed to a couple of slices of bacon, a spoonful each of grilled tomatoes and mushrooms, braised kidneys, with coddled eggs – on one plate – because that was how she wanted it.

At her second visit to the sideboard, she passed over the poached kippers, in favour of a rare slice of sirloin, which Hayton the footman did his utmost to dissuade her from eating.

To no avail, because Sophie was determined to prove little girls did like red meat, with a thick crust of bread to mop up the succulent juices. She made no sound, other than to emit appreciative grunts of approval whilst licking her fingers.

Charlie was ecstatic. "I can see Sophie is going to enjoy herself here, Josh. When we were in Dublin, Aunt Barleycorn would not let us have more than one slice of toast, and a smear of butter. Uncle Lucius was the only one allowed to have honey."

When they had eaten their fill, Joshua planned to set out on a tour of Linmore Hall. In assuming his cousins would look after Sophie, he wanted to show Charlie all the secret places they could hide, but his plan had to be adapted, because Sophie wanted to come with them.

Then he realised they must keep her safe, particularly after she had bested Matthew Norbery the previous day.

As far as Joshua was concerned, the timing of the house tour was crucial, and he wanted to walk through the downstairs rooms with impunity, knowing his brother never left his bedchamber until after midday.

They started weaving in through one door of the salon, and out through the hidden doors used by servants, then on to other rooms in sequence. It was important for Charlie to know of such things, because Joshua used them to escape from his brother's vengeful ways. Passing through the rooms, they encountered maidservants attending to their cleaning duties. Several smiled a greeting, but no one said anything amiss.

By the time Joshua crept up the mellow oak staircase to the first floor landing, the ormolu clock on the reception hall mantelshelf was chiming half-past eleven. At the top, he peeped around the corner of the balustrade.

Things had not gone entirely to plan, because of Charlie's fascination with detail. Joshua did not know all the answers to his questions. He had to think a lot, which meant the tour took longer than anticipated, and there were still many rooms to see.

He waited a moment, tilting his head to listen for any sounds that might indicate his brother was in the vicinity. The thought made his mouth feel dry.

"What are you doing?" Charlie asked.

Joshua hesitated, and then said in a quiet voice. "Just making sure there's nobody about."

"D'you mean him?" Charlie asked in the same, low tone.

He nodded and moved on again, thankful his friend understood. At the end of a long corridor, he stopped short and pointed at a solid oak door.

"My mother lives through there," he said.

"Are we allowed to see her?" Charlie wanted to know.

Joshua shivered. "No, you wouldn't want to. I only go when I'm summoned." He did not want to explain the reasons.

Charlie nodded. "Uncle Tom said Aunt Norbery was an invalid. What's the matter with her?"

It was difficult for Joshua to explain. "She hasn't been well since I was born, and blames me." There seemed nothing else to say.

"Can we go outside now?" Charlie said.

They hurried along a long corridor towards the nursery wing, down the back stairs and out through the door to the courtyard.

Joshua ran outside, took a gasp of air and let it go with a sense of relief. Then he had an idea. "Do you want to see where the kitchens are? They might find us something to eat."

It was less than two hours since they finished breakfast, but viewing the house was a hungry business. He skipped down the stairs to the stillroom on the lower floor, and found a woman, clad in black bombazine, sitting at a desk. On seeing them, she turned immediately to speak.

"Are these your new friends, Master Joshua?"

"Yes, Mrs Delbury," he said. "This is Charlie Cobarne, and his sister, Sophie."

The housekeeper looked from one to the other, and said in a precise voice, "I'm pleased to meet you both, and hope you will be comfortable at Linmore. I trust you will let me know if you have any problems."

Charlie nodded, but his attention was on an earthenware jar, reposing on a shelf. Then he turned his dark eyes and sunny smile on her.

"Do you happen to have any biscuits?" he asked.

"Of course I do, Master Charlie," the housekeeper said with an indulgent smile. "These are special ones I keep for Master Joshua." She lifted the lid and let them take two each of the fruity pastries made to a Shropshire recipe.

Joshua was so pleased that he could show Charlie someone liked him. His main problem was pleasing his mother, and he had long realised nothing he said or did would make any difference.

That night when Joshua went to bed, he could not find his nightshirt. He looked everywhere he thought it might be, but eventually, he asked one of the servants for a clean one.

The next day, his socks had gone, so he found another pair and thought no more about it. Then he noticed his scarf was missing, which was odd, because he had seen it the previous evening, hanging on the hook behind his bedroom door.

Thinking Charlie might have seen it, Joshua went through the adjoining door, and realised someone had moved Sophie's bed into her brother's room. She was sitting on the eiderdown, clad in his missing nightshirt, with a scarf around her neck and socks as mittens.

Charlie looked embarrassed. "I'm sorry, Josh. Can she have them for tonight? I will make sure she returns them in the morning."

Joshua burst out laughing. He had never seen anything so funny in his life. Then he realised Sophie took it as a sign of approval.

The following evening, he found two fruit-laden biscuits on the clothes chest by his bed, and guessed who had placed them there. Now he would have to pretend to the housekeeper he was to blame for raiding the stores.

Charlie came through the door, with similar biscuits in his hand.

"Did Sophie leave some for you as well? I've told her that she's not to go near the stillroom again."

Every day Joshua showed them something new. He went from the lower level of the nursery wing of the Hall, to the classroom on the top floor where he did his lessons. There was nobody there, because his father decreed studies should cease while Charlie and Sophie settled into their new home.

Assuming the girls would want to be friends, Joshua asked Lucy and Julia to join them when they took a walk in the gardens, but Sophie scowled at them and remained resolutely by her brother's side. Undeterred, he tried again, but each day was the same, until he realised that Sophie was not like other girls.

They were always neat and tidy, but despite having a bath and her hair washed, she persisted in wearing the black clothes in which she had travelled from Ireland – and the same scuffed boots. The only difference being her black hair was now in a thick braid that reached halfway down her back. That was all she would allow the maid to do to it.

For the first week they contrived to keep out of Matthew's way by taking long walks across the parkland; but as time went on, Joshua knew the chances of that continuing grew slimmer. He knew something would have to be done, but could not imagine what it might be. Then things came to a head.

It was halfway through the second week, as they slipped through the stable yard, that Joshua heard Matthew's bragging voice. He stopped, not wanting to be caught in the open, yet knew they should go on.

"I want a decent horse today, Shelwick. Not one of the dozy hacks you gave me last time my friends came. I'll take Thunderer, so you'd better have it saddled ready for when my friends come in half an hour."

There was a burst of laughter from the stable lads, before Shelwick spoke.

"That you won't, young sir. He is the master's horse, and it would take more ability than you have in the saddle to ride him."

"Do as I say, or my mother will dismiss you," Matthew Norbery screamed.

"No," said the head groom. "I won't do that, for if you fell off and broke your neck, she'd blame me for that. You will take whichever horse I think you are capable of riding. It's Squire Norbery's orders."

"When I'm Squire Norbery," he boasted, "you'll sing a different tune – and my brat of a brother as well, if he's still here by then."

"By that time, I'll be too old to care what happens to you."

Listening horrified outside the stable door, Joshua heard the familiar sound of clicking heels, and tried to slip out of sight, but was too late. As the door opened, he came face to face with his brother. Matthew Norbery gobbled with rage, and Charlie leapt into action.

"Come on, Josh, time to make ourselves scarce." He grabbed Joshua's arm as they hurtled through the stone archway into the park, with Sophie in tow.

Joshua dashed out across the park towards his favourite oak tree. He hesitated only a minute, debating whether it would hide them, but realised there was not enough leaf cover, and now wasn't the time to give lessons in climbing trees. He thought about the island on the lake, but could not be sure the boat was on the near side.

Deciding against it, he set off again, knowing that if they could reach Aunt Jane's cottage, they would be safe. Jessie was sure to be there, and she would find them some food. Returning home was a problem they would deal with later.

Whatever he did, Joshua knew there would be risks. It was too late to wish he had kept walking through the stable yard, but he knew that Matthew would want to humiliate him in front of his friends. It was what he always did, and would use this as a way of frightening Sophie.

"Where do we go now, Josh?"

"I'm trying to decide on somewhere he won't find us," he said.

"Don't be silly, Josh; he won't come after us."

Oh yes he will – and bring his friends.

"Well, if he does," said Charlie, hunting around for a stout stick to use as a weapon. "We'll be ready for him, won't we, Sophie?"

She nodded agreement, and picked up another stick. Joshua found another one, but it broke the first time he slapped it against his boot, leaving him to carry two halves.

"So where do we go?" Charlie repeated.

"The farm is in that direction," Joshua pointed, then turned around. "Aunt Jane's cottage is over there, or we could go to the river."

"What time is it?" said Charlie, glancing up at the sky. "We don't want to go too far away from food, so I think it should be Aunt Jane's cottage."

That was only half a mile away, but it meant crossing open parkland. Still they had to do it, and with luncheon on their minds, they set off.

Sophie saw them first, and tugged at Charlie's sleeve. Thinking about food had made him forget to be cautious.

"What is it?" he said, looking around, and saw a group of three men on horseback in the distance. Matthew Norbery he was sure they could deal with, but the other two looked somewhat menacing. He did not know what it was.

Charlie shivered, and looked at Joshua.

"What do we do?" he said.

"Run," Joshua said.

Charlie was already running, hauling Sophie behind.

"Where're we going?" he gasped.

"Split up," shouted Joshua, several paces ahead. "You go to the stables."

"What about you, Josh?"

"Never mind me. I will go where he can't get me. Keep Sophie out of his way," he huffed, throwing down a trail of his clothes in his wake – first the coat, then his waistcoat and neckcloth followed, leaving him stripped down to his breeches and shirt.

In the background, the sound of hoof beats grew ominously louder.

"No, Josh," said Charlie, "We should stick together. He can't hurt us."

"You don't know him as I do."

Reaching the edge of a fishpond, Joshua kicked off his boots and was half way down the bank. "I'll see you later," he said.

"I'm staying here," said Charlie. "So is Sophie."

She was out of breath, and her little legs could not have carried her any further. Charlie felt a sense of disappointment as Joshua dived into the water, and came up gasping, before striking out across the pond.

He gave one more glance and turned to face the horses. They looked huge and he felt small in comparison, but he was not going to show any fear. He braced his feet, gripped the stout stick in his hands and said, "Are you all right, Sophie?"

She took up a similar stance, held up her stick and grinned.

Nothing had changed. They were in this together, just as they always had been. Joshua would have to take care of himself, but it seemed chicken-hearted to run away from a fribble like Matthew Norbery.

The horses approached at a canter, one to each side with Joshua's brother straggling behind. Charlie scarcely noticed the one to the left, but the harsh-faced rider to the right seemed strangely moulded to the saddle, with his hands free. He saw the man's expression and felt a tremor of apprehension.

47

"Stand behind me, Sophie," he hissed, and then gasped in disbelief, as the rider raised a pistol, and took deliberate aim across the pond.

"No," he yelled, hurtling forward, but he was too late. There was a loud report, a puff of smoke, and the villain laughed.

Charlie stopped and looked fearfully across the lake, but there was no sign of Joshua. He felt tears threatening, but dashed them away, turning towards where Sophie stood at the edge of the pond, defiantly gripping her stick, her teeth bared in a grimace.

"Now, you interfering whelp," the voice rasped, "I'll deal with you, and then her, afterwards…" The man made to swing out of the saddle, but before his second foot left the stirrup, his horse bolted, dragging him across the park, with his head bouncing along the ground.

Inexplicably, the second horse veered off in a panic towards the far side of the pond, and the horse carrying Matthew Norbery, suddenly dropped its head and sent the rider hurtling over the grassy bank into the water. There was a terrified scream, a dull splash, and then nothing.

Sophie looked at Charlie, and said with a grin. "I did it."

Before he could speak, there were half a dozen grooms on horses milling around, scrambling down the bank to the water's edge, wading in and dragging Matthew Norbery to the side.

William Rufus came running up, "Where's Joshua?"

Only then did Charlie remember. He looked across the lake towards the island, and saw a slender figure, huddled against the trunk of a tree.

"He's there," he said, pointing, as tears of relief streamed down his face. He felt a little hand grip his own, and found Sophie looking anxiously up at him. He sniffed, and said. "It's all right, Sophie. Joshua's safe."

Then his knees went from under him.

"What happened, William Rufus?" Tom Norbery demanded. "I want the truth, not some story concocted by Matthew's friends about Joshua falling in the lake and Matthew trying to save him. We all know that is not true, for he cannot swim. Then you may tell me what the deuce Nathan Stretton was doing here?

Tom was in his library, trying to piece things together after Matthew had half-drowned in the lake, with Joshua sitting on the island, refusing to come off. He had heard several garbled versions of the events, with each trying to shout the others down. He knew the one individual was a family connection of Kate, from Norcott, but the other shifty character was unknown.

"Nor would I tell you that, sir. It was the other way around. Matthew and his friends were herding the little 'uns towards the lake. Whatever they said, Joshua is not cowardly for running off like that. He knew what his brother intended, and ran ahead of the others, chucking his clothes off, and dived in. Then he was off to the island, thinking Matthew wouldn't hurt the others if he wasn't there."

"I see," said Tom, under his breath. "Dear God, where do we go from here? All right, you might as well tell me what happened to Charlie and Sophie."

"Well, that's the funny thing. Charlie was carrying a big stick, and he stood at the water's edge, ready to defend his sister…"

"Yes," said Tom, beginning to laugh, "and what did Sophie do? I feel sure that she did something to bring about this penchant for swimming in the lake."

William Rufus shook his head. "I dunno, sir, but whatever it was, the horses didn't like it. Matthew and his two friends were riding hell for leather towards them, and suddenly the other two veered off to the sides; and Matthew's horse shied, and pitched him over the head, into the water. I never saw anything like it."

"Where were you when this happened?" Tom asked.

"I was coming across the park, and met the grooms exercising the horses. The little 'uns had slipped away earlier, and I was looking for them. As soon as we saw what happened, they helped me to drag Matthew out again. He's all right, but it will teach him not to go near the water in a hurry."

"Was the ambush deliberate, do you think?"

William Rufus stopped and rubbed his chin. "Oh, yes, sir," he said. "No doubt about it."

"I wonder what she did." Tom mused. "Something dastardly, I'll be bound."

"No, sir, the little wench couldn't have done anything to affect the horses like that. We'd have seen her."

"But could you hear her, if she made a sound? I begin to think that I have brought, one of the Irish *little people* to Linmore," said Tom. "From now on, William Rufus, I want you to make the children's safety your first concern, until I sort out Matthew's future."

Tom knew he would have to contend with Kate, blaming him for his lack of consideration towards her beloved son. The Cobarnes had been here for less than two weeks and Matthew was trying to kill Joshua. He could only hope that Jane's plan to send Kate and Matthew to Rushmore Hall would come to fruition, and then they might relax.

The underlying problem was more serious. Matthew's friend and cousin, Nathan Stretton had a pistol, lined up on Joshua swimming in the lake. The grooms had told him they saw that. Charlie might have spooked one horse, but not three. No, he would take a bet on it being Sophie who caused Matthew's horse to shy and the others to veer away around the side of the lake. It was bad enough for Matthew to try to hurt Joshua, but if a Stretton joined the hunt…things had turned nasty. They had no morals, scruples or fear of retribution.

It was just as well Nathan had a sore head to nurse for the next week or two. Taking a toss had slowed him down, but when the horse dragged him back to the stables… Tom wished he could have seen it.

CHAPTER 6

Two anxious hours later, after Joshua had been retrieved dripping and shivering from the island, Charlie sat beside his bed and finally had the chance to ask, "Why did you run away?" He realised his words sounded accusatory, but he felt aggrieved that no one had bothered to enquire how he or Sophie felt after the ordeal. The servants were more concerned with providing Joshua with a hot bath to wash the green slime and pond life from his hair.

"I didn't," Joshua said, shaking with the ague.

Charlie had no sympathy for someone who turned tail and ran, leaving him and Sophie to face the enemy unarmed apart from a stout stick apiece. They were the ones who prevailed, and yet they had missed not only their lunch but tea as well. Then they had to sit in the nursery while Joshua was cosseted by the servants, and given a cordial to ward off the effects of the cold, before slipping between the warmed sheets of his bed on which extra blankets had just been placed. He'd be well served if he had swallowed a few water beetles. It was more than Charlie or Sophie had to eat.

"If you'd stayed with us," he said, "they wouldn't have dared to shoot at you."

"No," said Joshua. "If I was there, they'd have thrown us all in the lake. It's happened before."

That silenced Charlie for a moment.

"What happened to the others?" said Joshua, burrowing his head into the pillows.

Sophie, sitting at Charlie's side, leaned forward and whispered in his ear.

"No, you didn't, Sophie," her brother said, patting her hand.

"What did she say?" Joshua asked.

"She says that she whistled, and scared the horses." Charlie lowered his voice, while Sophie glowered and sat nodding her head insistently. "It didn't happen like that. I whacked the gunman's horse, just as he was dismounting, and it bolted, dragging him with it. I would not normally have done it, but he was going to hurt Sophie. Who was he?"

"Nathan Stretton," said Joshua, yawning. "Matthew's cousin. They do not acknowledge me as family. I don't know who the other man was."

Charlie continued in a voice full of scorn. "Your bleater of a brother accused us of trying to drown him. If he can't sit a horse better than that, he needs to be on a leading rein." He stopped, realising that Joshua's eyes had closed.

"Well, look at that, Sophie; he's gone to sleep while I was talking. I must have a word with William Rufus. He looks just the man we need to toughen Joshua up."

Charlie hoped Joshua was not going to be timid about everything. He too was terrified when the man with the face of a rat levelled a pistol, but refused to show fear before the enemy. A gun he could understand, but Josh could not have known that when he started running. He sighed, and resigned himself to the task ahead. Guarding Sophie was one thing, but Joshua quite another.

They found William Rufus sitting outside Joshua's bedroom door, but it was a bit too public for Charlie to say what he wanted, so he bided his time, knowing there would be a better opportunity when Joshua recovered. That did not take long.

The physician visited once, stayed long enough for a quick examination, and then said, "He'll do, Miss Jane. Just keep him warm and ensure he has plenty of rest. Let him get up in a couple of days, and give him what he wants to eat. He will come to no harm. Now, I must see his brother… again."

Beyond the solid oak door at the far end of the corridor, servants were running around with mustard baths for Matthew Norbery, while the physician had called three times to attend him and gone away shaking his head in disbelief.

By the time Joshua recovered, and the Cobarne children similarly emerged from his bedroom, the house was a hive of activity. Everywhere they ventured above stairs, maidservants dusted and polished, while others bustled around carrying piles of bedlinen. On the lower levels, kitchen staff dashed back and forth to the storeroom, so busy that no one had time to tell them what was going on.

Moreover, on entering the stillroom in search of sustenance, they found an empty biscuit jar, and learned that Mrs Delbury, the housekeeper, was too busy to make biscuits. That was an unmitigated disaster, which could only mean one thing – visitors were expected. The question was… who was coming to stay?

For several days, they retreated to the nursery corridor, and found the answer when Hayton carried in a tray of supper.

When they finished eating, Joshua and Charlie dashed off to Aunt Jane's sitting room, with Sophie trailing two steps behind.

"Hayton says Lord and Lady Cardington are coming, Aunt Jane."

"Yes," she said. "They are bringing the family, en route from London."

"Who are they, Aunt Jane?" asked Charlie. "Are they mine and Sophie's relations as well?"

"Yes, Charlie, they belong to you both. Lady Cardington is my older sister, but you may call her Aunt Clarissa. Her husband is Lord Cardington, and I think it best if you address him as 'Sir'. He will expect that."

Charlie nodded his understanding, as Joshua took up the story.

"When Parliament is in session, Uncle Humphrey goes to London to sit in the Upper House. Papa is in the Lower House, because he does not have a title."

At least that was the way he understood it.

"When they are not making speeches and laws in the daytime," he said, "they dress up and go to balls and parties in the evening."

"Did you hear that, Sophie? They sound very important," said Charlie. Sophie sniffed.

"You will have a chance to meet your new cousins," said Aunt Jane. "There will be quite a houseful when they arrive. I'll leave Joshua to explain their names, so you know who to expect."

Joshua tried to remember the last time he had seen his relations. It was ages ago. Linmore was not like other country houses because it did not have many visitors, and those who came rarely stayed long.

The thought of having visitors was torture, because Joshua would have to pretend dutiful affection for his mother, whereas she made no such pretence. If he was lucky, she would ignore him, and he much preferred that to the acrimony to which she and Matthew usually subjected him.

Wanting to be first to see who arrived, Joshua and Charlie stood by the sash window at the end of the nursery corridor, while Sophie found a footstool on which to stand. From there, they all had a clear view of the front drive.

No sooner did they see a team of horses, drawing a carriage with big wheels, travelling at a thundering pace, than the lads hurtled down the back stairs to the lower floor, with Sophie running three steps behind.

They dashed through the back door and around the corner of the courtyard, to arrive at the front door just as the equipage swept to a halt. They gasped in delight as a groom leapt down and ran to the horses' heads.

Seconds later, Roundthorn the butler emerged through the front door, followed by a couple of footmen to collect the luggage.

"Who's this?" Charlie's voice was full of awe.

"That's my cousin, Moreton. He is the heir to Rushmore estate."

"Like Matthew Norbery?" Charlie asked.

"Oh no," said Joshua with a laugh. "Not like him at all."

They might share the position of being heir to their respective fathers' estate, but Lord Cardington's eldest son was everything Matthew was not.

As Viscount Atcherly, Moreton Cardington belonged to the Corinthian set. He was a notable whip and excelled in all kinds of sporting activities. Known as a hard rider to hounds, he could shoot and fence with the best, and regularly sparred in Gentleman Jackson's boxing club in London.

Whereas Joshua's brother was hard-pressed to drive a gig, his older cousin arrived at Linmore, in advance of the family party, driving his racing curricle with a team of four perfectly matched chestnut thoroughbreds, from the renowned Rushmore stables.

As Joshua gazed at the driver, clad in the uniform of the Four-Horse Club, with a proliferation of shoulder capes on his drab-coloured driving coat, his pride overflowed, and knew that Charlie was similarly impressed. Then he sensed they were not alone. Intent on being first to greet their cousin, Matthew Norbery stood behind them.

"Out of my way, you..."

Joshua realised his position, but was too late to avoid a ringing slap to his head, which knocked him to his knees. When he scrambled to his feet, he realised Moreton Cardington was watching. More than that, this magnificent apparition had ignored his older brother's overtures of welcome, and was speaking to them.

"Come on, brats, the team looks better from up here," he drawled, and reached down to help the two lads clamber up the steps. When Charlie and Joshua were proudly settled on the seat he gathered up the reins, preparatory to taking the curricle around the sweep of the drive towards the stables. Instead, he stopped. "Good God, what have we here?"

He raised an eyebrow in surprise when he saw Sophie waiting expectantly with her foot on the first step. He took one look at her ferocious scowl, boomed out a laugh and took hold of the little hand she extended for help. With one deft hoist, she was on the platform at her brother's feet.

"All right, little missy," he said. "If you insist, then it's the floor for you, and no squawking about me driving too fast. If you do, I'll put you out to walk."

If awe had a sound, then Sophie made it.

Joshua had never before known such kindness, but he knew he would have to pay for taking attention from his brother. If Matthew did not make him suffer, his mother would.

When the main party of visitors arrived, Lady Cardington immediately made her younger sister aware of her husband's displeasure at hearing that the family of a cousin had taken Tom Norbery away from his political commitments.

"My dear Jane," Lady Cardington said in her fussy voice for the third time in as many minutes. "Humphrey was absolutely shocked."

That was a degree of impertinence Jane would not allow, and one to which she gave a tart response. "Yes, I dare say he was, Clarissa, though what it has to do with him, I do not know. When I sought Tom's counsel, he took charge of the matter, and decided we could not leave the children in Ireland to be sent who knew where by their uncle – a man with no more sense of family than a stranger."

"But Humphrey says Tom should not have allowed it…"

There were times when Jane could cheerfully have shaken her sister. Instead, she said in the sweetest voice. "Would you rather have our cousin Charlotte's orphaned children treated like paupers, and be sent to a poor house?"

Being of a similar age to the daughter of her favourite uncle, Jane had a closer affinity with Charlotte than either of her sisters, and had lost a dear friend when she died.

"Of course not," Lady Cardington dissembled, "but surely, there was not the slightest danger of that?"

Jane chose her words carefully. "I don't know, Clarissa. After all, the man married his housekeeper. One doesn't know what else he might have done."

"His…?" Abject horror filled her sister's eyes. One did not do such things.

"To avoid paying her wages, I expect," she said. "It might well have been a prudent measure, for he did tell Tom his business was not in good heart."

Later in the evening, when Jane recounted the conversation, Tom said, "Did I ever tell you that you have a wicked imagination, my dear?"

"I cannot deny the truth of that," she said with a smile, "but I do thank you for being a dear, kind man. I shudder when I think of the life those children have led – especially Sophie."

"I think Sophie has developed her own resilient way of dealing with events. As you saw with Matthew, she is a formidable opponent."

"Mmm, I wonder what made her do that. It was almost as if she was punishing him for something." She stopped. "Do you think it was because he bullied Joshua?"

"But she had only just walked through the door."

"Yes, but he did make them welcome, when others in the family did not."

"I wonder if you are right."

Having planned the Cardington visit with one object in mind, Jane was prepared to endure almost any inconvenience, except the one to which she was subjected. Despite being told repeatedly that Kate lived on her side of the house and took no interest in anyone else's activities, Clarissa insisted that their elder step-sister be brought into the party, which Jane knew was at Lord Cardington's behest.

He had interfered many times over the years, for his notion of self-consequence knew no bounds. Jane also knew that Kate would not miss an opportunity to humiliate Tom, particularly in the light of recent events between Matthew's friends and Joshua.

Watching Charlie, when he met Lord and Lady Cardington, Jane knew her cousin Charlotte would have been proud of her son's good manners, whereas Sophie behaved towards the visitors with her usual degree of disdain.

At the outset, she wondered how Kate and Matthew would respond to Sophie, but she need not have worried. For a brief moment, the older black-haired woman subjected the younger pugnacious face to scrutiny; and then Sophie adopted the same attitude of unconcern as with Lord Cardington and walked away without uttering a word. Matthew, hovering in the vicinity of his Rushmore cousins studiously avoided her.

Inevitably, she had to listen to Clarissa's complaints. "I didn't know where to look, Jane. The child knew not how to behave in Humphrey's presence. She stared at him in the most insolent way."

Jane smiled to herself, and felt an affinity with Sophie. She too had the same problem maintaining a polite tongue in her head where Lord Cardington was concerned. He was a person who always knew best, and Clarissa was the perfect wife for him, because she never questioned his judgement, whereas Jane could not imagine a worse fate than being married to such a man.

She spent several interminable days listening to Clarissa's childhood reminiscences of life at Littlemore House, on two afternoons of which Kate deigned to visit them for almost half an hour, before suddenly standing up and leaving the room without a word. Clarissa looked astounded, but for once Jane was in accord for her sister's imperfect recollections brought her more pain than pleasure.

Normally active in household duties and visits around the estate, Jane found the perambulating schedule that Clarissa favoured unbearably dull, and her sister viewed the prospect of visiting the sick with distaste. How could two sisters be so different?

The only thing that alleviated her boredom was the knowledge that Humphrey Cardington was not of their number, having at the outset demanded of Tom a tour of the estate, during which he compared the ten thousand acreage of Linmore unfavourably with his property, which was half as large again. Tom bore his pomposity with greater equanimity than Jane would have done.

She knew that the peer had never understood or forgiven her poor taste in preferring the loving friendship of the heir to a lapsed barony, to an offer of marriage from an earl who was named after a royal duke of the Plantagenet line, whom he boasted amongst his ancestors.

When she declined, Lord Cardington had married Clarrisa on the rebound and Jane supposed with a chuckle that she was intended to regret it to her dying day. She annoyed him again, several years later, by refusing to marry his younger brother, a neck-or-nothing rider to hounds. It was just as well she did for shortly afterwards, Granville came to grief on the hunting field.

By then she was considered to be beyond redemption and relegated to the status of being called "Poor Jane" – a situation that suited her well.

"My dear Jane…" Clarissa uttered the same words each morning when they met to take breakfast.

What had Humphrey Cardington said now? Jane wondered, and knew that she was about to find out.

"Humphrey thinks it is most unkind of Tom to keep Kate locked on the other side of the house…"

That Jane would not allow. "The doors are not locked, Clarissa," she said, gritting her teeth. "Kate is free to run her household as she wishes without interference from us."

"No, you misunderstand, my dear. Humphrey believes that if Tom and Kate were reconciled, he would be able to accept a title, and life would be much more comfortable for everyone. Just think of the inheritance it would be for Matthew."

Everyone…? The thought almost deprived Jane of breath.

"Yes, just think about it," she said in a dry tone. Kate and Matthew would decimate everything at Linmore within five years, and they had no legal claim to it. She sighed, knowing what would come next.

"If only you could persuade him… "

"No, Clarissa," she said, resisting the temptation to raise her voice. "I cannot and will not do it. Nor will I argue with you. I will simply ask you politely not to intercede in things that you do not understand." She almost said interfere, but had no wish to offend before they had agreed to take Matthew and preferably Kate and Caroline to Rushmore. Until that was achieved she would tread softly. It seemed dreadful to be plotting to have a few weeks of freedom, but it was the only way.

She wondered what Humphrey Cardington would say if he knew that Kate's father, Matthew Stretton, had ended his days on the scaffold, after being convicted of deliberately shooting dead a young man who accused him of cheating at cards.

Clarissa had not known, for she was married before Martha told Jane about the ramshackle family of lechers at Norcott Abbey. She wondered what her own father had thought about it when he had learned the origins of his stepdaughter's violent tantrums, so characteristic of her family connections.

However difficult the present circumstances; it would serve no purpose for Jane to scream with frustration as Kate frequently did to gain attention. Nor could she reveal that she and Tom were trapped in a coil of Kate's making. They had lived with the intolerable situation for so long, she wondered if it would ever be resolved.

However tempting it might be to shock Clarissa by telling her exactly why Tom would never dance to Humphrey Cardington's bidding, there were young people whose lives would be ruined by such a revelation. The scandal would be immense.

It was all so complicated, and she was not going to create more upset when the purpose of inviting the Cardington family to Linmore was to resolve the problem with Matthew. The need to do that overruled everything else.

It was easier to pretend ignorance and change the subject.

"I presume that Fred will be joining the army soon."

Jane said it because she had noticed the increasing friction between Fredrick, Lord Cardington's second son, going on eighteen, and his father. She knew of his ambition to join a cavalry regiment and of his father's refusal to let him out of his control. It caused great resentment, which resulted in many arguments and subsequent humiliation. Everyone must be subjected to his Lordship's despotic command.

"Oh, no, you are mistaken," said her sister. "Humphrey will never allow it."

"Then he is a bigger fool than I thought," Jane allowed herself to say with asperity. "The time for that was last year, after he overturned the chaise and almost killed the groom."

Conscience-stricken, Fred had asked Jane to intercede when Lord Cardington dismissed the groom, whose head-injury reduced him to simplicity. Had Tom not shown compassion, Horace would now have been living in the poorhouse.

"But Fred might be killed…" wailed Clarissa.

"And he might do it driving too fast," said her sister, ruthlessly pursuing an idea she had. "Tell me, Clarissa; how much would a pair of colours cost in a cavalry regiment?"

"Oh Jane, you can't mean…" Clarissa said, her eyes widening in alarm.

"Yes, I do, Clarissa. I think I will ask Tom to make the purchase on my behalf. After all, Fred is my godson. It is only natural that I should want to help him."

"But Humphrey would never agree."

"Then he must be willing to pay the purchase price himself, and tell the world that he is proud of his second son. Otherwise, I will do it," Jane said, knowing that to challenge Lord Cardington was the only way to stop him interfering in things that were not his concern.

Having decided on her course of action, Jane raised the subject over dinner on a night when Kate was not present. She timed it to perfection. The servants had left the dining room and the ladies were not quite ready to leave the gentlemen to their port. She received a knowing look from Tom, who was already aware of her intention. Cardington gave a snort of dismissal, and Fred a grin of delight, when a lazy voice gave his approbation.

"That's an excellent idea, Aunt Jane. It'll be the making of him," said his half-brother Atcherly, who turned to his father. "You must admit, sir; Fred would look splendid in the uniform of one of the Guards' regiments. Apart from everything else, think of the benefits to the Rushmore horses if he learned to drive a team properly."

It was said softly, and in the driest tone, but Jane could see that Lord Cardington had taken heed of his heir's opinion. Only Moreton Cardington had the power to influence his father, and she knew he did it to save Fred embarrassment.

She also saw the look of mirth that passed between the brothers. Moreton Cardington had grown up with his father's second family, and was a kinder person. He had hardly known his mother.

Ultimately, Jane was sure that they had Sophie to thank for the hasty curtailment of the visit. Normally she might have expected the Cardington family to stay for three weeks, but a little over a week of Sophie's blatant disregard for his lordship's dignity was enough. He made a hasty departure, claiming to have pressing business to attend. He might well have, but the shorter visit exactly suited Jane's purpose, for Kate, Matthew and Caroline went with them.

Clarissa extended an invitation for the whole family to visit Rushmore Hall, but that was the last thing Jane wanted, and she couched her refusal politely.

"Regrettably, Clarissa, I must decline. I can think of nothing more detrimental to the children's welfare than for them to endure further travelling. It is no wonder Sophie has forgotten her manners; the poor child is exhausted. However, I am sure Kate would benefit from the change, particularly as you are taking Caroline and Matthew. It will help him to recuperate from his chill."

Before he left Linmore, Fred Cardington came to say farewell to Jane.

"Best of my aunts, I thank you for your efforts on my behalf," he said, saluting her cheek. He stopped and raised her hands to his lips. "How blessed I would have been if you had been my mother, and Uncle Tom my father."

"You are my favourite nephew," she said with a smile.

"But not, I think… the absolute favourite," he said with a knowing grin.

She flushed slightly and amended the statement. "One of my favourites, for we have Charlie now as well."

He grinned. "Of course, and we mustn't forget the incorrigible Sophie, who has entertained everyone, even his Lordship. It was a delight to watch her."

Jane gave a chuckle. "Yes, it was, wasn't it?"

The strained atmosphere had been considerably lightened by Sophie's total disregard for Lord Cardington's notions of self-importance. Where he considered he should take precedence, she walked before him, which had brought a hastily stifled shout of laughter from Fred.

The house seemed delightfully empty when the last of six travelling coaches loaded with baggage departed and quieter still when Lucy and Julia went to stay with their maternal grandparents in Westbridge. A visit already planned for August was brought forward at the twins' special request. There would be plenty of time for them to make friends when Sophie had settled into the household. For the moment, they seemed happy that she ignored them.

For Jane, it was a joy to be free of the responsibility of Kate's care, and more so to have time with Tom and the children. For a few weeks at least, it was a chance to be a real family.

CHAPTER 7

"Where is Hillend, Papa?"

It was only when Joshua posed the question that Tom realised how long it was since he had travelled that way. To him, Hillend was a sad, neglected place, and yet, twenty years ago, it was a pretty village, full of hope and joy. There was sadness too, but with the optimism of youth, he expected it to pass. Given a fair chance, it would have. At the time, his father was the Squire at Linmore, and he the eldest son.

Tom had spent the last two weeks driving around the estate with Joshua and the Cobarne children, travelling through the villages to meet the local folk, and listening to the boys talking. Charlie immediately took charge, by telling Joshua what to do – and Joshua, delighted to have a friend, let him. The smile on his face was evidence enough to show there was no sign of the fear he felt in his brother's presence.

Oblivious of the two boys, Sophie sat on the floor of the chaise, with her dark-eyed gaze firmly fixed ahead between the horses' ears. Tom was so pleased with the way things turned out that he left the Westbridge post-road behind, and headed for Hillend. Immediately, the name conjured up memories he would rather forget. Times of sadness, deceit, and an estrangement, which was never resolved, even on his father's deathbed.

"Hillend is a village that once belonged to the Littlemore estate, which Aunt Jane's father owned." That was the easiest way to describe it.

"How did it come to be ours, Papa?" said Joshua. "Did she give it to you when she came to live with us?"

"No," said Tom. "Your Grandfather Norbery bought it, when her father died, and merged the land with Linmore."

How simple it sounded, and how complicated it was. The monetary cost to Linmore was relatively small, a few thousand pounds, but it cost Tom everything he held dear.

It was in the summer of '76, when Tom and his brother, Jack, returned from their Grand Tour of Italy, and found their father had purchased Hillend

Estate, the property of his old friend and neighbour, James Littlemore, who died leaving his impoverished family dependent on the charity of others.

Having left the bereaved woman and her three daughters in possession of their home, his father, a widower, made regular visits to ensure the comfort of the widow – an attractive woman in her late thirties – taking his sons with him.

Tom remembered the idyllic summer when he fell in love with sixteen-year-old Jane, newly emerged from the schoolroom, and Mrs Littlemore's acceptance of him as a potential suitor for her youngest daughter. It was a magical time, but the mother's unexpected death, from typhoid, changed everything.

That was when his father ordered him, as the heir to Linmore, to marry one of the young ladies, and denied him the right to choose Jane.

"Think carefully before you refuse me, Thomas, in case you are the cause of all three young ladies being cast penniless on the district." Edward Norbery's harsh voice rang in his ears.

"How can they be penniless," he argued, "when you bought their estate, and allowed them to keep their home at Hillend?"

He had never seen his father look so uncomfortable, or so angry.

"Because James Littlemore's widow would not allow me to pay my old friend's debts. She insisted on doing that herself, and there was little money to spare from the sale. Would that I had paid double the amount, for if the lady had lived longer, she and I might have found another solution to their problems."

Squire Norbery did not say what that might be. Nor did he meet Tom's eye, but the realisation his father had contemplated remarriage silenced him.

"Now, you must marry the older daughter, so her younger sisters will have a home at Linmore. I will dower them and ensure they find husbands. My hands are tied if you refuse, for I cannot offer shelter when they have no female relation to act as chaperone, and Stretton, of Norcott Abbey, insists it is not fitting that Miss Jane should be married before her older sisters."

Tom had no wish to marry a bad-tempered woman, five years older than he, who in the eight months since her stepfather's death scarcely afforded him the time of day. There was no future in it, but his father was adamant.

Within a week, he married Kate Stretton by special licence at Littlemore House, in a ceremony shrouded in secrecy and conducted by an officiating cleric who was a stranger to the district, brought in by Elias Stretton.

Afterwards, his father said, "She may not be your first choice, but all you have to do is get the woman with child, so we may have an heir to Linmore."

Tom looked at his father and said, "You can force me to marry this woman, Father – but not to be her husband. If I die without issue, then Jack, my brother, is the heir."

Less than six months later, when Kate delivered a black-haired son whom she named Matthew, after her father, Edward Norbery summoned his son to ask, "This child, Thomas, is he…?"

"Mine?" said Tom, in a hard voice. "No, sir, he may have our name, but he does not have one drop of Norbery blood in him. You are well served for your interference, but I fear it is an ill day for Linmore."

His father blustered about annulment, but his words had a hollow ring. The scandal would have been too great. Nevertheless, Edward Norbery fulfilled his promise to the other girls, and before the end of her first season, Clarissa Littlemore married into the peerage.

A year later, Jane submitted to the same social process, but declined several offers of marriage, saying she preferred to stay at Linmore to support her older sister. With that, her benefactor had to be content.

It was never a marriage. While Tom treated her with courtesy, Kate repaid him with contempt. He did not know who fathered Caroline, born two years later, and yet he loved her as his own. To reject his wife for her blatant adultery would brand the child a bastard. He could not do it, which begged the question, how could he divorce a woman to whom he had never legally been married, yet who lived in his home as his wife?

Kate's wanton behaviour was not in doubt, only the validity of the special licence and the charlatan who purportedly conducted the marriage.

Tom discovered the fraud in the months following his father's death, when he visited the Doctors' Commons, and learned there was no special licence issued in his name, and no record of the marriage having taken place. When confronted with evidence of her guardian's perfidy, Kate laughed in his face and challenged him to tell the world.

Therein was Tom's predicament. In the eyes of the neighbourhood, Kate was his wife and the mother of his children. Legally, she was not. Had his father been alive, he might have insisted on a remarriage. Instead, Tom accepted his moral obligation to provide a home for his dependants.

Thus, she remained at Linmore, and the psychosis, which followed another pregnancy that appeared from nowhere, set the seal on her violent moods. Since then, Martha, servant to the Littlemore family, had been her constant attendant.

Faced with an untenable position, Tom stood for parliament in the by-election of '86, and won the seat for South Shropshire, which gave him a valid reason to stay away from Linmore. It was not a happy arrangement, but nowadays, Kate lived with Matthew in a separate wing of the Hall, and Jane looked after the rest of the family.

Setting his memories aside, Tom drove the chaise along the winding country lane and up the rising gradient, knowing that when he reached the crest he would see the village below. It was not a hill in the true sense, like Linmore, just an outcrop of higher land over which the road ran.

The view was much as he remembered, except the saplings had grown into trees, and bushes become thickets. He passed the village school on the slope with scarcely a glance, his attention already negotiating the approach to the corner, off which led the rectory drive.

It was fortunate the children sitting beside him were happy to talk amongst themselves. Lucky too the road was free of distractions, because he recalled the next bend was particularly sharp, and the high hedges prevented him from anticipating any oncoming traffic.

Having slowed the horses to a trot, his mind registered the overgrown trees in the rectory shrubbery. He supposed it should not surprise him, because the incumbent was the most cantankerous parson he had ever known.

It was no good blaming others when the fault lay with an absent landlord. Tom felt uncomfortable entering the village, knowing Joshua and Charlie would see evidence of his neglect. That was reason enough to instigate repairs, but it would not be easy. The last time his bailiff attempted to speak of restoration to the church, the rector rebuffed him.

For some obscure reason, Reverend Snitterfield approved of the leaking roof and an inch of draught under the main church door. Life was not supposed to be easy for churchgoers, and Tom was sure it was not.

Even in the height of summer, the atmosphere was depressing. He felt a stab of regret as he approached the church, and then forced his gaze beyond, looking towards the cottages beside the inn on the village green. He knew he should stop and speak with the innkeeper. It was what the villagers had a right to expect, but he did not feel disposed to tarry today.

Tom saw a sudden flurry of movement to the right side of his vision as a piercing sound shattered his reverie. "Squire Norbery, please stop…"

He hardly had time to react.

Hearing the shout, Joshua braced himself for the impact as a figure dashed through the churchyard gate into the path of the Linmore chaise. He hunched his shoulders and covered his eyes, not wanting to see the person trampled under the horses' hooves. If they were not dead, his father was bound to be furious with the person for causing him to snatch at the reins and hurt the horses' mouths.

By the time he opened his eyes, the chaise had stopped shaking and his father was down from his seat, calming the horses. Fear ebbed away, leaving him feeling foolish, but rather than admit it, he adopted a nonchalant attitude.

"Oh no," he said, "not more of them. I'm afraid you will have to get used to this now you are living with us, Charlie."

In truth, Joshua was proud of his father's popularity. There was nothing new about people waving and wanting to speak to him – but they did not usually risk life and limb to get attention.

"Who is that man?" Charlie asked.

"I don't know," Joshua whispered, "but I expect Papa does. He knows everyone in the area."

Charlie was awestruck. "Does Uncle Tom ever call them by the wrong name? I'm sure I would…"

"It's worse now he is a Member of Parliament as well as being squire."

"Be quiet, boys," an irascible voice said.

Joshua lapsed into shocked silence as his father turned to the hapless cause of the incident, cowering at the roadside. It was the church verger.

"What the devil do you mean by dashing into the road, Drakestone? You could have caused me to overturn the chaise. It was a damn fool thing to do."

The man was too mortified to speak, but the smartly dressed woman who swept through the lych-gate in his wake was not intimidated.

"I beg your pardon for stopping you, sir," she said, "but there is something we think you ought to see."

Squire Norbery immediately modified his tone. Joshua could not hear his father's words, but whatever he said made the woman's cheeks flush with pleasure, and she kept smiling. What a relief, he hated acrimony.

As he glanced towards Charlie, his attention fixed on the woman's hat. It was an amazing creation, the like of which he had never seen. It was formed in a dark blue material to match her pelisse, and trimmed with an array of flowers in various shades of pink, red, white, yellow and little trailing bits of blue, which looked so realistic he suspected they were hand-picked from her garden. He could almost smell the scent. Clearly, she was a person of some importance.

With an effort, Joshua dragged his attention back to the conversation, just as his father said, "About what was it you wished to consult me, Mrs Grimble?"

That was the name of one of their tenant farmers.

"Well, sir," said the woman. "I was just putting flowers on Grimble's mother's grave, and the verger called to me to come to the porch, because he had found a basket of rags."

Joshua giggled and bit his lip when Charlie nudged him.

"Be silent, Joshua," his father rebuked. "A basket of rags, Mrs Grimble, and is that all it contained?"

"Oh no, sir," she said. "There was a baby in it. Ever such a tiny tot and it don't look more than a few days old."

"Is the child still in the church porch?"

"Yes, sir, but it shouldn't be left there. We were wondering if you could tell us where we should take it."

Joshua waited to hear his father's decision.

"Where is Reverend Snitterfield?" Squire Norbery said. "I would have thought he was the proper person to deal with such matters."

"Well, sir," the verger cleared his throat. "He is... and he isn't, if you know what I mean."

"No, Drakestone," said Squire Norbery. "I'm not sure I do understand. Perhaps you could enlighten me."

Mrs Grimble interrupted. "It's because the Reverend's sister, Miss Petunia, doesn't approve of bastards, sir. She would send it to the Westbridge poorhouse, without any thoughts about its feeding needs. Unchristian, that's what she is – for all her prating hypocrisy about helping the poor."

That was strong language indeed, which left them in no doubt of the woman's opinion about the parson's sister.

"Do you have any suggestions on where the child should go, Mrs Grimble?" Squire Norbery asked in a quiet voice.

Joshua did not expect that. People in his father's position usually made decisions for other people. Luckily, the woman had an answer.

"Indeed I do, sir. The wife of one of Grimble's labourers had a stillbirth about a week ago, and I was wondering if you thought it might be a good idea if she was to look after the babe, seeing as she has milk to feed it. I wouldn't want to do that if you thought it was not the right thing to do. Of course, I doubt if she could afford to take it without some sort of recompense…"

"Is this woman a reliable person, who would care for the child?"

"Yes, sir, Peggy Walcote has worked for me on the farm for the last three years. She is a bit slow in the head, but is a kind soul, and hard working."

"Show me the child, if you please, ma'am. Drakestone, be so good as to stay with the horses."

"Papa, can we come with you?" Joshua could not wait to ask.

"Yes, Joshua, but you must behave yourselves."

With that, Squire Norbery and the woman turned towards the church.

Eager to follow, Charlie called for Sophie to join them, but she shrugged her shoulders and affected not to hear. No sooner did they pass through the lych-gate than she clambered up onto the seat of the chaise.

"She'll be all right sitting there with the horses, Josh, and the man's holding the reins."

The boys dawdled along the church path behind the grown-ups, kicking stones that came within their reach.

"Did you hear what they said?" Joshua asked.

"It sounds like they have found a baby, but nobody would leave a live one in a church on its own," Charlie said.

"Have you seen one of… what she said before? I haven't." Joshua was loath to admit the deficiency in his knowledge.

"Not that type," said Charlie, "but we did have several babies at home when I was young, but they didn't stay very long before going to live with Jesus. Everyone thought Sophie would go the same way, but she didn't, and look at her now – she's a real beauty."

Joshua would not have chosen those words to describe Charlie's sister, but he did not want to offend him. After all, they had only lived at Linmore for a few weeks, and Charlie was a better friend than his brother had ever been.

On reaching the church porch, they saw a basket of plaited rushes on a low stone shelf near the inner door. Rather than interrupt the grown-ups' conversation, the boys sidled around them and peered into the container.

All Joshua could see was a tiny face, surrounded by a ragged shawl. He assumed from the closed eyelids, the baby would remain sightless for several days like farm kittens.

"What a funny little thing," he whispered. "It has only a few tufts of hair, the colour of the chestnut foal born last month."

"They don't have much to start with, silly; but it grows if they survive." Charlie seemed to know about such things.

Joshua did not like to think the baby might not live. He had never encountered anything like it before. That was the trouble with being the squire's youngest son. Everything happened before he was born.

He wondered what his father would decide. The baby was ever so small, quite helpless, and from what he could see, it would not know how to feed itself.

When he reached out to stroke the baby's cheek, it brought a startling response. Two bright eyes opened, and a tiny hand grasped his finger.

"Hey, look," said Charlie. "He likes you. Be careful though, it might bite."

"Has it any teeth?" asked Joshua, touching the baby's bottom lip. No, he could only see gums. The little mouth started to work around the tip of his finger. Its tongue tickled. "What's the matter with it?"

"It's probably hungry," said Charlie. "Your finger won't satisfy it for long. Babies drink milk."

"Papa," Joshua called. "Charlie thinks the baby is hungry."

That drew the grown-ups' attention.

"Yes," his father said, "I expect it is. That settles the matter, Mrs Grimble. I think you had better take the child to your labourer's wife to care for. Here is some money for her trouble." He placed a handful of coins in her palm.

"But sir, there is five guineas here. Peggy won't expect that much," the farmer's wife said with certainty.

"I will leave it with you to decide how best to distribute it."

"If I find some clothes for the baby, and give the woman a shilling every week, she can bring the little one when she comes to work at the farm. That way I'll know she's taking proper care of it."

"An excellent idea, ma'am," said Squire Norbery. "Later, if the child thrives, she can be educated in the village school, and repay your good nature by working on your farm like the mother."

Relieved the matter was resolved; Tom dispensed a coin to the verger for his trouble, and climbed into the chaise. The boys settled back in their seats, with Sophie on the floor, apparently unconcerned by their absence.

He'd had enough mediating for one day. It must be the season for abandoned children. First, it was Charlie and Sophie, now a newborn baby.

Probably the mother was a country wench who found herself in trouble, and risked losing her home. There were always young men ready to sow wild oats. Tom hoped his eldest son was not the cause of this problem. It would not be the first time. He knew Matthew had faults aplenty, but did not think women featured prominently in his life – quite the reverse. He used them to be cruel.

With his mind filled with the events of the afternoon, Tom turned the chaise around and headed out of the village along the drovers' road that bordered the rear of Linmore estate. He glanced at Joshua sitting at his side, a look of deep concentration on his face. Eventually, he had to ask, "Is something bothering you, Joshua?"

"Why did you say, *her*, Papa? We thought it would be a boy."

"Mrs Grimble said it was a little girl, and she should know."

"Mmm." Joshua nodded his acceptance and turned to Charlie.

On reaching the back drive to Linmore, Tom drove the chaise through the gates into the park, and headed for his sister-in-law's woodland cottage, situated half a mile beyond the lodge.

The children were talking amongst themselves, and he was glad they showed no ill effects from when he'd brought the chaise to a sudden stop. It was safe enough when Joshua and Charlie sat together on the seat beside him, but not with Sophie huddled on the floor between their feet.

He had tried to insist that there was not enough room for all of them to sit in comfort, but she refused to stay behind. Truth to tell, she was no trouble when he let her do as she wished. She was definitely an original character, and Tom was growing accustomed to her quaint little ways. He wanted her to feel at home at Linmore.

Almost before he had drawn the horses to a halt in front of the stone-built single-storey cottage, Joshua jumped down and dashed along the garden path to be first to relate the news. Charlie followed close behind. The front door opened immediately and Jane emerged.

"Aunt Jane, we found a baby. Papa said it was a girl, but we don't know for sure." Joshua stopped to catch his breath, and then hurried indoors to impart the news to Jessie, the maid.

"Yes," said Charlie, "someone left it in a basket of rags."

Jane looked enquiringly at Tom. "Where was this?"

The sight of her always warmed his heart, but he kept his tone light.

"In the church porch at Hillend, of all places," he said, then stepped down from the chaise and handed the reins to the waiting outdoor servant.

"Thank you, William Rufus."

He looked back to the lone little figure squatting on the floor of the chaise.

"Are you coming with us, Sophie? I think we are staying for tea."

She scowled when he held out his hands, offering to lift her down. After a brief moment of deliberation, she shuffled towards him. When he set her feet on the ground, she dashed after the boys into the house.

Jane walked beside him towards the front door, but instead of entering the house, they walked around the side and traversed the length of the garden to an arbour containing a wooden seat. It was an idyllic spot, hidden amongst the trees and shrubs, sheltered from prying eyes, and a suntrap on a warm summer day, such as this year was producing.

It was always a joy to spend time at the cottage. It was Jane's home, and the only place where she could escape from Kate. That is why Tom built it for her – for them – and somewhere Joshua could come when life at the Hall became too much for him.

"Was it a newborn baby?" she said.

"Yes, a little girl, only a few of days old by the look of it. Drakestone, the verger, dashed out of the churchyard gate to intercept the chaise. It was a stupid thing to do, frightening the horses, which could have killed him. I was all set to give him a rare trimming but the farmer's wife from Oak Apple Farm was with him. She wanted to consult me about what should be done with the child."

71

"Did you advise them?" Jane asked.

"I simply agreed to her suggestion that she take the infant to a woman in the village who lost her baby, but was still lactating. Mrs Grimble said the young woman was one of her servants, and could be trusted, so I gave her five guineas for the woman's trouble. It saved the baby going to the Westbridge poorhouse."

"And the breast milk will be put to good use. Poor little mite, I wonder to whom it belongs."

"Apparently, there was a piece of paper with the baby's name, amongst the rags in the basket, but nothing to indicate from where it came."

Jane nodded and changed the subject. "I presume that would be the younger Mrs Grimble? At least, she was twenty years ago, when my father was alive. I imagine she has aged like the rest of us."

"She is decidedly matronly, whereas you don't look any older to me than you did then, Jane." His voice deepened as he raised her hand to his lips.

"Flatterer," she said softly, but her grey eyes shone. "Let us be practical. I am long overdue a visit to Hillend. Would you like me to drive over to see Mrs Grimble during the week to see if her plan came to fruition? Now you have taken an interest, I have a curiosity to see this little waif for myself. I am sure Jessie can find some baby clothes and linen to take for the child."

"But she was only the size of a doll. She was lost in the basket."

"All the better, they will fit her for longer. Did she have any hair?"

"Yes, Joshua described it as being the colour of the chestnut foal born last month. He was enthralled. He'd never seen anything like her."

"That's a wonderful tawny colour. I wonder what happened to the mother. How sad if she was forced to abandon her babe." Her voice wobbled.

"I doubt if we will ever know," he said. "Maybe she did not survive childbirth. We don't even know if the little one will thrive."

A shadow crossed her face. "We must do our best to ensure she does. I will leave some money with Mrs Grimble. How much do you suggest?"

"I've already given five guineas," he said.

"I will discuss it with Mrs Grimble," she said with a smile. "There are bound to be things she will need, and I can always go again to see how she is progressing."

"You would have loved to have a little girl, wouldn't you?"

"Yes… yes, I would, but… it cannot be." She bit her lip.

"In that case, my dear, you must indulge yourself, and adopt the little waif. Who knows, maybe one day she will come to work for you."

"Yes, maybe…"

CHAPTER 8

"Are you ready, Miss Jane?" a gruff female voice called. "I've packed the bag for Mrs Grimble, and William Rufus has the gig outside, but he doesn't want to keep the horse waiting."

The final words had the desired effect.

"I'm coming, Jessie." Jane stopped her musings about the unknown baby, and reached for her "Miss Littlemore" hat, the one she wore on visits around the estate. Dark coloured straw, plain and utterly respectable – just as she was – except that her wavy hair was anything but plain.

As a child, she had a riot of tumbling honey-brown curls that defied all attempts to control it. Her stepsister called it an abomination – but Kate never said a kind word about anyone.

Jane grimaced at the recollection and jabbed the hatpin through the fabric, then checked the contents of her purse to ensure she had enough coins for her needs. Now she was ready.

When they set out, Jessie sat with her in the gig, and William Rufus walked beside the horse. Jane was capable of driving without an escort, but it was something on which Tom insisted and she never ran contrary to his wishes.

The journey to Hillend was a matter of three winding country miles, and Jane knew every inch of the way to the village where she was born. A high redbrick wall bordered the drovers' road on one side and on the other, neat hedgerows and trees. Beyond that, the hay meadows merged with gentle wooded slopes skirting the western side of Linmore Hill.

Travelling by this particular route never failed to bring back memories of a series of tragedies that ruined many lives. It was bad enough when the sinking of an East India merchant ship lost her father a fortune. His death a few months later was worse, but at least no one doubted the shooting was an accident. It had to be, for James Littlemore was a man of honour, who would not have left his beloved wife and daughters in straitened circumstances.

When her mother died of a fever within a year of her widowhood, Kate's uncle said it was typhoid, caused by brackish water from the well. The servants had other ideas, but no one dared speak out. The outcome meant Jane's youthful dreams were shattered when the man she loved was compelled to marry another woman.

Whilst the church taught one to revere family members, it was hard to tolerate the older stepsister who usurped the position intended for her.

Jane might have accepted it better if Kate had made an effort to fulfil the duties of a landowner's wife. Even in the early days, her sister ignored the tenants on the Linmore estate, and not once in almost twenty years had she visited the poor and sick children. Having assumed the responsibility, Jane had a special relationship with servants at the Hall and estate workers' families.

She did it to help Tom, and in her father's memory. How else would anyone remember Squire James Littlemore, late of Hillend parish? If her father had lived, she would have been the wife of some great man of means, but she was content to live at Linmore. It was her life, her greatest love and would be until the day she died.

On leaving the drovers' road, Jane approached Hillend village along the narrow lane bordering the rectory grounds, turned right at the corner and continued towards the Lych-gate. William Rufus stayed with the horse, while Jessie carried the basket of flowers as they made their way to the porch.

It was so quiet that their appearance caused the verger to look up from his work in surprise, and Jane spent a few minutes hearing his news, before placing freshly picked flowers from the gardens at Linmore on her parents' grave.

As she drove towards the Bluebell Inn on the village green, several people came out of their houses to acknowledge her presence. She could do no less than stop to pass the time of day. Although many years had passed since she went to live at Linmore, they still remembered her family with affection.

From there, she moved on through the village towards the turn to Oak Apple Lane, its corner marked by the old tavern known as the Drum and Powder Monkey. A place frequented by the dregs of the social divide, who came seeking cheap ale, and who cared nothing for the rotting timber of the windows and warped roof as long as the drink flowed freely. A favourite haunt of the army recruitment brigades that passed through the area, and from where many local workers had disappeared over the years.

Reaching the junction, she gazed in the direction of her old home. It was little more than half a mile, and for a moment, she was tempted to go the extra distance. Then she remembered the reason for her journey, and turned resolutely up the lane towards Oak Apple Farm. Memories were all very well, but today she had a purpose to fulfil.

William Rufus walked ahead and made their presence known at the farm.

Mrs Grimble was effusive in her greeting. "Oh, Miss Littlemore, this is a surprise. To think you've come all this way to see me."

Jane smiled as she stepped into the parlour. "I must apologise for arriving unannounced, Mrs Grimble, but I was visiting the church, and thought it would be prudent to see you. Squire Norbery was anxious to know the outcome of your quest concerning the baby found in the church porch."

The woman's face creased into a smile. "In that case, ma'am, you may see for yourself, for the child is here." She indicated a crib in the corner of the room, near the fire. "The maidservant I mentioned to Squire Norbery is upstairs making the beds, but I told her to bring the little one here while she works. It's no trouble for me to keep an eye on her."

Before Jane could protest, Mrs Grimble lifted the baby from the cot and brought her forward. "Here she is, ma'am. This is Nell."

Jane's heart melted when she saw the little face. Tom was right, the baby was about the size of a doll she had as a girl. That more than anything brought back the force of her memories.

"She's beautiful, Mrs Grimble," she said tremulously. "Thank you, so much for showing her to me." She stroked the tiny hand with her finger, and felt an instant response as the babe opened her eyes, and her mouth started working.

"It looks like she's hungry, ma'am." The farmer's wife moved away to the door leading to the staircase. "Peggy," she called upstairs. "Come down here, and attend to your child."

Jane was not sure what kind of person she was expecting, but not a girl scarcely into womanhood. She could not have been more than sixteen years old, with a slow manner and good-natured face. Nevertheless, she was well-endowed to provide for the baby's needs, and a look of tenderness transformed her flat expression as she fixed the baby to the breast. Yes, she would probably do well.

While the young mother suckled the infant, Jane called Jessie forward with the supply of baby clothes and linen. Then, she donated a further five guineas to be dispensed at Mrs Grimble's discretion, and went on her way, asking the farmer's wife to keep her informed of the child's progress. She did not expect to have too much contact, but at least she could tell Tom that for the moment the baby was safe.

Once Lucy and Julia returned to Linmore from visiting their grandparents, there was no reason to delay the resumption of lessons. Joshua had shown Charlie the room where they would undertake their studies, and let him see the nursery classroom where Sophie would share lessons with his cousins.

After more than a month of freedom, it was hard to drag their feet up the three flights of stairs to the classroom, but if Joshua expected his tutor to be similarly reluctant to start, he was mistaken.

On each floor, they stopped and peered through the landing windows, and looked across the parkland.

"What shall we do after the lesson's finished?" asked Charlie.

Before Joshua could say a word, a stern voice responded from the upper storey.

"Before you make plans, gentlemen, you have to achieve that objective. Your lesson should have started ten minutes ago."

They looked at each other, and scuttled up the remaining flight of stairs, and through the classroom door. The holiday was over.

Having taken an unplanned sabbatical at Squire Norbery's request, the Reverend, Dr Edgar Hawley, was ready to resume his work, and test the new pupil with untried capabilities.

"As this is Master Cobarne's first Latin lesson with us, I will permit him to use my personal copy of Virgil, but I expect the book to be shown the same respect we give the subject. Now, gentlemen, repeat after me, if you please… *Amo…Amas…Amat…*"

Joshua rolled his eyes skywards. There was scarcely time to enter the classroom and introduce Charlie to his tutor, before the lesson began.

The language was dry as dust, just like the inside of his mouth, and there was at least another hour to go. It was bad enough reciting Latin on his own, but with a new friend to talk to, he could think of more interesting things to say.

At least with Charlie there, his mumblings would pass unnoticed. For once, he did not mind the restricted space in the little room on the top floor.

He supposed Matthew must have used it as well, but for all he learned the time was wasted. From what he could see, it was pointless to send his brother to university, for a more unlikely student would be hard to find. Then he thought about the benefits of his absence, and could not wait to be free of harassment.

"Master Norbery," his tutor's voice brought him back to reality. "I would be obliged if you would share your time with us. Your mind was clearly elsewhere."

Joshua sneaked a look at the wooden clock hanging on the wall, and resumed his droning. Fifty minutes more. Why did time have to drag? It was lucky Charlie was familiar with the subject, because his enthusiasm was as dead as the ancient language. *Morte,* he thought the word was in Latin.

He knew it was fatal for his lessons, but he began to wonder how Sophie was coping down in the nursery classroom with his two cousins. Charlie was starting to fidget, and he sensed his mind was similarly distracted. Then they had the first intimation all was not well below stairs.

The sound started as a faint squawk, coming from the direction of the lower nursery, which grew louder as it progressed up the back stairs to the landing, all the way to the attic classroom. Outside the door, the wailing was replaced by a thump, sounding suspiciously like a kick.

Dr Hawley stopped his recitation, and looked perplexed. "Was it you making the noise, Master Norbery?"

Joshua looked at Charlie and said, "I think there is someone outside the door, sir."

"Someone, or something, do you imagine?" The tutor asked. "Which one of you would care to ascertain the origins of the sound?"

"Please, sir," Charlie said, jumping to his feet. "May I be allowed to look?"

"Ah, the new student has a desire to be helpful. I commend you for your enthusiasm, Master Cobarne. You may proceed."

Joshua guessed what Charlie would find when he opened the door,

78

and he was right. Sophie sat in the doorway, awaiting her brother. At his appearance, she jumped up, hugged him and rushed into the room. Then she clambered onto the seat where Charlie had been sitting, and waited for him to come.

"No, Sophie, you can't sit there," he said. "I'm having lessons with Joshua."

Joshua felt her gaze turn to him, and sensed she expected him to give permission. He did not know what to say, so he waited for the tutor to speak.

"Do I deduce this… young person is a member of your family, Master Cobarne?"

"Yes, sir," Charlie mumbled.

"Elucidate your words, sir. They might one day have some significance."

Sophie sat, fascinated by the sound of the tutor's voice.

"Perhaps you would care to return the child to the proper place for her learning, Master Cobarne, and then we will resume your studies."

By the time Charlie obeyed the last instruction and opened his book, the wailing started again. Then they heard the running footsteps on the staircase and a kick on the door. Sophie was back.

Joshua looked at Charlie. He was tempted to giggle, but had to contain his amusement while the tutor continued his Latin phrases.

Dr Hawley gave an audible sigh, and then, vainly attempting to ignore the distraction, said, "Master Cobarne, would you care to tell me the extent of your studies whilst you were in Ireland? Did you perhaps study the classics, languages – or simply how to attend a recalcitrant sister? I would be obliged if you would convey to your sibling that my lessons are confined to young gentlemen. Miss Finchley attends the young ladies downstairs in the nursery."

Joshua felt Charlie's chagrin, and edged the textbook off the desk. It fell open on the floor with a thump, and succeeded in drawing his tutor's ire.

"When I said for you to treat *Virgil* with respect, Master Norbery, I did of course include the format in which it is contained. *Alas, the world is full of vandals…*"

Dr Hawley went off at a tangent, before adding a caustic rejoinder. "I wonder if it is your intention to destroy the means to study the classics, or whether your vandalism is a way of distracting my attention from your innate lack of ability?"

"I'm sorry, sir." Joshua caught Charlie's eye as he stooped to pick up the book, and winked.

"It would appear that your meagre imaginations have been stretched to the limit for today. You may dismiss, and I will see you here at the same time tomorrow, without the female accompaniment. Do I make myself clear, Master Cobarne?"

Charlie cringed. "Yes, sir, I'll do my best."

"We are all here on the earth to do our best, gentlemen. When we fail, we simply have to strive to do better."

As they opened the door, Sophie took her brother's hand and led him down the stairs. Joshua could not imagine his siblings showing such devotion.

"Is he always as bad as that?" Charlie said.

"I think he thought he was on his best behaviour today."

"It's not Sophie's fault. She's only a little girl, and I promised her when we came here, we wouldn't be separated again."

Joshua heard Charlie say that many times over the following weeks, usually when the tutor admonished his friend for his inability to control his sister.

Eventually, humiliated beyond his limits, Charlie said, "I'm sorry, Josh, I'm going to have to see your father and tell him we can't stay here any more. I do not know where we will go now. Nobody else wants us."

To see Charlie's bubbly spirits suppressed brought tears to Joshua's eyes. He did not want to lose his new friend, any more than Charlie wanted to leave. He was even prepared to have Sophie in the classroom during the lessons, if it meant they stayed at Linmore.

When she joined their afternoon pursuits, Joshua bowed to the inevitable. By now, she should have integrated with his cousins' lessons, but he knew she had no notion of doing girlish things, and suspected her absence from the nursery did not bother the governess.

Sophie became their shadow, and followed them everywhere, even back into the classroom. For some reason, Dr Hawley seemed to have reached a compromise, and agreed she could sit in on their studies for one hour a day. He stipulated she should remain at the back of the room, and listen, without making a noise whilst they did their lessons in French.

At first, she sat, looking from one to another, squinting as she listened to the sounds. Then she left her chair and sat on the floor at the back of the room, facing the wall and talking to herself.

When the tutor stopped to listen, Sophie continued speaking the words verbatim, oblivious of her watchers, or the significance of her uttering.

The tutor nodded his approval and said in the softest tone, "With a little more practice, she will have excellent diction, Master Cobarne. You may commend your sister."

On that day, Joshua relaxed and Charlie smiled again.

Lessons were fun with Charlie in the classroom. He had a question for every answer their tutor expected, and was soon entertaining Dr Hawley with tales of his father's military exploits. There was no doubt, in Charlie's mind: Major Fergus Cobarne was a hero of no mean achievement.

Joshua listened enthralled, and silently thanked his father for his forethought in giving him a new companion, and his only friend.

Apart from his father, Aunt Jane was the only person to show him affection, and he liked to pretend she was his mother. He thought his father wished it as well, because they were such good friends.

Anyone could see that, by the way they laughed and talked together. It was what made Charlie's friendship special, because he made people laugh, and there had been little enough merriment in Joshua's life.

CHAPTER 9

August 1794

Life at Linmore was much more peaceful without Matthew to spoil things. Joshua could rise in the morning feeling free to enjoy the day. It was a time when he didn't live in fear or have to constantly look over his shoulder to see if his brother was lurking around the corner waiting to pounce.

The summer was unlike any Joshua had known. The weather was kind with gloriously long hot days to spend with his special friend. Each one filled to the brim with exploration and adventure. So full he couldn't recall half, yet without enough hours to fill. Sleep claimed him at night, often mid-sentence, and he awoke to pick up the thread of conversation where he left off.

The sense of freedom made his cup of joy run over; but as the weeks progressed he gradually realised that he had simply exchanged one tormentor for another. It started as a sneaking suspicion, which he recognised as a prickly feeling between his shoulder-blades whenever Sophie was near – as she often was.

Initially, his lessons with Charlie were in the classroom, but then the tutor told them of his plan to study the local flora, fauna and geology. That caused great excitement because Charlie had a fascination with fossils, and Joshua knew of a disused limestone quarry on the edge of the estate, which he could not wait to show his friend.

When morning lessons ended, irrespective of the weather, the two lads dashed outside into the fresh air, hoping to slip away without Sophie seeing them. That was the problem, because she was always lying in wait for them. No sooner did she see them, than she trilled, *Charlie… wait for me…*

It was the strangest sound. The trouble was Charlie always waited, and excused his action with, "Sorry, Josh, I can't leave her in case she does something silly."

Of course she would – knowing he would do anything to avoid the situation occurring. It did not matter what they did or where they hid, Sophie would sense where they were. They knew from her crow of delight when she was coming closer. She had a better nose for tracking than the gun dogs, and they had to give up when they heard her warbling nearby.

Charlie was inordinately proud of his sister, even when she disturbed the trout they were trying to tickle in the stream. It spoiled everything.

"Why doesn't she stay with the other girls?" Joshua asked.

"She doesn't want to, that's why," Charlie said. "She prefers to be with us."

"But she's a girl."

"No," said Charlie; "Sophie isn't like other girls."

That much was obvious, but it never occurred to Joshua that girls might not like others of their kind. He thought his cousins, Lucy and Julia, were quite friendly. They probably would not mind having Sophie with them – so why should she object to their company?

It was the same when she persisted in watching him. She would fix him with her gaze, and not move.

"Why does she do that?" he asked.

Charlie sighed, and spoke slowly. "It's because she likes you, silly. Believe me, Josh; it is better to have her as a friend."

Joshua was not sure. It seemed unnatural. He could tell when her eyes were following him, because his skin crawled in the creepiest way. It was a bit like having a pet rat following you. It did not hurt, but set your teeth on edge.

He had only been polite, welcoming her to Linmore, and now she would not leave him alone. If he had known she would be like this, he would have remained silent.

One warm, summer afternoon they managed to slip away to a sheltered place Joshua knew by a bend in the River Linmore. He had gone alone in the past, to paddle near the riverbank, but with Charlie for company, he felt safe to wallow in the deeper water.

It was a magical place. Sunlight filtering through the silver-birch trees cast sparkling rays on the water. A gentle breeze cooled them as they floated around the pool. It was a joy to be free from interruption, but such perfection was too good to last.

Inevitably, Sophie tracked them down, and ran down the slope past the pile of abandoned clothes. She stopped several inches from the water's edge, but her feet slipped on wet grass and she toppled over the edge into the water.

Even before she sank beneath the surface, Charlie grabbed her by the scruff of the neck and heaved her squawking onto the riverbank. Instead of crying, she chortled with glee.

"Stay there, while I get dressed," Charlie ordered, as he hoisted himself out of the water and grabbed his clothes.

Unperturbed by her brother's lack of attire, Sophie sat watching as Joshua trod water, waiting for him to climb out, but he made no such move.

"What are you still doing in there, Norbery?" said Charlie, pulling his shirt over his head. "We have to get her home and into some dry clothes, before she takes a chill."

"You go on ahead," Joshua said. "I'm not coming out with her there."

"Oh, come on, Josh, you cowardly creature," Charlie taunted. "You're not afraid of Sophie, are you?"

No, but he was not going to expose himself in front of a girl either. He would rather freeze. To prove the point he sank further into the depths, which suddenly felt colder. Surely, Charlie did not expect him to explain the reasons. It was enough that Sophie made him feel uncomfortable.

It was disconcerting, the way she sneaked up on them. She did not say a word, but he knew she was there by the strange, spidery feeling touching the back of his leg. Charlie did not take any notice, but it curled Joshua's toes, and made him feel sick.

Charlie might call it affection, but at going on eleven years old, Joshua could not think of anything worse than having a girl touch him like that. It was weird. No, it was worse, because she left dirty finger marks on the back of their fawn-coloured breeches, which made it look as if they had been sitting in something objectionable.

"For pity's sake, Josh, she's only a little girl. She does not know boys are different to them."

Joshua stayed where he was. His legs were feeling cold now and he doubted if they would hold his weight.

"Oh, come on, Sophie, let's go home," said Charlie, grabbing her hand. "Let's leave him to freeze."

Joshua waited until they set off along the riverbank, before clambering out and making a dash for his clothes. As he dragged on his breeches, he looked up and saw Sophie peeping around a tree.

Most young girls would have run away squawking, but not Sophie. Her grin was beatific. Charlie was standing besides her, laughing at Joshua's discomfiture.

"Norbery's a chicken-hearted…"

"No, I'm not…" Mortified at being caught dishabille, Joshua hurled himself at his friend.

When the ensuing scrap ended in a draw, Charlie conceded, "I suppose she is a bit of a nuisance, but I don't think of her as a girl – she's just Sophie. All the same, you shouldn't be afraid of her."

It was not that. The other girls in the household knew better than to creep up on a chap when he was naked. Sophie did not.

After that when Sophie became too much of a pest, Charlie suggested using her as hostage in their battlefield games. She was happy to be tied to a tree while they slipped away to plan her rescue and sometimes only recalled her absence several hours later. Often they met her trudging home dragging the rope or sitting untied, happily crooning to herself, secure in the knowledge that they would come. And they did eventually…

Charlie never dreamed that his lessons at Linmore would include bare-knuckle boxing with a former pugilist. William Rufus, the second son of Aunt Norbery's nurse, was a big man, with a battered face, and long reaching arms. Yet when he spoke, it was with a gentle country voice.

It was one of the most exciting things he could imagine, but not the absolute best. That was having Joshua as a friend. He was like the brother, whom Charlie's ma and pa tried to give him, but their other baby boys died, and only Sophie survived. She was a skinny little thing for years, and he thanked God every day for saving his little sister.

When Uncle Tom took them out driving in his chaise, it was like having his pa back. There was nothing better than driving behind a pair of matched bays, unless it was with a team of four chestnuts, and Uncle Tom had promised to teach him to drive a team when he was older. He could not wait to start.

Charlie tried to tell Sophie there wasn't room for her in the Linmore chaise, but she didn't understand why, especially after Joshua's cousin,

Viscount Atcherly, let her sit on the floor of his curricle. So Uncle Tom agreed, and she was no trouble at all.

In Ireland, Charlie's life was predictable. He ate the same food every day, did the same things and met the same people. Everything changed when he came to Linmore. Classroom lessons were a bit of a trial, but when they were over for the day, life was full of excitement.

Charlie knew Joshua was proficient in several sports he had yet to learn. Fencing was one. He already took boxing lessons with William Rufus; outside when it was dry, or in one of the empty rooms in the stable block when the weather was wet.

Of course, girls could not do those sorts of things, but Sophie came to watch them strip to the waist, and took great delight in tickling Joshua. He hated it, and Charlie knew he should tell her to stop being a pest, but it made him laugh. Josh would just have to get used to such things.

Sparring practice was great fun, particularly when William Rufus brought another lad as an opponent for Joshua. One day, whilst waiting for the other pair to finish, Charlie decided to ask about something that bothered him.

"Why is Joshua so timid, William Rufus? He needs to be toughened up, and I'm going to see that he does."

The boxer looked down from his towering height.

"Are you really?" he said. "Well, let me tell you, young sir. You wouldn't be so ready to sport your canvas if you'd endured what Joshua has put up with from that brother of his."

"What do you mean?"

The pugilist walked away to the edge of the barn, and sat down on a wooden bench, leaving Charlie to follow – almost if he did not want to be overheard.

"Let's just say that Matthew Norbery wouldn't go out of his way to save Joshua's life."

"Oh, you mean the time by the lake with the pistol. It was his cousin, Nathan Stretton, who did that. Matthew would not have the nerve."

"You might think that to look at him," said William Rufus, "but he's sly, and has come closer to putting period to Joshua's existence than his cousin ever did."

"What… you mean Matthew would really kill his brother – but why?" It seemed incredible.

The big man rubbed his nose. "That's not for me to say, because it involves other folks as well. It wouldn't be right, even if I could."

That made Charlie more determined to find out, but when the man remained silent, he could only imagine it was something dreadful.

"Don't you go asking Joshua what happened. All you need to know is that my job is to keep you two lads safe out of harm's way."

"I don't need a nursemaid," Charlie said, full of bravado.

"Whether you want anyone or not, Squire Norbery told me to stay within reach." The pugilist lapsed into a brooding silence as Joshua approached.

Charlie's imagination ran riot. He imagined Matthew Norbery was just stupid, but now it seemed he was dangerous.

A few days later, the boxer seemed to relent. "I suppose you might as well know some of the things, seeing as you and Joshua are friends, for I doubt if he will tell you."

"Did Matthew Norbery really try to kill him?"

"All I will say is to keep away from the icehouse. It's out of bounds."

"You mean the one by the lake?" Charlie had wanted to look inside the building, but Joshua would not go near it.

"That's the one, and the door is always locked. One day, the key disappeared and so did Joshua. Then the key reappeared in its cupboard. The only way we knew to look in the icehouse was because one of the gardeners saw Mathew in the area. Normally, he's a hothouse flower. Wouldn't go out walking and get his fancy boots dirty."

Charlie was appalled. He wanted to speak, but sensed there was more.

"There have been other attempts as well – in the cellar and the attics."

"Why does he do it?"

William Rufus sniffed. "His mother tells him to do it – just as she orders him to flog the lad when his father is away from home, while she sits by and laughs."

Having lost his parents, Charlie could not imagine such a thing.

"I know it's hard to believe, but it is Mrs Kate Norbery I'm talking about. You won't have seen much of her yet, because she's afflicted with some very strange moods, and stays in her room."

"What can we do?"

"Your being here's a help, and I've taught him what I can about boxing."

"What about fencing?" Charlie racked his brains for ideas.

"I wouldn't like to encounter him with the foil off the blade, and for his age, he's better than most with a gun. His father made sure of that, and he can outrun folks with twice his years."

"You wouldn't think he was that capable to look at him." Charlie said with ruthless honesty.

"Joshua might not have a pretty face like you, young Cobarne, but he'll be a man as can be trusted, like his father."

Charlie was still puzzled. "I don't want to be nosy, William Rufus, but Joshua doesn't look anything like his brother."

"That's because he isn't," the man said. "He's a Norbery, through and through. The nose is proof of that, and you only have to see his light-coloured hair with the grey eyes."

"How does that make him different to Matthew Norbery?"

"That nasty black-haired creature follows a feral branch called the Strettons, and that is all I'm going to tell you. Don't dare repeat a word of what I've said."

In the dark of the night, Charlie recalled some of the conversation. William Rufus said there was no secret in why Aunt Jane looked different to her stepsister, because they had different fathers – and mothers. He thought about Aunt Norbery, with her black hair and pallid face. She was a Stretton, by all accounts, and Matthew followed her side of the family.

Left to himself, Charlie sensed the man had said something significant, but it did not make sense. Joshua did not look like either of them, because he was a Norbery, like his father. He thought about what William Rufus said about second marriages – then realised that could not apply, because Aunt Norbery was alive. Either, it was a coincidence – like his likeness to his ma, and Sophie, their pa – or there was some kind of mystery, but he was damned if he knew what it was.

"Why do you want to be a soldier, Josh?" said Charlie, one afternoon in the autumn when lessons were over for the day.

What kind of question was that?

"Because I do," Joshua said. "I always have."

"That's not a proper reason."

Why did Charlie have to spoil things, just when they were getting along well – making friends?

"Uncle Jack was a soldier," he said. That was a good reason. "And second sons in my family always join the army." That was even better.

"Yes," persisted Charlie, "but why do *you* want to join? I know why I want to do it. My pa was a hero and I want to make him proud of me."

Joshua did not want to admit his main reason was to get away from Linmore. Matthew said he did not belong there – and his mother insisted he was not her son – or some word that meant the same.

All the old bitter thoughts rose up in his throat, choking him, but rather than show his feelings, he did the only thing he could. He dashed out of the house, through the arch in the stable yard, and started across the park towards the back drive, without a backward glance. Somewhere behind him, he heard Charlie's voice calling.

"Where are you going, Josh? Wait for me."

Joshua wanted to be alone. He did not need friends who belittled him. He kept running until he reached his special oak tree, the huge one, which had hidden him from his brother, times out of number. With only a scant hesitation to catch his breath, he started to climb. He knew every hand and foot hold; even the ones worn shiny with use.

His foot started to slip, scuffing the toes of his boots, but he hung on, gripped harder and started again, more determined than ever to reach the canopy of leafy branches before Charlie came anywhere near. He did not know what he would do then. It did not matter as long as he was out of sight.

Just in time, he settled into his seat, his back against the big gnarled trunk, knees bent with his feet lodged against a branch, and held his breath. Without thinking, he pulled a handkerchief from his pocket; dropped it and watched it float down to the ground, revealing his position. Sophie dashed forward to retrieve it, and Charlie looked upwards.

"What are you doing up there?" he said. "You're not crying, are you?"

"No," said Joshua, in a gruff voice. "Of course, I'm not."

"Shall we come up?"

"No," said Joshua, protective of his den. "Leave me alone. It is all right for you to make decisions about joining the army. Mine was made for me, and I don't have anywhere else to go."

He did not want to admit that, but it came out, full of bitterness.

Charlie gave him an unhappy look. "I didn't mean anything, Josh."

He said nothing, but after a few minutes, he heard Charlie say, "Oh, come on, Sophie. Leave him to sulk. He'll come when he's ready."

When Joshua looked down the tree, he saw Sophie, squatting on the grass, with Charlie sitting beside her.

Knowing this could go on for hours, Joshua started to climb down.

When he reached the floor, Sophie held out the handkerchief. He murmured a word of thanks, and stuffed it back in his pocket.

"What did you mean, Josh?"

Joshua tried to shrug it off. "I do not belong here," he said. "My mother disowned me when I was born. That's why Aunt Jane looked after me."

"I didn't know…"

"Forget it," he said, wishing he had not said anything. "It doesn't matter."

Then, feeling he must make amends for his surly response, he said, "Come on, let's go for a ride. I should have offered to take you before."

They set off to walk across the park towards the stables. Joshua was used to Sophie not speaking, but Charlie was unnaturally quiet.

"It's all right," he said, anxious to break the uncomfortable silence. "Shelwick will easily find you a pony."

"No, Josh, don't ask him…please," Charlie mumbled. "I can't ride."

Joshua stared at him in disbelief. "What do you mean, you can't ride?"

Charlie flushed to the roots of his hair. "I don't know how. I've never sat on a horse."

"Then how are you going to be a dragoon?" Joshua could not help asking.

Lost for an answer, Charlie bowed his head, and looked at his feet. Full of defiance, Sophie moved to his side, clutched his hand and glowered.

Acutely aware of Charlie's embarrassment, Joshua tried to change the subject. "How did you manage when you were in Ireland?"

"Uncle Lucius only kept one horse, to drive the gig to his office in the village, and take Aunt Barleycorn to church. I used to walk to the rectory for lessons and twice to church on Sunday. It was only half a mile each way."

"What about Sophie?"

"She walked everywhere as well, until she went to the convent in the next village for her lessons." Charlie's voice sounded bitter.

At the mention of that, Sophie's gaze swept the floor.

"In that case," said Joshua, "you don't know whether you can ride or not."

"No," said Charlie, stopping to think. "I don't."

Each one having admitted their difficulty; Joshua and Charlie looked at each other with a new sense of understanding… and respect.

"Now," said Joshua. "Let's go and ask Shelwick, the head groom, to arrange some riding lessons for you. He wouldn't let anyone take a horse out, without knowing they could ride it."

CHAPTER 10

The following afternoon, Charlie went to the stables with Joshua and Sophie, feeling nervous. Yesterday was hard, because he finally admitted he had never ridden a horse. Today was his first instruction. What he made of it would determine his plans for the future. Knowing Sophie came along to offer support, spurred him on. He could not fail with her there. She relied on him.

Charlie looked at the pony Ed Salter had saddled for his use. It was the doziest animal, but every time he moved closer to put his foot in the stirrup, it sidled away. It was maddening, because Joshua, who had less idea about his reasons for joining the army, mounted with ease. The irony of the situation forced a laugh from him.

"It's all right for you, Josh," he said. "You were born in the saddle."

Some folk would have laughed at his failed attempts – or worse still, pitied him. Joshua proved his friendship by offering a practical solution.

"What about the mounting block?" he asked the groom, standing beside them holding the reins.

"Good thinking, Master Joshua," the lad said, leading the horse towards a solid block of stone steps by the stable door.

Joshua dismounted and walked the few yards with Charlie beside him.

"It's all right," he said. "You'll soon get the hang of it. I used it when I started to ride. I think everyone does."

It still was not easy. At first, all Charlie could do was to sit woodenly in the saddle, clutching the reins while the groom guided the pony around the stable yard on a leading rein. Joshua rode alongside in companionable silence.

After a few circuits, he started to relax.

Without the leading rein, it was obvious the horse knew more about this riding thing than Charlie did. To his chagrin, the animal determined how soon after mounting he left the saddle – and the head groom decided how long he stayed on the floor. It was not long. Failure was not an option, because Shelwick made no concessions for weakness, and Charlie was not going to admit defeat.

When he took a tumble, he gritted his teeth and muttered as he climbed back into the saddle, "Damn you, horse. I won't be beaten."

Eventually, Shelwick gave a nod of approval. "Aye, you'll do – for now."

Each night, when Charlie drifted off to sleep, he dreamed of challenging Joshua to a race across the park and never falling off. In the daytime, he was content to ride at the ponderous pace of a snail, whilst the tutor pontificated about the Latin names of trees and shrubs. He heard one word in three and understood less. His mind was on the future, and with Joshua riding beside him, he could believe anything was possible.

They never knew what caused Dr Hawley to change his routine, and take them through the west gate to the park. They continued along the road to the village, and stopped at the cottage opposite the church, which the tutor shared with his sister.

Miss Belinda Hawley was as unlike her tall, thin, reserved brother, as it was possible to be. She was a diminutive lady with a warm, friendly manner. More than that, she had the most extraordinary cooking skills, which earned her the slavish devotion of two young equestrians. Not least because she made the most delicious lemonade in the world, but she kept a store of homemade orange-zest biscuits that melted in their mouths.

One taste led to another, and before they knew, the glasses were empty. They did not need asking twice if they wanted a refill – or maybe two, if it was not being greedy. Then she opened her tin of fruit-flavoured biscuits and they were enslaved.

Even the thought was enough to guide their feet to the village – just on the off-chance of seeing her. Miss Belinda always made them welcome. The ponies received an apple, and she ushered the lads through the door to the kitchen for their refreshment. She never fussed about washing their hands as her brother did. Quenching their thirst was a priority.

From that day, Charlie's riding skills improved out of all proportion – as did his horse's behaviour. He could not speak for the animal, but he would have ridden through fire for one sip of that delicious drink.

Sophie seemed to understand the need for her to stay behind, especially when he brought back an orange-flavoured biscuit, and promised she would learn to ride when her turn came.

For several weeks, they set off in eager anticipation of their treat. Then one day, as summer started to turn to autumn, the direction changed. For some reason, Dr Hawley made them ride all the way to Middlebrook along the drovers' road.

"Sir," called Charlie. "We're going the wrong way."

"No," said the tutor. "My sister is visiting Westbridge today to purchase some lemons. Someone has drunk all her lemonade."

It came as a shock to learn that someone had to buy the fruit. It was a disaster. Without Miss Hawley at home, there was nothing for them to look forward to, and they felt mildly aggrieved about the lack of refreshments. Even worse, Charlie had nothing to offer Sophie as compensation on their return.

The following week, the tutor took them further afield, riding on the lower slopes of Linmore Hill. As usual, the pace was slow and deliberate, but Charlie had a plan in mind for when they reached the wider rides above Middlebrook village. If he could pretend his horse bolted, then Joshua was honour-bound to give chase. There were dozens of rabbits, which could cause such an incident.

The horses plodded up the first half mile of the rise. When it levelled out, they were above the tree line and the whole of Linmore Dale was at their feet.

Charlie glanced at Joshua, riding alongside. He was gazing out over the valley, lost in a world of his own. No one could blame him. On a warm, clear day like today, the view across Linmore Dale was unique. The memory was something Charlie would treasure all his life, wherever he went in the world.

He knew Josh felt the same, but what surprised Charlie was that he did not know anything about farming. Matthew Norbery had forbidden him to take an interest in the estate, on pain of death.

It was not fair, and yet Charlie could not make Josh realise his brother would not know what went on in his absence.

He was determined they would have a gallop to shake away the doldrums. They would have to do it soon because they had been riding for two hours and Charlie knew Dr Hawley would call a halt to return to Linmore. The most likely place would be at the convergence of the upper and lower rides that overlooked the village of Middlebrook. If they were lucky, he might let them ride part of the way along the upper level, which encircled the side of the hill, until they reached the path leading down to the drovers' road near the back gates to the park. There again, he might not.

Oh well, here goes, thought Charlie. *It is now or never.*

He practised the move in his mind, but there was no way of warning Josh this was the time to make a dash across the hillside. He hoped he would not take a tumble. *Serve him right if he did.*

He gave a quick glance over his shoulder. As he expected, Dr Hawley was engrossed in the slim book of verse he always carried. Charlie tightened his grip on the reins, dug his heels in the horse's side and gave a yell. To his ears, it sounded like triumph, and the startled horse threw him back in the saddle. There was no time to regret his decision; he had to retain control of the animal.

From the sound of thundering hooves, he knew Joshua was following. With his experience in the saddle, it would not take long to overtake. The thought spurred Charlie on.

He laughed in delight over his shoulder, and felt his thick black hair flowing free in the breeze. The black strip of ribbon must have pulled loose when his hat blew off, somewhere along the way. The freedom from restraint was exhilarating.

Their horses were neck and neck, each determined to win the race. They glanced at each other, laughing a challenge. Suddenly the unthinkable happened. Charlie looked ahead and saw, to his horror, a flash of colour right in the path of their horses.

He dragged on the reins, knowing Joshua was doing the same, but the closing rate of approach gave no time to do more than shout a warning.

"Clear the path ahead," he yelled, and vaguely heard Joshua's voice, echo the same desperate words.

It was too late. They were on the figure, and beyond as the horses thundered past, still neck and neck, with neither rider seeing what happened to the unfortunate person in their path.

Their flight ended in confusion a few hundred yards down the slope, beyond the brow of the hill. Charlie's hands shook so much he could scarcely grip the reins. He felt sick and icy cold. Joshua looked as ashen-faced as he felt.

One after another, they slid from the saddles and sat on the ground with head in hands while the horses grazed a short distance away. They had their race, but the pleasure evaporated. The warmth had gone from the day. What would they do if they had killed someone? They ought to go back but were scared of what they would find.

"Was it a man or woman?" Joshua said, glancing back over his shoulder.

"I couldn't be sure," Charlie replied. "Was it on your side – or mine?"

Joshua shook his head. Not knowing made it worse.

"Shouldn't we go back and see if they are all right?"

"I don't know," said Charlie. "Doctor Hawley wasn't far behind us. He would surely stop. He'd know what to do – wouldn't he?"

"I expect so." Joshua did not sound very sure.

Waiting was agony and the consequences of their actions assumed alarming proportions. Charlie's imagination magnified every sound and thought. Eventually, they could bear it no longer.

As one, they gathered their disordered wits together and looked for their horses. Seeing them grazing further down the hill, they plodded the distance, and were halfway back along the path when Dr Hawley rode into view – still reading his book of poems. They did not know what to think.

Surely, if the person were injured, he would not have left them there. Maybe he could not do anything to help – but he would at least have said a prayer. They waited, expecting the tutor to scold, but when he spoke, it was in the calmest voice.

"Now that you have had your gallop, gentlemen; you will take the next turn down to the village, and return along the drovers' road in single file."

"Yes, sir," they said in unison. However much they wondered what happened, it was obvious Doctor Hawley did not intend to indulge their curiosity.

After a while, Charlie wondered if they imagined the whole thing. They did not attempt to run away again, nor did they say a word to anyone. His greatest fear was that they might be deprived of future visits to see Miss Hawley with her lemonade and orange-zest biscuits. That was the worst punishment he could imagine. It did not bear thinking about.

Every day that Charlie took riding lessons, Sophie followed them to the stables, and in the months following when they went out across the park with Dr Hawley. They knew she watched them leave the stable yard and was waiting on their return.

Ed Salter had told them that her interest in Lucy and Julia's riding lessons did not extend beyond the second day, which led them to wonder what she did in their absence. Charlie was anxious when she missed several of Dr Hawley's classroom lessons.

"I wonder where she's gone. She's usually here with us."

"Maybe she went to the stables with the other girls." It was the best suggestion Joshua could make.

"You could be right," said Charlie. "We'll go there before luncheon."

When they arrived in the stable yard, Sophie was perched on the mounting block, enthralled by everything she could see. The next day they found her in the same place, and every day for the following two weeks. It became so predictable, it hardly seemed worth going, until one day when they went to the stables, she was nowhere in sight. Instead, they found Shelwick, waiting for them.

"We've got a problem with your sister, Master Charlie."

Charlie ruffled up at the gruff sound in the groom's voice.

"What do you mean? She's not hurt, is she?"

"No," the man snorted. "Quite the reverse, though it's more by luck than anything else. I've never known one so young be so contrary. Where the other girls ride ponies, your sister took it into her silly little head to groom the Master's bay gelding. That great brute could have kicked her out of his stall. He's done it often enough with the stable lads."

"What happened? Did he hurt her?" Charlie was beside himself.

"If I hadn't seen it myself, I'd never have believed it. There she was, crooning away in her weird little voice, and that old devil of a horse let her brush him, like he was the most docile creature in the stables, which he ain't."

They sighed with relief.

"The trouble was, young Jem saw her and told her to move away from the animal. She answered back when he went to pick her up, and the horse tried to trample him underfoot – almost as if it was looking after the girl. I dunno what she said, but it sounded like gypsy talk to me. They have their own language that animals understand."

"Where is she?" Charlie's voice sounded funny.

"We left her there, talking to the horse. It was more than we could do to get her to come out. I doubt she was in any danger."

Charlie tried to sneak past, but the groom caught his arm.

"Come you here, Charlie. You don't seem surprised. I reckon you know more about your sister's knowledge of horses than you let on. You'd better tell me first, because Squire Norbery will have to know."

Joshua looked at Charlie's troubled face, and guessed he was debating what to say. His muffled voice was barely discernible.

"There were gypsies on the hillside near the convent where Sophie went to school. When the nuns beat her, she climbed over the wall and ran away. They always found her in the camp. She did it several times in the year before we came here. Poor little girl, I think it was the only time she was happy."

Early summer 1795

When Squire Norbery summoned Joshua and Charlie to the stables, with express instructions to take Sophie with them, he gave no hint of what lay ahead. It was within a month of her tenth birthday, and Tom knew from his observations in the year since he brought the children from Ireland that Sophie would attend him, but on this occasion had no idea how she would react. That was why he wanted her brother to be there.

She drifted across the stable yard beside the boys, wearing the same grubby black frock and mutinous expression she always wore. No matter how many times she changed her clothes in a day, she never looked tidy. Her black hair seemed permanently tangled and her scuffed boots looked suspiciously like something Charlie might once have worn.

Tom waited until the head groom led a dark brown pony from the stalls. Not one smoothly brushed and neat, like the younger girls would have ridden. This was a perfect match for Sophie, with a suitably ruffled coat, and a disposition best described as truculent.

Sophie turned a wary glance in his direction, and for the first time since her arrival at Linmore, she cried. She did not know whether to run to the horse, or to him. She stood, looking from one to the other, her face a picture of disbelief.

"Is it for me?" she breathed, tears streaming down her cheeks. "Oh, Uncle Tom... thank you, I've never had anything like this before."

"Yes, Sophie, it's for you." Tom's eyes felt similarly moist, but to overcome his emotion, he said in a brisk tone, "Now, young lady, you have to play your part. Shelwick will teach you to ride and groom the horse, but it will be your responsibility to care for the animal. Do you understand?"

"Oh yes, sir – thank you, sir," Sophie said, her eyes shining, and then dashed off to hug the pony.

Tom knew he was right to suppose she would not want a quiet little filly to ride. She needed a mount that would test her resilience.

He called after her. "I think you'd better borrow some of Charlie's old breeches for when you are working in the stables."

The smile she turned on him was beatific.

"There is one more thing, Sophie. When Shelwick has decreed you are fit to ride to hounds; you may have a riding habit, but I will leave the design to you."

Sophie nodded, but her attention was elsewhere.

True to his reputation of being a hard man, Tom Shelwick gave her strict instructions about her duties. "Now, Miss Sophie, it is no good you thinking you can come as and when you feel like it. With Squire Norbery's permission, I'd like to start tomorrow. What time do your lessons finish?"

The girl scowled at him. "I can go to there anytime," she said. "This is far more important."

Everyone laughed, thinking Sophie would tire of her responsibilities, but she proved them wrong. The next morning, and every day thereafter, she was in the stables before breakfast, clad in a pair of her brother's old breeches, ready to break her fast with the stable lads.

She spent two hours following Shelwick's rigid training schedule, and then groomed the horse until its coat shone and brushed its shoes. Afterwards, she learned how to feed the animal, mix mash, cut chaff, recognise ailments, and apply compresses to strained ligaments. She had never looked happier.

None of the stable lads seemed surprised when the animal let her do as she wished. She forgot everything but the job in hand, and the pride she felt showed in the work she did.

On the few odd occasions when Sophie deigned to visit the nursery classroom, she arrived late for lessons, smelling of horses and shocked the governess with frequent lapses into the language of the stables.

One day, Joshua rode into the stable yard with Charlie. Usually, Sophie gave her brother first consideration, but on this occasion, she ignored them. Shelwick was in full flow, and her eyes did not leave his face for a minute.

Charlie stopped to watch. "D'you know, Josh?" His voice was strangely husky. "I haven't seen her look like that for years. Our pa was strict with her, and she would do anything for him. I reckon Shelwick has earned her respect; and knowing Sophie, that's not an easy thing to do."

Right from the first, Sophie knew no fear. Tumbles came thick and fast, but she climbed doggedly back into the saddle. Once she broke her collarbone, and Shelwick banned her from doing any grooming, but she was determined to make him change his mind. Even with her face grey with pain, she pleaded, cajoled and cursed. She stamped her feet with impotent rage, but to no avail, the head groom was immovable.

"Don't you come here shouting at me, missy," he said. "It's more than my job is worth to let you kill yourself."

When she snorted and turned away in disgust, the groom called after her retreating figure, "And remember to bring some better manners the next time you come, otherwise you won't ride any horse in my care."

Forced to capitulate, Sophie stalked out of the stable yard. For the duration of her stormy convalescence, she made everyone's life a misery, until Shelwick allowed her back in the saddle. Only then was she happy.

When Squire Norbery asked for a report on her progress, Shelwick shook his head. "I've tried me best, sir, but there's no stopping her. The silly little wench throws her heart over every time. Lucky it was only her that was hurt and not the horse."

The same obstinacy showed in the design of her riding habit. Sophie had no time for girlish notions of propriety. She knew what she wanted and stated her preference, but the dressmaker refused to comply. A battle of wills raged between them, which each was determined to win.

Eventually, someone had to adjudicate. Tom Norbery knew a side-saddle was an anathema to Sophie. The black riding habit she wanted was of a military style, with a divided skirt. The matching hat, a shako, was similarly severe.

Tom made his judgement, knowing he had given her carte blanche in the design, and was not about to renege on his promise. Admittedly, the style was bold for a female, but from what he could see, culottes were eminently suitable for riding. When he approved her choice, Sophie crowed with delight, but then he attempted to placate the dressmaker's offended sensibilities.

"I'm sure you will agree, ma'am, in the event of Sophie being unseated on the hunting field, such a habit would be more decorous than a skirt."

"Uncle Tom!" Sophie was outraged. "I almost never take a tumble nowadays."

"Do you not?" he said with a smile. "I felt sure preserving your modesty was your main reason for wanting the design."

With that, she had to be satisfied.

The finished outfit effected a remarkable change in Sophie's demeanour. With the training in horsemanship and improvement in her appearance, all trace of the clumsy, inept child of early years disappeared, and someone determined to be the best emerged.

Her real character showed when she was on the hunting field. She flaunted her divided skirts, showing contempt for women using a side-saddle. She was always happiest out in front with the leaders, taking her fences like a man, challenging her brother and Joshua to keep up with her. And they tested her to the limit.

Tom could see it was a matter of honour, for they could not afford to have a girl beat them, particularly one who was younger. If she fell at a fence, she cursed profanely, but was back on the horse in an instant.

There was no doubt her riding style commanded respect, and he noticed even Joshua agreed when Charlie said,

"Sophie's a good 'un."

CHAPTER 11

1798

Charlie's voice broke first. At fourteen and a half, he was the eldest. Joshua's tone deepened a few weeks later and he was easily the tallest and leanest.

Tom heard the news of the gruff voices in a letter that Jane sent to London. Although she made light of the event, it was obvious the lads were growing up and he knew before long that they would be kicking up all kinds of larks if they stayed at Linmore.

It was a good thing Matthew went straight from university to a tour of Italy; otherwise, there would have been confrontations – and might still be on his return home. The question was how to avoid it.

If it had not been for Sophie, they would have gone to boarding school. Another option was some kind of tour. As a young man, Tom travelled through much of Europe with his younger brother, and he wanted them to have the same opportunity to broaden their outlook.

It would be a wrench to send them away, but with their avowed ambition to be soldiers, the natural progression was something with a military slant, and Tom knew the erudite Dr Hawley was passionate about history. Before he could set plans in motion, something else took precedence.

In the previous spring season, a bout of influenza caused the cancellation of Caroline's presentation at Court. To delay her coming out further was unthinkable, which was why, a few weeks into the new year, the family from Linmore travelled to Cavendish Square, to stay in the Pontesbury household.

Tom's sister, Winifred, offered to bring Caroline out with her eldest daughter, Leticia. Then she extended the invitation to Lord and Lady Cardington for their daughter, Henrietta. Rather than leave the younger members of the family at home, Tom decided it was time they visited London.

Joshua and Charlie had no interest in presentations at Court or attending select dancing assemblies. They heard mention of Almack's Club until they were heartily sick of the name. It seemed a fool's errand for any girl to go there, simply to find a husband. From what they could see, it was an excuse to spend a vast amount of money on fancy frocks and frippery things of no value to anyone.

The house in Cavendish Square was in a state of flux, with three branches of the family in residence, and three young ladies preparing for their Court presentation. Nevertheless, Mrs Pontesbury was equal to the task of launching them into society – not least because when she requested attention, the world of milliners and modistes beat a path to her door.

Although considered eccentric by her contemporaries, every tradesperson who performed a satisfactory service for the lady knew they were assured of prompt payment. It was a powerful incentive.

For the young folk of the family, encountering the situation for the first time, it was a nightmare. The brass doorknocker on the black front door was never still, No sooner did the footman close the door on one visitor, leaving a calling card, than another arrived to make a morning call.

Below stairs, a porter was stationed by the tradesman's entrance to take delivery of clothes and hatboxes, which came several times an hour. Even worse was the profusion of floral offerings, inscribed with inane sentiments from a host of admirers. These were a source of amusement. Having read some of the ill-spelled sonnets and odes to the young ladies' relative blue, grey or brown eyes, Joshua and Charlie decided the writers of such nonsense must be touched in the head. Either that or they were bosky.

Aunt Winifred's youngest son made fun of everything, and thought it a great wheeze to swap the name cards around to cause confusion. When his mother demanded an explanation, Joshua and Charlie pushed him forward to receive his punishment. It was nothing to do with them.

The following day, Teddy Pontesbury retaliated by making an outlandish comment, which deprived Joshua of breath.

"D'you know chaps?" he said, including Sophie in their numbers. "I bet old Josh could write a better ode to Sophie's smile than this tripe."

Joshua froze at such a thought, and Charlie's brow puckered as he heard the words. Then he grinned and tapped his fingers to his head. Joshua nodded agreement. Pontesbury was a duffer.

"What d'you mean, Sophie's smile?" he said. Only a half-wit would suggest that. How could you pay tribute to something that did not exist? Everyone knew Sophie glowered most ferociously, and grimaced like nobody else – but she never smiled.

There was no peace for anyone. The lads watched the goings on in a state of bemusement from the upper floors. How glad they were not to be involved in what seemed a predatory occupation, which they likened to a foxhunt.

When Sophie curled her lip at such activities, they were in full agreement. They could only hope three determined females seeking a husband would not set their hopes on one unfortunate fellow and tear him limb from limb. Although the families purported to be friends, the degree of competition between the young ladies was beyond comprehension. If it were not for the risk of injures, they might just as well have let a prize fight decide the matter. It would be more interesting for the menfolk to watch.

It was a joy to learn that Lord Cardington's second son, Frederick, a Captain in the Life Guards, was on furlough. The sight of his military uniform made them restive. They wanted time to go faster, but were more than happy when he offered to take them to Horse Guards Parade. The visit was an outstanding success. They questioned him incessantly about his duties; and hung on his every word as he told them action-packed stories.

Most evenings, Fred and Augustus Pontesbury went off on the town with their friends or to social functions with the family, leaving the younger members at home. Teddy Pontesbury taught them to play cards. He was even more of a slow top than before, and had an irritating habit of waggling his eyebrows when he was talking, which amused Sophie. They were soon firm friends.

While Joshua and Charlie struggled to understand Teddy's version of Whist, which fell short of the original rules, Sophie grasped the essentials and was quickly engrossed. When she asked Teddy to show her how to play Loo, he was happy to explain.

"The general idea, Sophie, is that any card player who fails to take a trick has to pay a forfeit into the pool. In this case, we'll use tokens, so you won't be out of pocket."

"No," she said in disgust, "they're worthless. Why can't we use pennies?"

Being only a girl, Teddy decided to humour her, but he underestimated her aptitude. Sophie had a quick eye for detail and ruthlessly played to her own set of rules. When they exchanged cards for dice, she exhibited a deft turn of the wrist. By the end of the evening she clutched a handful of coins. No doubt a beginner's luck.

After the third such evening's occupation, Teddy Pontesbury viewed her balefully and asked, "Have you played before?"

Sophie glowered at him and went on counting her winnings, which left Charlie to speak in her defence. "Leave her alone, Pontesbury," he said. "She beat you fair and square."

"Too many times for a beginner," came the surly response.

Afterwards in the bedroom that they shared, Charlie said to Joshua, "I didn't say anything to your cousin, but I have a feeling that Sophie learned to play cards and handle dice with our pa. She was always pestering him when he was at home."

The following day she was in alt, when Fred Cardington offered to take them to the horse sales at Tattersalls. Girls did not normally go there, but nobody questioned her presence, when Sophie appeared wearing a pair of her brother's buckskins and boots.

With the military visit behind them, Joshua and Charlie felt honour bound to take Sophie to see the circus at Astley's Amphitheatre. Although they pretended it was for her benefit, they secretly revelled in the skills of the horseback riders, were spellbound, watching the acrobats and fell about laughing at the clowns' antics. The wild animals at the Royal Exchange intrigued them at the time, but after a couple of weeks, they were again suffering from ennui.

On the evening of the Pontesbury Ball in Cavendish Square, Joshua and his cousins escaped to the upper floors. Teddy led them along corridors to the back stairs, and thence through a door leading to a darkened balcony overlooking the ballroom. The room below was ablaze with lights and glistening crystal chandeliers.

Surrounded by the sound of a fine string orchestra, they watched guests dancing and milling around the reception hall en route to the supper room. The thought of food made everyone feel hungry, so Teddy summoned the servants to bring food and drink to the schoolroom.

While everyone else trooped away, Joshua stayed to watch his family gathered in the ballroom below. Even his mother was there, which surprised him for she was decidedly antisocial at Linmore.

All thoughts of the family elders receded when he entered the schoolroom. A bowl of fruit punch took pride of place on the table, surrounded by plates of delicacies; hors d'oeurves, potted meats and fish in light pastry cases, jellies and small cakes. On other platters were wafer-thin slices of ham and poultry, with a side of salmon.

Charlie looked up as he appeared. "Where have you been, Josh? You'll miss the food if you don't hurry."

"He's been wenching below stairs, I'll be bound," Teddy Pontesbury said with a leer. "Better not let my mater see you, coz, or you'll get a taste of her special birch."

"Just as you do, Pontesbury," Charlie growled.

They were disgusted with Teddy's habit of luring housemaids into dark corners. Sophie treated it as a joke, but she was too young to understand.

"Take no notice of him, Josh. Try some of the fish, it is particularly good."

Teddy handed him a goblet of punch, and said with a wink, "Have some of this special fruit cup to go with it, coz."

Joshua took a cautious sip, and almost choked as the liquid burned his throat. Teddy threw back his head and roared with laughter.

"It has a little addition of my own... which grows on you," he chortled, pointing at a bottle of his father's brandy.

Sophie giggled, and held out her glass for a refill. It was obvious the mixture suited her palate.

That night sleep came quickly. In the morning, Joshua and Charlie were up at dawn, dressed ready for riding. Parties or not, Sophie expected them to escort her to the park, and not knowing their way around, it was necessary for a groom to guide them through the bewildering amount of traffic.

This was the best part of the day, feeling free to gallop along the almost empty rides in Hyde Park. Then they made their way back for a hearty breakfast, before the rest of the family were awake.

After a month, Joshua, Charlie and Sophie were ready to return home. They went in one coach, while Aunt Jane and Joshua's mother travelled in another, accompanied by Martha, the nurse, who attended his mother's needs and carried her medicine.

Caroline stayed in London with Aunt Winifred and her family. Tom Norbery remained there as well, and however much Joshua wished otherwise, he knew that it was necessary for his father to attend debates or whatever it was that politicians did during the Parliamentary Session. Maybe he would even attend some of the social events.

Aunt Jane told him that Caroline and her cousins had taken well – whatever that meant. Realisation came after they returned home, and he learned his sister had received an offer of marriage from Richard Shettleston. It was the silliest thing he had heard.

"He lives within five miles of Linmore," he said to Charlie. "She didn't have to go through all this, just to meet him. Just think how much money they could have saved."

"You'd never catch Sophie doing that to find a husband," Charlie said with a grin.

Joshua looked at him, bemused. The thought of Sophie Cobarne one day having a husband almost made him fall about laughing. He stopped himself just in time, in case Charlie was offended.

September 1798

Having congratulated himself on the successful outcome of Caroline's wedding, Tom Norbery resumed his planning for Joshua and Charlie's tour. Knowing that the state of war in Europe would decide everything, he considered the options on how they would travel and where it was safe to go. Then, he spoke to the lads.

"Dr Hawley and I have decided you would benefit from some foreign travel. Not the kind of Grand Tour on which Matthew is engaged, but one with a military connection."

Joshua and Charlie looked delighted at the prospect.

"I am sure you are aware of Dr Hawley's interest in military history, so I will leave it with him to tell you the destinations. We were thinking sometime in March would be a good time to set out, so between now and then, you will continue your language studies."

That would be a few weeks before Joshua's sixteenth birthday.

"What about Sophie, sir?" Charlie asked the inevitable question.

Tom had his answer ready.

"She will remain at Linmore. The places where you will travel are not appropriate for her to go. Let us say, this is a practice for when you begin your military careers."

He could understand Charlie's predicament, feeling torn between loyalty to his sister, and his wish to travel.

In the end, Charlie said, "I understand, sir. I will have to explain she could not bring her pony. She fretted about him when we were in London, and we will be away from Linmore much longer this time."

Tom hoped she would accept this. Seeing the lads sitting in the classroom, at desks they had outgrown, he wondered if Dr Hawley noticed how they had changed since visiting London in the spring.

Charlie was almost sixteen, and it was obvious their gruff voices had not come alone. Long limbs and big feet brought their own problems as the two young men adjusted to their new maturity. At their age, female distractions were inevitable, but he must do his utmost to avoid any undesirable consequences.

Whilst out riding in the park, he saw the former pugilist walking towards him, so he drew his horse to a halt and waited for the man to approach.

"William Rufus," he said. "Joshua and Charlie are going travelling with their tutor in the spring, but I want you to keep them out of mischief until then. They'll have plenty to think about, once they are abroad."

"You mean the wenching kind of mischief, sir?" the man said with a grin.

"Yes," said Tom. "They're growing up fast. I don't want any bastards here, and they're too young for anything else." He could say it to William Rufus with impunity. Dr Hawley was another matter.

"I'll do me best, sir, but they're healthy lads, and popular with the womenfolk on the estate. A bit like a jam pot attracting wasps."

Tom knew what he meant, having seen how the lads drew many eyes in the congregation at church the previous Sunday. Most people looked favourably on them, but those with daughters had cause to be anxious. Sons of the gentry always drew attention; but these two were likely to set the neighbourhood alight.

"Do not give them time to get bored," he said. "Increase the pressure on them. Test them to the limit, and keep their competitive spirits directed against each other. Tell them these skills might one day save their lives in the army. They'll accept it from you."

William Rufus nodded. "I reckon whatever we do, they'll be having an audience, sir. Even when I was in the ring, there were wenches around the prize fights. Not out in the open, but behind the scenes they were."

Throughout the late autumn, Joshua and Charlie rode hard to hounds, and honed their shooting and fencing skills to competitive levels. Boxing became ever more intense – almost to the point where William Rufus ended the session with a well-aimed bucket of water. Neither would give an inch – they each had to earn the respect of the other.

Whilst there was little to choose between them, if either one was judged the loser on points, he demanded a rematch, determined to prove him the better man. Inevitably, the bouts attracted an audience of cheering stable lads and giggling dairymaids. Sophie, previously the only observer, was furious, and she drove them from the barn.

The snow, which came in January, was particularly deep and for a few weeks, Joshua was anxious in case it caused them to delay their journey. Thankfully, it melted by the beginning of March, but took another two weeks for the waterlogged roads to clear of floods.

With everything prepared for the journey, they studied the weather several times a day, desperately hoping for keen winds to blow away the storm clouds. Eventually, there was a lull, and on the morning of departure, Joshua went dutifully to take leave of his mother, but she refused to see him.

When he went outside, two coaches lined up outside the door. Dr Hawley stood waiting by the first, and Joshua looked around for Aunt Jane. Thank goodness, she was there, but the hardest part was saying farewell. Knowing it would be a long time before he saw her again, he gave her a quick hug and said, "I promise to write about our travels."

Then there was a delay of an hour, because Sophie was missing and Charlie would not get into the coach until he saw her. The servants looked everywhere inside Linmore Hall and out. Eventually, they found her hiding under a seat in the second vehicle containing the baggage, where Dr Hawley's manservant, and Gilbert, younger brother of William Rufus, were due to ride.

She looked so dejected when they tried to say farewell, Joshua almost wished they could let her go with them – anything to put a smile on Charlie's face. Then Shelwick brought her pony and she rode alongside the coach to the bottom of the drive. The last sight of her was when they reached the lodge. She waved a hand, as if in acceptance and turned away to gallop up the drive.

Charlie was hard-pressed to contain his sadness, but no one said a word, fearing to embarrass him. The thought of leaving Linmore touched Joshua the same way, and Dr Hawley, sitting with them, holding his book of poems, was similarly quiet.

By the time they had left rural Shropshire behind, and moved through the farming landscape of Herefordshire, both considered themselves seasoned travellers to be visiting London for the second time in a year. Despite this, not even the well-padded seats of the Linmore coach could alleviate the tedium, or jolting from side to side, along cart-rutted roads, and they viewed the coaching inn on the outskirts of Gloucester with relief.

Within an hour of arrival, they sat down to a meal of beef stew topped by herb dumplings, with lashings of gravy, followed by a spiced apple pie and cream. It was simple fare, but most welcome.

Their bedchambers appeared as if by magic, and they tumbled into the warm feather beds and slept the night through. They awoke refreshed, and after a leisurely breakfast, set off towards Oxford, through the Cotswold hill country with its green valleys and pretty villages of yellow stone houses.

They reached Mrs Pontesbury's home in London by the middle of the third day, and spent the next two weeks with the family, waiting for the ship to take them to Italy. It was a busy time, acquiring travelling clothes for their journey.

While Dr Hawley visited museums, Joshua's father took them to his tailor, Weston, and to have new boots made by Hoby. Aunt Winifred donated numerous items of attire, for which she claimed her two sons had no further use. Knowing her love of giving presents, Joshua suspected it was no such thing, but would never dream of saying as much.

Most poignant for him were the days his father spent with them in London before they embarked. During this time, they met a former soldier, named Sergeant Percival, employed by his father to act as tour guide to organise their travel and accommodation. It was clear the man had been in the army, but his bearing, manner and voice seemed too refined for a common soldier.

He was a tall man, with dark hawkish features, and strange green eyes, which gave him a natural air of authority. At first meeting, his disposition seemed taciturn, but his unerring knowledge of the vernacular in several foreign languages deterred anyone presumptuous enough to approach them. Two other men appeared with him, to whom he designated the title of assistants. Both were hard-faced, with wiry frames, clearly stamped with the mark of former soldiers.

When Dr Hawley met the tour guide, he froze him with a look of disdain and turned away. Later, when he needed to communicate on any matter, he sent messages with Gilbert, the Linmore servant. Joshua saw this and puzzled over the reason. It was strange, because their tutor always expected people to be polite to him, but he showed scant respect for the other man.

It was a cold morning in the second week of April, when Joshua and Charlie travelled to London Docks, to board a merchantman bound for ports along the Mediterranean coast, of which Naples was their destination.

They stood on deck, buttoned up in their greatcoats against the freshening breeze that filled the sails, as the ship slipped its moorings and slid into the deep-water channel on the morning tide.

Tom Norbery stood on the quayside, his hand raised in farewell. As Joshua returned the salute to his father, he felt the enormity of the increasing distance between the land and boat, knowing it would be many months before they met again. He sensed the same emotion in Charlie, standing beside him at the rail, but did not want to admit feeling scared.

"I suppose it will be like this when we go to war," he said. "Travelling across the Channel, I mean."

"Yes, I suppose it will," said Charlie.

They gave a final wave of farewell as the docks slipped out of sight. Soon, they were past the mouth of the river, heading down the Kent coast. Then curiosity took over. They never imagined seeing so many ships in the Thames estuary, or a lighthouse at Sheerness.

They saw the chalk cliffs of Dover on their starboard side, whilst across the water the French coast looked ominously close. They had not realised enemy ships had access to the same coastal waters through which they sailed. They were not alone in feeling nervous. Dr Hawley admitted he had not travelled before. Only Sergeant Percival was a seasoned traveller, but he kept to himself.

Once clear of the English Channel, Dr Hawley resumed their lessons. Each day he kept them apprised of the ship's position, and the captain's intention to keep the Brittany Coast well to port.

There were no problems until they were halfway down the Atlantic coast, approaching Bordeaux. The first intimation of trouble came when a lookout sighted a ship off the starboard quarter. Activity amongst the ship's crew intensified and Sergeant Percival appeared at Dr Hawley's side, to interrupt his discourse.

"Beg pardon, sir," he said in a blunt voice. "Can you take the young gentlemen down to their cabins?"

Ignoring the man, the tutor turned a haughty shoulder, with unexpected consequences. The former soldier raised his tone.

"For goodness sake, Hawley," he said. "Do as you are told for once. It's the captain's orders."

Dr Hawley was incensed. "You are impertinent, Percival. How dare you use that tone with me?"

Joshua and Charlie looked at the two men, aghast. What was going on? No one omitted the tutor's title.

"With respect, sir," the man said. "I am trying to impress upon you that Squire Norbery did not intend Master Joshua's tour to include an enforced ride in a French man-of-war."

The tutor's resistance collapsed as pallor replaced his previous facial flush.

"A French ship…?"

"Yes, sir," the guide pointed across the deck, "and it is bearing down on us. Now, if you don't mind, sir, the captain wants all English travellers to go below deck and stay there until further notice."

The ensuing panic induced an epidemic of mal de mer, as passengers rushed to their cabins, hailing servants to their side. This state of affairs proved of benefit when the advancing ship signalled the merchantman to heave to for an inspection.

Knowing the risk of the French taking his ship as a prize, the captain had ordered the fever flag be pinned to the yardarm, to discourage boarders. His hope being with only a handful of crew on the deck, the French sailors would wish to avoid contact with disease.

While the meeting went on above deck, Joshua, Charlie and others like them lay on their bunks, desperately praying none of the French sailors came aboard to put the heaving travellers to the test. For extra effect, Dr Hawley muttered his entreaties in Latin.

After what seemed an eternity, the ship was free to go on its way, and the lads vied with each other to decide which was most afflicted. In truth, relief left them feeling wan, and they stayed in their cabins from choice.

The nausea was anything but false when they went deeper into the stormy waters of the Bay of Biscay. Dr Hawley was worst affected, and Sergeant Percival, someone he scarcely deigned to notice, most adept at dispensing a swig of brandy to settle his system.

They rounded the coast of Northern Spain and were soon approaching Portugal, a fraction of their way to their destination, but the knowledge they had left France behind exercised a powerful effect.

They had no time to be bored when Dr Hawley found several new courses of study. A word with the ship's captain gained access to the charts, so they could learn how the officers plotted the route.

The following day, they had a lesson in the workings of sails, watching the sailors scrambling high above the deck in the rigging. They marvelled at the agility, yet knew it would not do for them.

When the boat stopped at Lisbon, they stepped ashore and looked around the town, before moving down the Spanish coast to Cadiz, from where the great Armada set sail. After a day there, they moved on to Gibraltar, where the ship entered the Mediterranean Sea.

At first, it seemed idyllic, with warm, fine weather every day. Then they remembered the military hostilities. That was the reason the captain took the ship on a more southerly course, but the wind dropped and left the vessel becalmed for several days on a shimmering sea within sight of the Barbary Coast.

Some travellers thought it seemed an excess of diligence when the captain ordered his crew to keep a strict watch in the heat of the day. A thought shared by Dr Hawley, until Gilbert brought a message from Sergeant Percival, explaining that a becalmed ship was as much at risk of attack from pirates as one sailing on the high seas. It was a tense time, waiting for a change in the weather, but the lack of wind similarly affected the barbarians.

In the first week of May, Joshua celebrated his sixteenth birthday on board the becalmed ship with a nefarious tot of rum, acquired for him by Sergeant Percival in the tutor's absence.

"Go on, lad," the soldier said with a dry laugh. "Drink it up before the professor comes back. It won't kill you, and more likely it will make a man of you."

Goaded by the taunt, Joshua swallowed it in a fit of bravado. Then he choked as the spirit burned his throat, and everyone laughed at his discomfiture. Charlie promptly did the same and drew their fire.

"Dear me," Percival said, with a wink at the Linmore servants, "I can see we will have to toughen your young gentlemen up if they are going to be army officers. Their subordinates won't respect them if they are abstainers – in anything. I wonder what other little treats we can find for them to sample."

The return of Dr Hawley from his promenade around the deck put an end to the ribaldry. Joshua was glad of the respite, and sensed Charlie learned as much as he did about strong drink and the former soldier's strange humour. No doubt, they would become accustomed to that when in uniform.

Heeding the captain's advice, the travellers arose early to restrict their exposure to the searing heat of the day, and retired to their cabins until well after the sun passed over the yardarm. The humid air lasted into the night, making sleep difficult. Nightshirts were an encumbrance, so they draped a sheet around them, toga style.

In the early hours of the fourth day, Joshua felt the blessed relief of a freshening breeze and movement of the ship as the wind filled the sails ready to take them around Sardinia and on to a safe harbour in Naples.

CHAPTER 12

Linmore Hall, Shropshire

Within a few weeks of Joshua and Charlie's departure, boredom was driving Sophie to distraction. She had nothing to anticipate – not even the fun of plaguing haughty Caroline Norbery. She could not understand how a man who sat a horse as well as Richard Shettleston could choose to marry such a prissy miss as her cousin. He was far too good looking for her, but she supposed there was no telling with men. They did the strangest things.

Lucy and Julia Norbery were insipid. She hated their dainty feet and nimble fingers. Dancing the minuet came effortlessly to them, as did pianoforte scales. Most of all, she detested the endlessly neat seams of embroidery they produced, and it was unnatural for both of them to write in a neat hand.

How dare that silly governess, Miss Finchley, commend their meticulous attention to detail and ignore the fact that Sophie could write sentences faster than either of them? True, her penmanship might not as legible, but Charlie wouldn't mind a few ink-blots on the paper, and once he had learned the trick of turning the letter sideways to read in the margins, he could work out what she intended to say. It wasn't as if he had letters from anyone else.

What did it matter if her handwriting was distinctly her own style, or her stitches looked crooked on a puckered piece of cloth? Such things did not concern her when she knew that she could ride to hounds as well as any man. It was not worthwhile teasing the twins about their paltry horsemanship, for they ignored her and comforted each other.

She needed comfort as well and there was no one to give it. Why had Uncle Tom sent Charlie and Joshua away? He should have known she would miss them. Even the horses could not compensate, so she looked around for things to do – and found mischief.

No one could be sure when Sophie's passion for horses waned, and her interest in grooms began. But it could have been about the time when she was discovered watching the stable lads having their weekly dip in the deep river pool, and laughingly told she was too young to participate. As a result, she gathered up their clothing from the riverbank, cast it into the water and ran away.

Of course, they chased after her – and she let them catch her…

She might have known Lucy and Julia would tell Aunt Jane, which was how Squire Norbery came to hear of it. Sophie laughed when he questioned her, and it seemed he shared the joke.

"You need company of your own age, Sophie. I will see what I can do."

Accordingly, he arranged for her to share lessons with the daughters of a neighbouring landowner, spending a week at a time with the family and returning to Linmore at weekends.

The arrangement worked well for almost two months, but one day when the groom travelled to collect her, he discovered Sophie had been missing for a week. Nobody knew where she had gone.

After searching for several days, they eventually found her in a gypsy encampment at the edge of the big wood on Linmore Hill. Although she was unharmed, Sophie claimed the gypsies abducted her. A charge for which, two young gypsy men were convicted and transported to the penal colony in the southern ocean.

Tom Norbery sensed it was unfair to evict the rest of the gypsy families from the land, but he could not take the chance of being wrong. What the deuce could he do with Sophie now?

With Jane's help, he explored every academic avenue, and discounted one school after another. Finally, after long deliberation, they decided to send her to Miss Pepperslade's Seminary for Young Ladies in Bredenbridge, which had the reputation for strict discipline, excellent refinement and achievement. Knowing how well Sophie responded to firmness from the head groom, Tom was optimistic of a good outcome, but Jane was less sanguine.

October 1799

"In flagrente delicto – what the deuce does she mean?" Squire Norbery was in his study, perusing a newly delivered letter when his sister-in-law entered the room.

116

"I would have thought the expression was self-explanatory," she said with a smile. "But to whom do you refer?"

"I know what it means, Jane," he growled. "The letter is from Miss Pepperslade, about Sophie."

"Ah," she said. "Couched in those terms, it can only mean more trouble of the same kind that we encountered before. I suppose we've been lucky to have a few months' peace from her antics, but it was too good to last."

"You'd better read the letter for yourself, and tell me where we go from here, for I'm dashed if I know."

Jane took the proffered sheet of paper and read the full page through twice before responding.

"We must go to the school at Bredenbridge, of course," she said. "The letter is a masterpiece of creativity if we ignore the underlining. Miss Pepperslade actually hints at a compromising situation with a member of staff, whilst remaining coy about the details. I thought all the teachers were female, although that doesn't guarantee anything."

"So did I, but from the way it is written, it would not appear so. How on earth did the wretched girl find a man in a girls' school?"

"I have long suspected Sophie has hidden talents in that direction."

Tom was not amused. He had sighed with relief when Sophie's first term at school passed without incident, but the autumn term had hardly started.

"Drat the girl," he said. "I hoped the episode with the gypsies was the last of such problems. Now I will have to see the headmistress and try to persuade her to let Sophie stay. It's a blessing the boys are not here, because Charlie would come out, fists flying in her defence."

"Would you like me to come with you for support?"

"For me, or Miss What's-her-name?"

"Both," she said. "I think the presence of another woman could prove helpful, because you will also have Sophie with which to contend. I will tell Kate I am going to the cottage for a few days, so we can set out from there with no one apart from Jessie and the coachman being any the wiser."

Some of the tension eased in his face.

"This matter must be settled quickly, because I need to be back in the House, early next week for the latest debate. Sometimes, I wonder if it is all worthwhile. When I am in London, I long to be here at Linmore; and yet when I see Kate, I cannot bear to stay. Her mind seems to be getting worse and more twisted with hate against Joshua, even when he is not here. I was afraid when he was a boy that she would do him harm."

"So was I," said Jane, "and it was most unpleasant."

Two days later, having informed the headmistress of their intention to visit, Squire Norbery and Miss Littlemore travelled in their coach to the county town of Bredenbridge, a distance of twenty-five miles. On their arrival, they went straight to a tall, red brick building in the town square – a former rectory, which was now a school for young ladies.

At twelve o'clock precisely, a maidservant admitted them to the building and conducted them to an ante-room next to the headmistress's study. Two minutes later, the interlinking door opened and a thin wispy person, clearly a secretary of some kind, appeared and bobbed her knees.

"Miss Pepperslade will see you now, sir," she said.

Tom entered the room and stopped short in amazement as a tall figure arose from behind the polished oak desk. His previous recollection of the headmistress was of a short, grey-haired woman of mature years, whereas this person was younger and of statuesque proportions, more suited to wearing a tailored, superfine coat, pantaloons and a pair of Hessian boots, than the black twilled silk gown and lace cap, which proclaimed her status as a teacher.

"Are you… Miss Pepperslade?" He could not keep surprise from his tone.

Fierce brown eyes met his gaze, as if daring him to challenge her authority.

"I am indeed, sir," the woman said. "I assumed the running of the school in September, when my aunt was taken ill. Previously, I was her deputy."

That explained the difference. The older woman maintained discipline with a firm hand in a kid glove. This person had yet to make her mark, but at least she remembered her manners.

"It is good of you to come, Mr Norbery," she said, and looked enquiringly at Jane.

Tom responded accordingly. "Permit me to introduce my wife's sister, Miss Jane Littlemore."

After the women exchanged greetings, he said, "We have come a long way, ma'am. I would appreciate if you could put us in possession of the facts."

The headmistress indicated they be seated, and took the straight-backed chair behind her desk.

"I will endeavour to do so, Mr Norbery, but this is an extremely delicate situation. My letter stated the facts, as they were known at the time. Since then, I have investigated the matter further." She stopped to consult a paper on her desk. "I mentioned one lapse… but have discovered there were three separate occasions when your niece indulged in clandestine assignations: with the music teacher, a young dancing master and… one of the under-gardeners. I have never, in all my years in teaching, had recourse to…"

Tom interrupted. "Indeed, ma'am. I trust you have irrefutable proof of this?"

"Mr Norbery." The woman visibly bristled. "I do not make such claims lightly to any parent or guardian. I have to consider the welfare of all my pupils, and protect the reputation of the school."

"Of course you do, Miss Pepperslade," Jane interceded. "We quite understand you have to think of what is right for everyone… including Sophie."

Tom sighed with relief when he saw the tension ease in the headmistress's face. He too felt the soothing effect of Jane's voice.

"I presume Sophie has provided you with some kind of explanation for these… um… untoward occurrences?"

The headmistress turned gratefully in her direction.

"She denies everything, Miss Littlemore, but I have to consider what other parents would say if they were aware their daughters were being placed in the company of someone with…" she moistened her lips, "such… potentially… loose morals."

Jane covered her eyes with one hand. "Oh dear," she said, her voice trembled. "My poor cousin, Charlotte, would have been horrified to think of her motherless daughter being in this situation. I trust you are aware that Sophie and her brother were left all but orphans whilst in their formative years." She looked towards Tom. "We have done our best, but it appears we may have failed…"

"Whilst I do not condone such behaviour, ma'am," Tom said, "I think it would be helpful to see Sophie, and hear her explanation."

"Of course, sir, it will be done immediately." The headmistress nodded and reached for a bell pull.

Within minutes, Sophie entered the room accompanied by a female member of staff, who remained standing by the door.

"Uncle Tom, it is so good to see you…" Sophie rushed into the room, hands outstretched, then stopped and scowled. "Aunt Jane, what are you doing here?"

"Like your uncle, I am here to see you, at Miss Pepperslade's request."

"Oh, yes… of course." She turned back to Squire Norbery. "This is the most appalling situation, Uncle Tom. I am being unjustly accused of… of… lewd behaviour." Her voice disintegrated in a flood of sobbing, as she clutched at his hands. It took a few minutes for her to recover her composure.

"It's not true," she sniffed into the handkerchief, which Tom provided for her use. "I only asked for extra music and dancing lessons, because I didn't want to disgrace myself at Linmore. It is not easy to compete with Lucy and Julia, because they do everything well. I did so want to make you proud of me, Uncle Tom… and… I miss Charlie," she wailed.

While Tom patted Sophie's hand, the headmistress blinked and looked away. Jane was the only person unmoved by the affecting display of emotion.

"Sophie is devoted to her brother," she murmured. "He is currently touring Europe with my nephew; Mr Norbery's younger son."

Knowing he could not leave the matter unresolved, Tom found overnight accommodation in the town and returned with Jane to the school the following morning. To his surprise, Miss Pepperslade's demeanour had changed.

Gone was the haughty assertion of authority of the previous day, and in its place a tremor of emotion. Tom could not tell what effected the change, but it was evident from her restless hands, fidgeting with her quill that the woman was struggling to compose herself.

"Mr Norbery," she said. "There has been a… development since you were here yesterday."

Tom sensed Jane's eyes on his face as they waited to hear the headmistress's next words.

"It seems I was precipitate in my assertion that your niece was complicit in the events that befell her. I apologise for my presumption, and the fact someone took gross advantage of her innocence. I would quite understand if you felt obliged to remove her from the school."

The woman took a deep breath. "Since we spoke yesterday, the father of one of Sophie's friends has interceded in her defence, and indicated he would be extremely displeased if she was blamed in any way. He said if you were agreeable, she would be most welcome to visit his family during the weekends and holidays."

Tom was astonished. "That is extremely generous, ma'am. Am I likely to be acquainted with the gentleman?"

Miss Pepperslade preened herself as she said, "He is the owner of Onnybrook's Iron Foundry, and Chairman of the Board of Governors."

Someone so influential, his wishes outweighed other considerations.

Having given permission, and said farewell to Sophie, there was nothing to delay their return to Linmore. As the coach started on its way, they settled back against the padded squabs and closed their eyes with relief.

A few minutes later, Jane said, "Poor Miss Pepperslade, I felt sorry for her. Yesterday, she was convinced she had right on her side. This morning, she was in the invidious position of having to compromise her principles. If one is to believe Sophie, her friend's father owns half the town so the headmistress cannot afford to alienate the man."

"I know, Jane. The woman was probably right in her assumption. Whilst this man's intervention means we have avoided a scandal with our niece; I am indebted to someone in trade, and he will expect me to return the favour."

"She is not your niece, Tom – her mother was my cousin."

"It's the same thing, Jane, as well you know." Tom lapsed into silence, looking through the window. Then he said, "Did Sophie tell you the girl's name? The headmistress evidently expected us to know the father by repute."

"All I heard from Sophie, amongst a lot of silly giggling, was that her friend was Annie Bell."

Tom frowned. "I knew of Josiah Onnybrook, when he was alive, but this man is new to me. However, I am sure we will hear more of him."

The resignation in his voice made Jane offer a suggestion.

"Do you suppose Winifred would help? Your brother-in-law, Pontesbury, has influence in the City, so that wouldn't tarnish you by association, would it?"

"Oh, Jane, where would I be without you? I will mention it to my sister, when I see her next week."

"We must be thankful Sophie can stay at school and visit her friends at weekends. I only hope she knows how to behave at their level of society –

whatever that is. Oh dear," she said with a dry chuckle, "I have just thought about the boys – but I suppose they are almost men now. Will they have a chance to mix with people on their travels?"

"Yes," he said. "Probably more than they realised when they set out. I gave the tutor letters of introduction to use for the various embassies where they travel, so they will be included in social functions. They may not have wanted a conventional Grand Tour, but Dr Hawley will arrange for them to have lessons in etiquette, protocol and dancing to ensure they know how to behave in society. If they question it, I suggested he told them that all army officers need to know such things."

CHAPTER 13

When Sophie was at Bredenbridge, she missed the freedom to gallop across the acres of Linmore parkland. Riding lessons at school hardly qualified for the name, for Miss Pepperslade's notion was for each class to mount the ponies in the stable yard, and ride in single file along a path behind the groom – never to break into a trot or extend the process for more than half an hour. It was pathetic.

The stables were considered dirty and dangerous places, and no young lady was expected to groom her horse – except Sophie, who rose early to spend an hour in the stables each day before breakfast. Similarly, her riding habit did not conform to the approved demure style. She alone wore black amongst an array of bright fashionable colours, but it was the military style, with divided skirts, that drew censure. She wore it just the same, saying her guardian approved it. Nobody argued with that. Whereas many pupils had wealthy parents, Sophie had a political contact.

As usual, there was a delay in starting, and Sophie knew if it took too long, Miss Pepperslade might curtail the exercise in favour of handwriting practice. That was futile, because she had her own inimitable style.

Tired of waiting, she was debating whether to whisper the gypsy words that would set her horse at a gallop, out of the stable yard and across the park. It would be worth doing penance afterwards, just to be free for half an hour.

Instead, her mind drifted back to the morning lesson of etiquette and protocol, before Miss Pepperslade sent the pupils to change into their riding habits. These topics were all the same to Sophie, with more things she could not do than she could.

It is not seemly for a young lady, to look directly into a gentleman's face. One must always lower one's gaze, Miss Pepperslade's glacial tone decreed.

That was nonsense. Eyes were essential. How else were messages to be conveyed, except with a smouldering glance?

Never grasp his hand in greeting – only extend the tips of one's fingers… Sophie almost snorted in derision.

You must understand that gentlemen have different desires to ladies, and it is most important not to arouse the beast in them.

That was plain speaking indeed for a maiden lady.

Of course they were different, and Sophie thanked God they were. She almost howled with laughter, wondering how many men Miss Pepperslade had known in the biblical sense. Precious few, she imagined.

One can always judge a gentleman by his mode of dress.

What nonsense. She had known impeccably dressed rakes, and thought the only true test of quality was the way a man sat a horse. In that, Uncle Tom was magnificent. Loyalty to Charlie demanded she set him high on the list, but honesty forced her to admit he would never be Joshua's equal.

The recollection of him sitting astride his father's bay gelding, the day before he set off on the Grand Tour with Charlie, deprived her of breath. It was the moment, she realised he was the epitome of everything she desired. Also, she was sure that once he shed the restrictions of his upbringing, he would be very good at being naughty – and she was just the person to teach him.

She closed her eyes, seeking to bring his image to mind… but the sound of tittering females broke into her reverie.

Looking around, she noticed a new girl to the group was having difficulty mounting her pony. When some of the other pupils started to laugh, the disruptive sounds transmitted to the animal. It sidled away, and became more restive with every attempt the groom made to assist the girl to mount.

Sophie's concern for the animal made her furious.

"Stop that at once," she ordered, striding forward to grasp the pony's bridle. "You're frightening the horse."

Ignoring the groom, she led the pony aside, whispering a few soothing words in its ear, and offering sugar lumps she kept in her pocket, while Miss Pepperslade looked on aghast. What did she care for a teacher's opinion?

Within minutes it was calm, so she beckoned to the girl and led the animal to the mounting block.

"Get on the horse," she said with authority, indicating the correct step on the block. "It's quite safe now."

The girl was still too scared to move, so Sophie placed a lump of sugar in the palm of her hand and showed her how to give it to the pony. A look of wonder lit her face when she realised her hand was empty.

"Take no notice of the others," Sophie said, casting a contemptuous glance over her shoulder, before showing the girl how to hold the reins and place her foot in the stirrup. "They don't understand horses. If you like, I will show you how I groom it afterwards. That way you gain its trust."

Within seconds, the girl was in the saddle, arranging her skirt. Sophie gave a low whistle, and her mount came to her side. A quick nod at the teachers and she was ready.

To her, it was a natural thing to help someone learn to ride, but it made her a friend, something she had never sought before. She did not particularly like the other pupils, but if she had to choose one, Annie-Bell, the new girl, was as good as any other.

That was not how other folk pronounced the name, but Sophie made a play on the sound, and the girl accepted it. They were an unlikely pair of friends. Annie-Bell was as fair as Sophie was dark, and quite tall, in a skinny kind of way, whereas Sophie had a towering presence.

It was a revelation to learn this insignificant wisp of a girl had the richest father in the town. The knowledge gave Sophie pause for thought. She learned the rules of etiquette and protocol by rote, but deliberately thwarted the teachers' attempts to instil discipline. Now she had the incentive to conform.

Life had been happy when her pa was alive. They only lived in a little house, in Dublin, but it was a joyful place when he came home on leave from the army. They did not need much money, for he filled the household with love and laughter when he tossed her in the air, calling her his beautiful girl. Sophie adored him.

It was a sad day when Charlie told her that Pa was not coming home again. That was when they went to live in Blackrock, and when Sophie smelled money for the first time. Charlie went for lessons with the local rector, which left her with little to do, except count on the abacus frame, which Aunt Tilda taught her to use. It did not occupy her for long, so she walked up and down the stairs, looking in all the rooms to inspect the contents of cupboards and drawers. Barleycorn followed everywhere she went, scolding.

One day, finding her uncle's study door unlocked, Sophie hid in there, but just when she decided to leave, Uncle Lucius entered the room, and took a locked box from a cupboard. She was enthralled, watching him stacking up piles of coins, setting them aside and moving on to bundles of paper, which he unrolled and counted before replacing them in the box. Her hands itched to reach out to touch, but the intensity of his expression made her stop. For quite ten minutes, he sat at the desk breathing in the scent on his hands. Beads of sweat lay on his brow, making him look almost feverish…or was it excitement? Whatever it was made her curious to know more.

It was the first time she did not tell Charlie what she had done. If she had, he might have understood the upset caused when Barleycorn, the housekeeper, caught her in the study, sitting on the floor surrounded by coins and piles of bank notes, sniffing the scent on her fingers. She was not stealing the money. It was simply a misunderstanding, and no reason for Uncle Lucius to send her to the convent in the next village to do penance. What was worse, they did not let her see Charlie before she left.

The nuns said the same prayers as Barleycorn, and tried to force Sophie to chant the words, but she knew what was right and used her own version. Then they beat her with sticks, and she climbed over the garden wall, and ran away to visit the gypsies in the hills. Each time the nuns found her, she ran away again. The last time it happened, they sent her home, and then Uncle Tom came to take her and Charlie to Linmore. He was wonderful, for he gave her a pony.

"Welcome to our little home, Miss Cobarne. I hope you enjoy your stay with us," said Annie's father on her arrival.

Sophie felt almost drunk with elation as she walked through the grand entrance, into a marble reception hall with an intricately painted high domed ceiling. The moment she climbed into the luxury coach that conveyed her to her friend's home, it had been like stepping into a different world, leaving the ordinary folk outside.

Glossy black paint trimmed with gold on the outside, but the interior covering on the thick padded seats and squabs was in burgundy velvet, a rich colour that reflected the comfort expected by its owner. Discreet half-drawn blinds enabled them to view their surroundings whilst ensuring their privacy was preserved.

The "little home" description Annie's father had given was inapt, for whatever Fallowfield Court might be, it was not small. Sophie had never seen a greater contrast between the quiet country elegance of Linmore Hall and the almost vulgar opulence of the mansion. Everything was designed to impress, from the crystal chandeliers and the abundance of gilt-edged furniture. Tables inlaid with ivory and display cabinets filled to the brim with ornaments. Chairs and sofas with ornate frames, covered in vibrant red stripes and dazzling shades of blue satin. Swathes of swirling fabric framed the long sash windows, with seemingly acres of deep carpet underfoot. It quite took her breath away.

"Oh my goodness," she gasped. "It's absolutely amazing."

The man looked pleased by her praise. "It wasn't always so, young lady," he said in a blunt voice. "Onnybrook House was almost a ruin when I took it in hand, and it cost me a pretty penny to set it as you see it today, what with one thing and another."

Sophie noticed the name he used was different to the one on the brass plate outside the door, but she waited until the introductions were over and her friend's father left the room before asking for an explanation.

"I thought this was Fallowfield Court."

"It is now," said Annie. "The other name relates to when Grandfather Onnybrook lived here. This was my mother's childhood home, but when her brother died, Grandfather had no other son to leave the business to, or the house where the family lived for generations. I'm afraid he let everything deteriorate."

"I see," said Sophie, not seeing things at all.

Annie cast a nervous glance around, before saying in a lowered voice, "I think Papa used to work in the foundry, but when my parents met and fell in love, Grandfather wanted him to change his name, but he refused. That is why we lived in a smaller house on the edge of town. I do not understand how Papa made the business profitable again, but when the old gentleman died, he employed an army of builders to restore this house, and when it was finished, he changed the name. It's rather sad, because only the foundry still has the Onnybrook name, and I much preferred it."

Thinking about the brash manner that Annie's father exhibited, Sophie was sure his love of money came first. Despite his expensive clothes, it was obvious he was not a gentleman like Uncle Tom. He was hard-faced and grasping, with a vanity the size of a mountain. He was everything Uncle Lucius Cobarne was not, except in the way his eyes shone when he talked of money.

This man had no need of false modesty, for his iron foundry processed the raw materials for the munitions the British army used in Europe, India and the Americas. It was a very profitable occupation.

Until she met him, Sophie did not know iron was newsworthy, but neither did the haughty pupils at Miss Pepperslade's Seminary – and she was not going to tell them, for fear they might usurp her position as his daughter's friend. It was her secret.

By contrast, Annie's mother was a gentle soul. Quiet and dignified, yet terrified of expressing an opinion, for fear of arousing her husband's ire. She was so fragile that she hid in bed to avoid annoying her husband. Sophie scorned the use of smelling salts, but she was fascinated by the silver vinaigrette boxes Annie's mother collected. Not for the pungent vapours they contained, but the intricate designs kept in a showcase like snuffboxes.

One visit to her friend's home was enough to give her a taste for a life of luxury. To achieve this, Sophie knew she would have to adopt a new stratagem. Whilst being naughty alleviated her boredom, she now had to be an exemplary character.

She went back to school feeling bemused by all she had seen, and ready to fill sheets of notepaper, telling Charlie of her adventures, which she had Uncle Tom's permission to send to Linmore for further dispatch.

Without saying how it came about, she wrote to tell him that Annie's home was like a palace, with dozens of uniformed servants to attend her every whim – even if she needed anything in the middle of the night. Her bedroom was perfect, as was the dressing room, and the screened, marble tiled alcove with a bath.

The first evening of her visit, she wandered round the room touching the plump downy mattress on the bed, two fluffy pillows and a coverlet of purple silk, and wished Charlie were here to see it. From there, another thought came to mind, which she added to her letter. *I wish you could meet Annie. I am sure you would like her.*

Having planted the seed, the idea came to fruition. Of course, Charlie would like Annie, and she, Sophie, would pave the way for them to meet.

If the first weekend visit enthralled her, the second and subsequent ones confirmed it was the best thing that had ever happened in her life. Thank goodness, Uncle Tom gave his consent. Not that he refused her much, even when Aunt Jane was there.

Some nights, curiosity kept her awake. Sophie waited until the last of the servants was asleep, before slipping from her bed to walk through the corridors, clad in her new silk wrapper, and revel in the atmosphere of affluence. A task aided by the plethora of candles in wall sconces, which burned throughout the night; she vowed one day, to have a home where cost was no object.

She had discovered that if the master of the house wished to visit his study, a footman sat on a chair outside, ready to open the door – and there the pretty boy was, exactly where he should be. Each night she approached on tiptoe, and heard the soft purr of a snore, but even if the minion awoke and saw her, he would never betray her, for he had too much to lose.

A sliver of light showed beneath the study door, just as it did the night before, but she could not risk opening it. Seconds later, the ormolu clock in the hallway struck three. Sophie heard the faint scrape of a key in a lock and melted into the shadows, as a shadowy figure came through the outer door at the far end of the corridor.

The servant was on his feet in seconds, ready to reach for the door handle, which confirmed that Annie's father came home at the same time every night. Most likely he had been to visit his mistress, a woman who would be treated better than his poor dab of a wife. Maybe, with a little encouragement, Sophie could persuade him to shower gifts on her. He could well afford it.

With each visit, there was more of the house to admire, and yet the only part she really wanted to see was a disappointment. When she visited the stables, she found a selection of horses suited to draw the carriages stored in the coach house, but not a single decent horse for riding. What a let down.

It made her restive. Sophie knew if she ever had real money to spend, the minimum requirement for her stables would be a pair of perfectly matched thoroughbreds for a high-perch phaeton, and a big black gelding for hunting.

There were compensations, for Annie, her mother and younger sisters much preferred shopping in the town, and Sophie found herself the proud possessor of new clothes, a hat or pieces of jewellery, the like of which she had never seen. Although Uncle Tom gave her an allowance, while staying with Annie, she did not need to spend it from one month to the next, so she hid it away.

It quite amazed her that everyone in the household gave her presents.

Annie's mother, her twin sisters, Eliza and Amelia, and the younger sister in the nursery, whose name she forgot. It seemed so natural, and yet Sophie sensed her visits were unusual.

"How many of your other friends come from school?" she asked out of curiosity.

"There's no one else. You are the exception, because Papa does not mix with other parents, or encourage me to have school friends," Annie said, looking embarrassed. "I'm glad you are at school with me, Sophie. It is not easy, having people say my father was made Chairman of the Board of Governors, because he invested money in the school."

Being a confidante was a new experience. While Annie's father was not a popular man in Bredenbridge, she had little doubt he would know exactly who Uncle Tom was. That, she suspected, was why she was accepted.

Sometimes, Annie's adoration became tedious, but it served Sophie's purpose.

"Oh, my," she said, espying a pretty trinket, and reaching out her hand to touch. "May I look at it? It is so pretty."

She did it to test the response, and it was always the same. Her friend would give her anything, and she quickly learned to handle Annie's pa, noting his roving eye and wandering hands with the housemaids, and playing to his vanity.

To amuse herself, she insisted his side-whiskers were exactly like those her pa had. They were nothing of the kind, but her words pleased him and he was willing to let her stroke them. After that, whenever she expressed a liking for some expensive little trifle, in his hearing, it became her own – and in thanks, she kissed him on the cheek and declared he was the kindest papa in the world, while his family looked on and smiled.

Although she found living with females a bore, it suited her purpose to stay there, until Charlie returned with Joshua. Once he was home, she would contrive to have him meet Annie and her family. That sorted the first part of her plan, after which, she would consider her next course of action – which involved Joshua.

CHAPTER 14

Early Summer –1799

No sooner did they land in Naples, than Dr Hawley's carefully laid plans suffered a check – then stuttered and virtually fell apart. The blame for that lay firmly with Bonaparte, for causing conflict between the aristocracy and lower classes. As a result, the King of Naples had moved his Court from Caserta, to the safety of Palermo, in Sicily.

Dr Hawley heard of this when he visited the British Embassy to present Squire Norbery's letter of introduction to the Ambassador, and learned that Sir William Hamilton was visiting the Bourbon Court. The junior diplomat to whom he spoke advised them to travel further afield, but it was too much to accept.

Before he left Linmore, Dr Hawley had set his heart on three things. To explore the city where Virgil, the Latin poet studied and made his home; meet an acknowledged expert in the study of volcanoes; and visit Pompeii and Herculaneum, the cities overwhelmed by the cataclysmic eruption of Vesuvius, which he heard were now under excavation.

Deprived of two of his three options, Dr Hawley was determined to visit Vesuvius. Mindful of his responsibilities, he considered it a good a way of keeping his pupils occupied, and ensured they would not be seduced in areas of the city where sins of the flesh were notorious – or so he had heard.

Whilst he was not averse to drinking a glass of wine with a meal, or playing a hand of whist with his sister; he did not condone licentious behaviour, and would do his utmost to protect his pupils from temptation. Cerebral occupation was the answer – keep the mind active and the spirit would follow.

Although Dr Hawley did not admit his disappointment, Joshua and Charlie recognised the way his mouth drooped at the edges when he heard the news. Then he sulked, like a child. Virgil was his hero, and he so looked forward to exploring Naples.

Without the ambassador to tell them about volcanoes, they would have to see Vesuvius for themselves. When the tutor pretended he was doing it for them, they accepted his word, knowing he would not admit his plans had gone awry.

They did not mind where they went next. Everywhere was new, and from what they could see of Vesuvius, across the Bay of Naples, the only sign of life in a near-cloudless sky were a few wisps of white around the top, which they hoped was steam – anything to show activity.

At Linmore, they had seen artists' impressions of volcanic eruptions in books. Vivid images of fire and brimstone. Savage acts of nature, which did untold damage. Now, they would visit the volcano, and two of the towns overwhelmed by lava.

The trouble was, when it came to arranging transport for the journey, Dr Hawley belittled every option Sergeant Percival offered. The man did his best, but there was little choice available, and what he found did not suit the tutor. Undeterred, the guide managed to find a conveyance – of sorts.

Within three days, they were on the move, passing through the city gates soon after sunrise, intent on travelling before the heat became too intense. They showed their identification papers when they left the city, and paid taxes for the surrounding district; a requirement for each border crossed.

Although the journey between Naples and Vesuvius was only five or six miles, it was tediously slow and woefully lacking in comfort. The hired coach belonged to a bygone age, its once plush seats tired and faded. Door hinges creaked and coach wheels suffered from a chronic lack of axle grease, and every jolt in the road jarred their bones. It was a miserable way to travel, and the heat made it worse, especially as the coach was overloaded.

There were five people travelling together, all breathing the same dry air, without permission to open a window, because of Dr Hawley's morbid fear of draughts. Apart from Joshua, Charlie and their tutor, two menservants occupied the coach – another grievance, for which Dr Hawley blamed Sergeant Percival, who rode alongside the vehicle.

Fortunately, it was only a relatively short distance, and there were compensations. All around, they could see orange and lemon groves covering the hillsides and valley floor, filling the air with the heady scent of citrus.

The sight teased Joshua's senses, making his mouth water and his memory recall the refreshing taste of Miss Belinda Hawley's lemonade and delicious citrus biscuits. In the dry, stuffy heat, the thought was bitter sweet – pure nostalgia and torment in equal portions.

When the coach stopped unexpectedly in the next village along the road, the door opened and Sergeant Percival appeared carrying a basket of oranges and lemons, together with a platter of large orange slices cut ready for eating. Sweet and succulent, it was nectar from the gods. Their grumbling discontent melted away in seconds.

The remaining miles passed unnoticed, except when Joshua and Charlie unfolded their long limbs from the cramped interior. Even so, they managed a laugh whilst vowing to walk back to Naples rather than enter the dilapidated vehicle again. After they dined and rested, they viewed the prospect with equanimity.

If nothing else, the view from the ridge of Vesuvius was worth enduring a four-hour ride on a mule and a half-mile trudge to the top. It was spectacular.

Up there, the world was untouched by military conflict. Below them, the Bay of Naples and the city, spread out like a painted picture. A blue haze of sky, far out to the horizon, and ships of the line visible on the sea, but they could not tell if the flags fluttering from the stern of the brigantines were the Red Ensign. In a just world they would be.

It was everything they expected it to be, and the mule ride was bearable in the early morning when they set off, an hour after sunrise. The heat increased, the higher up the slope they rode, and air became drier, which they presumed was due to the effects of volcanic ash and sulphurous fumes. An assumption, Dr Hawley did nothing to discourage.

Confronted with the beasts of burden, Joshua and Charlie decided future soldiers could ride anything, but they were concerned about their tutor's ability to cope. They need not have worried. The ponderously slow pace the animal moved suited Dr Hawley exactly, and he spent the time reading his copy of Virgil, just as he did at Linmore. At least he was happy, doing what he wanted.

God bless Sergeant Percival for anticipating their need for a bite to eat, when they dismounted and left the mules, half a mile from the top – and the most welcome of drinks – lemonade. Made from freshly picked fruit of the lemon grove – it was delicious. Even Dr Hawley seemed unusually grateful when the former soldier produced two stone flagons, one for their arrival, and a promise of the second before they began the descent.

Suitably refreshed, Joshua and Charlie waited while Dr Hawley fussed around and interrupted Sergeant Percival's negotiations with the Italian guides. Patience was a virtue at the best of times, but in the dry heat a few hundred yards away from the volcanic ridge, it was in short supply. The end of the path looked so close they could almost touch it.

Half the day was gone already, spent on the back of a mule. Their legs ached with inactivity, and their backsides from sitting on old, worn saddles. Joshua felt it most for his legs were too long for the stirrups.

Oh to be on the move. No sooner the thought than the deed. Claiming a call of nature, they slipped a few feet away beyond the trees that would shelter the horses, each knowing the other's mind and intention. Both knew it would take an age for their tutor to decide if he was ready, and by then they would be waiting at the ridge. They set off up the path, matching their steps to the other, but before they had gone a dozen yards, Joshua sensed the change and lengthened his stride, knowing that Charlie would try to outpace him. It was madness and yet he felt freer than he had for weeks.

"Gentlemen, stop at once…" Dr Hawley's voice hung behind them in the haze.

It was easy to pretend not to hear, but Sergeant Percival's authoritative tone could not be ignored. "Mr Norbery…" he bellowed.

Out of habit, the sound of his name brought Joshua to an abrupt halt and Charlie followed suit. They exchanged a quick shrug of their shoulders and a grin as they waited for the other members of the group to join them.

"Gentlemen…gentlemen," Dr Hawley chided, as if speaking to recalcitrant children. "You must curb your impatience, and prepare your minds for a truly awesome sight of nature."

"Yes, sir," they muttered in unison, and looked balefully at the former soldier. Sergeant Perceval ignored them and walked two steps behind at the rear of the line.

The final stretch they covered on foot was steep and slow. As young legs moved at the pace of old, Joshua felt hot and sweaty and he envied the Italian guides their clothes in lighter-weight material, but knew any attempt to remove his coat would be met with disapproval. He hoped that English country dress would be appropriate for other parts of the journey; otherwise they were in for an uncomfortable time.

The dry heat and frustration of the moment brought out Charlie's strange sense of humour. Separated from Dr Hawley by little more than a few feet, he muttered to Joshua, "I bet I could have reached the ridge before you."

"How much…?" Joshua said, striving to maintain a degree of the freedom he had been offered and lost.

"Half a guinea," Charlie retorted. "You would have lost for sure, because I'm more agile. Your feet are too big and clumsy."

Instead of arguing the point, Joshua said, "Which part of the ridge?"

"The rim of the crater, of course, you idiot Norbery."

"Having observed every clinker and charred blade of grass along the way, I suppose," Joshua intoned.

"Yes…something like that."

"I'll prove you wrong on that, Cobarne," said Joshua, determined to have the last word. "The bet is not off – only deferred until we return to Linmore."

Charlie nodded agreement and they continued the plodding pace in silence.

At the top of the path, a sense of unreality assailed them as they looked towards the rim of the hollowed-out mountain; and a sudden awareness of the need to watch where they put their feet amongst the black clinkered lava that littered the ground.

Remarkably, Dr Hawley seemed to come to life. "The guide tells me we have less than one hour, gentlemen. Then we must return, to allow other visitors to ascend," Dr Hawley, said over his shoulder as he hurried away to investigate the crater, adding as an afterthought, "Don't go too close to the edge."

Joshua heard the warning as he moved forward, and then hesitated before taking a step closer to peer into the crater. The sheer size and depth of the opening took his breath away, and yet he felt an irrational sense of disappointment at its quiescent state. Nothing below moved, or smelled unusual. He felt somehow cheated of the fire and brimstone he had been led to expect from pictures in books.

"Is that all there is?" he said.

Charlie looked for himself, and came to the same conclusion.

"Looks like it."

After all that time and spent effort, there was hardly a puff of steam to show a difference in temperature. The white wispy clouds they saw from across the bay really were clouds, not signs of volcanic activity.

Of course, there might be more going on, deep inside, but the crater was so vast and the clinkered black lava rocks near the edge blocked their view. It was five years since the last eruption, but lichen was already growing on some of the boulders.

They did not know what to do, so they picked up pieces of black rock, to take home – one to show Aunt Jane and the twins, and another for Sophie. Such thoughts inevitably took Joshua home to Linmore, which seemed far away from this barren place.

Dr Hawley seemed to have forgotten them. He was in discussion with the local farmer, who guided them to the top. One was speaking Italian in precise terms, the other fluent in a local dialect, too fast for anyone to follow.

Joshua turned back to look at the view. No one could fault that, but he had no idea how he would complete the report of the day's activities, which Dr Hawley insisted on.

"What do you think of the volcano, Master Joshua?"

Sergeant Percival's voice startled them. They had forgotten his shadowy presence, standing guard a step or two behind them.

Joshua would not dare to say what he thought to his tutor, but the former soldier was different. With him, you were not afraid of feeling silly, whereas academics could make you feel stupid, and frequently did.

"To be honest, Sergeant," he said, in a quiet voice. "We expected there to be more life in it than this."

A strange expression crossed the man's face, half-way between a smile and a grimace.

"That's understandable," he said. "But believe me; you wouldn't be standing here if it decided to erupt. I was in Naples, back in 'ninety-four, with a party of young gentlemen, similar to you, when it last put on a show – and when it does, Naples is close enough for anyone."

They looked at him, incredulous.

"What was it like?" said Charlie. "We've only seen pictures in books."

Sergeant Percival looked into the distance as he spoke.

"If I recall it right, it happened in the middle of July. There were several earth tremors within a few days, and some bursts of smoke and steam from the crater. Nothing much, but it gradually built up through the day, and the locals knew there was more to come. It was not dark at ten o'clock when the column of ash erupted, but it blotted out the light. Then a great crack appeared in one side of the rock, and molten lava started surging through the vents, one after another.

He stared into the mists of memory, gathering his thoughts.

"It was an eerie sight, watching from across the bay as the lava flow moved down the hillside, all through the night, burning and scorching everything in its path. It reached the centre of Torro del Greco at six o'clock the next morning," he said, pointing down the hillside in the direction of the town. "It's something I wouldn't want to see again."

They were transfixed. No written account could ever relate the event as Percival did, and continued to do so.

"I doubt if anyone in Naples slept that night. There was too much apprehension. The air was dry and dusty, from the clouds of stinking sulphur. The dust gets in everything – the food and water. In your ears and eyes, catches in your throat as well. It's hard to describe the taste. Acrid, I suppose is the best word for it. That's due to the sulphur." He grimaced, and changed the subject.

"There's nothing like that here now, but if you want sulphur springs, then Solfatara, on the Phlegraean Fields is the place to go. I think even you would agree it stinks just as a volcano should. Conditions in Naples are difficult now, but things might settle before we return home, and whenever that is, we will be sailing from Naples. If you ask the professor in advance, maybe he'll agree to take you there."

"How do you know all this?" said Charlie.

"Because I discussed it with Sir William Hamilton, the last time I was in Naples, and he's been studying the Italian volcanoes for thirty years."

"You... talked to the ambassador..." Joshua said in amazement, and then realised it sounded insulting.

Sergeant Percival gave a wry smile. "Yes, I did," he said. "He's a real gent, with a passion for the subject, and will talk with anyone who is interested."

"Dr Hawley wanted to meet him, but he's attending the King of Naples, in Palermo."

"I know," said the sergeant. "From what I heard, Bonaparte came a bit too close for comfort, late last year, so they moved the entire Royal Court to Sicily. I expect they'll come back again, when things settle down."

The depth of Sergeant Percival's knowledge was amazing. Dr Hawley gained his information by studying books, and the soldier, from observations of life, but the way he told it made it far more interesting. They were so enthralled that they failed to hear Dr Hawley's approach, until he spoke.

"If I may I have your attention, Masters' Norbery and Cobarne? It's time to leave."

As Joshua turned to find his tutor standing a few feet behind them, he sensed Sergeant Percival moving away. Neither man acknowledged the other, but it was obvious from his pettish tone that Dr Hawley felt aggrieved, having heard the soldier telling of his meeting with the ambassador.

It made Joshua feel sad that even in this remote place, Dr Hawley, who preached tolerance and courtesy to everyone else, should display such a bigoted attitude. It was a wonder Gilbert from Linmore had not been ordered to accompany them simply to convey messages.

He pondered it all the way down the dusty path on foot, and during the tediously long ride back to their lodgings. However much his tutor might sulk, Joshua could not regret talking with Sergeant Percival, for he brought Vesuvius to life.

Despite his avowed intention to explore Pompeii on the morrow, Dr Hawley felt the full effects of a day in the saddle and the extra altitude on the volcano. He was so fatigued that he spent the day in bed, with his manservant attending to his needs, and then tottered outside the following day, looking decidedly weary.

The effects of dry heat and riding the mules took its effect on all of them, and Joshua and Charlie were equally glad of the rest.

Mules, they discovered, were not like the horses at Linmore, any more than the ancient coach was comfortable. Sergeant Percival promised to find something better for the journey beyond Naples.

While their tutor languished in his room, they drank lemonade and talked with Sergeant Percival about what to expect from Pompeii and Herculaneum. Having visited these places before, he spoke of things that Dr Hawley had not mentioned – things of which to be aware. Or at least, Gilbert did. Sergeant Percival seemed to be asleep.

"Percy's been telling me about the Stabian Baths in Pompeii," Gilbert said.

Percy, being the name he used for Sergeant Percival.

"What about them?" Joshua said.

Dr Hawley had read from one of his books about the mosaics on the vaulted ceiling and walls. They had their sketchpads ready and pencils sharpened, for what their tutor considered would be a high treat.

"Very sociable places baths were in Roman times, by all accounts."

Their tutor said something similar, but not with a broad grin on his face. Maybe Dr Hawley did not understand something, and if so, things could be much more interesting. At least doing sketches meant their tutor was not droning on in what Charlie called his sepulchre voice.

It was lucky Gilbert got on well with Sergeant Percival, because they were much in each other's company, passing messages between the former soldier and Dr Hawley. It seemed so silly for grown men not to talk to each other.

"Not as sociable as the Lupanarium, it seems." Gilbert winked his eye.

"The Lupanarium…?" said Charlie. "What's special about that?"

"It is a place near the baths, with some very colourful mosaics, where the Romans took their pleasure." Sergeant Percival's voice filled in the details.

They had thought he was dozing in the chair. His broad-brimmed hat covered his eyes, obscuring his expression, but his voice sounded perfectly serious and yet Joshua suspected an innuendo, the meaning of which eluded him.

By the third day, Dr Hawley recovered sufficiently to emerge from his room, intent on spending half a day exploring Pompeii. He still looked pale and wan, but he was determined.

"I must not deprive you of my company any longer, gentlemen. I think an hour or two in the fresh air at the amphitheatre would benefit all of us."

Whilst Joshua and Charlie would happily have walked the short distance from their lodgings to the excavations, they knew that Dr Hawley needed to travel by coach. While he sat in the shade of his umbrella with his manservant nearby guarding a flagon of lemonade, they set off to explore the exposed parts of the amphitheatre.

Although the arena was open to the air, it was a strange feeling to be tramping up and down steps, weaving through doorways, around corners and sitting on dusty stone seats that until a few years before had been covered in lava. The knowledge that this had been hidden from sight made them reach for their sketching pads to note things of interest to discuss with Dr Hawley, and show the family at Linmore on their return.

Joshua could imagine his father viewing these scenes on his tour with Uncle Jack. Closer still, he wondered if Matthew had visited Pompeii, but closed his mind to the idea of meeting his brother on his travels. Some things it was better not to contemplate.

Everywhere they looked, Vesuvius was in the background, reminding them of its presence, and the fact that a few days ago, they stood on the ridge.

On subsequent days, they delved further inside the excavations, moving through tunnels, lit by lanterns, seeing more of the lava-buried secrets.

From there, Joshua took images in his mind of the relics overtaken in the disaster. Recording the visits in his journal, he found that words could not describe the feelings he experienced, when he walked through excavated chambers and corridors, sensing the terror of people trying to escape and seeing their petrified remains recreated in casts of concrete. It all seemed terribly depressing.

When they finally reached the Stabian Baths, there was scarcely time to do more than cast a glance over the wall frescoes, or note the nymphs and cupids on the vaulted ceiling, before Dr Hawley ushered them towards the Lupanarium. He stepped through the doorway, and stopped, rigid with horror.

"No," he said. "This is not what I wished you to see. Avert your eyes, gentlemen, and come outside – at once."

Between Joshua and Charlie passed a look of unholy mirth as the graphic extent of the mosaics dawned on their tutor, but the faces they turned to him were devoid of expression. This was the brothel about which Sergeant Percival told them, and if it was true to Roman life, it left nothing to the imagination.

Neither did the book of sermons to which they were subjected for the next hour, each quarter with the recurring theme. *There will be no fornication…* Every aspect of denial was explored, and Joshua was at a loss to know where Dr Hawley thought they would find the opportunity amongst the piles of volcanic dust and ancient relics.

Their tutor emerged from the lesson refreshed, but it left Joshua and Charlie feeling totally crushed, until Sergeant Percival said something aside that drew Dr Hawley's attention. In an instant their misdemeanours were forgotten. Almost as if the guide did it deliberately.

Their visit to Herculaneum was peaceful, and came as a welcome relief. Having recovered his composure, Dr Hawley related the story about how the great eruption had destroyed four towns.

Herculaneum was the first discovery, lying under a vast depth of volcanic debris. Artefacts provided evidence of a wealthy township: pieces of jewellery, elaborate wall mosaics and inlaid marble floors, as well as a street with paving stones, and remnants of lead water pipes.

When Pompeii was found at a shallower depth, the digging at Herculaneum was abandoned. In the sixty years since the discovery, the easier excavations in Pompeii had revealed a greater range of Roman life – a fact duly and dutifully recorded.

CHAPTER 15

"What's going on, Gilbert?"

Having returned to Naples, Joshua and Charlie were waiting in their lodgings to hear what would happen next, while the Linmore servant was dashing back and forth conveying messages between their tutor and Sergeant Percival.

"You might well ask." Gilbert checked in his stride. "I wish them two would make up their minds about the best way to travel."

"I thought Sergeant Percival said he was going to hire a couple of coaches and drivers."

"So he did, and the professor dismissed it out of hand. I'm just going to tell Percy," the man said as he strode away.

Bored with the tedium of waiting, Joshua and Charlie decided to follow, and arrived in the servants' quarters, just in time to hear Sergeant Percival say, with a touch of asperity, "Give my compliments to the professor, Gilbert, and tell him that I will reserve seats on the common diligence for him and the young gentlemen. You menservants can sit atop, with the baggage. I will ride alongside."

Minutes later, Gilbert returned, followed by the tutor, who was so incensed that he abandoned his dignity and confronted the guide, ready to convey his response in freer terms than was his custom.

"How dare you send impertinent messages to me, Percival?" he shouted. "Common diligence indeed; Squire Norbery will hear of your disregard for his son's comfort in my next report to Linmore."

Sergeant Percival raised an eyebrow and listened to the tirade in silence. Then he said in a quiet tone, "In that case, Dr Hawley, I take it you would prefer me to hire private vehicles to convey you to the Adriatic coast, and onwards to Macedonia."

"Of course I would," Dr Hawley said in a haughty tone, then realised he was outmanoeuvred. "I mean… yes… that would be the most appropriate mode of transport."

"Thank you, sir," said the guide. "I'll see to it today."

Joshua could not help feeling the soldier came out of the dispute best. He had noticed Sergeant Percival's quiet manner before. It was too refined for someone from the ranks – almost gentlemanly – but maybe his father employed the man because he was polite. Whatever the reason, it worked, and he hoped the acrimonious exchanges would lessen as the journey progressed. It must do, for this was only the start of their travels.

For the remaining days of their stay in Naples, Sergeant Percival maintained his urbane manner, and Dr Hawley reverted to sending messages with the Linmore servant. Apart from that, there were no problems.

In preparation, Dr Hawley showed Joshua and Charlie the planned route on his map, by which they would travel to Macedonia, the birthplace of Emperor Alexander. The name of the country was familiar from their lessons, but they had little knowledge of the terrain through which they would travel.

When the day of departure dawned, everything was organised with military precision. True to his word, Sergeant Percival hired two sturdy coaches, with horses and drivers, and declared his intention to acquire further transport when they reached the Dalmatian Coast.

Joshua and Charlie sat in the leading coach with their tutor, while Sergeant Percival rode alongside the second conveyance carrying the two Linmore servants and the luggage. Much to everyone's relief, the interior seating was a great improvement on the previous vehicle.

Although the distance to the coast was relatively short, there were few road bridges for river crossings. Sometimes, a ferry took them across, but failing that meant a diversion of several miles, and the anticipated journey of two days stretched to three.

At each delay, the tutor and former soldier entered into a battle of wills.

Dr Hawley became unusually vocal, insisting through his intermediary that the tour guide demand they take precedence over other travellers. Sergeant Percival responded respectfully, but carried on regardless.

Having dined on the second evening, Dr Hawley went to look at a local church, but refused Sergeant Percival's offer of an escort. The former soldier sent one of the grooms instead, and waited outside the hostelry for their return.

Gilbert stood in the doorway of the inn, watching the two men from a distance. "You wouldn't think them two was friends when they were lads."

Nothing seemed more unlikely.

"What happened to spoil it?" asked Charlie.

"Miss Belinda happened, that's what. Jim Percival grew up with the gardener's family on the Neathwood estate, in Linmore Dale. The old Lord Chetton wanted him to have extra schooling, so he paid the parson to give him lessons. Everything was all right until Reverend Hawley's daughter came home from school and fell in love with her brother's friend. Of course, that would not do for Parson Hawley, him being the son of a baronet. He did not object to Percy's humble connections, so much as his likeness to the old viscount. He is the living image of his father – from the wrong side of the blanket. It's not his fault, but he has to live with it."

"Gilbert…" From nowhere, a soft voice of authority growled a warning. Sergeant Percival had returned.

The manservant glanced over his shoulder. "That's me and my big mouth again," he said with a chuckle. "Talking about things as don't concern me. I'd better get on with me work."

With that, he walked away. Sergeant Percival went with him.

"What did he mean?" said Joshua.

"Maybe it was something like the baby we saw at Hillend church," Charlie said. "Do you remember, just after Sophie and I came to Linmore?"

"Yes," said Joshua. "The little girl who needed milk, and there was a woman who could feed it. The farmer's wife called it a name."

"She said it was a bastard, and the rector's sister didn't approve of them."

"It sounds as if Miss Belinda liked Sergeant Percival too much for the rest of her family."

Before they could say more, Dr Hawley returned from his walk.

When they set sail, Tirana was their destination, but when a storm blew up halfway across the Adriatic, nobody cared where they landed, as long as they had firm ground beneath their feet and shelter for the night.

Once they were safely ashore, Sergeant Percival set off to acquire transport and the relevant travel permits. He returned the following day, riding beside two coaches, with teams of four sturdy horses, and a complement of coachmen, grooms, postillions and outriders for each coach – eight in total.

No one questioned the numbers, and Sergeant Percival offered no explanation. Whoever they were, the men seemed to know each other, and accepted the tour guide's military rank as authority.

Everyone knew it would take time to reach Skopje, but three weeks later they seemed no nearer to finding it.

Each day, they maintained a steady rate through open valleys of pastureland and olive groves, broke their journey in the heat of the day to take luncheon and rest the horses, then continued until evening, when they found a wayside inn for food and a bed for the night. Sergeant Percival seemed unconcerned with the pace, for it meant they rarely needed to change horses.

From his recollection of the map, Joshua knew Tirana lay somewhere to the north of where they landed. They intended going that way, but looking at the morning sun, he suspected they were heading east, towards Thessalonica. He was loath to mention the fact to Dr Hawley. There was a fragile truce between the tutor and the guide, which he did not wish to spoil. There was only one person he could ask.

"Are we lost, Gilbert?"

"Well, I wouldn't say that exactly, Master Joshua," the man said, rubbing the side of his nose, as he always did when thinking. "Percy says in these foreign parts, we have to travel by the roads set on the permit."

"So where are we? By our reckoning, we should have reached Skopje."

"Now, that I don't know," was the servant's response.

"Does Dr Hawley know?"

"I reckon he has some idea of the way things are, but he'd never admit it."

Joshua had to be satisfied, for Dr Hawley did not encourage them to talk with the servants. They were almost entirely in his company – but sitting in a stuffy coach, with only the odd draught for ventilation, was intolerable.

If only he and Charlie could ride in the fresh air with the driver, even for a few miles. The problem was finding the right moment to interrupt Dr Hawley's rambling discourse to ask permission without him taking offence.

Eventually, Charlie could stand it no longer. "Please, sir," he said. "May we sit on the roof with the coachman?"

The request drew a pained expression from the tutor. "Ah, yes, you are bored. I should have realised that the wonders of ancient history would not hold your attention. Your responses to my questions have been so languid."

They wouldn't have minded if he'd let them open the window.

"No, sir," Charlie said. "It's just that… it's hot in here. We need some air."

"Then I must let you go first, Master Cobarne, as your need is greater. Master Norbery may go when you return."

With that as their only option, any pleasure they might derive was gone. It was for both of them, or neither, so they stayed where they were and forbore to ask again. It was almost a relief to revert to their Greek lessons, but Dr Hawley's passion for history proved as wearing as his petulant moods.

Usually so active, Joshua felt frustrated with the restrictions. He wanted to sprawl against the squabs and relax. Instead, he had to sit upright, with feet together, giving the appearance of listening to the epistle Dr Hawley was reading about Alexander. He heard his tutor's voice but hardly registered a word, yet he knew there would be questions to answer.

Sitting directly opposite, Charlie's expression registered the same degree of disinterest, except he kept his eyes open to contradict the impression he was asleep. They took turns on alternate days to face the direction the horses travelled, but neither sat opposite Dr Hawley. Listening to him was bad enough, without having him watch them like children. And if they lapsed they were read a sermon.

Joshua tried to stifle a yawn. Travelling today was the same as yesterday, as the day before, as tomorrow would be, confined in a stuffy coach when they wanted to be outside, breathing fresh air. His hand itched to reach out and grasp the window strap. To let down the glass an inch, maybe two, or even let it drop to the bottom – accidentally, of course. He sighed, unable to help himself, and caught Charlie's eyes flickering towards the window.

As he turned to look, one of the outriders rode past the coach, and he noticed the flap of the leather sleeve attached like a scabbard to the saddle was undone. Inside it showed a polished wooden stock. Only a glimpse, but enough to know the man carried a rifle. A strangely comforting thought.

His mind drifted from the gun to the man on the horse and his ability to use the firearm. He looked eminently capable, as they all did, which meant they must be soldiers, like Sergeant Percival. They knew what discipline was, and followed his lead. That was more relevant to the journey than how Alexander coped.

His mind jerked to attention, then slid away from what Dr Hawley was saying. As always, when he was bored, his thoughts turned to food, wondering what they would eat for supper tonight. Luncheon was three hours past, and the ship's biscuits with cheese and an apple was but a memory.

Maybe they would have some of the sweet dessert the soldiers once found whilst foraging in the marketplace of a little town they drove past. Baklava, he thought they called it. Whatever the name, it was delicious, and he imagined sinking his teeth into the pastry-like texture. He moistened his lips, willing the time to go faster.

A drink would be nice; some more of the strong coffee Sergeant Percival made earlier at the roadside – or tea with lemon, if they had any left. It was sharper than the milk, which Dr Hawley craved, and stayed fresh longer. The tutor insisted on sweetness, so the tour guide found him some honeycomb, which satisfied his taste, but he did not thank the man. Had it been anyone else, he would.

The sound of Dr Hawley's voice jerked Joshua awake.

"Do you remember King Philip of Macedon gave his son, Alexander, command of the army, when he was sixteen years old? The same age as you are now. Put yourselves in his position and try to imagine his feelings when he led the army into Thebes? Would you quail under responsibility, or quell the uprising as he did, and vanquish your father's enemies?"

Joshua wondered if Sergeant Percival knew anything about ancient Macedonia. Maybe he did, if Dr Hawley's father was his teacher. Now there was a thought. He certainly would not drone on, boring everyone. Even Charlie looked as if he was asleep.

"Mr Norbery, you are not attending." A peevish voice disturbed his reverie.

He could not argue with that. "Sorry, sir," he said. "It's the heat."

Knowing Dr Hawley was waiting for an answer, Joshua declared his wish to emulate the man who battled his way through Mesopotamia, and controlled most of Asia Minor, but who died of a fever before he was four and thirty years of age. It was a depressing prospect for anyone to contemplate.

"Of course, such a thing could not happen nowadays," said Dr Hawley. "Medical science has made great advances, so an Emperor would not be reliant on the primitive herbal practices which failed to save Alexander's life."

The lads nodded agreement, out of habit.

"Enough of such maudlin thoughts," Dr Hawley said, waving a nonchalant hand to illustrate a point he wished to make. "Let us look at the terrain through which the Macedonian army travelled, and consider how they fared. Where they would eat and sleep."

Joshua glanced through the window. What did he mean? There was no sign of habitation here. The last village he remembered seeing was several miles back, and from the state of the land, it was no wonder the folk were thin and gaunt. The scrubland was only fit for rabbits, which were in abundance, and a few scrawny sheep and goats on steep hillsides. He looked at the riverbed running beside the road, its flow of water reduced to a trickle. There was nothing here for horses to drink, let alone an army.

Looking around, he wondered when the landscape had changed. All of yesterday, they were in an undulating, fertile valley, and it was the same when they set off this morning. He had not noticed anything different when the group stopped for luncheon, to rest the horses, so they must have turned off the main road after that. He wondered why, and hoped the guide knew where he was going. Then he realised Dr Hawley was still talking.

"Be thankful you have better shelter at night and more food than the armies of Alexander did in their time. Remember that when you don the uniform to fight for His Majesty, King George."

"I remember Pa telling me an army on the march rarely had enough food, and men often went out to shoot rabbits for the pot," said Charlie.

"Who did the cooking?" said Joshua.

"There are always camp followers. Wives and such like." Dr Hawley pursed his lips, but did not elaborate.

They lapsed into silence, and listened to the sound of the coach wheels, grinding slower as the gradient of the track increased. The atmosphere felt oppressive, and in the distance the heavy sky threatened a rainstorm. Before it came, they would need to find shelter.

At the top of the slope, the coachman stopped to rest the horses. Joshua and Charlie climbed out of the coach and Dr Hawley wandered towards an outcrop of rock amongst the juniper bushes.

The lads would have followed him, but Sergeant Percival said, "Take care where you go walking, young sirs. You never know what dangers lurk out there."

"Dangers?" said Joshua. "But what harm could be there?"

"More than you would know about, young sir."

"Now look here, Percival…" The heat made him irritable.

"No, you listen to me," the guide said. "This isn't the English countryside. There are brigands in these hills, which is why we have guards. If that isn't enough, a snake or insect bite could cost you your life. Now, if you will pardon me, I had better find the professor and make him aware."

The man's abrupt manner left Joshua feeling stunned. He looked at Charlie for reassurance, but it was not forthcoming.

"I think he could be right, Josh."

Before they could say more, Dr Hawley came wandering back, looking perplexed. The soldier followed behind.

"Sergeant Percival tells me that I have been somewhat negligent of your safety, gentlemen."

"Certainly not, sir," Joshua said, "it's not for him to tell you what to do."

To their surprise, the tutor said, "I think it is, Joshua. The good sergeant has apprised me that he has your father's full permission to oversee your safety in any way he sees fit." He turned aside and said, "Sergeant Percival, I would be obliged if you would show them Squire Norbery's letter."

The soldier extracted a folded sheet of paper from his pocketbook and proffered it for Joshua's inspection. "I meant no disrespect to Dr Hawley, but as you will see the decision about everyone's safety lies with me."

Joshua studied the contents. The sight of his father's signature brought a wave of nostalgia, a sense that even this distance from home, a sheltering presence was with them. He took a deep breath, nodded agreement and returned the paper.

"Thank you, Sergeant Percival," he said. "That is most reassuring."

The soldier was already turning away towards the coaches.

"Right, gentlemen," he said. "If you are ready, we will be on our way."

The cavalcade moved on, its mood sombre. No one could think of anything to say. Dr Hawley started to speak, but lapsed into a drowsing stupor. Sometime later, he started muttering in his sleep. Incoherent wisps of conversation, unlike his usual logical talk, about *Belinda and a litter of kittens*. They knew about Miss Hawley, but such a lapse from a well-ordered mind was out of character. Then the rambling started again.

"Alexander – the fever…"

"He looks a funny colour," said Joshua. "Do you think he's all right?"

An unnatural flush had overcome Dr Hawley's normally pallid complexion. Beads of sweat glistened on his brow. A dull glaze coated his eyes, and on his breath, a strange, rancid emission.

The sight galvanised them to action. Charlie grabbed the tutor's walking stick and hammered on the roof to attract the coachman's attention, while Joshua shouted through the window.

Sergeant Percival appeared on his horse by the coach door. "What's the matter?"

"Dr Hawley's ill – he's sweaty, flushed, rambling…"

The soldier clambered through the door nearest the tutor, passed a hand over his brow, and turned the man's head sideways to reveal a vivid red blotch staining the side of his neck.

"You're right," he said. "It looks as if he picked up an insect bite in the undergrowth."

"Will he be all right, Sergeant?" said Joshua.

"He needs treatment, so I'll leave you to do the hoping and praying, and I'll see if we can find a gypsy herbalist. I doubt there's a physician in the area."

"But surely the Embassy would provide a doctor."

The soldier's laugh had a hollow ring. "Yes, they might, if we were within fifty miles of them, but he could be dead before we got anywhere near. We must find someone with knowledge of local herbs – and quickly."

"What can we do to help?"

"It would be best if you rode in the other coach," the soldier said. "Your man Gilbert can stay with the tutor, and his manservant can help until we find shelter in the nearest village."

The thought of their tutor being in danger struck Joshua to the core. He felt sick, and scared. It seemed easy when Dr Hawley was pompous about things, and for them not taking notice, but now…

"Come on, Josh. I think Sergeant Percival is right. We'll only be in the way." Charlie looked just as pasty-faced, but he grabbed Joshua's arm, and pulled him out of the coach, while the servants changed places with them. They had to accept the matter was out of their hands.

A distant rumble of thunder warned of the impending storm, matched by a flicker of lightning amongst the gathering clouds on the horizon. It was a matter of time whether they found shelter before it arrived – or not.

Hearing the order to move, the coachmen whipped up the horses and drove them onwards. Half a mile further on, a ramshackle collection of dwellings came into view, but before they reached it, the road went in separate directions. One track continued to the village and on into the hills, another turn led to a church, while the main road went down the hill out of sight. They waited while Sergeant Percival galloped ahead to seek shelter.

A woman peered out of one of the hovels, and pointed further along the road. Half a mile beyond, they found what appeared to be a tavern, in a much dilapidated state. It was not somewhere they would have stopped from choice, but there was nowhere else.

Somehow, the guide made his needs known and paid whatever money the innkeeper demanded. Only then did the man allow the guards to carry Dr Hawley from the coach to a dingy little room on the lower floor.

Conditions inside the inn were stark, but it was worse outside. The thunder rumbled overhead, but the rain held off until they carried their baggage indoors. Then the storm broke, lashing heavier by the minute as the coachmen and grooms released the frightened horses from the coaches and settled them under cover in a barn – just in time.

The two servants busied themselves in the improvised sickroom, using their own bedlinen to cover the thin straw mattress on a roughly hewn pallet in the corner. The only other item of furniture was a wooden chair.

Joshua and Charlie hovered around the tavern door, waiting for someone to tell them what to do – not knowing what would happen if Dr Hawley did not survive. They could not say the other word, for fear of making it happen.

By lucky chance, a local physician was visiting his brother in the area. When summoned to attend, he took one look at Dr Hawley and advised they called for a priest. Before he left, he proceeded to bleed the patient, and promised to return in the morning. Convinced he was dealing with a dying man, the priest came to sprinkle incense and utter a multitude of prayers.

Minutes after he left, a maidservant sidled into the room and approached Sergeant Percival, just as he was trying to persuade Joshua and Charlie to take some food. From the murmur of voices, they heard her telling him about a person living a few miles away – a Romany woman, skilled in dealing with local fevers.

He hardly waited for her to leave the room, before saying, "Mr Joshua, your tutor is likely to die unless we can improve on the care of this physician."

That stated the case baldly, but Joshua knew he was right.

"Did you understand what the maid said about the gypsy woman? I'm hoping she will give me some kind of herbal potion. There is no guarantee it will work, but you need to know the score, in order to tell your father we did our best."

"Do what you must," said Joshua. "We can't leave Dr Hawley as he is."

"Why can't she come here?" said Charlie.

The soldier stopped to consider his words.

"Because the locals think she's a witch. Neither the church nor the physician would tolerate us seeking her help, even if she saved his life. I want the chance to put her treatment to the test without anyone being the wiser. If we stop one before trying another, we'll give the game away."

Joshua could see the logic. The physician would continue to bleed the patient as long as they paid his fees – but unless Sergeant Percival found alternative treatment, Dr Hawley might die.

With one of the guards by his side, and a local boy as guide, Sergeant Percival set off into the darkness to find the gypsy woman.

Joshua and Charlie forgot their hunger until told by the innkeeper their dinner awaited them. It was a scraggy leg of mutton, roasted on the spit with herbs, and served with a few root vegetables, and chunks of bread. The juices from the meat tasted like nectar, but it seemed indecent to enjoy food with their tutor lying almost moribund in the next room.

They divided the joint and set aside food for Gilbert, and Priddy, manservant to Dr Hawley, and sent portions out to the coachman and remaining guards, whilst ensuring there would be ample for when the others returned.

Whilst they waited to see whether Sergeant Percival could achieve his aim, Joshua and Charlie took turns to sit in the tutor's room while the servants ate their fill and took a rest.

All the time, the tutor looked frailer and sank lower. Joshua had never seen anyone die, but he imagined this was how it would be. He felt helpless to intercede, wondering how his father would judge their action.

Please, please, please let the gypsy woman help.

He did not want to dwell on what would happen to Dr Hawley's sister if the unthinkable happened. She would be all alone.

Some hours later, Sergeant Percival and his fellow soldier returned, looking equally weary, with rain dripping off their hats and waterproof capes.

"Did you find the gypsy woman?" Joshua hastened to ask.

"Yes," Percival said. "She has given me something to try, but said to give no more than three doses. He can have the first now, another two hours later, and a final one in the morning before the physician returns. Any more might kill him."

After dispensing the first dose, the soldier and his guard went to eat. Joshua and Charlie went with them, and took a tankard of ale while Gilbert and the manservant returned to their patient.

They were incredibly tired, but sleep was beyond them.

"What will we do… if…?" Joshua did not want to say the words.

"If the potion doesn't work, you mean?" Sergeant Percival said.

Joshua nodded.

"Keep praying, young man, there are at least two more doses of the stuff in the flask, and it is not going to waste. If I'd had something like this to give your Uncle Jack, he might have survived."

"You knew my uncle?"

"I was his batman, and the tragedy was he sold out when his wife died. He bought my freedom from the army as well, and we were going back to Linmore to collect his daughters. I daresay he might have married again, but he didn't live long enough."

"I'm sorry," said Joshua. "I didn't know who you were…"

The man shrugged his shoulders.

"There's no reason why you should, except your father kept in touch and provided work for me. I've escorted quite a few young gentlemen on their travels. I even went to Oxford with your brother, but… um… let's say we did not get on well enough for me to accompany him on his Italian trip. There's not much of his father in him."

"He says the same about me."

"Oh no, anyone can see you're a Norbery."

Joshua felt comforted by the thought. "What about the other people here?" He nodded to the guards sitting beside the sergeant.

"Oh, you mean these ruffians? You could say they are old soldiers like me, between the wars and likewise recruited by your father."

Even here in Macedonia, there was evidence of his father's influence.

"Come on, young sirs." Sergeant Percival adopted a brisk tone. "It's time you were asleep, and there's a room upstairs awaiting you. Depriving yourselves of slumber won't benefit the professor."

The physician returned mid-morning, and was surprised to find his patient not only alive, but also swallowing sips of lamb broth. The priest similarly attributed his recovery to divine providence and went away to give thanks.

When Joshua and Charlie entered the sick room, Sergeant Percival greeted them with a grin. "Powerful stuff, that was, but it took a fourth and fifth dose to make sure."

"I thought she said…"

"Three, yes, but I never could count, and I had to make sure he'd had enough. Now I know."

CHAPTER 16

The time they spent at the inn seemed interminable, but by the end of the first week, Joshua was wishing for his tutor's recovery for different reasons. His initial fear of Dr Hawley's death had receded, together with the uncertainty of being in a strange country. Now, the reasons were personal.

His top clothes smelled musky from the odours of their surroundings, and in the summer heat, his sweat-stained linen beggared description. He had never wished so much for a bath in his life. He knew Charlie felt the same, although they said little on the subject. A wry smile and wrinkled nose was more expressive than a dozen words.

At Sergeant Percival's request, they made few demands of the innkeeper, accepted cold water for washing and eked out their supply of clean linen. Joshua vowed he would never again take so much for granted. The clothes cupboard in his dressing room at Linmore was neatly stacked with shirts, and linen was taken away to be washed almost before it was worn. He had so much, and yet here there were children in the village with ragged clothes and hardly a shirt to cover their backs. To flaunt such wealth to them was unthinkable.

He thought about it when he wrote in his journal. Every day, he recorded the happenings he intended to tell Aunt Jane.

Dear Aunt Jane. Another week has passed and we are still in the little mountain village.

He stopped, not wanting to cause alarm at home by telling about the problems. It was better to turn things around and make them sound humorous.

I do not know which one of us smells the worst. Charlie insists he holds the record, but I have my doubts. You may wonder why we do not change our shirts more frequently, but the truth is the servants are too busy caring for Dr Hawley, to worry about our needs.

We try to make one shirt and neckcloth last five or six days, so you can imagine the noxious state they are in when we change. It's lucky we don't have the same sense of our consequence as my brother. He would never cope with it.

The frugality of their use of linen was in sharp contrast to the number of failed attempts Matthew Norbery's valet regularly made whilst trying to achieve a reasonable effect in neck cloths.

You must not think it is a hardship. Sergeant Percival has arranged for women in the village to attend the washing, but they can only do so much. The sickroom linen must come first, and Dr Hawley's recovery is slow.

"Don't let go of too much linen, in case we need to leave in a hurry."

That was what the guide actually said.

Whilst the two menservants did most of the daytime caring, the former soldiers-cum-grooms took turns to sit through the night. Others in the group slept in the barn with the coach and horses, to see nothing went astray. Joshua and Charlie wanted to help, but Sergeant Percival limited their time in the sickroom to a couple of hours a day.

"I know you mean well, young sirs," he said, "but it would serve no purpose to have you in the same situation as Dr Hawley."

In the absence of any skills in healing, they read to the tutor from Virgil and his favourite book of sermons. For a time, they did not know if he could hear the words, but gradually they sensed his awareness and derived comfort from doing something useful.

Time was long and food scarce, so when Sergeant Percival sent two of his men out to shoot rabbits, the lads went with them. It was a relief to find something for which life at Linmore prepared them. They came back refreshed by the exertion and satisfied with their endeavours.

They returned, two hours, six rabbits and four pigeons later, to find their tutor suffering a relapse, caused by septic wounds from the bloodletting physician's practice. The gypsy remedy put paid to the original fever, but now they needed more supplies, which took another week to resolve.

Wishing to do something useful, Joshua offered to use money from his own pocket to pay for extra help, even going so far as to suggest he and Charlie practised their Greek language skills in the negotiations. To his surprise, Sergeant Percival declined.

"I know your offer is kindly meant, Mr Joshua, but I don't want either of you two young gentlemen going out talking to any females."

"But why?" they asked as one.

"This is a poor area, and some of the women might be tempted to offer you all kinds of services for money, and then we'd have their menfolk chasing us all out of the village before we're ready to leave."

It was obvious, from the expression on the soldier's face, this did not relate to the washing of dirty linen. Joshua sensed that the book of sermons would hold the answer.

Despite the frustration of having so much time to spare, and being restricted in what they could do, it seemed strangely companionable to sit in a flea-ridden inn, contemplating supper, smelling like a couple of tramps.

They did not complain, for the food was better some days than others. Several of the former soldiers had a flair for foraging. They went out three at a time to exercise the horses, and came back with bulging knapsacks. The contents usually guaranteed them a couple of meals with meat on the plate, then stew or a thin broth from the bones.

Pigeons and rabbits formed much of their diet, but on a good day the foragers might acquire eggs or poultry from a farm, and once, some river fish, which tasted like trout. It was a rare treat.

There was plenty of bread, but not the kind they ate at home. This was dense and dark, and took a lot of chewing, but at least it was filling, for it sat an unconscionably long time in the belly.

Tonight, the innkeeper shuffled into the room and placed a bowl before them on the hardwood table. It was always the man. The young maidservant they saw on their arrival seemed to have vanished without trace.

The first hint of tainted aroma told Joshua the rough-made vessel contained an indeterminate broth-like liquid. With luck, there might be a handful of herbs tossed in to mask the floating globules of grease, and a chunk of black, bitter-tasting bread on the accompanying platter.

It was just as well the low-beamed ceilings and little slits for windows prevented them from seeing the contents; otherwise, it was doubtful if they would swallow a mouthful.

Joshua stirred the lukewarm mess of potage, trying to force himself to fill his spoon and raise it to his lips. His belly rumbled in protest, anticipating the onslaught it was about to be dealt. Then he listened to Charlie, slurping one spoonful after another down his throat without a thought. He watched for a full minute and then said, "Do you like this stuff?"

"No," Charlie scarcely stopped long enough to answer, "but an empty belly's worse than this. My pa told me a soldier takes what he's offered because every meal might be his last."

Feeling ashamed, Joshua broke off pieces of bread and soaked it in the broth. After a minute or two, he gulped it down. Charlie was right – it was almost palatable, probably a third time rendering from the rabbit carcases. When he had drained the bowl and mopped it clean, he said, "I wonder what the others eat, out in the barn."

"From what Gilbert was saying, they have army rations; a bowl of gruel, a crust of bread and some broth every day."

The knowledge of how little others had to eat stunned Joshua. It was no good complaining. They wanted to learn about army life on the road, and their tutor's illness gave them first hand knowledge. This was the reality.

Descriptions of poverty could wait until their return home. What did it matter if the grease and smoky atmosphere in the tavern permeated their clothes? The hardships for people in the village were worse.

There was no colour. Everywhere Joshua looked, poverty showed its weary face. Old and young alike wore faded cloth, frayed to the point of destruction, and boots held together around splitting soles and gaping holes. Even at his dirtiest, he would never be in this state. Until now, it had never occurred to him to wonder if families in Linmore Dale lived in such poverty. He hoped not.

He thought back to the first day when they went out to shoot rabbits. A group of ragged children followed and vied with each other to pick up the carcases – anything to earn a reward. Their eyes looked so sad, he was tempted to dispense a coin to each in the group, but the former soldiers warned against it.

"If you give five of them a coin today," said Edwin, one of the grooms, "there'll be a dozen waiting tomorrow, and every time they see you. I doubt you carry that amount of money."

"He's right," Fredrick, the outrider, a one-time dragoon, agreed.

Joshua knew they were right, but he still wished he could.

"Are we lost, Sergeant Percival?" Joshua wanted to know.

Most evenings, Sergeant Percival came to sit with them in the tavern room, to drink a cup of coffee, and play cards by candlelight. Often, one or two of the soldiers joined them, while the rest of the men stayed outside with the animals. It was a friendly division, with different people every night, but Joshua and Charlie were rarely alone.

Percival concentrated on blowing cool air across the surface of his steaming cup of coffee. Then he looked up and said in a quiet voice,

"Yes, but only in the sense of having taken a wrong turn down in the valley. Once we did that, there was nowhere to turn around, so we came on, but I think we will probably pick up the right track about a couple of miles from here. The road to Thessalonica, I mean."

"But not by the route Dr Hawley intended. It can't be, because the storm blew the ship off course, and we went inland further down the coast to Tirana."

The guide glanced at the two soldiers sitting beside him, then back to Joshua.

"Having guessed half of it right, you might as well know the rest. The storm was providential, because it meant the professor could not argue with me about the direction we travelled. I never intended taking you the way he said."

Joshua and Charlie listened in amazement.

"Dr Hawley's notions about travel didn't take into account the political situation. It is my job to keep you safe, and Tirana was no place for you to go. The city belongs to Ali Pasha, and he's more trouble than you lads would want in a lifetime."

"Who's he?" said Charlie.

"He was the son of a brigand warlord. Now, he is a very powerful man, who contrives to serve his own ends, and the Ottoman Empire."

"I thought you said there were bandits in the hills."

"So there are, and pirates on the sea and slavers as well, down the coast; but Pasha's Court in Tirana is worse than any of them – for reasons you don't need to know. As soon as the professor is fit to travel, we will make our way to the capital."

"Does Dr Hawley know this?"

The soldier gave a wry smile. "Your tutor is an idealist, and I doubt he was aware of the hazards, even before he was ill. If he wants to believe this is the road to Skopje, then I'll not argue, if it keeps him happy."

"But we are in Macedonia – aren't we?"

Sergeant Percival smiled at Joshua's persistence.

"No, we are not," he said. "We've been in Greece all along, but if it makes you feel any better, we will cross the Macedonian border before we get to Thessalonica. I've arranged to send your father a report from there, and collect any messages from him. Then we will go to Athens."

How could they explain to Dr Hawley? He would never forgive them.

"Let me show you where we are," Sergeant Percival said, spreading out the map on the table, and tracing the route with his index finger.

"We're in this region here." He jabbed a point on the track. "The border is probably within twenty miles of here, and the capital, anything up to fifty miles beyond. How long it takes depends on a lot of things: Dr Hawley's recovery, the weather and the horses."

"What have the horses to do with it?" said Charlie.

"Having so many in one place attracts attention. The animals need food and exercise, just as we do; which is why I don't intend staying here too long. We could either lose the lot, or end up eating them."

"But it's so quiet here. There's nobody about," Joshua said.

"Oh yes there is. They are up in the hills, watching our every move. Their spyglasses catch the sunlight. The lads saw them when you went out shooting rabbits. We post guards at night, because if the horses disappear, we might find ourselves walking to Thessalonica. In that case, anything could happen…"

A cold shiver of realisation touched Joshua's spine. Sergeant Percival did not say the people in the hills were brigands, but that was what he meant. This might not be Macedonia, but there was still danger in this remote place.

"Tomorrow, the lads will go foraging for enough food for another few days. Then I want to be on the move, at least down into the valley. If things hadn't been so desperate, we would have moved long before now."

"Is there anything we can do to help, Sergeant Percival?"

"Yes," the guide said. "You can ride in the small coach tomorrow. It is the best way to exercise the horses without drawing attention to the fact. The drivers can find fodder for the animals, and bring extra sacks of flour and oatmeal. All I ask is you keep out of sight and let them do the talking."

On the way back, Joshua asked the coach driver to stop at the little stone-built church, on the edge of the village. Inside was a single room, with lime-washed walls. An alcove stood at one end, with a tiny altar and wooden cross. The sight filled them with a profound sense of peace and tranquillity.

Joshua dropped to his knees, bowed his head and without thinking, the right words came to mind.

Dear God, please help Dr Hawley recover his strength, and… Bless Sergeant Percival for keeping us safe.

Charlie's prayer echoed his own, and as they left, each placed a silver coin in the offertory box. It was the least they could do.

Two days later, Sergeant Percival was ready to move on.

The entire village turned out to see them leave. There were people of every age. Even the priest came and said a prayer for Dr Hawley's safe deliverance. Sergeant Percival expressed his thanks and gave him a handful of coins for the poor of the parish, together with the surplus sacks of ground flour. Ever practical, he stored a sack of oatmeal for gruel in the coach, with several loaves of bread, and animal fodder for a couple of days.

Then the children guided them back to the main road, and waved them on their way. Joshua added half the coins in his pocket to the collection. He wished he could offer more, but whatever else he saw on his travels, he knew he would take the memory of those skinny little faces back home with him.

On reaching the valley floor, Sergeant Percival continued until they reached a small town, five miles further. Clean lodgings and better food did much to revive their spirits and aid Dr Hawley's recovery. Best of all, it enabled Gilbert to find someone to wash their clothes.

After spending a week there, they set off in easy stages towards the Macedonian border. Of necessity, the days of travel were short, a few hours at most. Dr Hawley's gaunt frame, on which his clothes hung, was a constant reminder of what they endured. His lethargy added to the problem, and fretfulness made even the shortest day seem long.

To relieve the monotony, Joshua and Charlie took turns to read Virgil's poems about rural life to the convalescent. After a few minutes, Dr Hawley's attention lapsed, but he seemed to know if they stopped reading.

They talked in whispers for fear of disturbing the tutor's rest, or gazed through the window, looking at the scenery. After a while, all views looked the same. Joshua knew he should be grateful they were on the move, but it was not enough. More than anything, he wanted a bath, and knew Charlie felt the same.

Gradually, he noticed the land levelling out and the pace of travel increased as they covered more miles in a day. The air was fresher each time they stepped out of the coach, a sign they were nearing the coast. Their spirits rose at the thought of seeing the sea again, almost seven weeks since they left Italy. Where had the time gone?

When they stopped outside the British Embassy in Thessalonica,

Sergeant Percival drew Joshua aside as he stepped down from the coach. Tiredness showed in every pore of the man's face, and not even the thick coating of dust from the road could hide its presence.

"Mr Joshua," he said, "I'm going to ask if you will take your father's letter to the ambassador. I doubt if the embassy staff would let someone like me through the door, but they couldn't refuse you."

"Me? But I'm a bit… for visiting." Joshua twitched his nose and indicated the crumpled state of his clothes.

"They'd think nothing of that when you've been travelling. Most likely offer you the chance of a bath. The thing is the professor isn't in a fit state to see anyone, so it's up to you, sir."

This was the first time Joshua had taken adult responsibility on the journey. As the soldier said, they were his father's letters, which was why he and Charlie stood shoulder-to-shoulder, waiting to meet the British Envoy.

When Joshua explained his predicament, the diplomat offered Dr Hawley the services of his personal physician. At the same time, insisting that when the tutor was fit to travel, they must join his entourage en route for Athens. It seemed if they had delayed their journey even by a few days, they would have missed him.

Joshua accepted the offer with alacrity, but when he told his tutor, Dr Hawley said in a peevish tone, "Master Norbery, you must allow me to be the judge of where to go. Surely, you recall me saying two weeks ago that I wished to stay in the city."

Before Joshua could explain, Sergeant Percival held aloft a sheet of notepaper, "I'm sorry to interrupt you, sir," he said. "Squire Norbery has heard of your illness, and he insists we go straight to Athens. That's why the ambassador offered to take us."

"I beg your pardon," Dr Hawley said in a prim tone. "I was unaware… my memory of events is not what it was."

"That's all right, sir, I quite understand," the tour guide said, looking towards Joshua and gently lowering an eyelid.

They never heard another word of complaint.

The baths in the old city were unlike any they had seen before. It was Joshua's dream come true – a sheer indulgence to find a large room, tiled in marble, with screened alcoves along the walls, containing sunken baths filled with deep, oil-scented water, for each member of the group. There were servants in attendance, and in another room, minions waited to apply oil for massage.

They shed their begrimed clothes and sank down into gloriously warm water, and let the cares of the last few weeks slide away. After the meagre conditions endured whilst travelling, Joshua and Charlie would have been content to wallow all night, but for the invitation to dine with the ambassador's family. It was a foretaste of what was to come.

Joshua's political connection opened many doors. By the time they emerged from the water, their miraculously refreshed clothes awaited them in the bedchambers allocated for their use.

When they entered the dining hall, they found tables groaning under the weight of more food than they had seen for several months. Servants hovered around, waiting to serve them with succulent meats and varieties of fish cooked in spices and a dozen different sauces. To their delight, the choice included several varieties of baklava, and exotic fruits. It was a real treat for all.

Whilst the sight of the victuals revived their tutor's flagging spirits, Joshua and Charlie ate sparingly. They made tiredness their excuse, but in truth, the memory of the hungry children in the mountains blighted their appetites. The difference was too much to comprehend.

Within a week, the physician declared Dr Hawley fit for travel and they were on board a ship, sailing along the coastal route to Athens. On their arrival, the British Embassy staff found them a suite of rooms in a nearby hotel until they hired a villa in the locality.

Letters from home awaited them at the embassy, and they spent the first few days catching up with their correspondence.

Joshua received one each from his father and Aunt Jane. In the first, dated three months ago, he heard that his sister, Caroline, had given birth to a little boy called Master Henry Shettleston. He supposed that meant he was an uncle. It was a strange thought. He had only seen one baby before, the tiny foundling in Hillend village, but he presumed his nephew was larger.

A second item of news related to his brother, Matthew, returning to Linmore from his tour, the thought of which almost made it worthwhile being away from home – but not quite, for he missed it horribly. It seemed a long way away.

Charlie received several letters from Sophie, which filled him with joy, and Joshua could not begrudge his friend the enthusiasm, which bubbled over.

"Hey, Josh," he said for the third time. "Did I tell you Sophie is at school in Bredenbridge? She is having a marvellous time. Her special friend is the daughter of an industrialist, and the family invited her to stay with them at weekends and holidays." He chuckled. "You can tell she's excited. It's difficult enough to read her writing normally, without cramming so much on the paper."

Joshua felt quite envious. Compared to that, being a new uncle seemed mundane. He read his letters again in case he missed anything of significance. Yes, Aunt Jane mentioned his father taking her to visit Dr Hawley's sister on several occasions.

"Listen to this, Josh." Charlie looked up from the crumpled sheet of notepaper he was reading. *You would never believe it, Charlie. They have so... much... money and eat off gold plates. You should see their jewel boxes, filled to overflowing...*

It was more news of Sophie's friends. If she felt like that now, Joshua hoped she would not think life at Linmore poor by comparison.

CHAPTER 17

Athens – 1799

A year ago, when the French invaded Egypt, the news held Joshua and Charlie's attention for weeks, but much had happened in the intervening time and they looked at life differently. Every day since their arrival in Athens, they visited the British Embassy. Not to hear news of the war so much as to experience the reassuring normality they felt when they walked through the door.

Outside it was unbearably hot, but within the cool confines of the embassy drawing room, nothing seemed more important than entertaining the English visitors to afternoon tea and specially made scones. They could have been in England, whereas in the city, the Ottoman culture took precedence over Greek.

A mosque stood alongside the Parthenon. People in the streets and bazaars wore Turkish dress, and the air was heavy with aromatic fragrances. When Joshua and Charlie left their lodgings, Sergeant Percival and his assistants escorted them to ensure they were not tempted to enter the shops, which sold strange scented products.

The sea voyage from Thessalonica took its toll on Dr Hawley's health, so Joshua went with Charlie to present his father's letter of introduction to the British Ambassador. Once there, he found news of their misfortunes had preceded them, conveyed by the diplomat from Thessalonica.

The welcome he received from Sir Giles Stanmore was particularly warm.

"So you are Tom Norbery's son and heir. I remember your father and his brother as young men. My family are Salopians as well, and live only a few miles distance from Linmore."

Joshua noticed the oversight about his seniority, but the moment to repair the error passed without comment.

When they met the ambassador's wife, they found matters of great significance to gentlemen were of little interest to the ladies. Once they exclaimed at the news, they quickly passed on to other things.

Lady Stanmore was the first to express horror at the events that had overtaken them. "It must have been dreadful; Mr Norbery, to be confined in such conditions, and unable to seek proper attention for Dr Hawley."

Joshua would not want to do it again, but he tried to make light of the experience. "It was at first, your ladyship, but Sergeant Percival, our tour guide, acquired the services of a herbalist, who provided a remedy that saved Dr Hawley's life. Without her help, I fear the outcome could have been different."

A flicker of alarm crossed her face, but her manner remained benign.

"That is excellent news, but these things are fraught with danger, and one hears of some guides who are unreliable."

Joshua hastened to assure her. "Sergeant Percival is well known to my father, ma'am. I think the risk would have been greater, had he not been with us."

Sir Giles was not convinced. "That's as maybe, young man," he said, "but the area through which you passed is not commonly visited by English travellers. I thought the guide should have ascertained that first, and taken you along the Dalmatian coast. I will write to your father and tell him of this."

Joshua said nothing, in case he made things worse by admitting the guide used his initiative rather than follow Dr Hawley's instructions.

In the meantime, Lady Stanmore was eager to move on to things dearer to her heart. "Are you familiar with Almacks Assembly rooms, Mr Norbery?"

"Not personally, ma'am, Mr Cobarne and I were onlookers when my sister was presented at Court two years ago."

That was near enough without remembering the dates.

"Did she enjoy a successful season?"

He sensed the ambassador's wife was hanging on his words, but was not sure what she wanted to hear.

"I believe so, ma'am," he said. "Caroline is now married. So are the two cousins with whom she shared the season."

From her beatific smile, he had obviously said the right thing.

"How gratifying it must be for their parents. If only we can achieve the same for our daughters," she said in a wistful tone, and then asked a surprising question. "Did you share the pleasure with her?"

Joshua could hardly tell of the excruciating boredom they felt at the time, but Charlie was willing to elaborate.

"Oh indeed, my lady, there was great excitement in the household," he said. "It was a veritable whirlwind of daily visits by dressmakers and mantou makers. Almost every day, there were deliveries of bandboxes of every description, and bouquets of flowers by the score. And that was before they saw Queen Charlotte."

He had everyone's attention – even if he exaggerated.

Joshua caught Charlie's eye and was tempted to wink. Then he realised it was a most improper thing to do in the present company – so he did the next best thing, and smiled. That was perfectly acceptable.

By then, Lady Stanmore was speaking again. "The reason I asked, Mr Norbery, is because my husband and I will be returning to London next year, in order for Sir Giles to take up a new post in the Foreign Office. The timing is excellent, for it will enable our two daughters to be presented at Court during the following season." She hesitated before continuing. "Your arrival is most fortuitous, because we are seeking to prepare them as best we can with lessons in protocol, etiquette and dancing."

"How can we be of service, ma'am?" said Charlie.

"I wonder if you would care to join their lessons."

They readily accepted the invitation. It was not as if they felt in need of education, but after the rigours of their journey, it was a joy to mix with people of their own age. To laugh and talk again, and have young ladies consult their opinions on travelling in the hinterland.

When the ambassador's two daughters saw Charlie, their eyes widened with delight and they started to chatter amongst their group of friends, making plans to include their visitors.

"Mama," said Miss Eliza Stanmore, the younger daughter, a dainty little miss with fair, curly hair, "Emily asked if it would be in order to invite the gentlemen to our picnic party?"

Her older sister flushed with embarrassment.

When her mother agreed, the young lady turned to address Charlie.

"I'm so glad you have agreed to join our lessons, Mr Cobarne, it is beyond anything to have my brother pretend to kiss one's hand."

The Honourable Henry Stanmore, a young man of about eighteen years, rolled his eyes skywards, under the wayward lock of black hair that fell across his brow.

"Sisters, say the most embarrassing things," he grumbled in mock disgust. "All the same, I'd be awfully grateful if you fellows would support me; I can see they would much prefer your attention than mine."

Charlie chuckled and turned his roguish dark eyes in Joshua's direction.

"We are delighted to be of service," he said. "My cousin was saying only this morning, how much he enjoyed the present company."

That was the first Joshua had heard of it. Charlie was the one who enthused about them after the previous visit.

Lady Stanmore made no secret of her approval. "You must feel free to come and go as you please, gentlemen. The young ladies love to have your escort, and I am grateful that you find the time."

Several other invitations followed the first, and they soon found their store of clothes insufficient for their needs. A travelling trunk, containing many of the garments donated by Joshua's relatives, was still in Thessalonica. On hearing the problem, the visiting Ambassador from the city promised to have it returned to them.

When Lady Stanmore, heard of their predicament, she arranged for a tailor to attend them for fittings in the embassy. The thought of being beholden to strangers made Joshua embarrassed, but the lady waved his concerns aside.

"Good heavens, Mr Norbery, this is only a helping hand until your property can be restored. You must allow me to do this, for I have known your family for many years. In fact, your aunt, Mrs Pontesbury, and I were presented during the same season, so I am almost an aunt to you."

He supposed knowing the family made it all right.

Their first lesson in etiquette taught them formality ruled, but it was hard to maintain a straight face when Charlie emphasised every nuance and his exaggerated poses made the girls giggle in the middle of an introduction.

Joshua knew it was Charlie's way of hiding his boredom. He learned lessons fast, stored his knowledge and wanted to move on. He needed active occupation, not social posturing – they both did, but neither was so gauche as to admit to ennui in elevated company. Fatigue was permissible to admit, boredom was not.

In an attempt to impress on them the need to be serious, the ambassador's wife enlisted the help of her visitors, amongst which several members of the English aristocracy were new arrivals.

When the moment came, everyone passed the test. They answered questions correctly on points of protocol, maintained the correct demeanour, and afforded the assembled company the appropriate degree of respect.

Once they mastered the basics, they embarked on a series of dancing lessons. Had they been midgets, the master of the dance might have acknowledged their presence in a more gracious manner; but the appearance of two unknown, personable young gentlemen challenged his supremacy with the ladies.

Instead, he favoured them with a slight inclination of the head. Then he pranced around the ballroom, gesticulating and issuing orders in an unintelligible falsetto, to the accompaniment of a pale shadow of a woman on the pianoforte.

It was soon apparent the ambassador's children were familiar with the steps, but to Joshua, it was so complicated that it might have been a foreign language. He tried hard to follow the irritating little man's instructions, but always ended the dance confused.

Sometimes it seemed as if the dancing master deliberately set out to mislead him, and then belittled his efforts in his native, rapid-flow Italian, assuming Joshua could not understand the language.

At his side, Charlie nodded his understanding and tapped his toe in time to the music. "This must be the sort of thing Sophie was telling me she did at school. I can see why she enjoyed it."

Dancing was easy for Cobarne. Nobody would think his feet clodhopping, whereas Joshua had the problem of being two sizes larger, and was slower in the turns. Charlie could laugh at his mistakes, and frequently did. The young ladies forgave him, even when he stepped on the train of their gowns.

No matter how hard Joshua tried, he still felt foolish, and it did not make it any easier knowing that as the frequency of lessons increased, so did the number of spectators.

The Dowager Countess of Kenchester was visiting Athens, accompanied by her two granddaughters. One of which, Lady Rosemary Chervil, was an unusually tall woman, somewhat past the first blush of youth.

It was unfair of Charlie to call her a "Long Meg", but with her aquiline features, and russet coloured hair, severely braided around her head, she was unmissable, standing a head and shoulders higher than the gaggle of frippery young misses. Only Joshua stood taller and she immediately made her way to his side.

"Mr Norbery," she said, "I hope you will forgive me if I am direct, but it seems to me that you find the process of dancing somewhat confusing?"

He flushed with embarrassment, but could not deny the fact.

"It doesn't have to be that way, you know," Lady Rosemary said. "I have a suggestion to make. I love to dance, but seldom find a partner tall enough to make the process enjoyable. If you would be so kind as to lead me onto the floor, I will engage to see you learn the steps. In fact, it would be my pleasure."

She was an excellent teacher. Within half an hour, Joshua forgot to be nervous, and did everything right. There was not a word of dissention from the dancing teacher.

"I knew you had the makings of a dancer," Lady Rosemary said, "Now, I have another proposal. My grandmother has persuaded the ambassador to hold a ball whilst we are here, and I hope you will put your dancing to the test. I am sure you will be every bit as much in demand as your charming cousin."

Joshua was not so sure about that.

Long before the date of the ball, the diplomatic service restored the missing travelling trunk to its owners. With a wardrobe deserving of the name, Joshua and Charlie perceived the benefits of having a valet to keep their clothes in order.

In the first weeks, they had the excuse of wearing comfortable clothes, such as they used for travelling. Buckskins and top boots being their favourite dress, but their lessons taught them that for visiting, pantaloons matched with Hessian boots, and for eveningwear, knee breeches and silk stockings were the accepted mode of attire. The knowledge they were correctly dressed for the occasion made a difference.

Joshua knew Aunt Winifred had impeccable taste, and the array of clothes she gave them was ideal. The only problem they encountered being their size and having grown in stature on their travels, there was a need to use the garments before they were outgrown.

It seemed strange to dress in formal clothes. At Linmore, they laughed at Matthew Norbery aping the dandy set. Now, it seemed they were destined to be similarly dressed, but Gilbert, their valet, had no need to pad the shoulders of their coats and their smallclothes fitted their limbs like a glove.

The aptly named, calf-clinging pantaloons caused amusement at first, but they soon adapted to the change. Even buckskins had a smoother fit.

The proof of their success was in the reception they received from the ladies on the night of the ball. As he dressed in his new clothes for the occasion, Joshua hoped he would not disgrace himself. He moved his head from side to side, growing accustomed to the higher neck of his shirt, and crisp white folds of his neckcloth.

It felt strange, but in tying the cravat, Gilbert aimed for a simple design, perfectly executed, and to Joshua's mind, the result exceeded anything his brother's valet achieved in an hour of failed attempts.

For once, he was comfortable with his appearance and knew Charlie felt the same. Gilbert made a special effort in shaving them for the occasion. He started the practice soon after they arrived in Athens. Until then, it hardly seemed worth the effort, but their skin toughened during their sojourn in the hinterland. Now they were socialising, it was imperative they looked their best.

The valet explained the process as he worked.

"I daresay you'll have a batman to do this in the army," he said, showing them how to lather the soap on their faces before applying the open blade, "but it's as well to know how it should be done. You never know when it will come in useful. After all, you cannot go visiting ladies with stubble on your chin. They don't want to rub faces with a hedgehog."

At the time, it made them laugh, but smoothing his hand over his chin, Joshua could see the sense of it now. It felt good.

When he arrived at the embassy ball, Lady Rosemary tilted her head to one side as she scrutinised his appearance. Then she nodded approval.

"Oh, yes," her eyes twinkled appreciatively, "I think your Aunt Pontesbury would be proud of you, sir. Neither of her sons have your… um… presence."

"You know my cousins?"

She gave a wry smile. "I do indeed, sir. Would you mind if I called you Joshua? I hate all this silly formality, particularly when we might have been related."

Joshua's eyes widened with surprise. "You mean…?"

"Yes," Lady Rosemary said with a laugh. "My mother and your aunt had a strange notion when Augustus and I were infants that we might make a suitable match." She leaned closer and lowered her voice. "Complete nonsense, of course, but one day, we met and agreed to differ with our parents. I think Gus realised I might be as forceful as his mother, and he… well… let us say his lifestyle and mine are not compatible. I don't like the rackety people with whom he associates."

"I see," was all Joshua could think to say.

"I wonder if you do…"

The ball passed without incident. However much he might wish otherwise, Joshua learned it was not the done thing to mark a lady's card for more than two dances, so Lady Rosemary introduced him to several other women – friends, by all accounts – all of whom were older, and accomplished in the social arts.

He lost track of time, caught up in the flow of the music. At midnight, he saw Charlie, leading his partner to the supper room, and they exchanged a grin.

Dawn was breaking when they returned to the villa. The sun was rising over a blue sky, a sign it would be another warm day, but in their somnolent state, they would see little of it. Was this how their social lives would be when they were staff officers in the army?

Charlie was amused when they recounted their experiences of the evening. "D'you know, Josh?" he said, stifling a yawn. "We have a perfect arrangement. You seem happier with the older women, and I… think the young beauties like me. I reckon if we continue like this, we'll never have reason to quarrel over a woman."

Joshua stared, bemused. "Why would we argue anyway, when there are enough for us both?"

For the first time, he felt at ease talking to women. His partner's age did not bother him as much as his ability to complete the set piece of the dance, and he became more accomplished with each social event. He owed it all to Lady Rosemary – or Rosie, as she told him to call her.

Joshua knew from his lessons in etiquette that it was not appropriate for someone of his age to do that on such short acquaintance. She might do it with impunity, but he must observe the rules. To compromise, he maintained Rosie's title and shortened the name. In response, she called him, Mr Joshua Norbery with a laugh in her voice.

From what he could judge, Lady Rosie was about the age of his sister, Caroline, but much friendlier, and there was little doubt her independent nature was the reason she was not married. She was a delightful companion, as was her cousin, Lady Alice Silverdale, newly emerged from her widow's weeds, but several years younger.

As the weeks passed, hardly a day went by without them receiving invitations to evening parties, soirees, riding out to ruined temples with their friends, and dining alfresco in the embassy gardens. They were even included when visiting dignitaries came to the city.

When Dr Hawley recovered his strength, he too was included, and was present on the occasion when Lord Elgin, the British Ambassador from Constantinople, visited Athens. To their surprise, their tutor claimed a prior acquaintance with the peer, and was soon in animated conversation. The result of which: they were invited to join a group visiting the Acropolis.

Charlie was quiet when they left the embassy, but on one of the intervening days before the visit, Joshua came upon him standing in front of a mirror, raising an arched eyebrow.

He stood back and watched for a few minutes, wondering if this latest amusement had a purpose. Social posturing usually bored Charlie, and it showed in the flippant comments that rolled off his tongue.

"What are you doing?"

"I'm practising my look of disdain," said Charlie, as if that explained everything.

"You're doing what…?"

His friend shook his head and spoke slowly.

"In case I ever need to depress pretensions. Did you notice the haughty manner Lord Elgin used the other night at the embassy to deter people with whom he did not wish to speak? The Dowager uses it to good effect as well."

Incredulity must have shown in Joshua's face.

Charlie sighed. "I suppose giving a set-down comes easily to an ugly blighter like you, Norbery. Your face is naturally repellent, whereas my smiling countenance isn't." His merry laugh robbed the words of offence and dispelled any notion of vanity.

Joshua retaliated with a deft swipe of his hand, aimed at Charlie's ear and left him to resume his facial gyrations. All the same, he knew they were a perfect foil for each other, and friends could say things like that without offence.

On the appointed day, they joined Dr Hawley and a party of their friends to watch artists in the Parthenon sketching artefacts, and saw craftsmen making casts of statues – a practice cultivated to enable wealthy visitors to take home replicas with which to adorn their homes. Even had they been inclined, such indulgence was beyond their means. Instead, like many others in the group, they committed the statues to memory in their sketchpads.

Several times in the succeeding weeks, under the escort of Sergeant Percival and his assistants, Dr Hawley took them to an earlier temple of the Acropolis, the Erechtheum, dedicated to Athena and Poseidon.

"We are fortunate Lord Elgin has gained permission for us to visit this site of antiquity, otherwise, we might not have access to the area. I understand the interior of this temple has been used as a mosque, and…" the tutor gave a cough as he peered at his guidebook, "a harem…"

He moved on to inspect a single statue lying on the ground.

"If you look closely," he said, pointing upwards to the structure at the corner of the temple. "You will see this is one of the six figures that supported the Porch of the Caryatids."

The tutor caressed the marble figure as he spoke, drawing their attention to its construction. "Touch the marble," he said. "Feel the smoothness of the stone and appreciate the beauty of the artisan's craft."

The reverence in his voice radiated warmth, but the statue felt disappointingly cold to the touch. What did he expect them to say?

The tutor gave an exasperated snort. "I said touch it, not tickle it, Mr Norbery. If the thought of touching a female form bothers you, think of it as an architectural support. Note how the neck is the narrowest part and compare this with the other five statues that stood alongside it. Think of the strength in those six figures when they supported the entablature on their heads."

To think like that would be sacrilege.

"Do as the man says, Josh," Charlie muttered under his breath.

Joshua's hand moved of its own volition from the curve of the neck to the shoulders. Charlie did the same on the other side.

"Mmm," he said, "I can see what he means about the structure."

They were in full agreement. The flowing lines of the figure were perfection. Whoever created the statue was an artisan of no mean order.

Once committed to memory, the lush curves overflowed the pages of their sketchbooks and dominated their dreams.

After that, the marble statues in the villa garden took on a new meaning as they whiled away the hours, sometimes together, and there were times when Charlie slipped away to be on his own.

Often, on visits to the Acropolis, they met with their friends from the embassy, similarly occupied. They spent several hours exchanging opinions on the Doric architecture, fluted columns and marble statues that filled their sketchbooks.

"I think Mr Cobarne's goddess looks remarkably lifelike," Lady Rosie said, subjecting the drawing to scrutiny. "If you notice, the features of the face and…um…the body are so realistic; I suspect he had some help from a model."

Joshua looked over Charlie's shoulder at the scantily clad form reclining on the drawing, and recognised a marked similarity to one of the little dark-eyed maidservants from the villa. That must be why Cobarne slipped away into the garden in the evening to practise his artwork. No doubt, it was the same reason his Greek language skills blossomed – or maybe, it was Charlie's ability to speak in the Gaelic tongue as a child. That certainly must have helped. Whatever it was, it was far better than Joshua's stumbling attempts at conversation.

Charlie chuckled and said without a hint of embarrassment, "This little lady is Ariadne, your ladyship. But you're right in thinking that if you want authenticity, then you have to study the subject in close detail."

His words brought puzzled looks from the ambassador's daughters, but he forbore to explain. Lady Rosie, however, had no need to seek clarification on the subject.

"Your cousin is an original, Joshua. My grandmother calls him a charming rogue, but she ever had a fondness for them."

Joshua noticed how well Charlie related to the old lady. Despite the disparity in age, he shared the same sharp eye for detail, and wicked humour as the Dowager Lady Kenchester. They were soon firm friends, which left Joshua free to entertain the lady's keen-eyed granddaughter.

It was surprising how quickly the weeks slipped by between their arrivals in late August, to the middle of November. Joshua had written home in an earlier letter with news of Dr Hawley's illness and recovery, and Sergeant Percival did the same. His father's response was to order them back to Italy. With the uncertain military situation in Europe, he felt they needed to be closer to home.

Neither of the lads minded where they went next. They had not seen much of Macedonia, but it was enough to appreciate the difficulties Alexander experienced. They would forego the rest.

Dr Hawley could not hide his disappointment. While his pupils visited the embassy, the tutor indulged himself, soaking up the atmosphere of Plato's academy. Now, he would have given anything to follow clues relating to Santorini's eruption and the disappearance of the Minoan civilization, but his duty to Squire Norbery came first.

When Joshua imparted the tidings at the embassy, the Dowager Countess said, "That is splendid news, Mr Norbery, for it coincides with my own plans. I was saying to my granddaughters only this morning that we have tarried here long enough. It is time to be moving nearer home. Have you decided which of the Italian cities you wish to visit first?"

Joshua admitted he had not discussed the matter with Dr Hawley. He knew Sergeant Percival would be making the plans.

"In that case, you may join our party. Tell your man to contact my major-domo about the arrangements. What is the fellow's name?"

"Sergeant Percival, your ladyship."

"I presume the rank is genuine? You cannot be sure these days. People claim to be all kinds of things they are not."

The question annoyed Joshua and he felt obliged to protest.

"Sergeant Percival's honesty is not in question, ma'am. He was my late uncle's batman. My father has complete faith in him."

He caught Rosie's eye and she smiled.

Later, she told him, "Grandmama was impressed by your defence of a good servant. Few are given the credit they deserve."

"He deserves more than praise for bringing us this far. We were in a sorry state when Dr Hawley was ill. If it hadn't been for Percival's prompt action in finding the herbalist, he would have died for sure."

Joshua and Charlie had matured since they left Linmore. Prior to their tutor's illness, they viewed him as a fount of knowledge and person of unquestionable integrity. None of those things changed in their mentor, only their perception of his interaction with other folk.

On the outward journey, they became aware of Dr Hawley's shocking lack of tolerance. Now, they noted subtle changes in his demeanour and a greater civility towards Sergeant Percival. The fact they spent time in each other's company, walked, talked and even laughed together suggested their broken friendship was in a state of renewal. For that, they could only be thankful.

As far as Joshua was concerned, friendship was one of the most precious things in life and to lose it must be devastating. Thank heaven there would never be a similar rift between him and Charlie.

CHAPTER 18

"I am sadly out of favour, Joshua. I feigned not to notice when Sergeant Percival and his men physically carried Grandmama on board ship. My cousin is also blamed because she was similarly afflicted with deafness." Lady Rosie's tone sounded mournful but her lips twitched irresistibly.

Joshua had witnessed the masterful way in which the former soldiers prevented a repetition of the delaying tactics that Lady Kenchester used on two previous occasions.

Other factors dictated the urgency to achieve their objective. The increased traffic of enemy ships in the Mediterranean Sea necessitated the escort of a British Naval brigantine for the passage to Italy, and pirates were always a danger.

If the ship had not sailed from Piraeus harbour today, they might have remained in Athens until the spring, and who knew what the political situation would have been then.

"Of course," she continued, "the poor dear would never admit that sailing puts her out of frame. In her youth, a woman had to stiffen her resolve and endure whatever life threw at her."

When they embarked on the clipper, Lady Rosie accompanied her grandmother to her cabin, and then returned to assure Joshua that all was well. Now, they were standing on the deck, watching the city of Athens slip away into the distance.

"I mustn't laugh," she said, "but poor Dr Hawley looked most distressed – almost as if he wanted to cry."

"I expect he thought he would be blamed for standing by and doing nothing." Joshua was more interested in the fact Rosie had come to see him, than the tutor's anguish.

"My complicity was worse than his," she said. "I arranged it, and had the audacity to administer a dose of sedation to calm her fragile nerves."

"Was it laudanum?"

"Valerian, and only a small dose, but it will ensure she is able to sleep."

For the remainder of the journey the Dowager Lady Kenchester remained in her cabin, and her granddaughters seldom emerged for long.

Irrespective of the weather, Joshua and Charlie spent much of their time on deck, revelling in the fresh air and freedom from restraint. There were no social functions to attend, and little protocol to observe. Apart from going below deck to eat and sleep, they could gaze at the rocky inlets along the coastline, imagining slave-trading pirate ships lurking amongst the Ionian Islands. Fortunately, none was visible.

Sergeant Percival was never far away. He patrolled the deck with them, pointing out ships of the line, and the reassuring sight of a red flag fluttering on the stern of their escort.

Charlie was quiet, as if contemplating something. Then he said, "It's strange; this boat reminds me of when your father collected me and Sophie from Ireland."

That meant he was missing Sophie.

Dr Hawley spent much of his time in his cabin. They did not know whether he rested on his bed or peered myopically at his books, but it left them many free moments to go below to play cards and blow a cloud with the soldiers. Had he known, it was doubtful if the tutor would have approved of either.

When they met up with the ladies, promenading on the decks, Charlie usually offered his arm of support to Lady Alice and Joshua gravitated to her cousin's side.

"How is Lady Kenchester?" he asked. "Has she recovered from her malaise?"

"Yes, indeed, she is eagerly anticipating the strong arms that will carry her off the ship when we disembark. She cannot wait to see Sergeant Percival again. He earned her approbation by personally taking charge of her safety, and she wishes to make it known that he could apply to her if he ever required a testimonial."

Joshua heard the humour in her voice.

"We have been through this charade many times," she said. "Normally, no one dares quell her rebellion, but because of his audacity, she will scold and I will beg her pardon. All will be well until the next time. She fears the loss of dignity most, and relies on me to make the decisions."

Rosie clutched at Joshua's arm as the swell of the sea brought them closer together, and he covered her hand with his own. She looked up at him, grateful for the support. They stood thus for a moment beside the rail.

"I know Grandmama appears fierce, but she has the kindest heart. My father despaired of my independent ways. He said if I had an ounce of proper feeling, I would accept the husband he chose for me, but Grandmama would not let him force me into an unhappy alliance. Her marriage was extremely fruitful, but from things she has said, I do not think it was particularly happy. After my second unsuccessful season, my parents were glad to let me live with her. It was only fair, because they had my three sisters to establish. No," she said. "Don't pity me – the arrangement suits us well. I am in a fortunate position, and have the luxury to travel as her companion. She wanted me to know something different than a life with an endless round of pregnancies." Her voice shook with emotion. "If only she knew…"

She seemed to have forgotten to whom she was speaking. Joshua did not mind if she wanted to trust him with confidences. He would not betray them.

Then she recalled where she was and seemed embarrassed.

"Oh dear, I'm rambling," she said, looking around for her cousin. "It appears Alice has gone ahead. I must go downstairs. Grandmama will be wondering where I am."

"Rosie," he said, returning the pressure of her fingers. "I won't tell anyone what you said."

"No… I know that only too well."

When they arrived in Rome, Lady Kenchester took several days to recover from the journey. During that time, Joshua and Charlie presented his father's letters of introduction to the British Embassy. Whilst there, they took afternoon tea with the Ambassador and his wife and received their first invitations to meet Italian society, which promised to be rather grand.

After this, they visited the villa in which the Kenchester ladies were staying. The fact it was only two doors away from their accommodation was most convenient.

Having travelled together from Greece, it was natural for the two households to continue their association. On this, Lady Kenchester was most insistent, and despite Dr Hawley's modest demeanour, he was not averse to sharing elevated company.

The Dowager Countess treated Sergeant Percival with equal distinction, but the soldier was impervious to any entreaties to join her entourage. His loyalty was to Squire Norbery.

They celebrated Christmas in the household of their English friends, and yet they all felt the absence of family. A few days later, Charlie saw another birthday, and the New Year heralded in a new century.

The year was eighteen hundred, which sounded very different to the last decade. Maybe it was a foretaste of things to come, and they wondered how many more changes would there be before they returned home to Linmore?

In the weeks that followed, the weather was cooler than they were accustomed to of late, but significantly warmer than at home. Dr Hawley delighted in visiting art galleries and museums. Every week they visited another religious edifice with gold ornamentation and vivid coloured frescoes depicting warnings of retribution. The spiritual beauty of Michelangelo's work in the Sistine Chapel came almost as a relief.

The social calendar continued unabated, but there was an underlying nervousness about the changing military situation. They heard news of battles fought in other parts of Europe, and learned that if Rome was threatened, the ambassador and his entourage had plans for a move to Naples.

With fewer English visitors in the city, those who stayed seemed to cling together for their entertainment. It was evident, from the joint invitations they received, the Dowager decided that two personable young men were suitable escorts for her granddaughters.

As Easter approached, Lady Kenchester decreed a visit to Tivoli was a matter of some urgency, and arrangements were made. The journey, a matter of thirty miles, took two days to achieve at a leisurely pace.

On their arrival, the Dowager declared the accommodation somewhat rustic, but to Joshua and Charlie, it was sumptuous. There was an abundance of marble tiled floors and similarly clad walls, which kept the villa cool. It was perfect. Even in the spring, the weather was as warm as an English summer day.

The atmosphere suited the Dowager's mood, and in her somnolent state, she sent an apology with Lady Rosie.

"Grandmama begs you to excuse her, gentlemen. She is too fatigued to accompany us today."

When they expressed concern, she said, "Don't worry, she will be wonderfully indulged in our absence. I knew before we came that walking was going to be too arduous for her, but she has decided we can be trusted to bring back a good report of our visit. To ensure she has something to remember, I have engaged the services of an artist to record the scenery."

Joshua and Charlie were happy to act as escorts for Lady Rosie and her cousin. Dr Hawley went as well, as did the ladies' maid, and Gilbert, the manservant. At the last minute, Sergeant Percival joined them.

"Begging your pardon, ma'am," he said. "Lady Kenchester asked that you remember to take your parasols. She said the sun is extremely powerful."

Everyone laughed when Charlie stepped forward. "I have it here, my good man," he said, opening the shade he carried for Lady Alice, while Joshua did the same for Lady Rosie.

From the minute they arrived at the Villa d'Este, Dr Hawley was lost in wonder, and drifted off to contemplate the masterpieces of creation. In his absence, time had no meaning, and it was too warm to rush about, so the younger folk sat talking in shaded arbours, while the artist committed his sketches to paper.

"It says here that the man who caused this to be built was the son of Lucrezia Borgia." Lady Rosie studied her guidebook.

Joshua tried to remember what Dr Hawley had told him in preparation for the visit, but it was nothing like that.

"Her father was Pope Alexander."

Popes did not have daughters – did they?

"Yes," Lady Rosie said with a smile, correctly reading his mind. "This one did, and his grandson, was nominated several times to be Pope, but never chosen. When he failed, he created this beautiful garden."

Joshua watched her expression of increasing awe as they walked down the staircases between the terraces, then along the alleys to see hundreds of fountains and the Grotto dedicated to Diana.

Overwhelmed by the music of the water organ fountain, Lady Rosie turned towards Joshua, with head bowed near his shoulder; her voice muffled as she sniffed, inelegantly. Anticipating her need, he slipped a neatly pressed square of linen into her hand, and shielded her from view whilst she regained her composure.

Somewhere behind them, Charlie's voice drew the tutor's attention.

"Would you believe it, sir?" he said. "The whole system of fountains is supplied by a couple of aqueducts from the river. That architect fellow, Ligorio, was a genius and no mistake."

Lady Rosie raised her head. "Thank you," she said, returning his handkerchief. "I'm sorry to be a watering pot, Joshua. The sound is so moving."

He smiled at the description. How like Rosie to say that here, in a garden full of fountains.

"I'm glad you are here," she said in a gruff little voice, "but don't you dare say a word of this to anyone, Joshua Norbery. I never cry."

That night, Joshua lay awake remembering the little pavilions, situated at the crossing points of the staircases in the garden, the fruit trees and the air, heavily laden with the scents of aromatic plants.

It was a truly memorable day. He had never before felt so comfortable in a woman's company, nor talked with such ease. No artistic sketch could store the memory, but the sight of it would forever bring it to mind.

Their visit to the Villa Adriana later in the week was gentle by comparison. The Emperor's country villa was an hour's drive by coach from the d'Este garden. Whereas the fountains had been vibrant and living, the atmosphere amongst the sunken water gardens was incredibly tranquil. Although some of the original character of the ruins had been lost, its true beauty remained in the mosaic floors. Joshua committed several of the scenes to his sketchpad and before they left, each one took a little coloured stone from the broken mosaic floors to remind them, and Charlie took two for Sophie.

The following evening whilst they were dining alfresco in the garden, Joshua overheard the Dowager speaking with Dr Hawley.

"Will the young gentlemen be having their portraits painted whilst they are in Rome?"

He met Charlie's eye and raised a brow.

The tutor pursed his lips and said, "I think not, your ladyship. Mr Norbery made no mention of that in his letters."

Lady Kenchester seemed to have other ideas.

"All young men should have their portraits painted at least once. People change as they grow older, and it is good to remember one's youth. When my brothers were young, the Grand Tour was all the rage. Pompeo Batoni was the artist of choice then, but I imagine we could find someone just as good today."

What did she mean? It sounded as if she was involved.

Joshua was mistaken in thinking Lady Kenchester would forget the matter. A few weeks later, they joined the ranks of other young gentlemen travellers engaged for several sittings in an artist's studio. Batoni might be long gone, but his style of painting remained. Usually, it was a scene with the subject in the centre, and Roman antiquities in the background.

In Joshua and Charlie's case, the study was of two figures, their fencing lessons completed, leaning on their foils – and in the background between them, a replica of the sleeping Ariadne. All that remained was to give the picture a title.

"What shall we call it?" Joshua asked.

"Brothers at Arms, of course," Charlie said with a laugh. "What else?"

CHAPTER 19

I t was early summer and the British Embassy in Rome was in a state of high anticipation. On a recent visit, Joshua and Charlie heard news of the impending visit of the naval heroes of the Nile river battle, and received an invitation to the grand ball in their honour.

Whilst there, they met Sir William Hamilton, the British envoy from Naples, visiting with his wife, and thus remedied the opportunity missed when they first arrived in Italy.

On the night of the ball, the ladies were in alt, with everyone hanging on Lord Nelson's words. The menfolk were no different.

For Joshua, the presence of so many naval officers added a competitive edge to acquiring dancing partners, and he was surprised and pleased when Lady Rosie saved him two dances. He knew it was kindness on her part, and gratitude on his, and yet it felt like friendship, for what other interest would an earl's daughter take in him?

"Not all female hearts flutter at the sight of a naval uniform, Joshua," she said. "I have been on the social scene for a long time, and have met Horatio before. I will forgo the pleasure now, and let Emma Hamilton languish at his feet, which she is increasingly ready to do. When they are in Naples, Sir William spends much of his time studying volcanoes. It's debatable whether he does so because of her predilection for Nelson, or whether her husband's passion for volcanology has left Emma with too much time on her hands."

Whichever it was, Lady Rosie seemed happy with the present company, and Dr Hawley was more than ready to engage the interest of an acknowledged expert in volcanology.

A few weeks later, the tutor expressed an interest in visiting Venice, but Lady Kenchester immediately dismissed the idea.

"My dear sir," she said. "You must not think of depriving us of your company. How will we survive without your escort? In any case, what can Venice offer you, which Rome cannot give one hundred times more?"

The tutor tried patiently to explain, thinking the Dowager might not know the history of the city.

"Venice has many fine things, Lady Kenchester; most notably, the bronze horses, brought from Constantinople at the time of the Fourth Crusade, which adorn the parapet of the cathedral."

Joshua and Charlie watched the battle of wills, knowing their tutor could not win. It had happened before.

Lady Kenchester gave a tight smile. "If you wish to see those particular artefacts, sir, you will have to take your charges to Paris. I doubt that is your intention."

Doctor Hawley looked appalled. "Indeed not, ma'am," he said. "Paris is the last place Mr Norbery gave me leave to take his son."

"I thought everyone knew Bonaparte's army looted the city, three years ago, in 'ninety-seven," the Dowager said with ruthless candour. "Everything of value was taken including the plunder from Constantinople. All the paintings, jewels and exquisite artwork have gone, and the people left destitute."

Joshua watched his tutor's face crumble like a child losing a promised treat. He felt sorry for him. They missed seeing many things on the tour and this was another disappointment.

The Dowager's determination to retain their escort prevailed, so they remained in Rome. To compensate, the tutor enrolled Joshua and Charlie on a six-week course to study the antiquities.

To their surprise, Lady Rosie and her cousin elected to do the same, but while Dr Hawley intended the lessons to involve his students in serious study, the female company introduced an element of light-hearted rivalry.

"We don't expect you to be gentlemanly on our account," Lady Rosie announced. "Our ability to learn equals your own."

Said in the spirit of good humour, it was enough to spur them on. Some days Joshua and Charlie edged ahead, and the next the ladies recalled more detail. Another week, they worked in pairs, which worked out rather well when Charlie invited Lady Alice to see if they could beat the other two to flinders.

Lady Rosie had no compunction about the methods she used to succeed, drawing on knowledge acquired on previous visits.

Joshua was happy to go along with whatever she said, but Charlie protested. "That's unfair, Lady Rosie. I think you take advantage of us."

The lady looked him in the eye, and said, "Are you suggesting I'm cheating, Mr Cobarne? How very unhandsome of you, sir."

"Would I be so ignoble as to say a thing like that, ma'am?"

"If you are, sir," she said, "I must call upon my champion to fight a duel in my honour."

Charlie feigned to be terrified. "But he's larger than I am, my lady. It would be unfair to me."

"The choice is yours, sir," she teased.

He sighed and turned to Lady Alice. "Do you think I must make recompense for my hasty words to your cousin, ma'am?"

"I fear you must, sir. It would be more gentlemanly."

Dr Hawley looked pained by the interchange, but the light-hearted banter helped to uplift the content of their studies.

As the weeks progressed, they worked their way through all the sites of antiquity on Palatine Hill, the first occupied by settlers, and the place in Roman mythology where a she-wolf reputedly nurtured the children Romulus and Remus, from whom Rome acquired its name.

The Arch of Constantine reminded Joshua of the entrance gates at Rushmore Hall, and he assumed Lord Cardington's ancestors had seen the design on their Grand Tour.

A visit to the Circus Maximus taught him more about the speed with which a woman's mind changed direction than chariot racing, when a chance remark by Lady Alice started to escalate into a dispute.

"I wonder if Roman women used to drive chariots?" she mused to no one in particular.

When Joshua expressed doubt, Charlie disagreed.

"Why not," he said. "Sophie could have done it, and loved it."

Of course she would. He had forgotten about her.

"Who is Sophie…?" Lady Rosie interrupted.

Joshua looked at her, surprised by the touch of hauteur.

"That's Charlie's sister," he said, "his…younger sister."

"Yes, ma'am," said Charlie. "She's amazing on the hunting field. She's afraid of nothing."

In the next breath, Lady Rosie said, "Will we see your sister at Almack's anytime soon, Mr Cobarne?"

What a strange question. What did she mean?

"No, ma'am," said Charlie. "Sophie's not yet sixteen, and still at school."

Reassured on the point, Lady Rosie said, with a happy smile, "I see. She is an intrepid rider, who obviously challenges you and Mr Norbery, but is not yet old enough to be presented at Court. In that case, Lady Alice and I will have to wait to meet her."

Then, as if there had been no interruption, she reverted to their previous topic, saying, with a thinly veiled challenge in her voice, "So you doubt our ability to drive, Mr Norbery?"

"No," said Joshua, wishing he had considered his words better before speaking. "I…um…thought it unlikely…in Roman times."

"What difference does that make? I am accustomed to driving a high perch phaeton, and I will prove to you that we drive equally as well as men." The light-heartedness had gone. She was in deadly earnest.

"But Rosie," said her cousin with a laugh, "you never take gentlemen passengers."

"In this case, I will make an exception, Alice," said the lady, turning back to Joshua. "The next time you are in London, Mr Joshua Norbery, I will take you driving in Hyde Park, at the fashionable hour. That will be enough to set the gossips wondering about the identity of my handsome companion."

A stifled explosion of mirth followed as Charlie saw the joke, but her words left Joshua red faced, and not knowing where to look. If what she said were true, it seemed Lady Rosie intended to continue the acquaintance beyond Rome.

After a surfeit of culture, it was a relief to sit in the villa garden and watch the sunset. On evenings with no social functions to attend, Joshua and Charlie adopted the habit of wearing togas when they dined alfresco on the terrace. Dr Hawley made no complaint about their mode of dress, but he made it a rule none of the female servants were present to see them in a state of dishabille.

Another stipulation, on which he insisted, was his right to a few hours of privacy each week. They did not begrudge him the free time, for it meant they could do other things. They might chuckle at the thought of him spending hours whispering prayers, but decided he must derive some benefit, because he always seemed in a good humour the following day.

Dr Hawley had changed since his illness. He was still precise in his manner, but there was a difference in his demeanour. They speculated on the cause, but could find nothing to account for the secret smile on their tutor's face when he left the villa to take his evening walk. He set out at the same time every other evening with Sergeant Percival walking alongside.

Maybe that was it. The acrimony between the two men had gone. The question was – where did they go on their walks?

They knew their tutor was devout, but if he was going to church, why did the former solder go with him. It was almost as if they had an assignation.

The puzzle teased Charlie's mind. "I wouldn't have thought Percival was religious," he said one night.

"It all depends whether his inclination is for church going, or temple worship," said Gilbert, their manservant.

"What's the difference?" Charlie wanted to know.

The servant tapped the side of his nose. "Never you mind, young sirs. I daresay you'll find out before you're much older."

They might have accepted it if the man had not laughed, but now, Charlie wanted to investigate. "I think we are missing out on something, Josh. It is time we learned more about this other kind of temple."

The next evening, having shared their meal on the terrace, Dr Hawley left them to debate the merits between remaining in the garden, and walking towards the city walls – a matter already decided by their English attire.

The air was warm and it would be several hours before the sun was set. Charlie waited until the tutor closed the outer door, and then ran upstairs to the balcony, which gave a clear view of the street below.

"Can you see them?" Joshua called to him.

"Yes," said Charlie. "I'm going to follow. Do you want to come?"

"He said we're not supposed to."

"No, he said he wanted some privacy, but we are entitled to walk in the same direction if we want to."

"Why do you want to follow him?"

"Because I don't think he goes to church. I asked one of the maids about the directions, and she said there isn't a church near where he said he goes."

"Well, maybe he found somewhere else."

"I think Gilbert's right. He's found another kind of temple at which to worship," Charlie said with a grin. "Come on, Josh, or we'll lose him."

Soon they were clattering down the stone steps, out into the street. The light was changing, but it was clear enough to see what they wanted. One minute, Dr Hawley was strolling along the street ahead of them with Sergeant Percival beside him, and then they disappeared down a side alley. There was not a church in sight.

By the time Joshua and Charlie turned the corner, they were just in time to see their tutor passing through a dimly lit doorway. Charlie ran down the alleyway and said, "Let's have a look for ourselves."

Joshua was prepared to look at the entrance, but Charlie marched up to the door and gave a resounding knock, which echoed around the street.

"What did you do that for?"

"It can't do any harm. He's inside, and we'll say we are looking for him."

The door opened and a huge, dark skinned man in a turban loomed out of the shadows. Surprise made Charlie struggle with his Italian language, and he blurted out, "The gentleman who just entered. We're with him."

The attendant called into the interior, and Dr Hawley appeared at the top of a staircase, clad in a loose robe. He seemed unperturbed by their appearance.

"Good evening, gentlemen. I wondered when your curiosity would get the better of you." He spoke to some unseen person and the door closed behind them. "As you are here, you might as well continue your education. There is a first time for everyone, and tonight is your rite of passage."

Joshua blinked as two young women appeared, clad in flimsy togas. The one nearest beckoned to him, and Charlie went away with another. The candle-lit chamber he entered had a sunken bath and two women similarly clad stood waiting to assist him to undress.

One of the two seemed older, but that did not seem to matter. She knew what to do, and he forgot all his cares after he stepped down into the bath. Heady scents of aromatic vapours enveloped him. His head was in a whirl, but the rest of him was aflame…

When he came to his senses, he was sprawled on a couch. He felt so relaxed, it did not seem to matter how long he had been there. He yawned and looked around the candle-lit room, but the women had gone. What was he supposed to do now? Then he noticed his clothes on a chair, and quickly dressed himself. He wondered if Charlie was awake, and whether Dr Hawley was still there. How would they explain their curiosity in the morning?

Just as he was wondering where to go, the door opened and a Roman goddess beckoned. He followed her down the staircase, and saw Charlie emerge from another door; looking as dazed as he felt.

Dr Hawley awaited them downstairs. "Come, gentlemen," he said. "Your beds await you in the villa. I think in the light of your nocturnal activities, it is permissible for you to be excused the first lesson of the day."

The two lads looked at each other and silently followed their tutor through the door. Last night was an unexpected lesson, which they would never forget. On other occasions, they had seen the system of aqueducts, transporting water across the city. In the bagnio, they sampled the delights of the heated springs.

Joshua vowed never to underestimate his tutor again. He could not, because anyone who could rise refreshed from a night at the bagnio deserved his respect. On the other hand, maybe he only went for the bath. It was too perplexing a subject on which to waste time.

After a leisurely luncheon, their tutor said, "I trust you both slept well, gentlemen?"

"Yes, sir," they said with a broad grin. "Extremely well."

"That is good, because today, I would like you to commit your recollections of the Villa of Hadrian to your notebooks, and then recall your thoughts on the Mount of Vesuvius and the lost city of Pompeii."

It was no good thinking their knowledge of Dr Hawley's nocturnal visits meant they would be given extra leisure time.

"Next week, I thought we might consider visiting Lombardy, the area captured by Charlemagne. I don't know if I have mentioned this was quite my favourite part of history."

Many times, thought Joshua, stifling a yawn.

"The trouble with youth," Dr Hawley said in the driest of voices, "is that it is wasted on the young. You will both need more stamina, if you are to survive as army officers."

It sounded as if their tutor was making fun of their tiredness. Surely, even he must have been young once.

Charlie looked to be in the same state he was.

Joshua could not remember drinking any wine so the aromatic fragrances of the oils must have melted his bones. He closed his eyes for a minute...

Then he realised Dr Hawley was still talking.

"It is fortunate I sent my latest report on your progress a few days ago…"

What did he mean? Last night applied equally to Dr Hawley as for himself and Charlie. Then he realised he must have missed something his tutor said.

"If you wish to repeat the pleasures of last night, you must be aware of the hazards to your health and be prepared. I would be failing in my duty if I did not warn you that one must take precautions to avoid disease. It is something you must remember when you are soldiers."

Joshua was stunned. He could not imagine having such a conversation at Linmore. Charlie's expression told of the same degree of surprise. Then it dawned that Dr Hawley was taking advantage of their stupor to say things he did not normally say.

"You must beware another time of allowing curiosity to lead you into temptation. It is fortunate I was there last night to ensure your safety."

How could he say that when he was already at the bagnio when they arrived? And it was obvious he was known.

"I think it would be safe to exclude the events of last night from our next monthly report home, don't you, gentlemen?"

Joshua and Charlie nodded in mute agreement.

"Where was I? Ah, yes, Charlemagne, and our visit to Lombardy. I think that would be a fitting place to end our visit to Italy. Then we must set arrangements in motion for our journey home."

CHAPTER 20

Two days after their nocturnal adventure, they received invitations to a ridotto at the residence of an Italian diplomat. Given a choice, Joshua and Charlie would have foregone the experience in favour of another visit to the bagnio, but it seemed some unknown person had especially requested their presence – almost like a royal command.

The Villa Borghese was a mansion about which they had heard on their study tour, but not been permitted to enter. They had seen many museums, but this was a family home, with the finest art collection in the city.

Usually Sergeant Percival provided them in advance with information about the entertainments they attended. On this occasion, all he could elicit was that the wife of one of the family of diplomats was reputed to be the most beautiful woman in Rome.

"Ah well," said Charlie with a laugh. "Bring on the ladies, and let us see them. As long as there's one for each of us, we'll be all right."

Doctor Hawley's reason for attending had less to do with dancing than a curiosity to see the house where family connections of Pope Alexander lived. Having studied the subject in detail, Joshua and Charlie knew what that meant.

The staff at the British Embassy advised them on the mode of travel, and sent a carriage to transport them to their destination. The first intimation of the grandeur ahead came when the coach turned into the grounds and they saw the vast cavalcade lined up waiting to discharge the guests at the entrance.

So stately was the pace, they had ample time to admire the extensive grounds through which they passed. To catch a tantalising glimpse of shimmering water or a folly through the trees, and wish they could explore; to see a riot of colour and breathe in the almost hypnotic scent of the flowering shrubs that bloomed to perfusion, and observe the crisp white lines of the mansion with five arches at the entrance. It was magnificent.

When they finally moved inside, they found that the reception hall had marble walls and fluted columns, and was wonderfully cool after the enforced wait in the carriage.

While Dr Hawley enumerated the artistic treasures of Caravaggio, Titian and Rubens that he hoped to see; Joshua looked around with a sense of anticipation tinged with trepidation. It was a strange feeling for he had moved comfortably in aristocratic and diplomatic circles in Athens and other parts of Rome, and yet the elaborate invitation to the function that specified his name, came from an unknown source.

Before them and amongst the guests that followed, there was a vast array of elaborate masquerade costumes, while others wore fancy dress, and some plain domino cloaks in numerous colours. All were incognito and yet Joshua felt conspicuous.

Not being disposed to vainglory, Doctor Hawley wore a powdered wig, mask, and a black flowing cloak over his evening suit. He walked at Joshua and Charlie's side as they ascended a magnificent marble staircase, and stood waiting in line for the dignitaries to receive them. With the sheer volume of people, it was difficult to do more than bow and shuffle past the unknown people of importance – whoever they were, for they wore masks like everyone else.

Once the introductions were complete, their tutor left them to circulate and find their friends. They guessed he would spend the evening contemplating the artwork, and not reappear until the lure of the supper gong enticed him towards the Orangerie and adjoining terrace for the cold collation.

With the late invitation, there was little time for them to prepare for the occasion. Beneath his black domino cloak and mask, Charlie wore a bottle-green satin evening coat, with knee breeches, lace cravat and gold interwoven waistcoat, whilst Joshua favoured midnight blue, an embroidered silver-grey satin waistcoat, with his cape and mask of a darker hue.

Normally, they wore their hair au naturel. On this occasion, they opted for powdered wigs, but even with their unaccustomed disguise, they were distinctive amongst the hundreds of ornately attired figures, the painted society fops and portly Lotharios milling around.

The ballroom was huge, and magnificent, with a preponderance of gold in its decoration, though one could not tell whether it was gilt or gold leaf that edged the corners and cornices.

Although the evening was young when they arrived, an abundance of crystal chandeliers blazed overhead, running through the entrance hall, and down both sides of the ballroom, each lit by not less than fifty candles. Along one side of the ballroom, several pairs of glass doors opened onto long galleries exhibiting a vast collection of paintings and statues – all illuminated in the same extravagant manner.

In this light, the intricate artwork on the ballroom ceiling shone to advantage, but to appreciate it fully, Joshua thought one would need to stand alone on the floor of the room, not surrounded by upwards of five hundred guests in costume.

Forever after, he determined to judge a masquerade by this standard. While Charlie wasted no time in finding a partner, he was content to look at the elaborate costumes, and the intriguing selection of masks, some of which were of birds and animals. His appearance was plain by comparison, as was the outfit Charlie wore, which made him easier to recognise.

Having learned that Lady Rosie intended to dress as Queen Catherine de Medici, Joshua assumed she would be easy to find. How wrong he was. Now it seemed as if every tall woman in Rome wore a variation of the same regal costume. There was no easy way to find her in this throng of swirling figures. It was a process of elimination – and he might have to dance with them all.

The rules for dancing were different to those at a normal ball. Tonight, there was a free choice with a hint of mystery, not knowing the faces behind the masks until the unveiling at the stroke of midnight. Looking at the number of guests milling around the row of open glass doors leading from the ballroom to the terrace, it was unlikely some dancers would wait that long.

The night air was warm and redolent with heavy scents from the gardens. Outside in the grounds, temples beckoned, and lanterns flickered, illuminating the latest addition to the centre of the lake, the Ionic temple, dedicated to Aesculapius, the god of healing.

Joshua had never known such a crush. The heat from several thousand candle-flames, matched by vapour from half as many bodies in costume was intense, and the cloying scent of the floral arrangements set in recesses around the ballroom merely added to that. Then there was the dancing. He wished he could remove his cloak, and thought longingly of a bath in which he could immerse himself. Maybe he should have gone to the bagnio instead.

After several failed attempts, dancing with other ladies in a similar costume, he found Lady Rosie with her cousin, and engaged to dance two sets with each.

Charlie did the same, then entered into the spirit of mystery and headed for a group of ladies he thought he knew from the embassy. Joshua stayed for a while to talk with those with whom he felt comfortable. Eventually, he knew he had to leave them and circulate amongst the other dancers. What he had not anticipated was that a vision in gold silk would elect to dance with him.

He had seen the woman standing amongst the group of dignitaries when they arrived, and noticed her again when he was talking to Rosie and her cousin. He could not help doing so because she kept looking his way. At least he thought that, and looked around to make sure no one else was standing behind. They were not.

What was there about her that teased his mind? Then it dawned, she was Ariadne, in the flesh. The one the artist included in the portrait of himself and Charlie.

Tonight, she wore an upswept mask of a black lace design, its delicately woven frame studded with diamante. If the outline was smaller, he might see more of her face. All he could see were her rich red lips and pearly teeth.

When Joshua first saw her, he thought she was the most vibrant woman in the room. Where other costumes disguised the owner's identity, her outfit drew attention to her charms.

He did not know much about women's clothes, but he had the feeling that on anyone else, the drab gold silk she wore, fashioned in the deceptively simple lines of a toga, might have passed unnoticed amongst other more elaborate costumes. Instead, the slinky material shimmered as it flowed over her voluptuous curves, it could not help drawing the eye.

A floating wisp of gold silk fashioned as a hood moved his attention to her hair. It was as vivid as the setting sun, and twisted in a coil on the crown of her head. He had never seen such luminescence, or gems to equal the black pearls that encircled her neck and hung provocatively down to her waist.

Other eyes looked in her direction, and not only those of men. He noticed Rosie did too, with a strange expression on her face. Where most women looked with envy, her gaze held enmity, and he wondered at the cause. The woman was undoubtedly the more curvaceous, but that surely was not a reason to view her with hatred.

The goddess was neither tall nor short, but she had a presence that went beyond the clothes she wore. She simply oozed sensuality, and he was not the only one to notice her. Other men wanted to fawn over her, pay extravagant compliments.

Then he noticed the way she moved, and something vaguely familiar about the leisurely, feline sway to her hips touched his soul. Joshua could not keep his eyes off her. He had a picture in his mind of how her coiffured titian hair would look tumbling loose around her shoulders, and the thought made him feel hot and decidedly over-dressed. He closed his eyes but the tantalising image remained.

"What's the matter?" Lady Rosie asked.

"Nothing," he said. He could not tell her another woman was watching him. He did not have to. She could see for herself.

"Take no notice," she said tartly. "You'll only encourage her."

He took his leave of the ladies, promising to return for the appointed dances, and moved across the ballroom. There seemed a sense of inevitability about the way he met a uniformed minion half way to the door. The man bowed and spoke a few words. Joshua uttered an almost pre-ordained response and followed the servant to where his partner awaited him.

He bowed formally, carefully gauging the correct depth of deference, and she leaned provocatively forward. His mouth felt dry and he unconsciously moistened his lips. She smiled appreciatively.

Somehow, Joshua managed to match his steps to his partner, and to the set, but he could never remember what dance it was. When it was finished, he bowed his thanks and walked away across the room to speak a few words to Charlie.

Then he moved on for the first of his duty dances. They should not have felt like that, but they did. Lady Rosie conducted herself with stiff propriety and her cousin did the same. Soon it would be the supper dance. For some reason, he had not arranged to take either of the ladies down to the supper room. It was not intentional. It just happened that way.

He felt strangely isolated, so he made his way to where Charlie was standing. Midnight was the unmasking hour and people gathered around, waiting for the chimes to begin.

"I think the Countess likes you, Josh. She hasn't stopped watching you since you danced with her," Charlie whispered.

"She's married, isn't she?" He did not know how he knew.

"What's that got to do with it? Husband and wives rarely dance together. It just is not done, sir." Charlie's gift for mimicry perfected the lisping individual who struggled to teach them the rudiments of etiquette. "Surely, you have noticed the older menfolk favour the youngest maidens."

Joshua had seen that, but it was not the kind of thing to ask Dr Hawley, particularly after their recent adventure. He almost laughed at the thought and caught the woman's eye. She gave an almost imperceptible nod, pouted her lips and turned away towards the French doors leading to the terrace.

"There you are, Josh," said Charlie. "That's an invitation if ever I saw one."

If it were that noticeable, then surely everyone else would see him walk across the room towards her. He was hardly invisible.

A manservant appeared by his side. "Mr Norbery? The Contessa requested that you join her party for supper."

He looked at Charlie.

"Don't ask me, Josh. The invitation is for you, but if there's a party, it isn't as if you are the only one to be asked."

"If you care to follow me, sir…" The servant moved away, skirting the groups around the edge of the room with ease, and on through a corridor with doors on either side.

Joshua strode after the man, and found him waiting at the end of the hallway, holding open a door. He lengthened his step, and passed through several more doors, down a flight of steps to the outside of the building and across a flagstoned quadrangle, before entering into another maze of corridors.

This was silly. He was moving further away from the ballroom.

"Wait," he called, wondering if he'd used the right word.

"It's not far now, sir," the man said, scarcely checking in his stride.

When they finally stopped, the minion took a key from his pocket and passed through a door. Trailing several steps behind, Joshua found himself in a corridor, lined from floor to ceiling with marble tiles. It almost seemed like an extension of the main entrance.

A panel in the wall slid open, and Joshua passed through the opening and the outer door closed. Somewhere in the background, he heard the sound of running water and became aware of a sweet-smelling scent, reminiscent of sandalwood. Before he could discern the source, a servant appeared at his side, offering a goblet of wine.

Joshua felt better with something to hold, so he took a sip and a strange fiery substance scorched its way down his throat.

What the deuce was in that? He sniffed the contents and decided whatever it was, it was better not to drink any more of it.

"I'm so glad you came, Mr Norbery. You are most welcome."

Even before he turned, the sound of the sultry voice left Joshua in no doubt of her identity, and the sight of her titian hair tumbling around her shoulders evoked the same erotic response it did when he saw her in the bagnio – just before she melted his bones.

The realisation rooted him to the spot. With the removal of her mask, the goddess had shed the rope of black pearls and exchanged the gown she wore in the ballroom for a diaphanous shift, which revealed more of her voluptuous form than it hid.

What kind of outfit was that to wear when she was supposed to be entertaining guests for supper? More to the point – what was he doing here alone with her in a state of dishabille?

The absence of other guests and the lack of visible food struck him anew. So did the transparency of the scanty wisp of silk, which moulded itself to her form, outlining her taut nipples.

Distracted, Joshua took a gulp of wine and found the taste no better than the last time. If this was superior quality, then give him a tankard of ale any day.

"Come with me," she said, holding out her hand and moving towards an open door. "All is prepared for us."

He looked across the threshold of a bedchamber containing the largest, satin-covered couch he had ever seen. It was enormous.

How the deuce could he extricate himself from the situation? There was only one way. He would have to bluff it out.

"I beg your pardon for the intrusion, madam," Joshua said, struggling to regain his composure. "The servant must have brought me to the wrong place. I understood I was to take supper with the Countess… and her party."

"No," she said, with a little smile. "He followed his instructions to the letter."

"Where are the other guests?"

"They sent their regrets. I'm afraid they found the distance too much for their constitutions." She laughed at his look of surprise. "No, I confess that was my little ploy. There is only you, Joshua Norbery, and me, and we have the rest of the night to get to know each other."

Even he knew this was the height of foolishness.

"No," he said, backing away. "I must go back. My friends will miss me."

"I don't think so." She pouted and looked at him from beneath her sooty lashes. "I doubt if they have even noticed your absence. In any case, the door is locked, my dear sir, and the only key is here…"

She extracted a gold-coloured chain from deep in her cleavage.

"If you want to open the door, you will have to take it from me, by force, if you must, but I would much prefer to give it willingly. It would be a pity if I had to summon help to restrain you…"

"I haven't touched you."

"No, but you will," she said. "You won't be able to help yourself."

A sense of unreality invaded his senses. He did not know what it was, but he started to feel as if a drunken haze was seeping into his limbs, just like when he was at the bagnio.

Not that again… please…

"What was in the drink? It feels as if you've drugged me."

She gave a cynical laugh. "Don't be foolish. That would deprive your body of power, and I want you fully compliant. The cocktail will simply erase the event from your memory."

"You're mad," he said, and believed it.

She went on as if he had not spoken. "Not that you will ever forget what I teach you. In fact, it will give you a thirst for the unusual."

He stood, fighting a sense of unreality, yet unable to resist as the woman snapped her fingers for attention. Willing hands came from nowhere to ease the coat from his shoulders, and dispatch in seconds the necktie, which took Gilbert an age to achieve.

"No… Let me do it…" She moved forward, feverishly brushing hands aside when others would have unbuttoned his shirtfront.

With a low growl of delight, the woman ran her fingertips over his nipples, teasing them hard with anticipation, then she trickled her fingers down across his belly…

Hours later, Joshua awoke to the sound of Charlie snoring across the room, which told him he was in his bedchamber. The hour was early, but the sun streamed through the window.

He could not remember returning to the ball after supper, but he must have. How else would he be in his own bed? He looked around the room to where his eveningwear lay scattered across the floor.

His mind registered the fact Charlie had placed his neatly folded clothes over a chair. That must be the soldier in him, and it was something Joshua would have to learn.

The fancy dress clothes were there, so he had obviously been to the ball, but he could not recall how much of it was a dream. It seemed so real at the time, but surely, respectably married women did not go to bagnios, nor entertain young men alone in locked rooms – but then, she was hardly respectable.

The thought of her hands made his blood start to sizzle, and he knew if he ever met her again, he would never be able to look her in the face. It simply could not be true. It must have been the wine he drank or his overactive imagination…

Then the stark reality came back to him. The whore was wrong about the mixture erasing the event. He could remember everything she touched and his reactions. He broke out in a sweat. Even the thought of her sinking her teeth into his nipple set him on a cliff edge. He did not know what else she would do, had it not been for the interruption.

Thank God for the blessed interruption…

To Joshua, it seemed like an hour passed, but incredibly, little more than ten minutes ticked by between the time he entered the outer door and when the disturbance came. He was never more grateful to hear the patter of hurrying footsteps and an agitated, Italian-sounding voice, calling the Contessa's name.

The words were too fast and garbled for Joshua to follow, but the diplomat's wife heard and understood. She shrugged her shoulders, and said, "Of all the inconvenient times for my husband to come – now we will never know how good we were together…"

Then, with an urgency belying the woman's previous languid state, she was on her feet, pushing him through the door into a corridor. He straightened his smallclothes all by guess, as the barrier slammed behind him and he heard the key turn. Then there was silence. He looked down at his crumpled blue coat and necktie lying on the floor at his feet, alongside his cape.

Bemused, he reached down to retrieve the clothing, and his belly rumbled in protest at the lost supper it anticipated. He wondered if the supper room would still be open. It was strange how important it seemed. As he looked around the darkened corridor to gain his bearings, a hand grabbed his arm and pulled him into the shadows. Charlie stood before him.

"Cobarne, what are you doing here?"

"Rescuing you, me lad," Charlie said with a low chuckle, "but we'd better be making ourselves scarce – the husband is only minutes behind us."

"Where can we hide?" Joshua said, looking around the corridor for alcoves.

"We don't, but I've brought you the next best thing to an alibi."

"What?" Joshua turned and saw his aristocratic lady friend. He could not see her face in the shadows but he could imagine her expression. She would be disgusted.

Charlie had other ideas. "Her ladyship was telling me what a devilish place this was for getting lost. She thought you might need a bit of help in finding the ballroom again, so I'll leave you with her, Josh, and go outside to blow a cloud." With that, he melted into the darkness.

"I can explain, Rosie…"

"You can tell me later," she said in a fierce little voice. She grasped his arm and urged him forward as far in the opposite direction to where he had been, through a door into a lighted courtyard.

Seconds later, they heard irate voices and hurrying footsteps, as a door opened on the opposite side of the quadrangle. Three figures appeared. The Italian diplomat swept through first, followed by two waiters, one of which was the minion who guided Joshua's footsteps from the ballroom.

Before he could move, Lady Rosie took matters into her own hands, tangling her fingers in his hair and drawing his face down to meet her kiss, whilst his arms instinctively slid around her waist, drawing her closer. Seconds later, a rough hand caught at his shoulder and spun him around.

The diplomat railed accusingly at him in his native Italian tongue, and Rosie responded, equally eloquent. The man fell back, uttering profuse apologies.

"A thousand pardons, signor, I mistake," he said, and was gone.

Only then did Joshua recall his state of undress, and the fact that Rosie's hands were on his uncovered chest. In the time since he left the bagnio room, he had only replaced his coat, but his neckcloth was hanging loose around his neck with his unbuttoned shirt open to the waist, just as the seductress had left it.

For a moment, he felt sick with relief as he realised how close to disaster he had been. If discovered with the man's wife, as he surely would have been, the news of his involvement would have reached his father in London through diplomatic channels long before his return.

"How did you know where to find me?" he said.

"La Contessa is renowned for her penchant for naïve young men," Lady Rosie said. "She did the same to my cousin five years ago, but then, she was only the envoy's mistress. Her usual ploy is to claim to have been ravished if caught in flagrente delicto. Poor Peter, the scandal almost killed his mother, and all he was guilty of was naivety. The family sent him to India to weather the storm, and it has been the making of him. We made the journey to visit him and were en route back from India when we stopped off in Athens. Grandmama wanted to see him again before…"

Her bitter voice ended in a frustrated sniff. Joshua turned to confront a fiercely independent lady struggling to contain her emotions. He watched anger and distress vie with each other for supremacy. Wishing to distract her, he took her shaking hands and raised them to his lips.

"Lady Rosie," he said. "How can I thank you for saving me from the same fate? If you hadn't come when you did…"

She burrowed her face against his chest and he cradled her there. For a moment, he thought her shaking shoulders denoted she was weeping. Then she looked up and said with a throaty chuckle, "If you really want to thank me, Joshua Norbery, you can resume the delightful process I was enjoying before we were so rudely interrupted. I've wanted to do that with you for ages."

How could he refuse?

CHAPTER 21

The letter arrived whilst they were eating a hearty breakfast. Joshua was ravenous and determined to make up for the supper he missed the night before, when Gilbert entered the room.

"This has come from next door, Mr Joshua. The man said it was urgent."

He glanced at the flowing hand on the cover before breaking the seal. The contents were short and concise.

Lady Kenchester requests Mr Joshua Norbery to attend her at twelve o'clock.

Request…? No, this was tantamount to a royal command. He looked at the clock and saw he had less than an hour to prepare.

Charlie raised an enquiring eyebrow, and Joshua handed him the letter. There were no secrets between friends.

"I'd better come with you for support."

Time was short, but it was no excuse to attend looking less than presentable. That would create the wrong impression.

At precisely five minutes to twelve o'clock, they were admitted to the reception hall in the adjoining villa and were ushered into the peeress's sitting room. Rosie was sitting beside her grandmother, her face a mask of impassivity. She kept her eyes lowered, refusing to meet their gaze. Her cousin, Lady Alice, sat equally straight-faced in a high-backed chair on the other side,

Joshua looked at Charlie, unsure what to expect.

"Mr Cobarne," Lady Kenchester said, "I would be obliged if you would take a turn on the terrace with Lady Alice."

"It will be my pleasure, ma'am," Charlie responded with his usual charm, and they left the room, whilst Joshua waited in silence.

He felt as if he was in the classroom again, and prepared himself, out of habit to receive a scold. When the Dowager spoke, it was not what he expected to hear.

"I hope you have recovered from the most unpleasant experience of last night, Mr Norbery? No lady of quality would behave in such a way." She emphasised the last words.

Rosie sat with bowed head and flaming cheeks. Joshua looked from one to the other, his face suffused with colour. Hardly anything he experienced last night was unpleasant. Quite the reverse, it was illuminating, and much was due to Rosie.

The Dowager took his silence as agreement, and continued.

"To prevent any such recurrence, I would advise you to go home and take a couple of years to grow up – sow your wild oats or whatever it is young men are supposed to do. I understand you are a younger son, so you will need to find some occupation and establish yourself in life. Have you any plans?"

"Yes, ma'am," Joshua said. He was not sure where the old lady's comments were leading, but at least he could have his say. "My father has promised to purchase a commission for me and Charlie – Mr Cobarne, on our return home."

"Mmm, yes," she said. "I can see that handsome young fellow in regimental uniform. He'll be a heartbreaker, but I'm not sure how you will cope with military life, and I would not like to think of you putting yourself in danger."

"But ma'am," Joshua protested. "Charlie and I have always planned to join the army together. Why would we not do so now?" He looked from one to the other, hoping for enlightenment.

Rosie looked exasperated. "Grandmama has some nonsensical notion that…"

"No, Rosemary, I will not be interrupted." Lady Kenchester compressed her lips. "Very well, I will be succinct. It appears, Mr Joshua Norbery, that my foolish granddaughter has formed a tendre for you. Whilst it is understandable, she should know better at her age to choose a callow youth, but it would be unfair for you to form an attachment before you have seen anything of life."

Joshua looked at the old lady, stunned, as the enormity of her words sank in. Rosie sat, mortified by the exposure, while the Dowager continued her monologue.

"Young man, if you have any regard for my granddaughter's reputation, you will leave her alone. It is bad enough she felt obliged to rescue you from a harlot, without ending up compromised herself. Still, not all is lost.

I intend to spend the next few weeks visiting Naples, and return by the middle of next month. If your party is still here, we would be pleased to acknowledge you, but I suggest you think carefully about what I have said."

The Dowager sagged back in her seat, emotionally drained. Rosie looked anxiously on as the old lady waved her hand dismissively. "Yes… yes, take him outside to find his friend."

Keeping a respectable distance between them, Joshua and Rosie left the room through the French windows and made their way down the terrace steps.

"I do beg your pardon, Joshua," she said. "It was unforgivable of Grandmama to say what she did. It's just that she worries about me."

He walked at her side, pondering the situation. It was obvious, the way Lady Kenchester's mind was working, but it had not occurred to him to consider marriage at this stage. She was right in saying he was too young, but her thinly veiled hints confused him. He had only just acknowledged having feelings for Rosie. It would be years yet before he would be in a situation where he could consider an attachment.

Last night, Rosie had been kind, guiding his fumbling attempts at intimacy. Their emotions were high and it was a natural response then, but in the light of day, it seemed vaguely improper.

When they were out of sight of the villa windows, Joshua said, "I'm sorry, Rosie. I took advantage of you."

He reached out to take her hand, but she turned away, leaving him to follow her along the ornamental stone paths as she searched for somewhere private to go. Seeing a secluded little arbour set in the high garden walls, she entered the enclosure and sank down on a marble seat. Only then did she give him her attention.

"No," she insisted. "It was quite the reverse. I could have called a halt at any time, had I so wished, but did not. I have never felt this way before, about anyone. I knew what I was doing, and wanted to be close. Please do not worry about any consequences. Grandmama told me how to deal with such matters. She delivered eight babies before she found out."

Rosie's calm assumption of responsibility stunned him, almost as much as the fact she wished for a future with him.

"When are you leaving?" There seemed nothing else to say.

"Grandmama plans to make a start this afternoon, but she did agree I could speak with you." She reached for his hand and pressed it against her cheek. "Take care, Joshua. I hope you are still here when we return, but if you are not, I hope you do not take too long to grow up." Her voice broke. "Oh dear, I must look a complete hag."

"No, you don't," he said, wanting to comfort her. "You're a very special lady to me."

"Oh, Joshua, where were you when I made my coming-out six years ago? I imagine you were a young boy, playing with your friend at being soldiers. The years have been kind to you, but I fear that as many more will not favour me. I hope we meet again soon."

Joshua wished he could say something to reassure her. Rather than make promises it might not be in his power to fulfil, he gently wiped away her tears with a handkerchief. Then, he took her hand, pressed his lips against the palm and whispered, "Until the next time we meet…"

Joshua returned to the villa, his mind in a daze. He felt cold, despite the bright sunlight, which dazzled his eyes.

A sudden panic gripped at his throat. He felt sick, not knowing what to do. The Dowager's words pounded in his head. He had never considered marriage before. Some day he might, but situated as he was, with Matthew as heir, it was impossible to take his wife to Linmore – and if he joined the army, he could not expect her to follow the drum.

It was too late to think about the veiled warnings of indiscretions in the lessons. They only looked at things from a female perspective. It never occurred to anyone a woman might be the hunter – and he the prey.

Joshua berated himself for his naivety. He should have known better than leave the ballroom. If he had gone to down to supper, there would have been no need for anyone to rescue him, and none of this would have happened.

At least Charlie understood his predicament.

"Why do they want me, Charlie?"

"Well, it can't be for your looks, can it, Josh? Now, if it were me…"

He choked back a laugh. Of course, it could not be that.

"No, the Dowager is in the right. It is best for you to take a breather, and give the lady a chance to see sense. I'd lay you ten to one, the next time you meet; she'll be in love with someone like the dancing master – fine little fellow that he was."

There could not have been a greater contrast.

"What will we tell Dr Hawley?"

Charlie did not hesitate for a minute.

"Precisely nothing," he said. "For why would he need to know? It's not as if you're as important as Charlemagne, or our trip to Lombardy, so don't you go getting ideas above yourself."

"Thanks, Charlie." Trust him to put things in perspective.

"Think nothing of it, Josh. I know you'd do the same for me."

In the event, their plans for Lombardy came to nothing. Instead, a letter brought news from England, which caused their tour to be terminated, and threw their plans for the future into disarray.

Charlie would never forget the day Doctor Hawley summoned them to attend him. There was no warning of bad tidings, just a servant bringing a message. Naturally, they obeyed.

Joshua stood with him in the doorway, looking into the room where their tutor stood, holding a single sheet of paper.

"Joshua, please sit down." Dr Hawley looked pale. "I have received grave news from Linmore. There has been a terrible accident…"

For some reason, Charlie felt excluded. He heard the words, but was unprepared for the effect they had on Joshua.

"My father…?" His face was ashen.

"No," said the tutor, "it is your brother, Matthew Norbery, who is dead."

Joshua's shoulders sagged. "How…?"

Charlie felt an overwhelming sense of relief it was not Uncle Tom.

"Your father tells of a sailing accident whilst your brother was staying with friends in Ireland."

It was easy to imagine the type of characters they were, nasty brutes who bullied children, as they had when Joshua was a lad. Charlie could not understand why Joshua's mother welcomed such people, when she did not bother about decent folk.

"When did it happen?" said Joshua.

Dr Hawley paused to look at the paper.

"The date on the letter is a month ago. Your father asks us to return with all haste."

"I can't believe it." Joshua turned away to hide his emotions. "I have been free of him for a month, and yet I didn't know."

Charlie understood his friend's sense of release. He too felt relief, but doubted if the tutor knew of the indignity Joshua suffered at his brother's hands.

Sergeant Percival completed the travel arrangements so quickly that there was scarcely time to write a letter informing Lady Kenchester's party of the news.

On reaching Naples, they found that the British Ambassador had secured berths for them on a naval vessel leaving for England. They set sail, knowing all would be well, as long as the ship did not encounter the French fleet. That was in the lap of the gods.

It was a relief to be going home, not least because it solved the problem with Lady Rosie. Times out of number, Charlie had watched the lady's expression when she met Joshua. Her words of greeting might be formal, but the look in her eyes told a different story. He knew at first that his friend took her interest as sisterly, but it was much more than that now.

Charlie revelled in the drama of the rough seas, but he was concerned when Joshua spent several days heaving over a bowl, and when the mal de mer eased, lay on his bunk looking at the ceiling. He hardly spoke to a soul or ate any of the food Gilbert prepared.

He did not know what to do. In the end, he consulted Dr Hawley.

"Sir, what can we do to help Joshua?"

"I don't think anyone can at present," the tutor said. "His brother's death will have a profound effect on his life, and it will take time to adjust to his new status. It is hard for him, but I felt obliged to point out his new responsibilities."

"I don't understand, sir. What kind of responsibilities?"

"Joshua became the heir to Linmore on his brother's death, and in turn will be Squire Norbery."

"You mean Josh will have to stay at Linmore?"

"Exactly – he cannot join the army now. His father has no one else to take his place."

Poor Josh. All his hopes and dreams had gone. No wonder he looked sad.

"But that won't be for years yet. Uncle Tom…"

"Is a relatively young man, but Joshua will have to learn to manage the estate. I am sure once he comes to terms with the change, he will do his duty."

"I suppose you are right, sir."

The exchange left Charlie feeling confused. He had always wanted to join the army, but since coming to Linmore, his plans and Joshua's hopes were interlinked. Now everything had changed – for both of them.

When Charlie entered the cabin he shared with Joshua, he found him lying on his bunk. "Dr Hawley wanted me to ask how you are feeling, Josh," he said.

Joshua turned to face him, his eyes shadowed from lack of sleep.

"If I tell you that," he intoned, "he'll think I'm filled with grief, and say prayers for me. How can I be, when Matthew would have seen me dead many times, and my mother as well? I never felt anything for him but fear – and it dulls the senses. I keep expecting to hear his footsteps – the clicking of the raised heels he wore to make him look taller. I can't feel pity, except for my father for what it means to him, losing his oldest son. Someone has to feel sorry for him."

He fumbled in his pocket for a handkerchief, and blew his nose.

"You won't tell him what I said, will you?"

"No," said Charlie. "I'll say you were asleep."

After Charlie went away, Joshua lay on the bed, thinking. Amongst the jumble of thoughts filling his mind, Rosie stood out like a beacon, reminding him of the generosity of spirit and, he thought, something like love. He had never felt it before; nor did he understand why any woman would want him – yet she had, with an almost desperate need, which echoed his own yearning. So intense, it was easy to lose control. That is what scared him.

Sadly, she was in the past now. Linmore called him and he had to go. Dr Hawley told him of his duty and he could not fail his father. What was it Lady Kenchester said about finding occupation? His future was settled, but not as he thought it would be.

It was not his brother for whom he grieved, but the childhood dream he shared with Charlie. Honesty forced him to admit his wish to join the army started more as a desire to be free of Matthew Norbery than his wish to be a soldier.

Everything changed when Charlie came to Linmore. His soldiering was instinctive, and where he led, Joshua followed. They did everything together, so what more natural than being brothers at arms?

Not everything had changed for the worst, because his brother was gone. The knowledge that Matthew had lost his power to hurt gave Joshua a new taste for life, so he joined Charlie on the brigantine deck, and watched the stormy seas of the Bay of Biscay. Soon, they would be home.

"Do you think Joshua and Charlie will have heard the news about Matthew yet?"

Back at Linmore, Jane asked the question that had filled Tom's mind every day for the last week. No, longer than that, but he was realistic about the limitations in the delivery of mail.

"I'd hope so by now," he said. "I sent the letter to Sir William Hamilton, in Naples, asking him to ensure it reached Dr Hawley in Rome with all urgency."

How else could he send such news, except through diplomatic channels?

"What about Sophie?" she asked. "Should we tell her about Matthew?"

Tom shook his head.

"Knowing Sophie, I doubt it would bother her unduly. It's not as if they were friends."

"No," she said, "quite the reverse. As you say, it's better to leave her where she is until Charlie is home again."

"The waiting is the worst, and not knowing when to expect them. Feeling helpless to prepare them for what lies ahead. The changes will be significant. I think I should await them in London, and come back with them. I don't want Joshua to see Kate alone, and fear he may think it is his duty."

Jane nodded agreement.

"How is Kate today?" he said. "I don't think my presence helped her."

"It's not your fault," she said. "You didn't want him to go. Kate must accept the blame for encouraging Matthew to run contrary to your wishes. She will not, of course. It's not the Stretton way, to accept responsibility." Then she added. "How was it for you, in Ireland?"

Tom looked exhausted.

"It was horrible," he said, "knowing what it would do to Kate's state of mind. Yet, when I considered what she and Matthew would have done to Linmore, had he lived, I couldn't help feeling somewhat relieved. Is it wrong to leave him buried in Ireland, knowing that now, Linmore will have its rightful heir?"

"Stop tormenting yourself, Tom. You could not bring him back in the state he was. He'd been in the sea for three weeks at least."

"I know, but the sight of him will never leave me." Tom shivered and changed the subject. "I'll be glad to have the lads home again. I've missed them."

"So have I," said Jane. "I wonder what they will be like. They have grown into men, and I suppose there will have been women in their lives. When the bereavement year is over, we will need to plan for Sophie to have a Season, but I think Winifred would probably organise it."

"Yes," he said. "I'll broach the subject when I see her."

He stopped, debating aspects of the situation he had not told her.

"What is it, Tom?" she said, sensing his dilemma. "There's more to this, isn't there?"

He nodded. "I didn't tell you at the outset, but the letter I received informing me of the accident was addressed to the father of Matthew Stretton. That was how his friends knew him, and how I had him buried. You see, Jane – in his final hours, Matthew rejected Linmore. Maybe that makes it easier to understand."

He hesitated, trying to gather his thoughts. "I was told there were a number of women in the water as well. It seems the orgies at the castle were well known, but in the past, they always brought harlots in from outside the district. This time, several local girls were involved. Maidservants, I believe, but nobody knows whether they went willingly, or were coerced. Their families were devastated – not knowing whether to shun or grieve their daughters. At least for me, it was straightforward. I knew what Matthew was."

"Oh, God, not more signs of the Stretton heritage," she said. "Will we never be rid of them?"

"Yes, we will…eventually," he said in a weary voice. "Matthew was not the only one of Kate's family to drown. I saw the names of Nathan Stretton and one of his younger brothers in the burial register, but didn't dare tell Kate. I hope that no one else does. Another of their friends lived in London. His father was there a few days before me. For all I know, we might have passed at the docks, without knowing we were on the same sad errand."

Jane shook her head, tears welling up in her eyes.

"What a tragic waste of young female lives, and another old Irish title, given to the English Aristocracy, brought into disrepute."

CHAPTER 22

Late Summer – 1800

They reached Portsmouth in the middle of a thunderstorm, heartily sick of the sea, and anxious to be on their way, but the lateness of the hour forced them to seek lodgings in the town.

They set off the following day, with more than a hundred and fifty miles ahead. It was a journey dogged by delays, and despite regular changes of horses, took four days of bone-shaking travel before they reached Linmore. Charlie's heart lifted when he saw the Hall then fell again, for the dreary, overcast sky made it look more than ever a house in mourning.

Apart from the servants, Aunt Jane was the first person they saw. She looked tired, but wrapped her comforting arms around them in welcome. From her, they learned that Squire Norbery, expecting them to disembark in London, was waiting at his sister's house in Cavendish Square. He had planned to travel home with them.

When Joshua asked to see his mother, Aunt Jane demurred. It was so unusual, and Charlie hoped his friend would not insist, but he did. Aunt Jane deliberated for a moment, before saying, "Your father wanted to be here with you, Joshua; but if you feel you must, I'll see if Martha thinks it is advisable."

"Waiting won't make it any easier," he said. "I'll have to do it sometime, so it might as well be now."

Aunt Jane sighed. "If you insist, but I really don't advise it."

"I'll come with you." Charlie wanted to help, but felt uncomfortable, going against Aunt Jane's advice.

The dressing room where Aunt Norbery sat was dark and gloomy .The single candle on the side table shed so little light, it gave an eerie feeling to the room. Even the fire burning in the grate did not lift the dismal atmosphere.

Charlie wished they had not come. He knew Joshua wanted to do the right thing, but if Aunt Jane expressed concern, he was not sure this was a good time.

Aunt Norbery sat in an armchair, seemingly oblivious to their presence. Her deep-set eyes looked vacant and her skin waxen as if she too was preparing for the final journey. Then, Joshua entered the room.

"Mama," he said, "I'm so sorry."

The sound of his voice effected a startling change. Two spots of colour seeped into Kate Norbery's sallow complexion, and her lacklustre eyes erupted sheer malevolence.

"You…" she shrieked. "It should have been you who died, not Matthew."

Charlie recoiled back to the door in horror, but Joshua took the full force of the venom that spewed from her lips. He stood, rooted to the spot, until Martha the nurse took his arm and drew him back.

"Master Joshua," she said, "it's no good you trying to comfort her. She doesn't want you – or your father here."

He looked bewildered.

"Aunt Jane said that, but I thought, just for once it might help. I'm sorry, I won't come again." He left the room without a backward glance, to where Charlie waited outside the door.

When he spoke, there was raw grief in his voice. "Do you see how impossible things are, Charlie? I hoped to get away from here, and live a normal life. Now he's dead, I'll have to stay and be duty-bound to look after her for as long as she lives – and every day, I'll know she hates me."

Even allowing for grief, how could a mother say that to her remaining son? It was hard, but Charlie finally understood what afflicted his friend. Whereas he would have given anything to see his mother again, he knew that in Joshua's case things were different.

It did not take many weeks for the mood at Linmore to lighten. The house was still in mourning, but with Matthew Norbery gone, the servants started to walk with a spring in their step. Maidservants that he molested dared to smile again. It was no wonder they welcomed Joshua home, for he had long been their favourite, and was now in his rightful place as heir.

Charlie watched the tentative steps Joshua made towards acceptance of his position, but no one else knew what it cost him to hide his frustration.

Well, maybe Aunt Jane did, for she was the one to welcome them into her sitting room to take afternoon tea. Charlie liked going there. It was a homely place, simply furnished with a chaise longue and armchairs set around the fire, and a little table to one side from which she dispensed the tea.

When Uncle Tom returned to Linmore, he joined them. It was a real family feeling, a sense of being together, which reminded Charlie of the special time he spent with his parents before Sophie was born.

After they related some of their adventures, Aunt Jane told them about the events surrounding Matthew Norbery's demise. She sounded weary, but was remarkably detached, and Charlie honoured her for the honesty of not pretending sentiments towards someone whom no one but his mother liked.

"Matthew came home from his tour a few months after you set out, thoroughly dissatisfied with life demanding money to indulge his…um… whims, and those of various friends he brought here. He introduced his mother to the opium habit. Kate had taken small doses of laudanum before, for her nerves." She hesitated on the word. "Now, she cannot live without it, and Doctor Althorpe tells us she will be like this for the rest of her life. He is the new physician in Middlebrook, and assistant to Doctor Tilbury, who is long overdue to retire."

"Where was Sophie?" said Charlie.

"She was at school in Bredenbridge – thank goodness."

"You were saying about Matthew…" Joshua prompted.

"We sent the twins and their governess to stay with Caroline. It was not safe to keep them here with Matthew causing havoc in the house, smashing furniture if he could not have his way. William Rufus and his brother Sidney did what they could to control him, but even they suffered. Kate wouldn't hear a word spoken against him when he grew wilder and more violent towards the servants. It is a characteristic of her forebears. I suppose the end was inevitable."

Charlie did not like to ask what she meant.

"He was invited to stay with friends in Ireland. Your father forbade it, fearing the worst, but Kate gave him money to travel – just to be spiteful, so she must accept her share of blame. I don't know if you have any idea of the kind of profligates he called his friends…"

Strong emotion forced her to take a breath before resuming.

"I doubt they could sail a boat when they were sober, but we learned they took a yacht out in one of the Atlantic storms when they were inebriated and soaked to the brim with opium. The boat foundered on the rocks and no one survived. It took three weeks to find all the bodies and

Matthew's was the last. Your father went over there for the burial. Poor Tom, he blamed himself for everything."

Aunt Jane's words triggered a childhood memory of a time, soon after Charlie arrived at Linmore, when a friend of Matthew Norbery tried to shoot Joshua by the lake, and he wondered if the same bully was involved in the accident. To him, that would be justice.

Sophie came home a few weeks later, blissfully unaware of the events that caused turmoil. She had returned to Linmore only once during the whole time Joshua and Charlie were on their tour, at the end of her first term at school. She had written feverishly to her brother, and the letters continued on his return.

Joshua knew Charlie wanted to see her, but she wrote incessantly about her busy life, and they assumed she was happy to stay. They could hardly think anything else, considering the bundle of hasty scribbling that came almost every week.

Yes, she was happy, and her friend's father was most obliging as to frank her letters. They were the most delightful people, and she could not wait to introduce them to Charlie. She had so much to tell him…

All they had to do was wait. They anticipated her return on three separate occasions, and each time Charlie was disappointed.

Sophie arrived at the most unexpected time. Each morning, Joshua and Charlie took a ride across the park in a different direction, but it always ended with a race to see which one would reach home first. Sometimes, one or other won by a horse's nose but usually it was a dead heat.

They were half way back across the park when they saw a strange coach lumbering up the drive. Although too far away to identify the conveyance, the wish to know more spurred them on.

If Joshua's father been there to witness the event, they would have dismounted sedately and handed over the reins with a word of thanks to the grooms. Instead, they galloped into the stable yard, threw themselves from their mounts, and hurtled around the side of the house to reach the front door before the vehicle came to a halt.

They stopped, gaping in amazement as the coach door opened, and a tall, shapely figure, clad in a fashionable dark green pelisse, over a matching gown, tumbled out, straight into Charlie's arms.

"Charlie," she squealed with delight, hugging him. "I've missed you so much."

216

"Let me look at you." Her brother held her at arm's length and his jaw dropped. "Sophie," he growled with obvious disapproval. "What the deuce are you wearing?"

"Isn't it dashing?" she said, unbuttoning the coat, to reveal a low-cut bodice, which clung to her form. "It's a present. My friend bought a new outfit, so her parents insisted I had one too."

"It's indecent," he said. "Go and find a scarf to cover your chest."

Sophie stopped, looked mutinous and then laughed. "Don't be silly, Charlie. You and Joshua are dressed up to the nines, so why shouldn't I?"

"That's different, Sophie. You're a girl and must have a care for your reputation." Charlie's mouth worked as he tried to find words to describe his feelings. "It's too small. They should have bought you a larger size."

She pouted and turned aside. "What do you think, Joshua? Do you think I've grown?"

His tongue stuck to the top of his mouth. He nodded, trying not to meet her eyes. He lowered his gaze, and wished he had not. Yes, she had definitely grown. She might have sprouted horns as well as a voluptuous bosom, but he did not stop to look.

Sophie gave a gurgle of delight and moved closer.

"Now," she said, "it's time I looked at you…" Her eyes widened in amazement. "Ooh…my…word, Joshua…"

She stopped to let her tongue encircle her lips, and then, boldly, extended her hand to stroke across his shoulders right down his lower back. "You have grown so… tall… You're even bigger than Charlie…"

Out of sight of her brother's vision, she slyly let her fingers trickle teasingly across his derriere, whilst waiting to see his reaction.

Heat immediately surged through him. Startled, he turned and met her smouldering gaze, but not wanting to think what it meant, dropped his eyes to the coating of dust on his top boots. It was better to do that than acknowledge her blatant invitation. Luckily, Charlie's mind was on other things.

"Don't encourage him, Sophie," her brother grumbled. "His head's big enough as it is, without you giving him ideas of his importance. You wouldn't believe the number of women that chased after him these last few months."

For some inexplicable reason, Sophie flounced off in a sulk, leaving Charlie to explain his state of agitation. He was beside himself. His hands fluttered across his chest – hardly knowing which part to touch, and yet, clearly his sister's décolletage was the cause.

"Oh, my God, Josh," he said. "What are we going to do? She has no more notion of the world than a newborn. Fancy her thinking it's all right for a girl of her age to expose her chest, wearing clothes like those. What kind of people are they to buy such things?"

Joshua knew from his encounters with Italian women the look Sophie gave him was anything but innocent. It was wanton, but that was not what Charlie wanted to hear.

"You'll have to help me look after her, Josh; otherwise we'll have some loose fish giving her a slip on the shoulder. It doesn't bear thinking about."

Sophie had changed beyond their expectations. Whilst they acknowledged their maturity, it never occurred to them she was similarly growing up. Joshua did not want to think of her as a woman, but knowing Charlie expected an answer, he nodded like a loony. Speech was impossible, even if his life depended on it.

While his breathing returned to normal, Joshua concentrated on his second impression – that the hat Sophie wore was too old a style for a girl her age – and if he was not mistaken, she wore makeup, but on that he remained silent.

It seemed inevitable that Sophie's behaviour would cause Charlie embarrassment, but Joshua determined to play no part in the process. His friendship with her brother was worth more than Sophie's fleeting amusement.

Within minutes, she returned to plague them.

"Look at her, Josh."

Sophie seemed delighted her appearance struck her brother speechless. A throaty gurgle of laughter erupted as she slipped between them and linked her hands through their arms. "I have so much to tell you…"

"What's that?" said Charlie, when his sister drifted into his bedroom.

A soggy strip of leather fell to the floor when Sophie took a handkerchief from her pocket. Charlie picked it up and recognised it as the leather tassel from Matthew Norbery's boot, which Sophie took when they first arrived at Linmore. He looked at her in disbelief. Surely, she had not kept it all this time. It must be at least eight years.

"Why is the tassel wet, Sophie?" It gave him a sense of unease.

"Oh, that old thing?" she said, not meeting his eye. "I threw it in the lily pond at Annie's home, and forgot it; only, one of the gardeners found it, and gave it back to me this morning." She sounded aggrieved. "I don't want it now it is spoiled."

"Matthew Norbery is dead, Sophie," said Charlie. "He drowned in the sea."

She looked at him, and said without interest, "Is he? In that case, Joshua won't have to leave home."

"No," said Charlie. "Nor can he join the army, as we always planned." Then an awesome thought struck him. "Did you put a curse on this?"

She gave a half laugh. "Don't be silly, Charlie. I do not know any spells. I just wished something would happen to let Joshua stay at Linmore, so we could always live here. It's our home, and it would be lovely if you could meet Annie, and she could come to live with us."

With Sophie at home, Squire Norbery had to organise some kind of entertainment. Whereas nothing official was permissible in a bereavement year, there was no reason to avoid informal gatherings where the young people could meet without offending convention.

Joshua met his nephew on the baby's first birthday. They travelled to Shettleston Hall for the occasion, and he saw immediately that marriage had changed his sister. Caroline was happier than he had ever seen.

Something about her reminded him of Lady Rosie. He could not say what it was, but seeing the baby jolted his memory. He hoped her assurances were correct, otherwise, he would no doubt hear from her…

He had not realised that Caroline was a great organiser of social events. She knew many families with young folk of similar age to Charlie and himself, and decided it was acceptable for young people to attend dancing classes.

"Can you dance, Joshua?"

"Yes," he said with a smile, remembering how he learned. "Charlie and I took dancing lessons whilst we were in Athens."

When she looked surprised, he said, "It's true. We were guests of the British Ambassador's family. They know Aunt Winifred."

No one could dispute that.

"That is excellent," she said. "Several female members of Shettleston's family are in need of dancing practice, in preparation for their presentation."

She looked dispassionately at Sophie. "Did your lessons at school include dancing?"

Sophie met her eye and smirked. "Of course, Cousin Caroline; and I have lots of practice whilst staying at my friend's house. Her parents are extremely sociable people, and with their position in society, they regularly entertain."

Caroline Shettleston's nose twitched.

"Then I trust you will have no trouble assisting the young men in the Shettleston family to learn the correct steps."

Joshua sensed an undertone in his sister's manner, but could find no reason for it. He knew Sophie used to challenge Caroline's authority, but surely, nobody held a grudge that long.

It was easy to see the difference between Joshua and Charlie's proficiency and the country folk who received only the basic instructions. Charlie was in his element, charming the young ladies with his natural ability in the dance, whereas Joshua gave his attention to the quieter girls, lacking a partner. After all, someone took pity on him, so the least he could do was return the compliment.

Several times he noticed Sophie watching him, and heard her say in conversation with his sister, "I don't mind dancing with the other young men, Caroline, but I mustn't neglect Joshua. It would be most impolite."

To his surprise, she was remarkably good, and everyone commented on how well their steps matched. Then Sophie bobbed a saucy little curtsey and moved on to her next partner. Later, when she returned for a third dance, he was ready. "No, Sophie; only two dances are permissible. Three are not allowed."

She scowled, and insisted. "Yes, but this is only a pretend dance."

"No," said Caroline, overhearing the exchange. "It's a preparation for Almack's, so we must do things correctly."

After several sessions at Shettleston Hall, they went to other country houses for birthday parties, which always ended with dancing. It was the first time Joshua had met many of the young members of his community, and yet he supposed he would have to know them. Maybe, one day, he might even marry one of the girls. He looked around to see if he could remember who they were, but their names escaped him. Never mind, there was plenty of time.

Once Joshua started to dance, he was too engrossed in the enjoyment of the set to give anyone a second thought, until Charlie appeared, looking anxious.

"Have you seen Sophie?"

No, he had not and did not particularly want to – but Charlie did.

"You'll have to help me, Josh. I can't look everywhere."

Joshua thought of the obvious. "She might have gone… well, you know."

Realisation dawned on Charlie's face. "Good thinking, I'll see if she's upstairs, and you can look in the garden. She might have felt hot and gone outside for some air."

There was no sign of Sophie when Joshua stepped out onto the terrace, so he walked down the steps to the garden.

"Sophie," he called, all the time looking around.

Hearing voices, Joshua walked down a cobbled path, but with evening merging into night; it was not easy to tell if he was moving in the right direction.

"Sophie, where are you?" Then he clarified his reason for being there. "Charlie is looking for you."

He heard a low laugh, coming from the bushes, and Sophie emerged, adjusting her skirts. "What are you doing there?" he said.

"Were you worried I might get lost, Joshua?"

"No, of course I'm not," he said, "but Charlie was."

"Liar," she said softly.

He turned away to walk back to the house.

"Aren't you going to offer me your arm?" she said in a complaining tone.

"You came out here alone, so you can find your own way back." He did not believe she had for a moment.

"How ungallant you are. I thought you were a gentleman."

The scorn in her voice forced him to comply. It was not what he wanted, but he was not going to argue the point, in case she fell returning unescorted.

It was only as they passed through the French doors into the ballroom that he saw the ruffled state of her hair.

Then he heard a footstep behind them, and a languid voice declared, "I don't know if you've noticed, Norbery, but your young lady has mud on the hem of her gown. I suggest the next time you walk in the garden; it would be wiser to stay on the stone paths."

Joshua turned, and recognised the sleek black hair and hawkish features of the Honourable Robert Chetton, from Neathwood Park – which answered his query about Sophie's escort on the outward trip to the garden. What the deuce was she doing with a man like Chetton, who was at least his late brother's age, and had been on the town for years?

"Don't let me keep you, dear boy," Chetton said, "her fierce-looking brother is even now advancing." With that, he was gone.

It was a relief when Sophie went back to school. The trouble was, Charlie insisted on going as her escort to ensure she came to no harm. Not that she would, for Squire Norbery always provided a coachman, a groom and outrider for support.

When he returned three days later, he looked dazed.

"Are you all right?" Joshua asked.

"Mmm, yes," was his only response.

"Where have you been? We expected you back yesterday."

"I… um… Sophie wanted me to meet her friend…s."

"What are they like?"

"Wonderful." Charlie breathed the word.

"All of them?"

"No, just the one, and she is beautiful."

"What's her name?"

"What?" Charlie was in a stupor. "I call her Diana… like the goddess."

Joshua knew all he wanted to know about Roman goddesses.

Charlie made several visits to Bredenbridge in the next few weeks to take various items that Sophie claimed to have forgotten. Joshua guessed it was an excuse to see the other girl. Usually, he was a sensible chap but now he walked around with a silly grin on his face, uttering the most inane sentences, which were supposed to be poetry. It was painful, listening to him reciting it, or having him say, "D'you think she will like this, Josh?"

Joshua uttered words of agreement. It was not the time to say the rhymes made him feel nauseous, and Charlie needed a physic to set him to rights.

It was even worse when Charlie returned from Bredenbridge, declaring, "I'm in love, Josh."

"You mean like the time you loved the red-haired girl in the village, and the gardener's daughter, because you couldn't make up your mind which you liked best?"

"No," said Charlie, his voice ragged with emotion. "This is different. If you'd ever felt like this, you'd know."

"Give me old-fashioned lust," Joshua started to say, with a laugh, but the glow in Charlie's eyes silenced him. It made him wonder if love was the same feeling that kept him awake at night, thinking of Lady Rosie. He thought it might be, and felt sad, not knowing if he would ever see her again.

"It's all right. I believe you," he said, knowing he would have to wait for Charlie to recover. If the past were anything to go by, he would be back to normal in a few weeks.

Then he recalled what Charlie said when they had their portrait painted in Rome. *We won't fight as long as the goddess remains in the picture.*

Joshua did not argue about Charlie's notion of a goddess – nor did he intend to languish whilst awaiting his friend's return to sanity.

In the event, time was long and lonely without Charlie for company. William Rufus tried his utmost to test Joshua's mettle with boxing practice, but it wasn't the same without the need to win and prove he was the better man. When Charlie returned to Linmore, it was clear his mind was elsewhere. Joshua could tell by the little smile that played on his friend's lips, and felt sad.

Even from afar, he felt Sophie's influence. Why couldn't she and her friend leave them alone? If his brother had not died, he and Charlie might have been in uniform by now, and no females could interfere. Then he realised that Sophie Cobarne would have found a way to make her presence felt.

He drifted from one thing to another. Riding around the estate only made him realise how little he knew about farming, and he could not bear the pitying looks if he showed his ignorance by asking questions. He didn't even know what was normal or what to ask.

One evening, he made his way to the dairy and waited for Millie to finish her work. A comely wench, older than him by three years, Millie was kind and Joshua liked her better than the younger milkmaids, for she didn't make him feel stupid. When he and Charlie returned from Rome, she had kissed them both without favouring one more than the other. Now, she gave her time to Joshua, and comforted him so well, he decided that Charlie could take all the time he liked to recover.

CHAPTER 23

Spring – 1801

In the event, Joshua had plenty of time to indulge his interest through the winter months. Charlie's ardour for his goddess was unabated. He either languished around Linmore, singing her praises, or found an excuse to go to Bredenbridge to see her. Left alone, Joshua tried to understand his feelings, but it was hard.

Christmas likewise came and went, and when Sophie returned to Linmore at Easter, he noticed that she seemed filled with a kind of suppressed excitement, uttering silly giggles whenever she faced him across the dinner table. It was disconcerting to have Sophie smile at him, but her brother seemed oblivious.

With Charlie undecided about his future intent, Joshua wished they could have joined the family for a few weeks in London during the Season. Caroline had suggested it as a way to help distract Charlie from his obsession with Bredenbridge. Now they would have to wait until they were a year older.

Joshua – I need to see you. It is urgent. I will be in the usual place. M

When the message came, Joshua headed straight for the hayloft. Usually, he met the dairymaid at dusk when the barn at the back of the stables was quiet. Today the midday sun lit the yard, and the stable block was alive with voices.

Scrambling up the ladder, he found the loft unusually dark after the brightness outside; then realised that the door over the yard through which stooks of hay were tossed, was closed. How stupid; it was always left open in the daytime.

"Millie," he called into the gloom. "Where are you?"

There was no response. "Millie?" he called again, but there was no answer. "Oh well," he said. "I'll let some light in before someone gets hurt."

As Joshua moved forward to sweep back the bolt, a sound arrested his progress – a giggle that brought a smile to his face. Teasing, tantalising and so erotic, he blundered into the darkness without considering the pitfalls. Stopping to listen halfway, he heard an intake of breath, and caught the hint of a familiar scent. He would know Millie anywhere.

He reached out, but she was before him, catching his hands and slipping them inside her open bodice, without even a shift to hinder them.

"What's the matter," he murmured, "couldn't you wait until tonight?"

Words seemed beyond her, but the moan of ecstasy was eloquence enough. Joshua savoured the moment, caressing her breasts, feeling her nipples harden as passion rippled through her. He felt an answering response, deep within and heard her panting breath as she began to stroke his thighs. Slowly, then with increasing urgency, she moved to his belly and slid her hands deftly past the clothing barriers to arouse him to fever pitch.

Whatever the reason for the summons, it would have to wait for this was Millie as he had never known her. The gentle girl who normally yielded to his every need had become a wanton.

He stood, biting his lip, and let her take him to the heights of fantasy, just as an older, bolder woman had done in the bagnio. Then, with a low moan, she slid down to the floor, drawing him with her.

Determined to take control, Joshua exerted his strength and rolled her in the hay, tugging at her mobcap. Millie had too much of her own way with him, now it was his turn, but he knew the ghastly truth even as he heard an unmistakable crow of triumph and felt mortification wash over him.

Oh God, no… Not that…

His befuddled mind cleared like a bolt of lightning as the girl's laugh confirmed his worst fears. Lax in the pursuit of his own pleasures, Joshua was, like most men, puritanical in the belief that women of the family did not behave likewise.

The realisation that, by some means, Sophie contrived to be with him in this act breached the unwritten code of conduct between friends. Sisters, or girls brought up as family were sacrosanct. He would no more have seduced his friend's sister than his own.

"Get away from me, Sophie." Revulsion goaded him to violence and he flung her across the floor, not caring how she landed, as long as it was far away from him.

Stunned by her feral behaviour, Joshua sat in the hay feeling sick with self-disgust and berating himself for not acknowledging the difference. The trouble was he was so used to meeting Millie and the suspicion never entered his head that Sophie might seek to take her place.

It was only when he gathered his disordered wits together and climbed down to the lower floor that he realised where his tormentor had gone.

"You bastard, Norbery – what the bloody hell do you think you've been doing to my sister?" The harsh voice came from nowhere.

Joshua saw Charlie standing in the doorway, riding crop in hand, his expression satanic. Sophie stood beside him, and smirked, while in her red-tipped fingers, she held back the tattered edges of her bodice to reveal several scratches gouged across her chest.

He was appalled, knowing that Sophie must have inflicted the marks herself to spite him for the rejection. "She wasn't like that when she left me," he burst out, but realised his mistake even as he uttered the words.

The riding crop struck full force across his face, splitting his lip and knocking him sideways against the wall. Stunned disbelief turned to anger with Sophie, and then erupted into action as Charlie raised his hand to take a second strike. He was damned if he would be thrashed like a dog.

Conscious thought disappeared as Joshua launched himself at his attacker. William Rufus had taught them discipline in practice sessions, but they had never before fought in anger.

This was real. It was vicious and Charlie was beyond reason.

It started as a scrabbling bout, sparring wildly, with both hampered by their coats as one aimed to inflict punishment, the other to protect himself and hold his opponent back until he tired. Then they might talk sense.

Despite Joshua being taller with the longer reach, Charlie was solid and threw a couple of punches to the head that made his eyes water. Time after time, Charlie milled in again, fists flying or aiming his foot. Joshua took a pummelling, then sidestepped, caught the outstretched boot and threw his opponent sideways to the ground, where he landed with a sickening thud, grasping his elbow. Pain creased Charlie's face, but he refused to acknowledge it as he struggled, wheezing, to his feet.

Joshua stood upright first. The blood from his split lip was the least of his troubles now. His ribcage, fore and aft, was a mass of hurt, and he could hardly breathe for the pain.

Suddenly, Charlie scrabbled away through the stable door and snatched up a hoof-paring knife, with a vicious blade that could slice through leather.

"Now I'll deal with you as you deserve, Joshua Norbery," he said with a humourless laugh, as he returned to the attack, slashing the air back and forth.

Joshua backed away without taking his eyes from Charlie's face. He saw murder there, and knew only his death would satisfy the lust for revenge. Somewhere in the background, he heard jeering and saw vague shapes moving forward through the corner of his eye. He dared not blink in case it gave Cobarne an advantage to gore him like a bull.

From nowhere, a commanding voice roared, "What is the meaning of this disgraceful exhibition? Stop this nonsense at once."

Relief almost swept Joshua's legs from under him as his father entered the stable-yard astride his big bay gelding. But it was short-lived, for Charlie, distracted by hands that grabbed him from behind, swung out in his rage and caught Ed Salter a glancing blow to the face. Joshua, standing only a foot away, felt the man's pain on impact, and saw blood spurting out as the knife dropped from Charlie's fingers, and clattered on the cobbles, from where one of the grooms snatched it up out of harm's way.

"I didn't mean it," Charlie said in a voice hoarse with shock, and was promptly sick on the ground, but no one took any notice. Everyone's attention was on the groom rolling on the floor, screaming with pain, the side of his face a mass of blood.

"I don't care whether you meant it or not," Tom Norbery blazed at them as he dismounted. "Get out of my sight, the pair of you, and don't speak to each other until I call you."

"He raped Sophie," Charlie protested.

"No, I didn't, she – " Joshua, similarly sickened by the sight, interrupted.

"I haven't time to listen to your bickering, this man needs help," Squire Norbery snapped, as someone led his horse away. "You," he said to one of the grooms who looked on. "Ride to Middlebrook surgery for the physician. Tell him that there's been an accident and I need his services immediately." To another, he said, "Ask Miss Jane and Jessie to bring clean dressings for the wound, quickly."

He stripped off his gloves and pressed a couple of clean folded handkerchiefs to the man's face.

Joshua and Charlie looked on in stunned silence as Squire Norbery said over his shoulder to the assembled gathering, "Not a word of this situation leaves the yard. The man has been kicked by a horse. Is that clear?"

There was a murmur of assent as Joshua and Charlie slunk away to sit in their rooms, a mere fifteen feet apart with the interlinking door locked and the key removed to prevent access, where normally it opened at will from both sides. Now the door was a barrier.

Quite how they reached the house, Joshua couldn't remember. Side by side, he thought, but several feet apart as if repelled.

Time seemed endless. It was torture to be isolated, not knowing the outcome, and even luncheon, without which they normally could not survive, was left uneaten.

Having hastily washed and changed his dirty clothes, Joshua lay on his bed, listening to Charlie walking around the floor in the adjoining room. The footsteps stopped at the door, and the handle half-turned, before the steps resumed their endless pacing. He felt bereft, for there had scarcely been a day since Charlie's arrival when they had not talked endlessly.

Joshua went to his side of the door, wondering whether to rattle the doorknob. He reached out to touch but the realization that it might have been him lying in Ed Salter's place stopped him. What maggot in Sophie's brain possessed her to behave as she did? He wondered where she was. He couldn't hear her talking to Charlie, so assumed that she must be in her own room across the corridor.

He couldn't remember whether she was still in the stable-yard when his father arrived. If not, he wondered if she was aware of the consequences of her actions. Somehow, he thought that she would care, for the grooms were her friends.

Joshua closed his eyes and then opened them, hearing again his father's voice, as he leapt from his horse and strode forward. "Silence," Tom Norbery had bellowed, "Get out of my sight. This man's injury is more important than your petty squabbles."

He had never known his father be so angry, but he realised that at a stroke, Tom Norbery had quelled Charlie's accusations, and ensured that no one had time to listen. The grooms sprang into action, responding to their master's orders and their wounded colleague's need. For that he was grateful, but he felt anger at his stupidity for being caught in a coil not of his making.

Ed Salter's injury should never have happened. The sight of blood sickened him, but not so much as the accusation of rape – and of whom?

It was incredible that a girl of Sophie's age should have carnal knowledge of the kind that he gained from a harlot in a bagnio. From where had she acquired it?

Honesty told him that, even in the darkness, he should have realised it wasn't Millie. Her breasts would have overflowed his hands, whereas Sophie…

Joshua would have given anything to erase the memory of how responsive her pert nipples were, and the lustful feelings generated when she touched him. It was just as the Contessa had said. Damn the woman. That ensured he could never look Sophie Cobarne in the face without embarrassment; or Charlie without regret.

Three hours later, Squire Norbery summoned them downstairs. They emerged from their separate rooms at the same time, but neither spoke nor exchanged glances.

In the library, Joshua's father sat at the desk writing, and continued for several minutes without acknowledging their presence as they stood before him.

"How's Ed?" said Joshua, hating the silence.

"The wound has been stitched, and he is under sedation, but where there are horses, there is always a risk of lockjaw," Tom Norbery said, looking from one to the other. "Now I want an explanation for the vulgar display of brawling that precipitated that poor man's injuries. I hope you realise that you have both brought shame on Linmore by your actions. Charlie, I would like you to explain for what reason you picked up a hoof-paring knife as a weapon."

"He raped Sophie," Charlie repeated the accusation.

"No, I didn't," Joshua interrupted, "she –"

"One at a time," Tom Norbery barked out. "You, Joshua, will be silent and allow Charlie to explain, and he will remain mute when your turn comes."

When Charlie hung his head, Tom Norbery said, "In that case, I will ask questions. When did this incident take place?"

"It was late morning, and Sophie came out of the hayloft with her clothes in tatters. She told me that Joshua had –"

"Yes, as you said before, that he had molested her. Can you recall which clothes she was wearing at the time? I must ask you to bear with me, for I think it could be relevant," he said, drumming his fingers on the desk.

"I've not seen them before," said Charlie, with a puzzled frown. "I didn't know she had any like them."

Joshua watched as his father reached down behind his desk to lift a tattered, dirty white bodice and a skirt with blue stripes. "Would these be the ones?"

"Yes, that's what she was wearing," Charlie said in triumph.

Tom Norbery nodded. "These were given to me by Millie, the dairymaid, who found them dumped in the dairy after luncheon, apparently having been borrowed from her earlier in the day by your sister."

"She's lying. Sophie had no reason to wear such clothes."

"I would agree with you, Charlie. No reason at all, except that she was wearing them with black riding boots when she climbed the hay-loft ladder this morning. Boots that no dairymaid would wear, clearly visible under a striped skirt made for a shorter woman. She was seen by one of the coachmen. He also noticed that the door of the pitch-hole over the yard was closed before Joshua's arrival, ten minutes later."

"No," said Charlie, appalled. "You're making excuses because he's your son."

Squire Norbery gave an exasperated sigh, and rubbed both hands over his eyes. "No, I am saying it because it is the truth as I was told by a particular groom who had no reason to lie, and an extremely irate dairymaid who will have to be found new clothes to wear at work. I will call her to speak for herself," he said in a weary voice, and rang a handbell.

The door opened immediately, and a footman looked into the room.

"Hayton, please ask Millie to come in, and request Miss Jane to bring Sophie."

"No," said Charlie in rush. "I won't have her interrogated."

"Very commendable, if you think it would injure her sensibilities, but I fear she has none. Never mind, I have already spoken with her and she claims to have no recollection of the time to which this relates," Tom Norbery said, watching Charlie's look of astonishment. "Hayton," he said aside. "I trust that you know how to keep your tongue between your teeth. This is not for servants' hall gossip."

"Beg pardon, sir?" said the footman with the air of one afflicted with deafness.

"Good man. Now send in Millie, and wait outside."

Millie entered the room looking concerned, and then glowered at

230

Charlie and gave Joshua a quick smile of support. She inspected the clothes on the floor, and confirmed without hesitation that they were the same ones borrowed by Sophie. No, she hadn't asked for what purpose they were required, because she hadn't thought it was her place to question what the gentry did. But in the light of all the trouble it caused, she was of a different opinion, as she quickly told Charlie.

"That sister of yours ought to be ashamed of herself, borrowing my clothes to entrap a young man, and then to ruin them. Unlike her, I don't have any more to replace them," she said, a picture of moral indignation.

"Millie…" Squire Norbery warned, but the woman hadn't finished.

"If I'd known she would do what she did when you two was off on your travels, I'd have told her to sling her hook, and find summat better to do with her time. Calls herself a lady," she said in a voice full of scorn. "She's no better than the light-skirts who walk the streets in Norcott Town."

"You're lying," said Charlie, outraged.

"No, I'm not," she retorted, "as anybody who was here before she was bundled off to school will tell you. I never thought to see such goings on at Linmore."

"Be quiet, the pair of you," snapped Squire Norbery.

Joshua was agog with curiosity, while Charlie, separated from him by the length of the desk, quivered with anger, as the dairymaid lapsed into silence.

"That will be all, Millie. I will ensure that your garments are replaced," said Squire Norbery. "But remember, I do not wish you to repeat a single word of what has passed in this room to anyone. Do I make myself clear?"

"Yes, sir," said the dairymaid with a sniff as she bobbed her knees. "I beg pardon for speaking out of turn, but I'm that moithered by what 'appened, and didn't want Joshua to be blamed when it wasn't his fault."

"Nor will you discuss anything of what occurred outside today." Tom Norbery's voice was icy cold. "You may go, but I will speak again with you on this matter later."

Suitably chastened, the woman bobbed her knees and scurried from the room.

Tom Norbery let out an exasperated sigh as the door closed behind her.

"We will be extremely lucky to keep this unpleasant episode quiet," he said. "Now we will proceed with something that should have been resolved last year when you returned from Europe. I thought it best after Matthew's death to leave the pair of you together, but evidently I was mistaken." His tone expressed his disappointment.

In fact, they were rarely together, for Sophie had introduced Charlie to her school friend in Bredenbridge, and he made frequent visits in the intervening months to see the girl that he called his goddess.

"You, Charlie, will join the army and be trained to use weapons properly. That, as far as the household is concerned, is why you will go to London. It has ever been your intention and only Matthew's death delayed it."

"What will happen to him?" Charlie interrupted in a truculent tone. "Why should he get off without punishment?"

Tom quelled the outburst with a glare. "Joshua will leave Linmore for a different destination, but the fewer people that know the true reason for your separation the better. If it were a simple case of the two of you brawling over some wanton farm wench, I would flog the pair of you and be done with it. But the minute Joshua was stupid enough to go to the hayloft, for whatever reason, and you in your anger picked up a knife, you did so with intent." Tom Norbery let the words sink in before he continued. "Personally, I believe that you were both victims of the same misguided notion of a prank that went horribly wrong, and it could get worse if Ed Salter's wound becomes infected. An inch higher, he might have lost his eye, but if the wound goes septic, he could lose his life.

"As a magistrate, I can tell you that if he dies, questions will have to be asked, but if you are not here you can't be compelled to answer. In the first instance, the physician was more interested in repairing the wound than probing the cause…"

"What about Sophie?" Charlie asked, chalky faced.

"Your sister will accompany you to stay with my sister, Mrs Pontesbury. I will inform the headmistress of her school that we have decided that Sophie is going to London to prepare for her coming out in the small season of the autumn. I will leave it to Sophie to break the news to her particular friends.

"That will satisfy idle curiosity. I daresay that many pupils will envy her, as most of the girls, whose parents are in trade, don't have access to such refinements. I will also make it known that Joshua will join you later, because it will be expected, but he will not."

Charlie lapsed into silence, looking stunned. No doubt, thought

Joshua, he had realised that there would be no more visits to his precious goddess in Bredenbridge.

He was astounded by the completeness of his father's plans. Tom Norbery had obviously not wasted a moment since the scene in the stable-yard.

Whilst Joshua couldn't deny having touched Sophie, he knew that she had molested him more than he her, and revelled in so doing. He cringed at the thought of his complicity. Why the hell, when he felt the prickly feeling between his shoulder-blades halfway across the hayloft floor, hadn't he recognised it as a sign that she was near, when he'd always known before? Or gone out early to ride with his father, instead of turning over and going back to sleep? Better still, why hadn't he stayed in bed all day and ignored any notes that purported to come from Millie?

If he had done that, Ed Salter would be safe, his friendship with Charlie intact and he wouldn't now be awaiting banishment from home. How he wished that he could wake up from the nightmare and find that everything was normal again.

"Joshua…" His father's blunt voice interrupted his reverie. "There are things that I wish to discuss with Charlie that don't concern you. Take this note to Gilbert and stay in your room until you are told to leave."

"Yes, sir," he said, taking the folded sheet of paper that his father offered.

He made his way upstairs, wondering if Aunt Jane was still with Ed Salter. He wanted to see her to explain. If anyone could make things right, she could.

Gilbert read the note and left the room without a word. He returned minutes later carrying a portmanteau, which he proceeded to fill with clothes from the dressing room cupboards. Joshua watched him count out a number of shirts for the day and a similar quantity for night, then a pile of neck-cloths, underwear, handkerchiefs and several pairs of hose. A spare jacket, waistcoat and breeches followed in turn, before he closed the case and placed it by the door.

"Is that for me?" he said.

"Yes," said the valet.

"Where am I going?"

"The note doesn't say. Just to get a few essentials together, and then I'm to bring you something to eat up here."

"Do you know what happened?" Joshua ventured to ask.

"No, and it doesn't concern me," said the man.

Martha's family were loyal to the last.

"Do you know where Aunt Jane is? I'd like to see her."

"Busy, I expect," came the blunt reply that didn't really tell him anything.

Not for the last seven years had he felt so bereft of friendship. People moved around him with kindly intent but it wasn't the same, nor would it ever be again.

Joshua didn't have to protest his innocence or admit guilt for his father had conducted his investigations before they went downstairs to the library. That took everything out of their hands, for it was obvious that the matter with Sophie, serious though it was, lacked the urgency of what followed.

His father had swept it aside, but Joshua knew that in having given his word to help protect Sophie, Charlie saw the illicit meeting in the hayloft as a betrayal of their friendship, whereas nothing could have been further from his mind.

CHAPTER 24

Charlie turned away as Joshua left the library, not wanting to look on him. He heard the door close, and suddenly felt bereft. When he awoke in the morning it was a day like any other. He'd opened one eye long enough to debate going for an early morning ride with Uncle Tom; decided that he would do it tomorrow and fell asleep to dream of Annie.

After they shared breakfast, Joshua disappeared and Charlie went to the stables looking for Sophie to find out when she would see Annie again, intent on going with her. How he wished that he'd stayed in bed, then none of this would have happened, or if it had, he wouldn't be involved.

All he could think of was that Ed Salter, who helped him learn to ride, lay injured. Charlie would never have harmed any of the grooms. He'd worked hard to earn their respect, just as Sophie had. Now they looked on him with loathing. Millie, who had always been free and easy with her favours, made that clear when she berated him about the note to Joshua.

"How could it be from me," she had said, "when I don't have the letters?"

Of course she must be able to write. Surely everyone could… couldn't they? He'd never thought about it before. But if she hadn't written the note that took Joshua to the hayloft, who did? The paper Millie claimed to have found was dreadfully crumpled, so it was impossible to tell.

Thankfully Salter wasn't dead. A minute later it could have been Joshua, and would have been the way Charlie was feeling. He wished they had been flogged, for that way he knew Joshua would have been punished. And so he should be.

She wasn't like that when she left me…

Joshua hadn't denied being with Sophie in the hayloft, although he did later in the presence of other people. What else could be said when he'd admitted his guilt?

That's what hurt most and made Charlie angry. Now, if what Squire

235

Norbery said was true, Sophie had denied any knowledge of the situation, just as she did as a child. Where did that leave him in the light of what had followed? He shook his head feeling overwhelmed.

The sound of someone clearing their throat broke through his reverie. When he opened his eyes, he saw Tom Norbery still sitting at the desk, watching him, a handkerchief in his outstretched hand. Not wanting to be beholden, Charlie fumbled in his pocket, determined to use his own.

"Are you ready to continue?"

The voice was kindly as it always was; deceptively so. Charlie wanted to believe that nothing had changed, but knew that it had, for the Uncle Tom of old would never have let a servant berate a member of the family.

He blew his nose whilst waiting for Squire Norbery to speak. Until a few minutes ago, he thought of him as Uncle Tom, but could not be sure of their relationship now.

"I'm sorry you heard about your sister's previous behaviour like that, Charlie. I would much rather not involve the servants, but whether you like it or not, the young woman had a point to make. Somewhat vociferously, I admit."

He seemed to realise Charlie was still standing.

"For goodness sake, boy, sit down," he said gruffly. "I can't talk with you standing there, looking at me as if you're about to go to the gallows."

The expression so echoed what Charlie was feeling that he remained woodenly on his feet, even though his legs threatened to let him down. He hated to be at odds with Uncle Tom, but it was easier to maintain what remained of his dignity when he stood to attention. He dared not let it go for it was all he had left to support him.

"Very well, stand if you prefer," Squire Norbery said, sitting at his desk. "Maybe you can tell me whether you wish to see Joshua before you leave and speak man to man?"

"No, sir," he said. "I never want to see him again."

There was a silence before Squire Norbery responded. "As you wish, Charlie, but I am saddened that this occurred under my roof. Civility is clearly out of the question, so I think the best course of action is expedite your entry into the army. I also think that Sophie might benefit from a sojourn in town to help her to make a recovery from this shocking event, and prepare her for her future life."

It was strange how the emphasis changed when they were alone.

Courtesy was everything, and Uncle Tom implied that Sophie's needs were being considered, whereas when Joshua was there they were told what would happen. The difference was beguiling, but Charlie knew what he must say.

"The sooner it can be done the better, sir," He raised his chin and thrust his shoulders back to stop himself wavering, "but I would like to know if my father left sufficient funds for a pair of colours. If not, I'll enlist as a common soldier; in fact, it might be my best option. I don't want to be beholden to anyone. All I ask is that you think kindly of Sophie."

Charlie met the older man's gaze squarely. It was hard, but he was determined not to weaken. Leaving Linmore was like losing his pa all over again. Last time it was beyond his control. Now he blamed the friend he had thought of as a brother, and it left an acrid taste.

"Well said, young man, but I will ask you not to be hasty, or too proud to permit me to make enquiries on your behalf. Would I be right in assuming that you wish to join your father's old regiment? The King's Own Irish Dragoons, was it not? I imagine he will still be remembered with respect."

His uncle's words brought Charlie closer to tears.

"I want you to know that Aunt Jane and I held your parents in great esteem, and have a fondness for you and your sister. Be assured that I will investigate the matter of funding, and let you know the outcome."

"What… will happen to…your son, sir?"

"That need not concern you, unless you wish to see him." The voice was cool and controlled.

Charlie shook his head. He knew if he laid eyes on Joshua, he would still want to throttle him. He told himself that because he did not want to accept the possibility that Sophie might not have been honest with him. To think badly of her would be a betrayal of his promise to their pa, which kept him strong at a time when she was all the family he had.

Just when he thought the ordeal was over, Squire Norbery added, "What I suggest is a temporary matter, Charlie. As far as I am concerned, Linmore is still your home, and you will be welcome to return. I hope you feel able to keep in touch with me."

When Charlie had left the library, Tom walked slowly around the back of the bookcases to where Jane was sitting in an alcove. He sat down beside her on the sofa, feeling older than his years.

"Where do we go from here?" he asked wearily. "Charlie doesn't want anything to do with Joshua, which is why I let Millie have her say. I would not normally let a servant be so outspoken, but better it came from her than me. After all, Sophie involved her, but I have to deal with the aftermath."

"I know," she said. "He's so conditioned to fighting Sophie's battles, he won't believe ill of her, even when he must know it's true."

"It might have been easier for Charlie to understand if I had explained about the problems we had with Sophie before we sent her away to school," he said, "but I didn't want to humiliate him when he was close to breaking point. He already thinks that everyone is against him."

"And they're not, but he wouldn't believe it," Jane ended on a sniff, and gratefully accepted the handkerchief that Tom offered. After a minute she said in a stronger tone, "What are your plans?"

"If it can be arranged in the time, I'll go to London tomorrow, and take Charlie and his sister with me," Tom said. "No one will remark on my departure for I should be there with Parliament in session. Thank God I wasn't, for I shudder to think how you would have dealt with this appalling situation in my absence. I daresay that their hasty departure might be remarked upon, but to delay, we risk further problems if Kate heard of it."

"It will have to be done, but this has come at a most unfortunate time," said Jane. "We might have sent them to Shettleston Hall if Caroline's second confinement hadn't been due. As it is, her antipathy towards Sophie would complicate things dreadfully, and gossip would inevitably spread like wildfire about the reason for them being there. Wherever you send Joshua now, he will have to live at Linmore in the future, and to have the accusation of rape levelled at him would taint him for life. Nobody would want to know him."

Tom nodded grim agreement.

"I ought to stay here with Ed Salter," she said, "but for appearances' sake, I must accompany you. Not that Sophie will appreciate my presence for a moment. The foolish girl needs to be spanked, but Charlie needs our support. He sounded so sad, I wanted to wrap my arms around him and give him a hug, for he desperately needs some affection. He believed in both Sophie and Joshua but knows that one betrayed his trust. The problem is that he is blaming the wrong person."

"I sent for Percival when it happened," said Tom. "He's taken charge and will work with Jessie and William Rufus in conjunction with Dr

Althorpe. He suggested that Miss Finchley might take Lucy and Julia down to his cottage for tonight in his absence, and go to their grandparents tomorrow. I thought it was an excellent idea. If everyone is moving, it will draw attention away from the others."

"I will go to the cottage shortly to arrange with Jessie for Joshua to sleep there," said Jane, "and remind her about our gypsy friends on the hill. Their remedies will be invaluable if there is any fever."

However hard Tom tried to keep the subject impersonal, it veered back at every turn. "Percy knows about dealing with infection, for he went out of his way to acquire herbs to save Dr Hawley's life in the wilds of Macedonia."

"Yes, Joshua and Charlie told me about it on their return. Their friendship was so strong then, and it's sad that Sophie's wanton behaviour has spoiled it."

"Yes," said Tom, "she always was a strange girl."

"Thinking of the events of today has reminded me of the first time Sophie came home from school in Bredenbridge. She used to talk to me then, and tell me about what she had learned. I know that her mother would have been pleased." Jane sighed at the recollection of her cousin. "It was never the same after she started to visit the girl with the Onnybrook connection. From then on her behaviour became ever more grasping and outrageous.

"This time she has overstepped the mark, and left Joshua and Charlie no time to resolve their differences, for with Ed Salter's injury it's impossible for them to remain together at Linmore."

"After Matthew's death a parting of the ways was inevitable," Tom said, "and Joshua needs to be brought to a sense of his responsibility to Linmore. I will consult Thomas Coke when I am in London. He's the best source of advice on land management. I don't know why I didn't think of him before.

"Purchasing Charlie's commission will be easy, compared to arranging for Sophie to be presented at Court. I daresay Winifred won't thank me for taking her to London halfway through the social season but she will understand the need when she knows the reason. I've never known her to be daunted by a challenge."

"Poor Winifred," said Jane. "I don't envy her the task ahead."

"Nonsense," said Tom, "my sister positively thrives on conflict."

"Maybe she does, but she's never had to deal with Sophie as we have."

The sound of the stable clock striking three reminded Charlie of the events that occurred to make this the last time he would sleep at Linmore. He remembered the first night he had slept here, and awoken to the open door that led to the room next door where Joshua Norbery slept.

Now there was a deathly hush where once a friendly voice had bid him welcome. Charlie shivered, knowing how close to being true that word had come. When he closed his eyes, he saw the knife in his hand, and felt again the power at his command to cause terror. He saw it in Joshua's eyes as he edged away.

Coward, he thought, slashing the knife back and forth. *Stand still and take your punishment.* But what happened wasn't a fight, and the man he hurt wasn't his enemy. He would do anything to wash away the memory.

It was an accident. Not that it was judged so by the onlookers for he had been heard to make a threat. He'd never felt such anger. Almost jealousy, if he probed deep enough. Joshua was his friend and for him to turn to Sophie, having promised to help guard her, was betrayal.

"Charlie…" Sophie whispered across the bedroom that she still insisted on sharing when she was at home. "Are you awake?"

"Yes," he mumbled, feeling as if he'd never sleep again.

"I'm cold, can I join you?"

Wanting company, Charlie turned back the bedclothes to let her share his bed, just as they used to as children in Ireland and when they first came to Linmore. Then it was supposedly to save on linen. The bed was larger now than on their arrival, but the need for warmth and reassurance was the same.

"I don't want to go, Charlie," she said in a subdued voice after a few minutes.

Charlie made what he hoped were comforting noises, not daring to admit that the thought of leaving the place that he had made his home tore him apart. If he had spoken he would have cried, and he learned long ago that was unmanly. His pa had told him that when he grieved at the age of seven for the mother he dearly loved.

Be a man, Charlie me boy, and leave the weeping for the womenfolk. It's what they are good at. The words were indelibly imprinted in his memory.

He hadn't cried since that day, not even when he heard his father grieving for his lost love in the dark hours of the night, or in the morning when he found him lying in sloth beside the empty whiskey bottle. That had frightened him, for he did not know how to help. Sophie did, for she hugged their pa and shed childish tears with him, but she had been dry-eyed since, not showing her feelings.

He tried not to mind when his pa had turned away, saying that Charlie reminded him too much of Charlotte, and yet he took Sophie of his knee and called her his beautiful girl, and they laughed and cried together.

Uncle Lucius had liked Charlie, but couldn't cope with Sophie, and he'd never explained why she had been sent to the convent. She just went one day when Charlie was at his lessons. When she returned, Uncle Tom came to Ireland to collect them; and in the morning, he would take them away.

Despite what Uncle Tom said, Charlie couldn't return. He'd never before appreciated Linmore as he did now. He hoped that Aunt Jane wouldn't disown them for Sophie had no one else if anything happened to him. That's what bothered him.

"Are you going to join the army?" Sophie sounded a long way away.

"So they tell me," he said.

"Can I come with you and follow the drum?"

"Yes," said Charlie. "It'll be you and me together again, just like it was before."

"Mmm…" she murmured in a sleepy voice. "I'll tell Aunt Winifred that's what we've decided we're going to do. Don't worry; I've got plenty of money…"

CHAPTER 25

It was after dark when the word came for Joshua to go downstairs. The Hall servants were all at supper, so none but his father and Gilbert saw him leave the house in William Rufus's company, or set off across the back drive towards Aunt Jane's cottage in the woodland.

She greeted him with a hug, and spoke for a few minutes before departing with William Rufus, in the gig, for the Hall.

"I don't know how much you are aware of our plans, but tomorrow morning, your father and I are taking Charlie and Sophie to stay with Aunt Winifred. He must remain in London because Parliament is in session, but I will return as soon as can be. We will talk then. What you must know is that Ed Salter is here in the cottage. Jessie will nurse him with help from William Rufus and Sergeant Percival. We felt this was the best place to maintain discretion, and allow Dr Althorpe to visit in private."

"How is Ed?" he said, terrified of what he might hear.

She hesitated before saying, "The physician has stitched the wound and he's under sedation."

"Will he be all right? I mean…"

"Yes, I know what you mean, and we must pray that he is."

With that Joshua had to be content. Sleep was long in coming. He felt empty inside but he relived every moment of the previous day and felt every punch and kick to his ribs that Charlie had given him that would show as a bruise in the morning.

His mind was fixed on the moment when Charlie snatched up the knife; seeing Matthew Norbery all over again, on that far-off day as a child when his brother had similarly threatened him and Jessie stepped between them. William Rufus had interceded a few minutes later to save his sister's life, but she still bore the scars.

He felt sick to the core, knowing that someone else was the innocent victim of an attack intended for him, but now it was Ed Salter who had borne the brunt…and every time he saw the man in the future he would remember.

In the morning when Jessie gave him breakfast, she said. "I heard you moithering in the night, so you'd better come and see Ed for yourself."

Joshua blessed her for knowing what had bothered his sleep. He knew that her words were well intended but the prospect scared him.

"When was he brought here?" he said.

"Soon after the doctor had stitched the wound," she said. "Your father decided that it was easier for the physician to visit without being seen. The story is that he's been kicked by a horse."

It was a feasible cause of injury, even if it wasn't the right one in this case.

"How long will I stay here? My father said I'd be sent away."

"Yes, I know," she said, "but he's got to find somewhere to send you. Until then, you can make yourself useful."

Ed Salter lay perfectly still in the big bed where Aunt Jane normally slept. Joshua had known the cottage from a little boy and had often crept into this room, and felt safe as he slipped beneath the covers. Now it felt anything but normal.

The curtains were half-drawn to ensure the room was in shadow. The sound of the man's steady breathing might have implied a healthy sleep, if the awkwardly placed bandages were not visible around his head, and Joshua hadn't been told that the groom was given a dose of laudanum to control the pain. The soporific effect was the result of sedation.

He sensed another presence in the room. Turning, he saw Sergeant Percival sitting beside the bed, his eyes apparently closed, but as Joshua watched, the man stood up and approached. There was not much that passed his notice.

The sight of him in the sickroom evoked memories of the time in Macedonia, when Dr Hawley's life lay in the balance. They were dark days, in appalling conditions, but Joshua had companionship. The recollection brought home to him what he had lost.

Feeling choked, he made his way towards the parlour. Sergeant Percival followed, and Jessie remained in the bedroom.

"How is Ed?" Joshua asked, striving to stifle the memories shared with Charlie.

"The sleep will have done him good, but I want to be prepared in case there's any fever. Jessie tells me there's a herbalist in these parts, so I'll be going out later to seek her advice."

"Will I be able to come with you?" Joshua said, feeling lost and craving the company of someone he respected.

"It's best if you stay here in case your father wants to see you before he goes to London." Sergeant Percival's voice held a hint of regret.

Joshua nodded, knowing that it was unlikely for he had seen his father before he left the Hall last night. Ten minutes was all he was allowed but it was enough to reassure his father on the subject that was bothering him.

"There's just one thing I wanted to ask you, but in the uproar there was no chance for private speech," Tom Norbery had said.

It wasn't easy to admit that he wasn't entirely blameless, but when he had, Joshua learned that Millie was the first person to bring her complaint, closely followed by Jack Kilcot the assistant-coachman, who said that he recognised Sophie immediately. She was too conspicuous to pass unnoticed climbing a ladder, wearing buckskin breeches and top-boots under a skirt made for a shorter woman.

If only Joshua had insisted on opening the door in the loft wall above the yard, he would have seen her hiding in the shadows and guessed her intent.

The discussion gave him much to think about, particularly his father's comment that caused him to squirm. "Your mother and I had noticed Sophie's preference for you, but we did not think it was reciprocated. Now we have to decide what to do with you. I will give the matter some thought and will let you know what I decide. Before I leave, is there anything you wish to say to me?"

"The matter with Sophie was not something I planned, sir. I would never have touched her in that way."

His father looked at him. "No, I didn't think you would intentionally, Joshua, but I have to know if you did unintentionally – just in case there are unforeseen… complications." The inference of a pregnancy was obvious.

"No, of course not…" he said, indignant, while hoping that he wouldn't be asked what Sophie had done to him.

His father looked relieved and the conversation ended, but at the library door Joshua looked back and said, "I'm truly sorry, Father."

"Yes, Joshua, I know, we are all sorry that this has occurred."

Thinking of the sadness in his father's voice, he lay awake in the middle of the night, running the conversation through his mind many times before he realised what his father had said… *Your mother and I noticed Sophie's preference for you but we did not think it was reciprocated…*

Of course it was not. *Your mother and I…?* The words screamed at him.

Joshua could not believe that his father, who normally only talked with Aunt Jane, had discussed such a thing with his mother. Would he also, knowing how she hated Joshua, tell her of the latest episode?

For much of the first couple of days, the only person he saw was Jessie, and she never said a lot. He sensed she did not know what to say, but at least she applied salves to the cuts on his face and sore ribs. The bruises soon started to fade, but the grief inside was raw as ever. Aunt Jane's absence made things seem worse.

Every day, Joshua heard the physician arrive and stayed out of sight until he left. Sergeant Percival had decreed it must be so. No one was taking a chance on Joshua being questioned. No doubt it was really on his father's orders.

Hearing a familiar voice in the kitchen, he learned that Gilbert had walked across the park to bring him clean clothes and to sit with Ed through the night, and would return to the Hall in the morning.

"Aren't you tired?" Joshua asked.

"There's not much to do with Squire Norbery away," he said.

No, he supposed there wouldn't be. Gilbert had lost his other charges as well. "When did they set off?" he said, wanting to glean the information.

"On the first day at about twelve o'clock, so I reckon that they'd have a couple of nights on the road. Jack Kilcot and Horace took them in the big coach. Daniel Salter stayed here this time…"

Of course he would with his son lying injured…

That meant they should be in London by now. Joshua wondered how many days it would be before Aunt Jane returned.

"What are they saying at the Hall?" he said.

"Folks at the Hall know better than to gossip," said Jessie, bustling into the kitchen to interrupt. "They know which side their bread is buttered."

He took the comforting thought to bed, that the servants' loyalty to his father held firm even in his absence, and slept properly for the first time since he arrived.

In the morning, Jessie scolded when he got under her feet in the kitchen.

"It's no good you moping about, or starving yourself, Joshua," she said. "You need to eat and get outside in the fresh air. Things will look better there."

If only they did. He knew she meant to be kind. She had always been good to him. Rather than argue, he started to eat. He couldn't taste the flavours, but felt the benefit. Outside, he had to dodge the April showers on his walks in the woodland, and often came back soaked.

"When do you think Aunt Jane will return, Jessie?" he asked for the third time.

"Stop moithering me," she said in her blunt way. "I've told you before that she won't stay any longer in London than is necessary. She never could abide the place."

No, she promised to come back and talk and she'd never disappointed him.

This went on for almost a week, and every day, he watched the rain running down the windowpanes. They looked like the tears of sadness he felt inside, but was not supposed to show. Females could do that sort of thing – just as they could twist the truth to suit their ends. As long as he lived, he would never trust another woman.

One day at breakfast, Jessie said, "Mr Weyborne sent word he'll be over to see you later, Joshua."

He frowned at her, and then realised it was the Linmore land agent.

"Why is he coming to see me, Jessie?"

"That's for you to find out," she said, and went on with her work.

It was late morning before a gig drew up outside the cottage and the agent knocked on the door. Jim Weyborne was a man of few words, but those he spoke were to the point.

"Good morning, Master Joshua," he said. "Squire Norbery has sent word that he wants you to stay with me and Mrs Weyborne. If you'd like to get your things together, Francis will pick you up later today."

At last, there was news, but he wished his father were here to tell him, not send messages with the servants.

The morning sky was overcast, but the afternoon sun began to shine when Francis Weyborne arrived at the cottage. Joshua's low spirits started to improve in the company of a younger person, and as they talked, he learned that Francis, of a similar age to him, was in training as bailiff on the estate.

The journey to the Home Farm took them within sight of Linmore Hall, but halfway across the park, a fork in the back drive made a sweeping detour towards the stone-built farmhouse where the agent lived.

Joshua liked the Weyborne family on sight, especially Mrs Weyborne, a plain-speaking, motherly soul who was a wonderful cook. In the absence of Aunt Jane, she was a good substitute, who made him welcome and prepared a meal of his favourite roast mutton. After that, the world did not look quite so dark.

His bedroom, which was next to Francis, was smaller than the one at home, but the linen was fresh and the feather mattress comfortably warm.

The agent's family did everything they could to make him welcome. No one in the household mentioned Charlie and Sophie although he was sure everyone on the estate knew the story. It was as if they had never existed.

Sitting in the dining room, Joshua listened to Francis talking with his father about estate work they were planning. Although the two men included him in the conversation, he did not know what questions to ask without sounding ignorant.

Instead, he concentrated on his food and complimented Mrs Weyborne on the excellence of her meal. It was evident from her smile that his comment gave pleasure, and in return, the agent's wife insisted they introduced other topics to discuss besides farming.

When the meal was over, the family took prayers with the servants, and at nine o'clock, a servant brought a tray of tea to the drawing room. This comfortable family life was so different to what Joshua was accustomed.

An hour later, the agent said, "Come on, Francis, we'll need an early start in the morning."

Out of interest, Joshua said, "What time's early, Mr Weyborne?"

"Half past five."

That came as a shock, for at the cottage, Joshua used to lie abed until all hours of the day. "Does that mean me as well?"

"It does, young man," said the agent. "Your father wants you to see something of the estate and find out the kind of work we do."

The following morning, Joshua mounted his horse and set out from the Home Farm with the agent and his son on their rounds. Until then, he had not realised the long hours worked. They rose at dawn, and apart from an hour for breakfast, kept going until daylight was fading. Through all the villages to inspect parcels of land for repairs, some of which he could hardly remember seeing.

By the end of the first week, he started to look at farm buildings differently, to see things he would previously have missed – recognise a dislodged roof slate and know the portent. It was little enough, but he was glad to have learned. He had not been aware of the need for him to know, because he assumed that was why they employed an agent.

The ride through Hillend village brought back memories of the last time he had been there, eight years ago, just after Charlie arrived at Linmore. On that occasion, they stopped at the church and then drove home.

This time, he rode with the agent and Francis, past the inn on the village green and continued out the other side. Half a mile beyond, they stopped the horses beside a pair of high metal park gates in a sadly dilapidated state.

Joshua looked for some identification, but the weathered wooden sign attached to the stone pillars gave no clue. Rusting chains barred their way, as did a metal plate bearing the faded words of warning. *Private Property. Keep Out…*

This must be the only place on the estate to have a notice threatening to prosecute trespassers. The land looked coldly remote – barren even – apart from the overgrown coppice of birch, beech and hazel. Individual tree trunks melded with brambles and weeds to form a barricade, leaving no hint of what lay beyond.

"Where is this, Mr Weyborne?" Joshua pointed to the sign.

The agent cleared his throat before speaking. "It's where Miss Littlemore used to live when she was a girl, Master Joshua."

"Why are the gates locked?"

"There's nothing there. The house was demolished years ago."

Before he could ask more details, the man said, "We'd better be on our way. This can wait for another time."

When Joshua attended Evensong on Sunday, he walked up the aisle towards the empty Linmore Hall pew by the pulpit. Then he remembered and turned aside to follow the Weyborne family. Others in the congregation must have noted it, but no one remarked on the lapse.

Aunt Jane returned home in the middle of the second week, looking tired. Joshua was so thankful to see her, but there was no question of him stopping work. He visited in the evenings, and learned that Ed Salter was still weak, but he had started to recover.

"Come into the bedroom, Joshua. He'll be glad to see you," Aunt Jane said, leading the way. She stopped for a moment at the door. "Don't be alarmed by Ed's appearance. The wound looks puckered but it is healing. It's just that there was a lot of infection, but the herbal remedies worked."

Just as they had for Dr Hawley in Macedonia. The thought crossed Joshua's mind as he entered the room. It was lucky that Aunt Jane had warned him; otherwise he might have shown more of the shock he felt.

The man he saw in the bed looked frail, but he was awake. Before the accident he was a handsome man, but now, a jagged scar ran down his left cheek, disfiguring him. Joshua felt sick, but not at the image before him as much as the fact it could have been his face he was looking at.

He was glad the room was half in shadow to hide his feelings.

"Hello, Ed," he said, reaching for the limp hand on the sheet, and felt a slight squeeze of the fingers.

"Hello…Josh." The speech was slurred. "They tell me… that you're over at the… Home Farm."

"Yes," he said, "showing how little I know about farming."

"Don't worry, you'll soon learn… Squire Norbery'll be proud of you…"

There was a silence and Joshua realised the effort of speaking had exhausted the man. He looked at Aunt Jane for guidance, and she nodded towards the door.

"I'll come to see you again," he said, looking back from the open door with tears in his eyes. In that moment, Joshua decided that when Ed Salter recovered his health, he would be his personal groom. He owed him nothing less.

"Will he recover…?" he asked.

"It will take a long time," said Aunt Jane, "and he won't be quite the man he was, but Dr Althorpe is hopeful… as long as there is no more infection."

When Joshua rode slowly back to the Home Farm, he realised that he had not asked Aunt Jane about either Charlie or Sophie Cobarne. When he thought about it, their absence ceased to be of significance compared to Ed Salter, but he wished they could see as he could, the damage that their actions had caused.

The sight of the injured man had a profound effect, making Joshua determined in the days that followed to fulfil the words that Salter had spoken in Aunt Jane's bedroom. "You'll learn…"

He vowed to do his utmost. After all, there was nothing else for him to do, or more important than to regain his father's good opinion.

After the second week, he heard a whisper, which increased to a shout in his mind. *Squire Norbery will be home tomorrow.*

He waited and waited for the summons to go home, but it did not come. Several days passed while Mr Weyborne attended to other matters, so Joshua rode around the estate with Francis. During these hours, they cemented a working bond of friendship.

When the summons finally came for Joshua to see his father, he had to wait outside the Linmore estate office while the agent conducted his meeting with Squire Norbery.

In his father's absence, the agent held weekly meetings at the Home Farm, and many times Joshua was encouraged to express an opinion. Today, he was on the outside, awaiting his father's pleasure.

It was strange to think he had not been inside his home for more than three weeks. He walked in from the stable yard, and everything on the lower ground floor seemed the same. It was quiet, and yet, in the background he could hear the murmur of servants' voices. There was always someone bustling about. Kitchen staff sent on errands to collect stores or laundry women chattering on their way outside to hang out the linen. Familiar sounds, and yet, he sensed it would never be normal again. His belly rumbled, but he had felt too anxious to eat a proper breakfast.

The office door opened and the agent and bailiff emerged. Francis gave a wink of encouragement as he walked past, and his father said, "Squire Norbery will see you now, Master Joshua."

He nodded and walked through the open door and saw his father reading a bundle of papers on the desk. Squire Norbery did not lift his head, but with a sweep of a hand, pointed towards a chair opposite to where he sat.

Instead, Joshua remained standing, feeling as he did when the tutor passed judgement on his behaviour when he was a lad.

"Sit down, boy," his father growled, and continued reading.

The tone did not invite argument. As he obeyed, Joshua looked at his boots and wished he had given the leather an extra layer of dubbing. He was not too adept at achieving a shine. It was something he would have to practise.

Through his reverie, he heard his father's voice: "You will go to Norfolk…"

What…when…how? The words ran through his mind. He opened his mouth to speak but nothing came out. Then he saw a look of exasperation on his father's face.

"Did you hear what I said, Joshua?"

He heard part of it, but why Norfolk?

"What is the matter with you?" The edge to his father's voice finally penetrated his consciousness. "Does my plan not meet with your approval?"

"I'm sorry, sir," he said. "I don't understand what you mean." He wished he had been listening.

"I was hoping for a better response than this." His father sounded annoyed. "It is not every young man who has the chance to spend a year on Thomas Coke's estate at Holkham."

Joshua gasped as the significance sank in. "Do you mean Mr Coke of Norfolk, the agriculturalist?"

It was the name Francis Weyborne had mentioned reverently in passing.

"Yes, he is my political colleague. We met whilst I was in London. He told me about a project he has started to teach the young landowners of the future about the changes in agriculture. He already has two students this year, and didn't plan for any more. I hope you realise he only agreed to take you as a favour to me, and it is on condition you do not waste time. You are there to work, Joshua, so please don't let me down, ever again."

Flooded with relief, he said, "Thank you, sir, I won't let you down." He added as an afterthought, "Of course, I will miss everyone."

"You won't have time to miss anyone, not even Millie," his father said. "You leave in three days; everything is arranged."

PART 2

ORDER
AND
METHOD

(1801 -1802)

CHAPTER 26

Early May 1801

"I'm so glad that you are here with me," Joshua said as he climbed into the coach. "You must be tired of travelling after your recent visit to London."

"Not really," Aunt Jane said with a smile, as she settled herself on the opposite seat. "You forget that it is rare for me to leave Linmore. It gave me the chance to see Aunt Winifred, albeit for a short time."

Joshua was at a loss to know what made her suddenly decide to visit her sister, Lady Cardington, when she usually described Rushmore Hall as the most boring place in the world. Whatever the reason, acting as her escort made his journey to Norfolk seem less like banishment. That is what it was, no matter what they called it. Irrespective of the challenge ahead, he was determined to see it through. He had to, for he was the heir to Linmore.

"How far is it?" he said, unable to recall the last time he had visited his relatives.

"About twenty miles," she said, stifling a yawn. "With luck, we should be there by three o'clock."

Joshua supposed that it took four hours because of the winding country roads, and the need to stop several times to water the horses. Thank goodness they were travelling in the well-padded comfort of the Linmore coach.

"Will you stay long?"

"Two weeks at the most," Aunt Jane said, closing her eyes preparatory to sleep. "I rely on Jessie to send an urgent message for me to return to Linmore."

Saying farewell to his father was hard, which was why he welcomed Aunt Jane's presence. She had always been there for him, right from the beginning. His journey to Norfolk was about two hundred miles, but he had never before travelled alone. Other times, people were with him to deal with arrangements.

The plan, when Joshua left Linmore, was for Jack Kilcot, his father's coachman, to drive Aunt Jane to Rushmore, and the following day, take him to Lichfield, where he would stay overnight in readiness to board the stagecoach that would take him to Norfolk. Mr Penn, his father's secretary, had organised everything in advance. He gave Joshua sufficient money to defer expenses, and a list of hostelries with guaranteed accommodation en route, which was so easy to follow, a child could use it.

Joshua said as much to Aunt Jane when he showed her the letter in the coach, and then briefly closed his eyes, feeling a gnawing sadness in his gut as he thought of the acrimonious parting with Charlie. One minute they were brothers-at-arms, and in the blink of an eyelid, deadly enemies. It should never have happened. He took a breath, deliberately turning his mind to the purpose of his journey. Whatever else the year at Holkham involved; he hoped there would be no women to cause trouble.

His thoughts ran together and he dozed; lulled by the drumming of coach-wheels on the roads that became progressively smoother the further they travelled. Reaching the halfway point, they stepped down from the coach to take a drink, before resuming the journey to their destination.

Rushmore Hall was a sprawling edifice, built in the Jacobean era, situated about five miles beyond the cast iron bridge constructed over the Severn Gorge.

Approached through an arched gateway, the front drive passed through two miles of parkland studded with oak and beech trees, before the house came into view, and another half mile to the entrance.

Although suitably impressed, Joshua secretly thought the building oozed the same pomposity as his uncle, Lord Cardington. He much preferred the friendly informality of the Linmore estate, a mere ten thousand acres, as opposed to Rushmore, which was half as big again, and twice as self-important.

Royston, the stately butler, met them at the door. He was flanked by two footmen and a similar number of uniformed maids, to be worthy of their consequence as family connections of Lady Cardington. Had it been the master who arrived, the entire staff would have been in evidence.

Aunt Jane went away to talk with her sister. To Joshua's surprise and delight, his older cousin, Fred, Lord Cardington's second son, was on furlough from the army. The last time they met was on a visit to London, three years before, when he took Joshua and Charlie Cobarne to Horse Guards' Parade, and the horse sales at Tattersalls. Sophie had inveigled her way into the visit, more was the pity. She encroached on so many things.

When they finally escaped from the welcoming party, Fred took Joshua to visit the stables, to see the thoroughbred horses for which Rushmore was renowned, and to choose a horse for his use. Dinner that evening was a long-winded affair, with Lord Cardington dominating the conversation, probing the reasons for Joshua's visit to Norfolk, for which Aunt Jane supplied answers that bore no resemblance to the reality.

Having a congenial relationship with his father, Joshua imagined everyone else did the same, but after the ladies withdrew from the dining room, he sensed a strange acrimony between Lord Cardington and Fred, which ensured the drinking of port was not prolonged. It was a relief to escape to his cousin's apartment, a substantial set of rooms in the west wing of the house.

Used to army life, Fred's notion of a quiet evening was to play cards and imbibe several bottles of burgundy. Joshua joined him in this, but tired from travelling, and unused to the quantity of alcohol, or quality of Lord Cardington's excellent wine cellar, he lapsed into a stupor and spent the first part of the night on a sofa.

Sometime in the early hours, he blundered back to his bedchamber and fell into bed, not knowing how he found his way. Hearing birdsong, he cautiously opened one eye, felt the room spin round, and closed it. He tried again, and it stopped spinning. The next time, he smelled the aroma of coffee and found a valet looking incuriously down at him.

"Would you care to take your bath now, sir? Captain Frederick asked if you would join him in the breakfast room when you are ready."

"What time is it?" he mumbled, blinking.

"Half past ten, sir, and everything is ready."

Joshua sat up very carefully, feeling a runaway horse had trampled him. He touched his head to see if it still sat atop his body, and risked a nod of agreement. When nothing fell on the floor, he took a deep breath, slipped his feet out of bed and stood up.

A welcome cup of coffee removed the sawdust from his mouth, while the bath helped ease his discomfort and revive his flagging spirits. Half an hour later, he entered the breakfast room, and found Fred looking disgustingly fit, devouring several slices of red sirloin. He shuddered at the thought of food, but nodded when Fred insisted, "Eat some of this, Josh; it will do you good."

Surprisingly, it did.

"It was probably the brandy you drank," Fred said with a laugh. "I daresay that you're not used to it. Better stay with the burgundy tonight."

Joshua could not remember drinking brandy, but he bowed to Fred's superior knowledge of his inebriated state.

His aching head cleared during a day spent riding a magnificent bay gelding around the estate, while Fred chose a chestnut. One could not fail to appreciate the bloodlines, and whatever else one might think of Lord Cardington, his stables were infinitely superior to any Joshua had seen before.

When they returned, he bathed again and donned formal dress, in readiness to endure another evening in Lord Cardington's company. Fortunately, it was not of long duration, for Fred's acerbic humour ensured that his lordship retired early to his library and remained there. After that, they escaped.

Although by nature Joshua was dutifully respectful to his elders, he admitted, by the time Fred opened a second bottle of burgundy, that it was a relief to be free of the sound of Lord Cardington's booming voice. At five years his senior, Fred became equally more loquacious as the wine loosened his tongue.

"Have you heard about Atcherly being caught in the parson's mousetrap, Josh? The sooner he produces a couple of sons, the better I will like it."

What he meant was that Joshua's cousin, Viscount Atcherly, had finally married. Fred made flippant comments about *a suitable bride, with a substantial dowry and lands that marched alongside those of Rushmore.*

A cynical viewpoint indeed, but he learned it was no more than the truth.

"That should let me off the hook, unless he produces a clutch of daughters, for I'm next in line for the illustrious honour. Who wants a damn title and a fifteen-thousand-acre millstone around their neck? Marriage is not for a military man like me. I like women well enough, but prefer the decorative kind. Why take a wife when I have a little ladybird in keeping, who knows exactly how to keep me happy, and one can always avoid bastards.

"In due course," he rambled on, "the parents will expect me to do my duty. That was why his lordship remarried, to have another son, when Atcherly's mother died in childbirth. Of course, I don't compare to the first-born, for I'm only the spare – his lordship's guarantee for the future, to prevent the name dying out. I daresay you might have felt something like it when Matthew was alive."

"No," said Joshua, perfectly honest. "He said I was the family bastard."

"The devil he did. It was just like him to say that, when everyone else knew that he was the cuckoo in the nest."

Joshua looked at him hard. "What do you mean?"

"Part of the family secrets, I suppose," said Fred, with a rueful grin. "It was something Atcherly told me when we visited Linmore, just after Uncle Tom brought those scrubby brats from Ireland. I think they were in some way related to my mother and Aunt Jane. The lad was polite enough, but his obnoxious sister quite upset his lordship, by not showing the proper respect for her betters. How we laughed…"

An apt description if ever Joshua heard one. The momentary recollection of the life-changing event that occurred when he was ten years old distracted his thoughts. When Joshua asked more of what Atcherly had said, Fred abruptly changed the subject, and he was no wiser.

"Keep out of my parents' way as long as you can, Josh. They will be seeking a bride for you, before you are much older. It stands to reason, with Matthew gone. Have to say that I think you will make a better job of running Linmore when the time comes. Not that one would wish it to be soon, for Uncle Tom's a splendid fellow. I always envied you your father. He is gentle in the real sense, whereas his lordship always took his parental duties far too seriously – particularly the floggings. Devilishly savage, when I was younger."

Fred was well into his stride now, and Joshua let him ramble. He was learning more about the family than he knew before, and it helped to keep his mind off what would happen when he left Rushmore.

"Gilbert, his brother, was of the same harsh disposition," Fred said, looking around for another bottle to broach. "Poor Jane…" he mused. "Did you know that is how my mother speaks of her sister, because she did not wish to forge close links with the Cardington family? My father intended her to marry his brother, but she laughed in his face. They consider her a sad case, but for my part I think it showed amazingly good sense."

Joshua shook his head, wondering what else he would hear.

"A fine life she would have had if married to Gilbert," Fred said, meaning exactly the opposite. "I like her best of all the family."

"So do I," said Joshua. He had not realised that Aunt Jane's sister, Clarissa, was Lord Cardington's second wife. It explained so many things.

He stayed three nights at Rushmore, during which time Lord Cardington decided to change Tom Norbery's plans, and, without telling anyone, sent Kilcot home with the Linmore coach. Joshua only learned of this on the final night, when he sat down to dinner with the family.

Hearing the pronouncement, Joshua looked questioningly at Aunt Jane, but she simply raised her eyebrows. He guessed it was news to her, and wondered if her annoyance stemmed from a dislike of causing a dispute in front of the servants, or reluctance to be beholden to Lord Cardington for her transport home.

On that occasion, he met his cousin, Atcherly, with his wife, who dined with the family. *Suitably meek*, he thought, and someone who would not argue.

As usual, it was an over-long, formal affair of pomposity, in which Lord Cardington's opinion took precedence over everyone else, and he depressed the pretensions of anyone with the temerity not to agree. Lady Cardington nodded approval to every word he uttered.

When the ladies retired from the dining room, the butler brought in the decanter of port, and the talk became more general. Fred called across the table to Joshua, an action that elicited a frown of disapproval from Lord Cardington. His cousin's mocking grin warned Joshua not to take his words literally.

"I'll be returning to London tomorrow, Josh. Had I known of your visit in advance, I could have driven you to Lichfield, but it appears that his lordship has planned a delightful surprise for you. Wigmore, his head groom, will take you in the chaise, instead. You must be sure to express your dutiful thanks to him."

The following morning, after Joshua had thanked his hosts for their hospitality and said a fond farewell to Aunt Jane, he realised the significance of those cryptic words.

The day of departure started cold, with hazy sunshine, but Joshua was suitably clad for a ride in the open air. His low-crowned beaver hat, leather-caped greatcoat and gloves might be too warm later in the day, but were exactly right for the drive to Lichfield.

When he climbed into the chaise, Joshua imagined the splendid team of four matched chestnut horses would cover the distance in record time – but he had not accounted for the stately pace the senior groom thought fitting for such an equipage. Within minutes of meeting Wigmore, he realised the man belonged to the same school of thought as his old nanny, and irrespective of anything else, the old retainer would do things his own way – or rather, Lord Cardington's way.

As they set off down the long drive, Joshua checked his timepiece to calculate how long the journey would take.

"Wigmore," he said, politely. "How far away is Lichfield?"

"Oh, let me think," the man said, suiting the word to the deed. "It must be all of fifteen to twenty miles, give or take a mile or two."

"How long will it take us to get there?" At the present rate, Joshua could imagine them stopping for the night along the road.

"We'll get there when we get there, young sir," Wigmore said, in a patronising tone.

Joshua lapsed into exasperated silence, and then, to relieve the tedium, looked over the hedges of the enclosures. Within minutes, his eyelids drooped and he was wishing Lord Cardington had not sent the Linmore coachman home. He would not have been half so bored with people he knew. Then he started to watch the trained hands of the groom holding the reins and for a time, subconsciously mimicked the action.

"Wigmore," he said, "have you always worked for Lord Cardington?"

"Indeed I have, young sir. I grew up on the Rushmore estate and was lucky enough to get a job when I left school. A better place I couldn't hope to find." Wigmore's loyalty to his master was unshakable.

That much was apparent in the number of stops made to water the horses. Although the groom politely enquired if Joshua needed sustenance, it was obvious that his first consideration was for Lord Cardington's horses.

Having accepted a tankard of ale with a crust of bread and cheese, Joshua wondered how he would fare travelling on his own. Intent on refreshing his memory of his travelling schedule, he opened his pocket book and to his chagrin, realised the list of instructions prepared by his father's secretary was missing. A search through his pockets brought the same result. Where was it? Most likely he would find it in his valise when he reached Lichfield.

Joshua knew that one part of the missing papers itemised the towns and hostelries where he would stay overnight, with payment guaranteed. The next was a neatly written letter, requesting whomsoever it concerned, to provide Mr Joshua Norbery with whatever assistance he required during his stay.

He distinctly remembered reading it to Aunt Jane in the coach from Linmore, and had memorised the names of the towns.

Lichfield, the first on the list was a few miles off Watling Street, an old Roman road. Market Harborough was next, then Peterborough, Wisbech and Kings Lynn. Reassured by this, Joshua decided that the loss of the paper was not a disaster. He did not need anyone to find him accommodation. He could ask if a room was booked in his name. Payment was not a problem either, for his pocket book was literally stuffed with bank notes, and Aunt Jane had given him an extra ten guineas for emergencies. What could possibly go wrong?

CHAPTER 27

A church clock struck three times as they turned into the stable yard of the Red Lion Inn on the outskirts of Lichfield. Wigmore hailed an ostler, and exchanged a greeting, while Joshua jumped down from the chaise and stretched before approaching the front of the half-timbered building.

He pushed open the solid oak door, and stepped from bright sunlight into a dark interior with low oak beams. A log fire burned in an inglenook fireplace, making the atmosphere seem unbearably close. Somewhere in the background, he heard the publican speaking to another customer.

"I'm sorry, sir, I have to keep my best room for a member of the nobility, but I can offer you the second best at a reduction."

"If I take it, I want my dinner free as well," said the man.

"I'm afraid not, sir. It's the room or the meal, not both."

After a grumbling hesitation, the person agreed.

Joshua looked around the room and found himself under the scrutiny of a sharp-featured woman, dressed in a frilled cap and black bombazine, whom he presumed to be the innkeeper's wife.

"Yes, sir, and what can I do for you?" Her blunt tone was the first indication to challenge his belief in a warm welcome.

"My name is Norbery. I understand a room has been reserved for me." Joshua quietly stated the fact, convinced his word was sufficient to prove his credentials. It worked in foreign embassies, so he anticipated no problems here. The woman glanced in the direction of her husband, and then peered doubtfully from the reception book, back to Joshua.

"I'm sorry, sir," she said. "We have no reservation in that name."

"Are you sure?" he said, but it never occurred to him to advertise his family connection with Rushmore Hall.

He could see his question flustered the woman, but she was unyielding. "We are definitely not expecting anyone by the name of Norbery, sir."

Rather than make a scene by challenging her dictate, Joshua thanked the woman, and went back to the chaise. An ostler was attending the horses and the groom stood ready to take the corded travelling trunk inside the hostelry.

As he approached, Wigmore said, "Is there a problem, Mr Norbery?"

"There must have been a mistake with the booking. They haven't got a room for me." Without the letter of confirmation, Joshua was at a loss to know what to do.

"No room," said Wigmore, "when Lord Cardington asked for one? You let me go in and talk to them. I will sort this out."

Under normal circumstances, the groom's outrage might have been amusing, but Joshua was in no mood to compromise further.

"No, Wigmore," he said, in a decided tone. "We will go somewhere else. Where do you suggest we look first?"

A lifetime of obedience forced the groom to comply, but he was not happy, and his state of agitation increased when the next two hostelries returned the same negative answer. At the third, a tiny wayside inn, all but hidden away amongst the trees at the side of the main road, Joshua acquired a bed for the night, and meagre stable accommodation for the horses, but he could see from Wigmore's look of disgust what he thought of the conditions.

By the time the groom made things tidy to his satisfaction, and their evening meal, such as it was, was ready to eat, Wigmore had recovered his power of speech, sufficiently to catalogue the deficiencies of the half-witted lad acting as ostler. Every other sentence started with, "Lord Cardington wouldn't approve…"

Eventually, Joshua's patience snapped.

"For goodness sake, Wigmore, stop moaning," he said. "I don't like the situation any better than you do, but it's only for one night. Tomorrow, you can take Lord Cardington's precious horses back to Rushmore."

Immediately contrite, the groom said, "I'm ever so sorry, Mr Joshua, but those horses mean more than anything to me. Oh dear, I knew I should have gone to see my sister at the Red Lion, and made her understand about the room. Then we would have had some decent food and accommodation."

Joshua could not believe what he was hearing.

"Wigmore…" he growled. "Are you saying that your sister was the landlady at the Red Lion? Why did you not tell me when we were there?" He should not blame the man. If he had looked more closely at the miserable-looking woman, he might have recognised the family likeness. It was plain to see.

"Is it too late to go back again, sir?" Wigmore half pleaded.

Perversely, Joshua refused to consider the option. He had paid for a bed, and intended to use it. All he wanted was to sleep, but the colony of fleas occupying his mattress, and the cacophony of snoring emitted by Wigmore in the next room, ensured he did no more than close his eyes – and scratch.

Apart from the company, he could have been back in Greece. As he listened to the noise, Joshua thought how he and Charlie would have laughed, then sadly realised such companionship was at an end. How he wished they could have talked and resolved their differences – and more than anything, he yearned for Sergeant Percival's presence to sort out the difficulties.

Eventually, with little hope of sleeping, he got up and dressed, then huddled in a rickety armchair waiting for the dawn. At some point he must have dozed, for he awoke moderately refreshed, and took a breakfast that hardly warranted the name.

By nine o'clock, he was standing outside the inn with the Rushmore groom, watching the stagecoach approach. So relieved they would have a successful conclusion to their association, he had bestowed a handsome largesse for the groom's services. Wigmore, seemingly eager to be on his way, was prepared to risk life and limb in his haste to stop the oncoming vehicle.

Stepping into the roadway, the groom frantically waved his arms, but to no avail. Passengers on the roof waved and shouted warnings, as the stagecoach trundled past them, gathering speed down the slope until it disappeared around the corner at the bottom of the hill.

Joshua looked at the groom in disbelief, and then turned towards the handyman-cum-ostler, who lounged against the inn doorway.

"I told him last night, the stagecoaches don't stop here," the man said with a nod in Wigmore's direction, which the groom ignored. "It's not on their list."

From that, Joshua deduced that he meant the company schedule.

Angered by the groom's duplicity, he stalked back to the Rushmore chaise, and Wigmore followed, looking suspiciously cheerful.

"I'll take you back to Lichfield now, to wait for the next coach, sir," he said with almost a smirk. "I'll make sure there's no trouble with the room this time."

From the thinly veiled insolence, it was obvious the man was testing Joshua's authority. His father's air of command was instinctive, but it was something he had yet to acquire.

"No, Wigmore," he said, with a touch of hauteur. "Lord Cardington would expect you to take me to Market Harborough. If you do not wish to do that, I will drive the chaise myself. Alternatively, we can return to Rushmore, to consult his lordship…"

Red faced with outrage at the thought of anyone driving his precious horses, the groom opened his mouth to protest, and then as the significance of the threat dawned, closed his lips, and replaced Joshua's baggage in the chaise.

Having made his point, Joshua climbed into the passenger seat. He did not intend any such thing, but guessed that if Wigmore believed the possibility, he would behave. Secretly, he wished they had returned to Lichfield last night, but it would achieve nothing now.

"Where do you wish to go, sir?" Formality ruled again. Wigmore had regained his composure.

"Onwards, Wigmore, to the next picking-up point on the sacred coaching schedule. Tomorrow, when I am on the stagecoach, you may return to Rushmore and tell his lordship that all is well."

The journey continued in silence, at a tediously slow pace. After travelling a distance of about fifteen miles, he felt obliged to stand the expense when Wigmore pleaded the need to stable Lord Cardington's horses, and listened to the groom's niggling complaints about the poor quality of replacement horses all the way to Market Harborough.

At the first hostelry Joshua entered, it became apparent that Lord Cardington's well-meaning interference in changing his travelling plans had lost him the room booked for his use on the previous night, and he suspected that it would be the same when he reached Peterborough.

His second enquiry also drew a blank, so he sent Wigmore to ask at another inn further down the street, and was relieved when he saw the groom's sour expression lighting up to almost a smile. By the end of the evening, the groom had lapsed into a fretful state of uselessness, worrying about the care given to Lord Cardington's absent horses.

Joshua lay in bed, grumbling to himself, and hoping things would improve. Their meagre supper tasted better than it looked, but from the musty smell in the room, it was weeks since anyone changed the bedlinen. He could not even open a window to clear the air. It was nailed shut. Morning could not come too soon.

When the grey day dawned, Joshua was already dressed, awaiting his breakfast. Wigmore went to the stables to inspect the Rushmore chaise, and returned looking pleased.

"I've taken the liberty of ordering horses for the chaise, sir, and if it is all right with you, then I'll be on my way as soon as the stagecoach arrives."

"How much will it cost?" Joshua said, reaching for his purse.

Wigmore's response rendered him speechless, for the second time in three days. "That's all right, sir," the man said. "His lordship always gives me money when I go out, in case of emergencies. I have plenty for the return journey."

Despite having paid to ride inside the coach, Joshua decided in a fit of chivalry, to give his seat to an elderly woman, and took his place on top by the driver and guard. From there, he gave a cheery wave to Wigmore as the transport set off along the road. He guessed the man would return to Lichfield, to apprise his sister of her error – but how would he explain to Lord Cardington?

For a time, he enjoyed sitting in the fresh air, watching the rolling Leicestershire landscape unfold. All too soon, the novelty of clutching the rail and being jolted from side to side wore off, and he thought longingly of the well-sprung chaise and four of his earlier journey. Even Wigmore's company would be better than the strange sense of isolation that gripped him amongst strangers.

The first stop to change horses came as a relief, and Joshua watched the process with interest, but within ten minutes the coach was gathering speed again. Then the wind changed, bringing rain. Slow at first, and light, then with increasing severity. Within half an hour, his shoulder capes were drenched, and water dripped miserably off the brim of his hat.

As if the weather was not enough to contend with, during the afternoon, one of the leading horses cast a shoe when they were two stops away from Peterborough, and the driver needed to seek a farrier. By then, the effort of sitting upright made Joshua long for a cushion, and he descended outside an unknown village inn with the gait of a man forty years older.

267

The rain had ceased by the time he re-emerged, but the afternoon light was fading. As he prepared to climb back onto the box, the driver informed him that the old woman had left the coach, so he was able to regain the relative comfort of his rightful seat and doze until the vehicle reached its destination.

The following day was another one of heavy skies and pouring rain. Joshua was thankful that he was inside the coach, and pitied the poor souls sitting on the roof that bore the brunt of the weather. Compared to them, his discomforts were insignificant. Arriving late in Peterborough the previous evening, he learned that a lone traveller had to share with a stranger, or pay extra in advance for a single room. He chose the latter, and was grateful for somewhere to lay his weary head.

It was little more than a box room, set at the back of the inn overlooking the stables. After eating his evening meal, Joshua lay fully clothed on the truckle bed, and closed his eyes, meaning to undress later. Several times during the night, the sounds of coaches entering the stable yard disturbed him, with drivers calling to ostlers for a change of horses, and then sleep claimed him again.

He awoke with a start, feeling dishevelled when the early call came to rise for breakfast. Removing his crumpled coat and neckcloth, he made shift to wash his face and shave using the hot water the servant brought, but his dusty boots remained unpolished. Halfway down the stairs, he remembered hiding his wallet under the mattress, and dashed back to retrieve it.

Beyond Peterborough, the coach entered the Fenlands, a vast area of low lying marshland with a desolate aspect that added to the tedium of travelling at a pace that was, of necessity, slower than the previous day, for fear of running off the road. Joshua was indebted to a scholarly man with a passion for history, sitting in the corner seat opposite, who enlightened his ignorance about the surrounding district.

Listening to the man's well-modulated voice, he crossed the centuries, hearing of the Roman-built causeway on which the road ran, and the massive drainage works undertaken by a Dutch engineer, whom the Duke of Bedford employed on his Peterborough estate in the seventeenth century.

The drainage works project was interrupted by the Civil War, between the Royalists and Parliamentarians, and resumed when it was over. Finally, he learned that the Lord Protector of England, Oliver Cromwell, was born at Huntingdon, a few miles to the south. Joshua listened with interest, but after an hour, his eyelids became increasingly heavy, until lulled to sleep, he didn't notice the coach stop to change horses at Wisbech. When he awoke a few miles beyond, the man had gone, but the coach rolled on, seemingly forever.

After that, he had little to do but look around him, and observe his fellow passengers. Whilst he realised that most people, of necessity, travelled this way; some without consideration lit up a pipe and filled the coach with smoke, or took furtive swigs from hip flasks, and became argumentative. Others coughed, wheezed and belched incessantly. Women travelling alone, or those with young children, were particularly vulnerable.

Waking from a doze, Joshua turned his head and saw a young mother in the next seat, suckling a babe in arms under the enveloping cover of a shawl, whilst another weary little soul stood clutching her knee. Looking away, he met the disapproving stare of a prim-looking female sitting opposite; though whether she was chastising him, or the woman, he did not know. Rather than argue the point, he closed his eyes again, and let his thoughts drift back to Lichfield.

There had been no trace of his father's booking at the Red Lion – only one from a member of the nobility. Recalling the Rushmore groom's dog-like demeanour, he wondered if the request had come from Lord Cardington; and had he, in thwarting Wigmore's determination to obey his master, made his journey unnecessarily complicated. He would have to write to Aunt Jane, expressing his thanks for the servant's efforts.

For the rest of the time, Joshua divided his thoughts between listening to the conversations going on around him, and worrying about making his money last. So far, he had managed to strike a balance between being too open-handed and miserly with his tips to people who gave good service, but he must be careful until he reached Holkham. Once there, he hoped that Mr Coke would act as his banker and cash any drafts on his father's bank.

By the time the coach reached Kings Lynn, he felt so weary, he would happily have slept in a barn, but when the coach stopped outside the largest hotel, he learned to his delight a room had been booked for the young man travelling to Holkham Hall, and that a coach would collect him the following day.

For the first time in almost a week, Joshua enjoyed the luxury of dining at an individual table, and sleeping in superior accommodation, undisturbed by any of the irritations encountered along the way.

CHAPTER 28

Refreshed by his night's sleep, Joshua savoured his breakfast and set off to walk the half mile to the sea front. It was exhilarating, feeling the sea breezes blow away the tedium of travelling. The near-cloudless sky, reflected in a palette of aquamarine, triggered memories of other seascapes, but they were long gone, and there was no time for regrets. Today, everything began again.

The harbour was a hive of activity, with all kinds of boats at anchor – fishing, sailing and whaling – and many strange smells he could not identify. If only there was more time to explore, but he had to return to the hotel before the transport from Holkham arrived. He made it, with half an hour to spare.

The driver of the gig was a young man of about his age, with tawny hair and a shy smile. Joshua took to him on sight.

"Good morning, Mr Norbery," the groom said respectfully, "Ben Waters at your service. I've come to take you to Holkham Hall."

The formality made him laugh. "I prefer to be called Joshua."

With the introductions over, and his baggage stowed, the gig set off through the town traffic at a dawdling pace, but when they reached the coast road, Ben spoke again.

"Sorry to be slow, Joshua; I'm not used to driving in so much traffic where I come from, but it will be all right now we are out of the town."

As the pace quickened, the two young men exchanged information about their origins. Joshua told the groom about his home in Shropshire, and Ben admitted he had never been out of Norfolk.

"I was born on the Holkham estate, and have always worked there, like the rest of my family. I would not want to work for anyone but Mr Coke. Have you heard about the wonderful things he's done for farming?"

"That is what I am here to learn about," Joshua said.

"You couldn't learn from a better man," Ben told him. "Mind you, Mr Blakeney the land agent is the one who implements Mr Coke's ideas."

271

"What is he like?"

"A bit strict, but he's all right. He came down from Scotland a good many years ago, and stayed here after he married my mother's sister. I expect you will meet him tomorrow morning."

The areas of flat land and scrub vegetation along the coast road made Joshua nostalgic for the lush green Shropshire hill country where he lived, and the neat dwellings of brick and flint looked quaintly different to the limestone cottages near Linmore.

After a few miles, the groom halted the vehicle beside a water trough next to an inn. "I usually stop here to water the horses, and get a drink for myself. I hope it's all right with you?"

They were both ready to stretch their legs, and sit outside the inn with a tankard of ale to wash down a crust of bread and cheese. Joshua leaned back on the wooden bench and took a deep breath.

"I can almost smell the sea. Where is it?"

Ben laughed, and pointed to the far side of the inn.

"The salt marshes are out there beyond the stone wall. Go and have a look if you want to, but the tide will be out for a while yet."

The sight that met Joshua's gaze was vastly different to his recollections from his Mediterranean travels. Beyond the sea defences there was a coarse meadow, which gradually merged into an expanse of tufted greens and browns until he could see a line of sand in the distance.

"Where's the water gone?"

"I told you, the tide is out, but by the time we get to Holkham, it will be back almost up to the level of the dunes."

Ben hesitated before resuming the journey. "There's something I'd better tell you, Joshua, just so you don't ask. Mr Coke's wife passed away a year this summer. Lovely lady she was." He turned aside as his voice muffled. Then he sniffed and blew his nose. "Right, we'd better be on our way."

The afternoon shadows were lengthening by the time the gig turned up the long drive to Holkham Hall. Joshua could not remember where the spare landscape had changed, but everywhere he looked now, he saw a proliferation of trees.

Ahead of them, a herd of deer raced away across the rolling acres of landscaped parkland, and gradually, around a bend in the drive a Palladian mansion came into view. The ochre-coloured edifice glowed in the sunlight. Spartan in its simplicity, it was magnificent.

Seeing it, Joshua felt a wave of nostalgia for the time he spent in Italy with Charlie…and Lady Rosie. The one friendship was in the past, and only time would tell if the second survived, and deepened into anything stronger.

Rather than brooding, he recalled the story that Ben Waters told him, about how the first Earl of Leicester built Holkham Hall, to house the vast collection of art treasures and statues acquired during his extended Grand Tour of Italy.

During the thirty years it took to complete, the earl and his only son died, so his widow, the Dowager Countess, completed the project. The title lapsed when the earl's nephew inherited the estate, and when he died, his son, the present owner, carried on the work.

That evening, Joshua dined with Mr Robertson, the steward, and learned that Mr Coke was in London, attending his political duties. They talked of many things, but he was so tired, he could not remember a single topic.

He rose early, feeling refreshed, and took a walk along the side of the lake. On his way back, he lost his way and arrived late for breakfast, a matter highlighted when the steward outlined the strict protocol of the house, and informed him of the meeting arranged with the agent, Mr Blakeney, at ten o'clock.

Joshua approached the meeting with trepidation. By his late arrival at breakfast, he had already broken the rules pertaining to timekeeping, and hoped to avoid any further lapses.

When he entered the agent's office, a dark-haired man of medium height and spare frame rose from behind the oak desk to meet him.

"Good morning, Mr Norbery," James Blakeney said, his soft burr emphasising the sounds. "I trust you slept well."

Joshua grinned. "Yes, thank you, sir. I went for a walk in the park and lost track of time. I'm afraid I was a bit late for breakfast."

"So I heard," the voice cut in dryly. "There is one thing to remember whilst you are at Holkham. An estate does not run itself, and there are certain rules, which have to be complied with."

A sweep of his hand indicated a large framed inscription on the wall behind his desk, which bore the inscription "The House Rules", in copperplate writing.

"Learn them well, Mr Norbery, and you will not go far wrong."

There was no time for Joshua to give them more than a cursory glance before the agent moved on to other things.

"This morning, I would like to outline your training schedule for the next year. It may sound complicated at first, but when you understand the routine it is quite straightforward."

"Yes, sir," said Joshua, hoping he was right.

"Sit down, and I'll explain," the agent said, indicating a wooden chair on the opposite side of the desk. Then he pointed to a board on the adjacent wall, covered by charts. "It's easier to show you than fill your head with a lot of words you will forget as soon as you leave the office."

Joshua nodded and waited for the first instruction.

"In brief, I divide each half-year into four sections of six weeks, representing estate management, crop rotation, animal husbandry and forestry, the latter including woodland management and game-keeping. You will undertake the first rotation to learn the basics, and the second to consolidate what you have learned. Is that clear?"

"Um… yes, I think so, sir." In truth, he was confused. The agent's enthusiasm for the subject made him feel as if he were back in the classroom. Joshua doubted if anyone would flog him if he failed to learn, but he knew his father expected results.

"If there is time at the end, you will have the opportunity to spend a week or two on one of the best farms on the estate. Egmere, which is tenanted by Mr Danby, is a fine example of what can be achieved with good management."

After a further hour of talking, Mr Blakeney removed his spectacles and placed them in a case on the desk. "That's enough paperwork for now," he said. "After luncheon, I'll show you some of the estate."

At the mention of food, Joshua's early breakfast seemed a long way away, and he felt quite light-headed. He was in need of a break, for his mind was reeling with the enormity of what he had undertaken.

He waited whilst the agent locked the estate office door, and followed him across a courtyard to the servants' entrance to the Hall. Once indoors, they made their way to a room adjoining the servants' hall, where a table set with four placements of cutlery awaited them.

The agent took his place at the head of the table, and waved Joshua to the chair on his right-hand side.

"I take my meals here during the daytime," he said, "and it is where you will dine with the other students. On the occasions when you work different hours you need to speak with the kitchen staff and they will provide for your needs."

The tantalising aroma of meat roasting in the kitchen caught Joshua's attention. His mouth watered in anticipation of the treat, but when he sat down to eat, he found the luncheon consisted of a cold collation of generously sliced ham from the bone, a platter of fresh bread, creamy butter, cheese and pickles, with a tankard of ale. It was plain food, but it was welcome and remarkably satisfying.

The agent waited until they cleared their plates before speaking again.

"There are a couple of points I intended to mention. Your daily hours of work are from seven o'clock in the morning, until six at night, and on Saturday morning, you finish at midday. The rest of the day is your own, as is Sunday. You will, of course, attend matins, and afterwards, Mrs Blakeney is most insistent you join us with your colleagues for luncheon."

Joshua noted the details and said, "Thank you, sir."

"The second matter is with regard to your personal finances. Your father has provided Mr Coke with money drafts to be cashed in your favour. Mr Robertson, the steward, deals with that, and his usual arrangement is to issue sufficient funds for a calendar month. In the unlikely event you outrun the constable; you may apply to me for an advance on the next month's monies. I will then put your case to him."

That was a relief. Joshua had wondered how he would replenish his depleted supply of funds. The agent then cleared his throat.

"I trust I do not have to warn you about fraternising with any females on the estate, or in the locality, Mr Norbery."

"Absolutely not, sir," Joshua was vehement in his denials. The encounter with Sophie Cobarne ensured that.

"Good," said the agent. "Mr Coke will be glad to hear of your assurance."

Joshua wondered how much the agent knew of his reasons for coming to Holkham. He was here to work.

They walked to the agent's gig, parked outside the estate office, and set off at a steady pace down the front drive with the Hall on their left, and the lake opposite. Joshua had seen this view on his early morning walk, but it was unfamiliar then.

As they passed a right-hand fork in the road, Mr Blakeney pointed to a building beyond the lake. "You will need a horse to ride, so we will come upon the stable block another way."

He drove on, indicating a single-storey, thatched building on a grassy slope. "The ice-house is apparently the only remaining part of the original landscape at Holkham."

One glance and a nod was enough for Joshua. He could not speak. The memory of another such cold place haunted him. Luckily, the agent drove the gig up the slope to the obelisk. From there, they looked back down the drive at Holkham's finest view of the Hall.

It was breathtakingly beautiful, and the perfect setting for the simplistic lines of a Palladio design. Again the sight brought back memories of similar structures in Italy, and was one view Joshua vowed to look at many times.

"If you look to the right, the next time you come up the slope," said the agent, indicating the direction with a sweep of his hand, "there is a temple in the trees. It was one of the first structures built, along with the obelisk."

They moved on at a brisk pace over the rise and down the slope, before turning off the main drive along a track towards a large building, built in the same local ochre brick as the Hall. The agent stopped the gig in front of the big wooden doors and stepped down. Joshua followed.

"This is the Great Barn," he said, "one of the improvements Mr Coke made when he inherited the estate. It is where we hold the Holkham sheep-shearings, but I will tell you more on the subject later. I want you to meet two young men who began their studies last autumn."

It was a brief meeting, but sufficient for Joshua, standing a head and shoulders taller, to note that the two lads were of a similar age to him. Jack Syderstone was of medium height, dark haired and taciturn, with a weathered complexion; whereas Harry Bircham was shorter and more outgoing, with sandy hair and fair skin, which caught the sun.

The agent was anxious to be on the move, and in minutes the gig re-joined the main drive and passed through the arched structure at the south lodge. From there, they travelled along a country road towards the farmhouse where the agent lived, before returning along the estate road past the walled garden to the stable block.

Once there, they descended from the gig to meet the head groom who promised to find Joshua a suitable horse for the following morning. With the matter arranged, he expected Mr Blakeney to climb back into the gig. Instead, he followed as the agent entered the stable block through a side door, and ascended a staircase to the upper floor. "This is where you will sleep and live," he said.

The door at the end of the corridor opened into a communal sitting room with a wooden table and three chairs. There were three bedroom doors beyond, and a fourth revealed shared washing facilities. To Joshua's unpractised eye, his allocated room seemed to be of monastic proportions – neat and tidy, with basic contents, sufficient for his needs.

It contained a narrow bed, on which a feather pillow in striped ticking reposed on top of a pile of clean linen, awaiting the making of the bed. To the one side, there was a candlestick on a small table; a screened hanging rail for coats in an alcove, with ample shelving for clothes, and storage underneath for boots. Seeing his travelling trunks beside the bed, he guessed the groom must have placed them there, and made a note to thank the man.

"Come, Mr Norbery, we have more work to do." The agent walked down the stairs, leaving Joshua to follow. It was only four o'clock. He might be tired but the working day was not finished.

By the time Joshua had shared the students' evening meal, and walked back with them from the Hall to the stable block, he knew that Harry lived on an estate near Bedford, and Jack was the son of a Staffordshire tenant farmer.

Anticipating a task he had never attempted before, he entered his room and found to his surprise and relief that some kind soul had made his bed – no doubt at Mr Blakeney's behest. Similarly, his coats hung on the rail, with piles of shirts, neck cloths, and underwear on shelves, and his polished boots beneath.

He recalled the House Rules as his head touched the pillow, and determined to write them down at the earliest opportunity. He was still thinking about it a week later when he joined the two other students to dine with Mr Coke.

Although Joshua had not mentioned his father's political connection with their host, it was apparent from the warm welcome he received from Mr Coke that they were acquainted. It seemed the gentleman knew a great deal about him – far more than he had imagined.

Mr Coke was a tall man, of equal height to Joshua, and quietly spoken, but his presence filled the room. He was the father of three daughters, and Elizabeth, the youngest, at six years old, was his favourite. His eldest daughter, a widow, spent much of her time at Holkham, acting hostess for her father, since her mother's death the previous year.

For such a grand house the food was plainly cooked, but well presented. A succulent joint of beef sirloin, tender squabs roasted on the spit, with half a dozen root vegetable side dishes, followed by a large fruit tart, an assortment of cream jellies, and a selection of local cheeses.

The talk during dinner was of a general nature, but when the meal was complete, the ladies left the room. The servants placed decanters of port and brandy on the table, but to Joshua's surprise, they added three tankards and a jug of ale, and withdrew. He waited to see what the other lads did, and then filled his tankard with the local brew. For students, this was clearly the thing to do.

While the agent and steward sipped their port, Mr Coke took the opportunity to talk to his students. When the other lads nodded agreement, Joshua sensed it was for his benefit. They had obviously heard it before.

"I don't know how much you know about agriculture, Joshua, but I was deplorably ignorant about the subject when I inherited this estate." Mr Coke took a sip from the glass in his right hand, and then continued.

"When one of my tenants told me he couldn't make his farm pay, I decided, with the optimism of youth, to take over the management for myself. In so doing, I sought advice from knowledgeable people in the district, and anyone in the country who was willing to share their expertise. Every year since, we have held gatherings at Holkham at the time of the sheep-shearing. It is only by the exchange of ideas that agriculture improves, so you have come at the right time. The next meeting in July is probably our twenty-fifth, and nowadays we have visitors coming from all over the world."

That explained Mr Blakeney's reference to the Holkham sheep-shearings. It meant a quarter of a century of sharing knowledge on agriculture. No wonder Mr Coke was an acknowledged expert.

Afterwards, Mr Coke took the students on a tour of the house. The magnificent marble staircase, alabaster pillars and the splendidly ornate roof of the entrance hall evoked memories for Joshua of similar examples in Rome.

The statues in the long gallery reminded him of the time he watched Greek artisans making similar casts for English travellers to bring home.

He stopped short on seeing the name Batoni adorning the portrait of a tall, handsome young man in masquerade costume. Yes, the goddess was there in the background, as Lady Kenchester said was the artist's practice.

Mr Coke noticed his hesitation. "Do you know the artist?"

"Yes, sir, I heard his name mentioned when I was in Italy."

"Your father told me that you spent some time there, but you went further afield, I think."

"Yes, sir, to Greece and Macedonia." Joshua's nose wrinkled as he recalled the time he spent in the mountain village.

"I think you travelled with… a cousin, wasn't it?"

He nodded, not knowing what else to do.

"That is obviously the young man who has joined the army; which was why your father said you needed occupation, and why you are here."

Joshua nodded again. How strange that other people knew more about Charlie's whereabouts than he did.

CHAPTER 29

Two months after Joshua left Linmore, his father received an urgent message from his sister, which demanded an immediate response. On arrival at her Cavendish Square home in London, Tom was ushered into her private sitting room, and saw Winifred prostrated on a chaise longue, her vinaigrette in one hand. It was unprecedented for her to show emotion, but his formidable sister, who could face down an ogre and walk away unscathed, was close to tears. Not since she was a girl had he seen her so upset.

"Thank God, you have come, Tom," she said. "I am at my wits' end, trying to decide what to do about Jane's wretched niece. I cannot take her anywhere without her ogling men. I never know what she will do next."

It was amazing how quickly Winifred disowned Sophie when she caused trouble. "Come, Winifred," he said, in a brisk tone. "It can't be that bad."

"You are wrong, Tom. It is worse. Sophie opposes me in everything," she said, twisting the fringe on the Norwich silk shawl draped around her shoulders. "I told her a girl of her age should have a care for her reputation, and yet when we drive in the park, she encourages every rake, reprobate and rattle in uniform to stop by our carriage. She even waved to that dreadful courtesan, Harriet Wilson, and had the temerity to laugh when I reproved her. I thanked God there were so few people in town to see it."

Rather than interrupt, Tom let Winifred ramble on, releasing her thoughts.

"One must be thankful we are not in the season. It would be impossible to acquire vouchers for Almack's," she said, warming to her theme. "I dare not think of taking her to Brighton for the summer, for fear she attracts the attention of one of Farmer George's sons. They would be bound to notice her, which would be ruinous."

He too was aware of the consequences of that connection.

"Mistake me not, Tom. She has the soul of a courtesan. Our only hope is to get her married, very soon; otherwise, she will join the demi-monde. She will disgrace herself, and bring us down with her – and that, I will not allow."

"What about Charlie? Does he know of this?"

"I doubt he would believe it of her, Tom," she said, her expression softening. "He is a delightful boy. I only wish that my sons were so charming, but have to live with the fact that they are not," she ended on a sour note.

"Has he settled into his regiment?" he said, wanting to change the subject.

"Yes." She sounded comfortable imparting the news. "He often visits his sister, and tells us that he is enjoying his officer training. I try to see that he receives invitations to informal gatherings, outside the family, and have good reports from friends of his reception. I wish I could do more, but he is very protective of Sophie, and I am sure he thinks we are punishing her."

"That makes the situation more difficult, Winifred. How can we find a husband for Sophie, one who will be acceptable to her brother? Particularly as most people have left the capital for the summer."

Winifred veered off the subject.

"It would be so much easier if Augustus was married," she said. "I could have handed the wretched girl to his wife to add a touch of respectability – show her how to behave. It was a pity about Lady Rosemary. I always thought she would have had a stabilizing effect on him."

"Lady Rosemary?" he said, grappling with her change of direction.

"Surely you remember? She's Lord Kenchester's eldest daughter – a delightful girl, if a trifle eccentric. She spends most of her time with the Dowager Countess, her grandmother. Apparently, they returned from a trip to India a few months ago, and promptly went off to stay with a cousin who breeds horses in Ireland, to recover from the ordeal. The last I heard, they were still there."

Tom nodded agreement, but his mind was on other things.

"Where would you suggest we look to find Sophie a husband?"

Winifred had obviously given the matter considerable thought.

"We have to be realistic in our expectations. It is no good thinking Sophie will attract a man of breeding, in need of a wife. She has no background, apart from Linmore, and her recent behaviour has tarnished her reputation. The best we can hope for is to find someone in trade. No, Tom," she said, when he would have demurred. "Don't discount the option too quickly. There are some quite respectable people nowadays, who are remarkably well heeled."

Accepting the fact, he said, "Do you have anyone suitable in mind?"

"It is hard to judge a person's suitability when you meet them socially. Pontesbury's banker is a widower, who is looking to remarry. His only son and heir died at about the same time as Matthew. He lives in London, but has a small country estate a few miles from Linmore."

"What age is he?"

"He's probably no more than five years older than you, and is an extremely wealthy man."

That made him just over fifty. Tom was hoping for someone younger.

"Money is not the only consideration, Winifred."

"No, but if what you told me about the situation with Joshua was true, and I have no doubt it was, then this man is our only option. His age is not ideal, but with the present crisis…"

"Are you sure this is the best we can do?"

"In the available time, yes, and time is something we do not have. If Sophie were like her brother, we would have no problems."

"That is my concern, Winifred. We must be very careful in how we proceed with this. Despite his love of Linmore, Charlie forced himself to leave, because he could not believe ill of Sophie. He considers it his duty to care for her, and if she marries an older man, he will blame me."

Tom knew he could not avoid making a decision; and irrespective of what Charlie thought, he would have to live with the outcome.

"Very well, I'll leave it to you," he said. "Obviously, I would like to meet the man, and I'd better see Sophie as well."

"I need a few days to make arrangements, but if I invite a few friends and some of Pontesbury's associates to dinner, let us say Wednesday or Thursday of next week, and include Edward Teale in the numbers. You can meet him socially and decide whether you think him a suitable candidate. If so, we will proceed from there. Charlie must come as well, for I think he will accept it better if he meets the man at the same time as does Sophie."

Now she was calm, Winifred was back in control.

"It appears you have thought of everything, but then you always were good at organising things, Winifred."

"It's not settled yet, Tom," she said in her blunt way, "but she'd be a fool to refuse him. He is older than I would wish for a girl of her age, but she will not do any better. With his financial situation, she will be extremely well looked after, and he won't expect a dowry, which is a consideration, because I expect she has nothing."

Tom shook his head, feeling weary. "There was nothing left when her father died. Apparently, he left considerable debts, which his brother cleared, using his own money. By all accounts, Fergus never did understand finance, and he went to pieces when Charlotte died."

All they needed was to gain Sophie's cooperation.

Tom was dreading the meeting with Sophie, but could not avoid it. The Cavendish Square library was an ideal situation. It was quiet, and today felt unusually warm, but he put the latter down to his anxiety. A lot hinged on how he handled a delicate matter, and with Sophie, there was no telling.

She was already late, no doubt, because Winifred planned for her to be here by two o'clock. It was now twenty past the hour. He would give her ten more minutes. If she failed to come, he would go to his club. In the meantime, he stared at the bookshelves. Row upon row of leather-bound books, most of which had never been opened. Winifred's family were not a studious lot.

He turned as the door opened behind him and Sophie entered the room.

"Aunt Winifred said you wanted to speak to me, Uncle Tom," she said in a sulky voice. "I expect you will scold me, just as she does."

"No," he said. "I'm not going to scold. I simply wondered what we were going to do with you, for I'm dashed if I know."

She stood before him with the same pugnacious expression as when he first saw her. Wooden… wary… and waiting…

"I told Aunt Winifred that I wanted to follow the drum with Charlie," she said.

So this was what the battle was all about. Tom guessed that his sister's outraged response was the cause of Sophie's determination to force the issue. He waved her towards a leather armchair, but she doggedly remained standing, leaving him no choice but to do likewise. As he waited for her to speak, a gamut of emotions flitted across her face, highlighting her uncertainty.

"What do you think I should do, Uncle Tom?" she said in a quiet voice.

"I can't answer that, Sophie," he said. "When I met you and Charlie in Blackrock, I judged your uncle harshly for failing you. Now, I am standing in similar shoes, waiting for Charlie to judge me accordingly."

At his words, all signs of defiance crumbled.

"No, it's not true," she said, shaking her head. "I would never let him criticise you, Uncle Tom."

He held out a conciliatory hand and waited for her response, but Sophie stared unseeingly at the floor, her lips tightly compressed. When she finally spoke her voice was strangely gruff. "How… is Ed Salter?"

Tom looked at her, surprised, wondering why she had chosen this moment to ask. "He's recovering," he said, noting relief in her expression, "but he'll be scarred for life."

"I'm sorry about that," she said. "He's a good man."

Tom thought that was the moment when Sophie realised that she had gone her length and there was nowhere else to go. Her next words confirmed it.

"I won't plague Aunt Winifred any more," she said. "Not if it reflects on you."

He felt touched by her response. It was the nearest thing to an apology he would receive, but he was content knowing that she wouldn't deliberately step outside the accepted standard of behaviour and cause him embarrassment. For the moment, it was the best he could expect.

"Thank you," he said. He would have loved to ask why she tormented Joshua, but their truce was too fragile to spoil. He hoped that, one day, she would tell him the truth, but would not hold his breath.

By the time the banker dined in Cavendish Square, a week later, Tom found Sophie's demeanour had undergone a remarkable change. All trace of the hoyden had disappeared, and the appearance of civility existed between her and Mrs Pontesbury. She was even amenable to his sister's suggestions on the latest fashions.

He was glad that with Sophie's commanding height and dark colouring, his sister had the sense not to dress her in pastel shades or frills and furbelows. Wearing a gown of dusky rose, she looked older than her seventeen years, and more assured than Winifred's daughter of a similar age, brought in to balance the numbers. If only they had presented the two girls at Court in the spring season, Sophie might have received an offer of marriage, and avoided this trouble.

When Tom met Edward Teale, he realised this was the man who purchased, Ravensbury Manor, a run-down property situated a few miles from Hillend village, and about which he had heard good reports of the changes made.

During the evening, he noticed Charlie with the younger members of the Pontesbury family, and thought he saw a touch of sadness – almost as if he was looking for someone with whom to share his thoughts. Knowing the camaraderie with Joshua would be hard to replace, he questioned his decision to keep them apart. At the time, with Charlie's avowed antipathy, it seemed the only option. Now, he was not sure. Maybe, they should have had the chance to make peace.

A few days after the dinner in Cavendish Square, Tom met the banker in his office to discuss a number of financial investments; and a week later, Mr Teale hosted a dinner party in his townhouse, with a select guest list that included Tom, his sister and brother-in-law, together with Sophie and Charlie.

Arriving at the house, Tom met Mr Teale's cousin, a mature woman of middle years, who acted as hostess at the dinner, and who, he learned, managed the household. The knowledge reassured him, for Sophie would need support. He only hoped she would accept it. He need not have worried for the evening passed without event.

In her elegant attire, Sophie's behaviour was so good he could almost suppose that another person stood in her shoes. Then he realised for the first time the benefits of her Bredenbridge education and wished that Jane was here to see her. No, some of it must come from staying with people with money.

"I was almost proud of Sophie last night," said Winifred, when they took breakfast the following morning.

"Indeed," said Tom, "her appearance said much for your excellent taste."

Winifred acknowledged the compliment with a smile, and then asked, "What did you say to Sophie to effect such a change in her behaviour? One cannot credit that she is the same girl. Even Pontesbury noticed the difference, and as you know he normally only sees the food on his plate."

"Sophie asked me about the injured groom who had been her friend," he said, ignoring the rest. "I told her that Salter would recover, but be permanently scarred, and she was sorry."

"Did she give any explanation?"

"No," he said, "but she was greatly moved, so I didn't press the matter."

"Nor do I relish another confrontation. Did she tell you that she wanted to follow the drum with Charlie? It's an absolutely ridiculous idea."

"Is it?" he said, a smile teasing his lips. "I can just see her on the march, impressing the generals with her riding prowess. She's better in the saddle than Charlie, you know."

"How can you be so nonsensical? Of course it is impossible."

"She probably told you that to provoke you, in the hope that you would be glad to see the back of her."

"No, she meant it, because Charlie was aware of it. When I told him it was not at all the thing, he accepted my word but she did not. Of course the foolish girl cannot do that. A wife might go with her husband or a daughter as part of the family, but it is not appropriate for sisters to travel with their brother. What would she do if, heaven forbid, Charlie were killed?"

"I don't think we need to stretch our imaginations to find an answer for that, Winifred. Sophie would find a protector."

"As she will here, without any trouble, but she needs to be protected from her own folly," Winifred shuddered at the thought and reached for her vinaigrette, which had been forgotten.

"I seem to recall another young lady who wanted to follow the drum," he said.

"That was different," she said. "I was older and wiser than Sophie, and it is unkind of you to remind me. However, it was probably a mistake for he got himself killed in that horrid American war, before we could be married. I'm sure that Pontesbury is a better husband, even if he is not very dashing."

"Less than half-a-year in age, if I recall," he said with ruthless accuracy.

"Oh, you are provoking, Tom. Was I really so young and light-hearted? One forgets as time goes by…" Winifred sighed at the recollection.

"Very dashing you were," he said.

"Yes, I was, everyone said so, but that is nothing to the point, Tom," his sister said. "Sophie would be absolutely ruined if she did that, and you would be blamed for she is your niece, or at least, her mother was Jane's cousin…"

"I'm sure that Sophie realises it for she was impeccably behaved."

"Did you see how she deferred to Edward Teale's judgement? I think she must have done that when she was staying in Bredenbridge. From what she said, her friend's father was greatly impressed with her common sense."

"Men often are, Winifred, but I find that ladies are not, and you must admit that Sophie is unusual."

She shuddered. "You don't have to tell me that, Tom. It wouldn't do for him to hear of her plan to follow the drum; or her previous escapades."

"Forget it, Winifred. I think that Sophie will surprise us."

She gave him a quizzical look. "What do you mean?"

"I watched how she cast an appraising glance over the contents of each room that we entered."

"How vulgar," she said. "I must speak with her about it."

"No, Winifred," said Tom, "I've seen many people do that when they think they are unnoticed. Ladies are especially critical, and Sophie has been accustomed to staying in an extremely wealthy household. I think she was mentally comparing the value, but to Edward Teale she expressed her admiration, which pleased him."

Tom had noticed the adroit way that Sophie conducted herself. He wouldn't be surprised to see Teale giving her everything she asked for. Whereas Charlie was without guile, he knew that Sophie could turn most situations to her advantage.

"You're very observant, Tom."

In his position he was supposed to notice things.

"I need to satisfy myself that they have a chance of being compatible, Winifred; otherwise I will not allow her to marry him."

"You wouldn't want her to marry Joshua, would you?"

"No, he's far too young for the responsibility. That's why he's at Holkham, to be away from the temptations that women might offer."

To Tom's relief, Sophie quickly recognised the benefits of marriage, and responded favourably when Edward Teale made his wishes known.

She returned from her second visit to his London home, full of enthusiasm about the luxurious furnishings, and the promise of having her own glossy black phaeton and pair of perfectly matched chestnut horses. That was the deciding factor.

"It's just like my friend Annie's house," she said in an excited voice, "only better, because it will be my home, and Charlie can live with us."

Hearing the sound of satisfaction, Tom felt happier. Sophie never took the slightest interest in house furnishings at Linmore, but it seemed that the idea of being mistress of such a lavish establishment held great appeal for her. The prospect of having a wealthy husband overcame any other desires, and from her perspective, his advancing age was no impediment to the match.

Tom left the purchase of bride's clothes to his sister, and duly paid the accounts when they arrived. He also funded the engagement ball at Cavendish Square, which Winifred considered necessary for a member of the Norbery family. It was modest by her usual standards, but no one could say she did not do things properly.

Caught up in the excitement of the event, Sophie was happy to marry her banker, by special licence, little more than a month after they met. Due to the bridegroom's working commitments, neither deemed a bridal trip necessary.

Punctilious in her duties, Mrs Pontesbury ensured an entry appeared in the *London Society Gazette*, recording the marriage between Miss Sophie Cobarne, of Linmore Hall in Shropshire; and Mr Edward Teale, a banker in the City. After which, the report stated the couple would divide their time between Mr Teale's London home, and his country estate.

CHAPTER 30

When Tom left London, it was with the intention of travelling to Holkham to see Joshua, before returning home to Linmore. In his pocket was a copy of the *London Society Gazette,* containing a report of Sophie's wedding; a second one having been sent to Lucius Cobarne in Ireland, together with a letter of explanation.

I took the liberty of purchasing a commission of Second-Lieutenant for Charlie in his father's former regiment. As he is unaware of the state of your brother's financial situation, I implied that monies were left in a trust, which you have managed. He may well write to express his gratitude. Similarly, for Sophie, I provided a dowry for her marriage, the details of which are in the magazine.

What else could he say? It was nobody's business that he took out a mortgage of ten thousand pounds, using Linmore as security, with five thousand for each invested in government funds. Edward Teale had agreed to manage them.

It was not exactly how he intended his guardianship to end, but he had fulfilled the legal obligations he promised to the best of his ability. All that remained was for him to maintain contact with the Teale household, to assure himself that Sophie had the support she needed.

Tom had great hopes of his investment in Joshua at Holkham. Linmore money would pay for improvements to the estate, and if the war continued as seemed likely, farming profits would increase and the mortgage could be repaid within a few years. There was no reason for him ever to know.

The last month had been a trial, but they had brushed through it without too many problems. Quite unexpectedly, Sophie had shed a few tears when saying farewell.

"Please don't abandon me, Uncle Tom," she whispered when, quite out of character, she gave him a hug of farewell.

"No, Sophie," he said, "I won't. If you need to consult me… about anything, send a message to Aunt Winifred. She will ensure it finds me."

It was the only hint of any anxiety Sophie might feel, and was quickly gone.

"I will send news of your marriage to your uncle in Ireland," he said.

She gave a little crow of delight, hastily subdued, and said with a rueful grin, "He'll never believe it of me. Thank you, Uncle Tom, for everything…"

If, as Tom suspected, Sophie had wanted to remain at Linmore, he thought that the relative proximity of Ravensbury Manor, might have helped sway her judgement.

Having satisfied himself that all was well, he turned his mind to how Joshua was faring. He'd travelled to Holkham before at the time of the sheep-shearings, but not for several years. Now Joshua could explain what was going on.

Afterwards, he would make his way home to Linmore. He couldn't wait to tell Jane the news that Sophie was safely married and in a few weeks, Charlie would commence his officer training.

In Jane's last letter, she had mentioned Ed Salter's continuing progress to recovery, and a problem that she wished to discuss with him about Millie. This puzzled him, for he had ensured the girl was amply rewarded for her honesty in speaking in Joshua's defence, so what else had occurred?

If Sophie was ecstatic about the turn of events, Charlie was appalled when he heard news of her impending nuptials. He looked at her in disbelief.

"You can't marry him, Sophie. He is far too old. The Norberys have no right to make you do this."

"Don't be silly, Charlie," she said. "Nobody is forcing me to do anything, least of all Uncle Tom. He was kind to me from the beginning, and I will not have a word said against him. I am doing this, in part, to make up to you what you have lost. Mr Teale has agreed you can make your home with us."

"It's not necessary for you to go to these lengths, Sophie," he said, running an agitated hand through his hair. "I would have been leaving Linmore anyway. It's what you want that matters."

Sophie gave a wry grin. "Believe me, Charlie," she said. "This suits me very well. I've never had money, and he has more than enough for all of us. He's old, and might not live long, so we'll make of it what we can. In any case, I have other friends."

"But you told me that you had money before we came to London."

"Oh, Charlie," she said with a gurgle of laughter. "That was the allowance Uncle Tom gave me when I was at school. Living with Annie, her parents paid for everything. I saved every penny, but it was chicken-feed compared to the amount of pin-money Mr Teale will give me every quarter."

In Sophie's eyes that made it right but as Charlie could offer no alternative, he had to accept it. "It's Joshua Norbery's fault. He's reduced you to selling yourself to the highest bidder…"

She turned on him fiercely. "Don't even mention his name," she said in a gruff voice. "Try to forget what happened at Linmore, and let me do the same."

"I can't forgive him for what he did."

She was equally determined. "If I can, then you must. I don't want you to bear a grudge. It's over now. Linmore is behind us."

"I promised Pa I'd take care of you. This makes me feel I've failed."

Sophie took his hand, and nursed it to her cheek.

"No, Charlie," she said. "You always looked after me, and now it is my turn. Please, say you will accept it – to please me."

Charlie could not refuse her entreaty. He was not entirely happy, but at least she had a home, and he must trust that Edward Teale would treat her well.

At Sophie's wedding, he felt a sense of loss, but not only for his sister. It was probably the last time he would be part of the Norbery family. On the day, only Uncle Tom came from Linmore. Aunt Jane sent her love, and a letter asking him to keep in touch, but it was not the same. He would have dearly loved to see her again. She was the only person to whom he could have admitted his anger had gone, and now he felt sadness.

It was hard to believe the silver-haired banker was his brother-in-law, when the man must be thirty years older. Still, Sophie seemed excited about the style of the London town house, and Charlie was impressed with the man's generosity in showering his wife with the finest clothes and jewellery. All she had to do in return was present her husband with an heir.

For the first month, he shared their home and watched Sophie settle into her new role, which she did with remarkable ease. Then he heard news that his regiment, the Eighth Company of Dragoons, was moving to a training camp in the north of England. Until now, he had been a soldier in name only, sold short by his cussed independence, which insisted on a commission as Second Lieutenant, where Uncle Tom wanted, on his uncle's behalf, to give him the full title. A letter of thanks must be his first action, with an explanation of his intention to earn the extra rank.

In his heart, Charlie felt haunted by his actions in the Linmore stable yard. He always fought fair before, but to his shame, took unfair advantage of his opponent, and things went horribly wrong. Worse still, Squire Norbery saw him do it, which was why he refused a higher ranked commission.

Taking leave of Sophie was hard, and he struggled to shut out the memories of the last time they parted, when he set out on the Grand Tour. This time however, she was dressed in fine silks, and stood beside her husband, looking elegantly defiant. All would be well as long as the man was prepared to understand her foibles.

He set out in the company of other newly commissioned officers; but where many of them travelled in a covered wagon, he rode his horse in all weathers, while the enlisted men marched every step of the way. To justify the decision, he recited the words his father, Major Fergus Cobarne, had spoken on his last visit home before his death.

Remember this, boy: if your men can see you at their side, they will obey you, wherever you order them to go.

He was thankful the rain on his face covered the emotions that would not stay hidden. The sturdy mount from the Linmore stables was proving its worth, as was Rushwick, the former soldier, recommended by Sergeant Percival for the position of his batman-cum-groom. That, no doubt, was Uncle Tom's gift as well.

If he had been travelling inside the wagon, Charlie would have been prey to his thoughts, and memories of other confined places. Even so, he was not proof against the letter he received from Uncle Tom, telling him about financial investments made on their behalf. He must tell Sophie that, irrespective of her marriage, this was their security for the future.

The weather worsened the further north he travelled. Deluge after deluge echoed his weeping heart as he remembered he had lost contact with everyone for whom he cared. Never had he felt so low.

Sophie always showed him parts of the letters she received from her friend in Bredenbridge. In the latest one, Annie, his dearest love, was distraught. She did not know what to do, because her father had forbidden her to contact him. All he had left was the little cameo picture his golden goddess had given him.

Rather than weep for his loss, Charlie damned Joshua Norbery for destroying his chance of happiness, as well as a precious friendship. It did no good, for he had always known that Annie's father was a wealthy man with rampant social ambitions.

With Uncle Tom, and the Linmore connections, he might have been acceptable as a possible husband, but without them, his lack of background made him *persona non grata* to a man of means. Now, he would have to earn his promotion on the battlefield, and pray his dearest love was still free when he returned – or die in the attempt.

CHAPTER 31

After the first couple of weeks at Holkham, Joshua felt overwhelmed by the sheer volume of information. The agent's schedule was strict and unremitting. Some days he felt so tired that he almost fell asleep over the paperwork.

Estate management took precedence over everything else. On his daily rides with the agent, he saw farmhouses of palatial proportions and animal sheds that would have looked like mansions to country folk in Shropshire. The Great Barn was one such example.

"Mr Coke made rebuilding a priority when he inherited the estate," said the agent. "By improving the quality of accommodation, he attracted a better class of tenant, willing to pay a good rent to live in such style."

In his novice state, Joshua felt stupid at not being able to answer the simplest of questions. Many times, he wished himself back at Linmore, but gradually the mistakes grew fewer.

The first time the agent said, "Well done, Mr Norbery, that's very good," he felt his eyes water with pleasure.

It was still hard, trying to sort the details in his mind. Eventually, he asked the other students when they met for their evening meal, "How did you manage when you came here first?"

Harry and Jack laughed aloud. "Order and method, old chap," said Harry. "Order and method."

Joshua frowned. "Isn't that one of the House Rules?" he said.

"Indeed it is," said Harry, "Rule number two on the list, but you must realise that without discipline, all else fails."

When he was next in the agent's office, Joshua sneaked a look at the picture behind the desk. They were right about the second rule. *Without discipline, order and method, all else fails.*

It was one of Mr Blakeney's favourite sayings.

Good, that was one out of the way. To simplify matters, he decided to write them in his notebook, and allocate one for each day of the working week. Then he read them through.

Monday declared – Cleanliness is next to Godliness.

Tuesday decreed – Without discipline, order and method, all else fails.

Wednesday taught him – Manners make the man.

Thursday's reading told him – Time is a valuable commodity. Use it well, for you do not know when you will need it.

Friday advised – At the end of each day, make peace with your God.

Having completed his list, Joshua realised that Thursday's rule about time applied when the agent planned the farm leases, which could be anything between eight and twenty years. In these, the tenant had to follow the exact clause for the preparation of soil, and use the specified rotation, for which Mr Blakeney gave them ample time to make improvements and achieve a profit.

Now it was beginning to make sense.

The list of House Rules looked quite straightforward when Joshua read it aloud, which he often did when he was alone. He became so proficient, he could have recited the words in his sleep, and for all he knew he might well have done.

He thought Aunt Jane would agree with the sentiments, but was not sure about the other lads, particularly the evening Harry wandered into his room and found the open notebook. When he saw the list, he chortled with glee.

"What have you written them down for?" he said. "You surely don't believe those rules belong to Mr Coke, do you?"

That was exactly what Joshua assumed.

"No," Harry said, "Jack and I decided at the outset it was Blakeney who wrote them, and he uses them to keep us in order."

Jack looked on and said nothing.

"Listen to the words. *Manners make the man…* Can't you just hear him?" Harry tried to mimic the Scotsman's accent, and failed miserably, due to his laughter.

"I was sending them to my aunt," Joshua said. "I think she would appreciate them."

Harry had the grace to look shamefaced. "Oh well, in that case, I daresay she will. Ladies like that sort of thing."

After that, things started to improve. In the weeks leading up to the sheep-shearing, Mr Blakeney kept everyone occupied with the planning.

Joshua saw little of the other lads during the daytime, but he was glad of their company in the evenings. It helped alleviate his loneliness and took his mind off the reason that had brought him there.

On a Sunday morning, they rode their horses from the stables to the church on the hillside, overlooking Holkham Park. Afterwards, they galloped across the park to dine with the agent and his family. The rest of the day belonged to them, and this was when Joshua began to know his fellow students.

They were friendly chaps, but Joshua didn't expect the camaraderie he shared with Charlie. He doubted if he would ever find another friend, and felt the loss of friendship worse than bereavement. In any case, they had almost completed their placement year. By August, they would have left Holkham.

Before that, they showed him different aspects of the estate to ones he travelled with the agent. If he thought Mr Blakeney's work schedule was intense, he found that Harry and Jack seemed determined to use every spare hour of daylight for their pleasure. No sooner was their evening meal over than they set off to ride across the park to one of the country inns around the estate, many named after the ostrich, which adorned the Coke family Coat of Arms.

Harry insisted it was the best way of introducing Joshua to the locals, but from the enthusiastic welcome they received wherever they went, it was obvious the other lads spent their money freely, knew the taste of all the local ales and were on friendly terms with every barmaid for miles around.

Irrespective of the reason for the visits, Harry always took the lead.

"This is our new friend, Mr Norbery," he said, settling a serving wench onto his knee. "You must be sure to look after him when we leave."

"Where does he come from?" the girl asked, as if Joshua was not there.

"Shropshire, near the Welsh Border," Harry said.

She frowned, and then came up with a suggestion. "Is it near Norwich?"

That was obviously the limit of her geographical knowledge.

"No, my pretty wench," Harry said with a laugh, and pointed to a spot on the edge of the wooden table. "We are here, in the east of England, and Shropshire is two hundred miles away in the west of the country."

"Ooh," she said, her eyes widening. "You're quite a foreigner then."

Yes, he supposed to her, he was.

"You're not leaving us yet, though," she said, turning back to Harry.

"Not until after the sheep-shearings in July."

"Oh, I know when they are," she said. "All our rooms are booked for the week, and everyone around that has beds to spare."

After three weeks, Joshua had met more barmaids than in as many years at Linmore; some were pretty and slender, while others looked as if they would make a comfortable armful. Harry loved them all, Jack laughed and joked, and Joshua nodded acknowledgement, knowing that he had plenty of time to get to know them.

Some people and places were more memorable than others. One inn stood out in Joshua's mind; a strange little place, hidden away down a country lane off the beaten track. Its ivy-clad walls and weathered thatch of Norfolk reeds blended so well into the surrounding woodland, one could be forgiven for passing by without seeing it. And yet when they arrived, an ostler appeared and took their horses to the stables at the back of the building. Almost as if they were expected.

"Do you know something, Josh?" said Harry, giving an elaborate shiver as they entered the low-roofed building. "I have a feeling that this place is haunted."

"If you're trying to scare me into paying for the first round, you won't succeed," said Joshua, concentrating on avoiding low oak beams for the second time that evening. "I bought one at the last place."

"He said the same thing to me, when we first came here," said Jack.

They all laughed at the notion, but when Joshua thought about it, he couldn't deny that the building had a strange presence. Not that it seemed to bother a couple of farm labourers that had stopped for a tankard of cider on their way home from work.

Their welcome was predictably good, and within minutes Harry disappeared outside with one of the serving-girls. A few minutes later Jack strolled over to chat with the barmaid, leaving Joshua to drink his tankard of ale.

When it was almost finished, he sat back on the wooden settle with his long legs stretched out before him, feeling the warmth of the blazing logs on the hearth. He laughed to himself, thinking of Mr Blakeney's dictates about fraternising with local women, and realised that hidden away as they were, it didn't matter for no one would know what they did or with whom.

At half past nine, he contemplated ordering another pint before the others returned. Deciding to wait he closed his eyes and let the cares of the day slide away. Almost immediately, he felt a heightened sense of being watched, and became aware of a swish of skirts and a soft tread crossing the bare floorboards that stopped before his table.

"Good evening, sir," said a delicious voice that sent a shiver of anticipation down his spine, "what kind of entertainment can I offer you?"

With a voice like that she could offer whatever she liked and he'd accept it.

Joshua opened his eyes and met the appraising gaze of a woman, slightly older than the girls who attracted the other lads, with tawny tresses tumbling around her shoulders. Before he could respond, she said, "I'd say that you look in need of cheering up, sir; maybe I can help you relax."

Aware that he was gawking, Joshua took a long drink to moisten his suddenly parched throat, and almost choked as she placed her hands on the table and leaned closer to give him a better view of her generous breasts nestling between the creamy flounces of her bodice. She was temptation incarnate, and for a moment she reminded him of the goddess in the bagnio. Oh…yes please…

"Look all you like, sir," she said, running the tip of her tongue around her rosy lips, "but if you buy me a tot of rum you can touch as well."

Joshua hastened to oblige, but as he fumbled in his pocket for a coin, she stroked his cheek with a touch, soft as gossamer, which took his breath away. Then she laughed, low and sultry, and he was bewitched. Her eyes held him in thrall, her lips tempted him, and time ceased to have any meaning. And then from somewhere in the distance, he heard a voice calling his name… *Joshua*…

Go away, don't disturb me. He wanted to stay with her, but the voice was insistent. Joshua looked at her with a profound sense of regret. "I must go…"

"Maybe you'll come again," she said. "Be sure to ask for Polly. I'm always here."

He nodded, but wasn't sure when that would be. When he looked again, she had glided away without speaking to anyone else. In fact, nobody seemed to notice her.

"Come on, Josh, it's time to go," Harry called impatiently from the doorway.

298

Joshua drained the tankard and made his way to the bar. "Goodnight," he said to the landlady. "Tell Polly that I'll see her the next time I come."

"Polly…?" the woman said in surprise. "Oh, you mean Sarah, the dark-haired girl who was talking with your friend?"

"No, I mean Polly, a tall girl with reddish hair. She came over to talk with me at the table in the corner by the fire." He pointed to the far side of the inglenook.

"Are you certain?" she said, a worried look creasing her homely features.

"Yes," he said, annoyed at the doubt. "She asked me to buy her a tot of rum."

"Joseph," the woman called to her spouse, "this gentleman says he's seen Polly."

The landlord came forward, nodding dismissal to his wife; then he said in a lowered tone. "You couldn't have done, sir. Polly was our daughter, and she was drowned in the sea five years ago."

"But I did see her," Joshua protested, "as plainly as I see you or your wife. She asked me to buy her a drink."

"No, sir," the landlord's tone was firm. "With respect, I think that you must have been dreaming. This local brew is strong and it has that effect on some people."

Joshua didn't believe that he had been asleep, for he could still feel the tingle in his skin from when the woman stroked his cheek. *You can touch if you buy me a drink.*

He cursed his stupidity for not availing himself when he had the chance, then he would have known for sure.

Ask for Polly, I'll always be here… But she wasn't here now and apparently hadn't been for years. Joshua walked outside to the stables where the other lads awaited him, not knowing whether to mention what he had seen.

"What kept you, Josh?" said Harry. "Have you been talking with the local ghost? The ostler reckons that the wench ran away with the smugglers, and that's why they say she drowned – but she might have come home – just to see you."

"I think you could be right," he said with a rueful smile. He didn't know if Polly was real, but she had stirred him like no other woman and left him hungry for more.

After that, they changed their evening routine. The first time that they rode down to the seashore, Joshua gazed in wonder at the wide expanse of Holkham beach, which ran along the coast as far as the eye could see, with a line of sheltering dunes of the finest sand imaginable. The other lads rode steadily on, and Joshua had to chase after to catch them, but as he drew closer, they spurred their horses on. Two could ride together; three made it a race, and with no winning post, they galloped on for the sheer exhilarating fun of doing it.

It was a close run thing, but Harry won by a nose.

"It was easy for you," said Joshua, gasping against the onshore wind. "I started from way back there." He pointed to the row of pine trees in the far distance that served as a windbreak.

"All right then, we'll race you back," said Harry. "The last one to reach the Ostrich at the bottom of the drive pays for the first round."

Joshua's horse lagged behind when he stopped to pick up his hat that had blown away, so he paid the forfeit. After the other lads had each paid for a tankard of ale, he found they were better acquainted with the various stages of inebriation in which he was a novice. Maybe it was tiredness from the unaccustomed work routine, or his obsession with trying to remember everything the agent told him, but whatever it was, after a couple of tankards of ale he could hardly keep his eyes open, or sit straight in the saddle riding back to the stables. They brought him back, in need of help from the grooms to drag him upstairs to his room. He felt ashamed when they let him know the next morning.

"You're working too hard, Josh," the other lads told him.

"You don't understand," he said. "I have to do it."

He would not tell them the reason was to drown out the loneliness he felt. Homesickness for Linmore was one cause; but the driving force was the need to redeem his self-respect after the trouble at home. He had so many secrets.

When Fred Cardington started his education with wines on the journey to Holkham, Joshua realised how little practice he had on the European travels. Strong black coffee and anxiety about Dr Hawley's illness put paid to that.

Then he recalled that Sergeant Percival ensured that neither he nor Charlie imbibed too much of the strange-tasting brews in Greece. Whilst they drank champagne at various grand social events in Rome, it was the excitement of the moment, not alcohol that went to his head on a visit to the bagnio, and his friendship with Lady Rosie.

After the first attempt at racing, Joshua was prepared for the next; and all the hours he spent galloping across Linmore Park with Charlie Cobarne came into play and he won, time after time. In the end, they laughingly decided he needed a handicap.

"It's an unfair contest," protested Harry. "You were obviously born in the saddle, unlike us ordinary mortals."

His challenge was to join the stable lads, when they raced the horses on the beach, half a dozen at a time. A crowd of locals came to watch, and a tanner apiece went into the betting hat, with the winner taking the prize. Joshua entered into the spirit and hurtled past the winning post ahead of the field.

Whilst it seemed unfair to take their money, a bet was a bet. To refuse would offend and set him apart, so he accepted his prize with good grace, and stood them a round of drinks at the Ostrich – a move that won instant approval.

From the beach, the three lads moved on to a race meeting at Fakenham, five miles across the estate. Although he started well, Joshua's luck with betting did not hold with other riders in the saddle. By the end of the day, his pockets were to let; an experience he was loath to repeat, for he had squandered the equivalent of his allowance for two months.

It was only early June, with three more weeks before he could anticipate a single shilling more from Mr Blakeney. How would he survive?

Several times, he declined Harry and Jack's request to join them for a drink, claiming he had letters to write, or his work diary to complete. Pride would not let him plead poverty, however temporary; but they saw through his pretence.

"If you're short of cash, we can lend you some till next month."

"No." Joshua was appalled at the thought. "Thank you, but it's unnecessary."

They grinned, and said, "Come anyway, and let us buy you a drink. You can repay us if you like, when you claim an advance from Mr Blakeney. It is all right; we have both done it several times. He might make you wait a day or two, but he doesn't refuse."

Relief spread through him like a wave. How silly to have forgotten the agent's words on his arrival. Deciding that a guinea or two would make a huge difference, he made his application to the agent.

The weather was balmy the next Saturday afternoon, so they rode to the beach, tied up the horses and walked down to the sand dunes.

"What kind of boat is that?" Joshua asked, pointing out to sea.

Harry turned to survey the horizon.

"It's probably the revenue cutter from Yarmouth," he said. "A few miles down the coast from Cromer."

Joshua looked blank and shook his head.

"Oh, I forgot, you're new to the area," Harry said with a laugh, and proceeded to draw the shape of Norfolk in the sand.

"Look," he said, marking a straight line to illustrate the direction, followed by a curve, than jabbed the sand with his riding crop. "We're here on the north coast; whilst Cromer, Yarmouth and Lowestoft are around the corner. Suffolk is the next county to the south and Lincolnshire, up the coast, beyond the Wash."

Joshua recalled studying the area on the map at home.

"What are they doing here?" he asked, reverting to his original topic.

"Patrolling, I suppose. Looking for smugglers; but don't ask anyone else about them. Nobody talks about such things around here."

"Why?" It did not make sense.

"It's safer that way…"

"But this beach is on Holkham land. Surely, nobody would be as stupid as that… would they?"

Harry shrugged his shoulders and grinned.

"It's as good a place as any other part of the coast. Admittedly, it doesn't have the waterways of the Broads to take the contraband inland, but once beyond the salt marshes, it would quickly disappear. After all, none of the locals would admit to seeing or hearing anything on a dark night."

Joshua laughed, thinking Harry was teasing him, but later, he wondered. Parts of the beach were so isolated, anything could happen. He shivered at the thought, unsure why he felt this way. When he looked again towards the horizon, the boat had gone, and so had his companions. Without saying a word of their intentions, Jack and Harry had left their clothes in the dunes and dashed down to the waters edge.

After a quick look around, he followed the other lads through the rolling breakers and plunged headlong into the deeper water. He surfaced with a shiver, shook his head and laughed. Bathing in the sea was infinitely preferable to using a tin tub in the servants' washrooms at the Hall.

Refreshed by his dip, he left the others to wallow and dashed up the beach to retrieve his breeches, before throwing himself face down in the sand, and letting the gentle breeze waft over his back. Once there, he could relax, safe in the knowledge the sandy dunes shielded him from view.

That was the best kind of privacy.

On their regular evening dips in the sea, Joshua quickly shed many inhibitions he'd brought to Norfolk. It was not as if any women might see them. In fact, apart from the time when the grooms exercised the horses, he had not seen a soul near the pine trees that formed a windbreak.

Work inevitably intervened, but as Joshua grew to know the other lads better, he became the recipient of confidences from one or the other. Harry, in Jack's absence, told of his family background, and the reason he was at Holkham.

"I expect your family were born to the position," said Harry. "Until two years ago, my father was an army major; a younger son with no expectation of inheriting a country estate. When his godfather died without heirs, he resigned his commission to become the squire, and the family have had to learn to move in different circles. We're lucky in having Woburn so close to home. The Duke is a friend of Mr Coke, and he suggested Holkham to my father, as a way for me to learn about estate management. You and I will have the full responsibility one day, but it's different for Jack, because his father is only a tenant farmer."

Joshua nodded, whilst thinking of what Jack had told him one night in a tavern when they were sitting waiting for Harry to return from his tryst with a serving wench, his tankard of ale abandoned on the table before them.

"Is he always like this?" Joshua had said.

"Chasing wenches, you mean? Yes, most of the time," said Jack. "From what he said at the outset, his father told him to conduct himself like a gentleman."

"I'd say that he's doing exactly that," said Joshua, with a dry laugh.

"Yes, but you know how they behave, don't you?" said Jack, "Whereas, I'm only a tenant farmer's son. More of a non-commissioned officer compared to the likes of Major Bircham."

"Did Harry say that?" said Joshua appalled at the suggestion.

"Not in so many words," said Jack, before changing the subject. "He said that he'd be flogged if his parents' heard of his behaviour, but the closer we get to leaving Holkham, the worse he is, and I'm no better. I don't know your reasons, but I was sent here because I was becoming too friendly with the parson's daughter."

Joshua nodded his understanding, but was saved the need for further confidences when Jack added, "I'm glad it gave me the chance to come to Holkham. My father may not own the farm, but the need for sound management is just the same – more so, when the landlord is Mr Coke's son-in-law."

CHAPTER 32

After the visit to Fakenham, Joshua needed something else to occupy his time, so he wrote a letter to Aunt Jane, telling her things he felt would be of interest; he wrote another to Francis Weyborne, with extra details about his work, which he planned to send to Linmore when he could afford the postage.

I wish you could see the Holkham estate. It is hard to imagine the sheer size of thirty thousand acres, of which the park accounts for three thousand. Compared to Linmore, the land in Norfolk is flat, and they use a system of crop rotation, which replaces the need to leave one field fallow in four years.

First, they plant a grain crop, such as wheat, corn or barley, then one of the root crops, swedes, turnips or mangelworzels, followed by either grasses or clover on the remaining two fields. I will tell you more when I understand the process.

Everything is new to me. I had not realised there was so much to learn about the preparation of soil, or that seed drills cover several rows at a time to ensure a uniform depth and better coverage of the land.

Teams of oxen do the ploughing, but the Suffolk Punch breed of heavy horses is replacing them, because they cover half as much land again in the time. They are such placid creatures. I doubt there is an ounce of vice in them.

By the way, the agent asked about the type of rock at Linmore, and I said it was limestone. I hope you will correct me if I am wrong.

Sharing the knowledge made it easier for Joshua to understand, particularly when he drew diagrams to represent fields like the quarters of a clock. The four sections equated to the rotation of crops. Preparation of the soil and addition of fertilizers took a little longer to understand, but as his knowledge increased, he added notes to his diary.

It has much to do with acidity. Being on the coast, the soil is light and sandy. I think marl was used initially, then clay. Bonemeal is used now, but the most natural addition is the manure taken from the animal wintering sheds.

He used other diagrams to illustrate the additions, but did not realise the agent had noticed, until a voice said, "That is very good, Mr Norbery, I see you have a receptive mind."

Wishing to explain his reasons, Joshua said, "I was telling my friend, the trainee bailiff at home, about the work here."

Mr Blakeney nodded, but it was hard to know what he was thinking.

Joshua added another note to his letter to Francis Weyborne.

I have learned that Viscount Townshend, of Raynham, lived near to Holkham. In case you are wondering, it was Turnip Townshend who introduced turnips as the fourth course in the rotation.

I am sure you know all this, but as the growth of root crops for winter fodder increased, the old practice of slaughtering animals in the autumn decreased, which ensured a better supply of fresh meat throughout the year.

When Joshua looked at the six pages of double-sided writing, he thought twice about sending regular epistles of his work. There was so much and he had only touched the surface of the subject. He could not expect his father to pay extra postage, so he would have to think of another way.

It seemed no time at all before the long-awaited Holkham sheep-shearing arrived. Three days, in which Mr Coke of Norfolk opened his doors to like-minded agriculturalists. The event gave Joshua the opportunity to observe his patron at his best, when he was centre stage in the arena, meeting and talking with everyone.

The visitors numbered several thousand from all parts of Britain, with many from the Low Countries of Europe, and further afield. In agriculture, the aristocracy stood on equal terms with landowning politicians of different parties, tenant farmers, and royalty, the Duke of Sussex amongst them.

"You should see the huge gathering at Woburn," Harry said proudly, when pointing out the Duke of Bedford as one of Mr Coke's particular friends.

The three days felt more like a sennight. So much was crammed into every hour, rising early and retiring late in the evening.

Everyone gathered around the Great Barn for the sheep-shearing. In the early days, the emphasis was on improvements in sheep breeding, but now, the process was a celebration of the best of the breed, of prize-giving, speeches, and after-dinner talks on every aspect of farming, with Holkham a showpiece of innovative practice.

Joshua spent his time watching, listening and meeting people. Harry's father came from his Bedfordshire estate, as did Jack's father from Staffordshire; but nothing could have surpassed Joshua's delight when his father arrived, all unexpectedly but doubly welcome, bringing with him an extra trunk of clothes.

He talked himself hoarse, showing his accommodation, the estate office, the farmhouses and the great barn. His father stayed at the Ostrich Inn. Joshua joined him and together, they walked to the beach.

On the day before his father returned home, Joshua showed him his work diary. Tom Norbery read the work with interest and nodded approvingly.

"I'm impressed, Joshua," he said. "It looks as if you will have a great deal to contribute to Linmore on your return."

Joshua then handed his father a bundle of papers. "I've written these letters for Francis Weyborne," he said, "telling him about the work here, but they are so long, it would cost you a fortune to frank them – and there are a couple for Aunt Jane as well."

"I'd better take them with me," Tom Norbery said with a smile. "Next time, send them to me at Linmore, and I will ensure everyone receives them."

The mention of money made Joshua hesitate to reveal a problem, but honesty forced him to tell the truth.

"There's something else I should tell you, sir. At the beginning of June, I went to the races at Fakenham with Harry and Jack…"

"Been sporting the bustle, have you?" his father said. "How much money did you lose?"

Joshua was astounded. "Twenty pounds, but how did you know I lost?"

His father laughed. "It's obvious, because if you had won you couldn't have kept it to yourself."

"You're right, sir." Joshua said. "Actually, I did have a couple of small wins to begin with, and put everything on a horse – a sure winner – only he fell at the first fence and I lost everything."

"What did you do then?"

"I was out of pocket for the month and had to apply to Mr Blakeney for an advance on this month's allowance. He spoke with Mr Robertson, the steward, and he made me wait a sennight for his answer. It meant Harry and Jack paid for me when we came down here for a drink. I don't like to borrow from friends."

Tom Norbery extracted two crisp five-pound notes from his pocketbook, and counted out ten guinea coins. Before he gave Joshua the money, he said, "Have you learned anything from the experience?"

"Yes, sir, I have," Joshua said with a decided nod. "Racing is not my forte, and I won't do it again – being in debt made me feel horribly uncomfortable."

"Then something good has come from it," Tom said, handing the money to his son. "Just remember if you are ever tempted. The next time I might not be near enough to help."

Twelve weeks through his first rotation, Joshua began his placement in stockbreeding. He spent most of the first week, poring over the cattle breeding books in the agent's office, learning about stockbreeding methods pioneered by Robert Bakewell of Leicestershire, and discussing refinements made by his apprentices, the Collings brothers, to include the short-horned breed.

The event in early July taught him a great deal about sheep. He met John Ellman of Glyde, an improver of the Southdown sheep breed, from whom Mr Coke bought a flock of ewes and four rams, back in '92.

When it was over, he returned to work.

"What do I do now?" Joshua asked when the agent took him out on the estate and made him known to the head shepherd.

"You observe the shepherds at work, Mr Norbery."

The agent's tone was patient, but Joshua felt stupid for asking what later seemed obvious. Whilst he accepted the dictate, he soon realised that a whole year spent watching people work would leave him with too much time to think of things he wanted to forget. To save his sanity, he must find active occupation.

He had started the placement too late to see the shepherds washing sheep before shearing, to clean the fleece. Now he learned of the practice of dipping, several weeks later, to kill ticks on the skin. From what he could see, it could not be that difficult, for even the most simple country yokel could do the work – so why should he not achieve the same result?

When he tried, and found it was not easy, he blamed his clumsiness on the bulky working smock they gave him to cover his clothes, and gaiters over his boots. Deep down, he knew it was his ineptitude, but resolved not to be beaten. Although the Holkham shepherds had years of practice in washing sheep, Joshua derived immense satisfaction from eventually catching a single animal, and guiding it through the water dip.

He failed many times, and then, wearing the dirtiest smock of all as a badge of office, he took the laughter of the other workers in good part, and received a cheer of approval.

"I reckon we'll make a shepherd of you yet, young sir," the head shepherd said with a rare smile. "You've got from now till lambing time to get some practice. I expect you'll be coming back to us about that time."

When he took the filthy smock to the laundry for washing, one of the workers, a pert young woman, not realising he was of the gentry, mistook him for a farm labourer and sent him on his way.

"Don't you know any better than to bring that dirty thing here?" she said. "Your mother should do your washing for you, my lad."

Had he been at home, Joshua might have laughed at the suggestion of his mother's involvement, but at Holkham, he was perplexed. Nobody had refused to wash anything before, so he rolled it up and hid it away, intending to ask Harry or Jack what he should do. Then he forgot.

The warm summer evenings of mid-July drew the three lads down to the water's edge. Each time, they wandered further along the beach, determined to ensure nobody from the village was within sight when they took to the water. Sometimes, it was almost dark by the time they fell into bed, but at least they washed the sweat away.

They went back at the week's end. Sometimes, after their swim, Jack and Harry wandered off in different directions, leaving Joshua lying in the sand, letting the drying sea breeze waft across his back. He drifted off to sleep and awoke to find himself alone. He listened to the gulls overhead, and the sea in the distance.

Closer still, on the other side of the sand dune, he heard laughter and female voices, and realised the other lads must have met a couple of local girls – no doubt some of the tavern wenches.

Joshua was in a dilemma, not knowing how close the females were. He was not completely naked in his undershorts, but wished he had replaced his breeches. It might be safe to come out from under cover, but he would feel a fool if anyone saw him wandering around in a state of undress.

He closed his eyes, and thought longingly of the warmth he shared with Millie, which left him with an empty feeling. Probably by now, she would have found someone else to amuse her. He lost track of time, but it seemed only minutes later he heard Harry's voice, rousing him from the mists of sleep.

"Come on, Josh. The tide's coming in at a rate of knots."

They dashed back up the beach to the row of trees where they'd left the horses. As they rode back up the drive, Harry said, "Sorry, Josh, we forgot you might want a woman. We will have to see if we can find another wench for the next time the girls come."

Although Joshua disclaimed the need, Harry was adamant. Finally he agreed, and persuaded himself that it would be easier with a stranger.

The following weekend, his friends found a third girl to provide for his entertainment. When the other couples had gone further along the dunes, the black-haired wench stood ogling him, running a lazy tongue around her lips.

He focused on her mouth, waiting for the stirrings of a response, as she made a play of unlacing her bodice to the waist, letting her breasts slide temptingly forward, before lifting her skirt in bunches, to expose her ankles. But he felt nothing. What the hell was the matter with him? Then he realised, that although her features were unfamiliar, something about her reminded him of Sophie Cobarne. The thought killed any fervour stone dead.

"No," Joshua grunted. He hunched his shoulder and turned away to hide his frustration. He could not bear the thought of touching her, let alone…

"What d'you mean, "no", when I came here a' purpose?" she screeched.

"No, thank you." Joshua turned back and thrust a coin in her direction, and felt her grasping claws snatch it from his hand.

The girl shrugged a disdainful shoulder, and swaggered back along the sands, clutching the easiest guinea she had ever earned.

Bitter though it was, the experience told him that he must be more selective. Conversely, he knew that he wouldn't have turned aside from the girl called Polly that he saw at the inn. She was everything that was warm and welcoming. Her hand was soft when she stroked his face, and he wished that he had touched when he had the chance.

Even the thought of her aroused him more than the other girl had. No matter what they said, he could swear she was real. How could he have been mistaken when the thought of her lush curves set his blood pounding in his veins, and his breath quickened with the memory of her scent? He would happily have drowned in her eyes.

Not today, you won't, he thought as he ran down to the breakers, and dived into the deeper water before allowing the incoming tide to sweep him towards the shore. Suitably invigorated, he walked back up the beach to where the other lads awaited him by the dunes. As he approached, he read the question in their faces and prepared his answer.

"Was it your first time, Josh?" Harry ventured to ask.

"No, of course not," he said, affecting a bravado he did not feel. "That was with an Italian countess, who invited me back to her home a couple of days later…"

What a bouncer… Harry and Jack looked at each other in utter disbelief.

Joshua gave a wry smile, knowing that in making the truth sound like an elaborate boast, he had distracted their attention from the third wench of whom there was no sign. Then he laughed. "Well, not quite the first," he amended, and endured the pitying looks that assumed it was all over in thirty seconds, if it lasted that long. Nor the second or even the worst encounter, but it was preferable for them to believe that, than for him to admit the reason he walked away. The prospect was humiliating.

"Don't worry," said Jack, with a sympathetic grin, "the next time will be better."

"I don't know about you, chaps," Joshua said, striving to salvage his pride, "but I could do with a drink. I'll stand the first round."

CHAPTER 33

"I trust that you were not down at the Mermaid Inn on Saturday night, getting into bad company, gentlemen? It seems there was trouble in the village, some time after nine o'clock. An incident between a group of the local fishermen and Preventive Officers from the Revenue Cutter from Yarmouth, caused, if rumour is to be believed, by someone who tempted the locals to drink gin – or "blue ruin" as it is known – which might have come to these shores as contraband. This suggestion the innkeeper's wife vociferously denies, and few men hereabouts are brave enough to challenge her assertion face to face."

Having seen the woman in question, Joshua could almost hear her strident voice denouncing the slur on her character.

August had finally arrived, and the students were at their regular monthly meeting with the agent. The last one Harry and Jack would attend before leaving Holkham in a few days' time. The tavern to which Mr Blakeney referred was in one of the fishing villages, three miles along the coast.

Discretion kept the lads silent. The day was right, and their Saturday evening visit was to say farewell to Patience and Prudence, the black-haired wenches who served in the bar, and "obliged" Harry and Jack, but by nine o'clock, they were back at Holkham.

Joshua had been to the inn only once before, but it looked different at night. With several hours to sunset, it was light outside, but the taproom was dark, and the two lanterns hanging by the bar had little effect on the smoky atmosphere. Nor did the oil lamps in wall sconces, or the kindling spitting on the flagstone hearth, brighten the gloom.

Despite the earliness of the hour, trade was brisk, but on their entry, an uneasy silence fell over the room. Several men occupied each of the wooden settles along the walls, and Joshua felt numerous other eyes in dark corners turn to watch them. He saw the two wenches that Harry had come to see, but under the watchful gaze of the innkeeper's wife, Prudence and Patience showed no sign of recognition.

In fact, the formidable dame with a penetrating voice stopped them before they reached the wooden bar counter.

"Begging your pardon, young sirs, but we have no parlour for the gentry."

There was still an empty table by the window, but the finality in her tone left them in no doubt that their presence was unwelcome. Harry looked stunned, Jack bemused and Joshua said, with all the dignity he could muster, "In that case, chaps; we'd better try the Ostrich."

But rather than risk further rejection, they rode silently back to the stables.

Recalled to his surroundings, Joshua realised the agent was still speaking.

"I must have forgotten to tell you, Mr Norbery, that the Mermaid is known to be one of the smugglers' haunts. It seems that the crew of the Revenue Cutter came ashore for a drink, and two of the Preventives have disappeared."

The agent's words made Joshua remember the thriving trade at the inn, and two newcomers, wearing black-peaked caps and jackets, that stood waiting outside the door, for him to leave.

He wondered what had happened after they left. Who was the man who made free with his money to buy gin? Was he already in the tavern when they arrived? Had the innkeeper's wife sent the lads away because she anticipated trouble? Were the missing Preventives the two men he had seen outside the inn – and were they still alive?

Jack and Harry left Holkham in the middle of the second week of August.

Mr Coke entertained them to a farewell dinner, and the two lads said their thanks to their host. They extended an invitation to Joshua to visit their homes when he was in the district. He said the same to them, but doubted if anyone would venture as far as the Welsh borderlands.

Their absence left a void that was hard to fill. He missed their cheery laughter, and acceptance that he was not like other men. Sober, they had never questioned it, but sometimes in their cups, they teased him. If only he could have told them the reason why.

Work left little time for maudlin thoughts during daylight hours, but he felt lost in the evening, listening to the silence of the stables. It was a strange time, when the light of the waxing moon found a chink in the blind and disturbed his sleep.

At Linmore, he was unaware of the effect moon cycles had on the tides, but with Holkham village almost on the seashore, everyone knew when to expect a high tide. He heard whispers about the dark of the moon being the likely time for a smugglers' drop of contraband; and after recent events, knew well enough to keep away from the shore. He would have loved to spend his evenings riding on the beach, but the last thing he wanted was to encounter any trouble when he was alone. The same applied to drinking without company.

His sense of isolation was worse the second Sunday he was alone. He did not know whether to head for the salt marshes, watch the birds on the shore, or swim in the sea. In the end, he rode a couple of miles along the beach to the end of the plantation of pine trees, which formed a windbreak at the edge of the salt marshes. Once there he tied the horse to a tree, stripped to his underclothes and walked down the beach to the waterline.

The beach looked as it normally did, except that a strip of sand on the landward side of the dunes seemed uneven, almost as if someone had dug holes in it. He puzzled about the cause, and then realised that it would disappear after a couple more high tides.

He paddled ankle-deep for a while, and then wallowed in the surf, letting the little waves ebb and flow over him to wash away his sense of inadequacy. It felt so good, but after about half an hour, he went back up the beach as far as the sand dunes, and sat down knowing the tide would be out for a few hours yet.

It was strange to think he was alone, and nobody knew where he was, but the sense of peace was worth it. He mused, noting how the rich colour of the sky merged into the sea. Within minutes, he was asleep.

The sky was darker when he awoke, and a keen wind blew across the sand. He shivered, realising the tide had turned and was rippling closer. It looked grey now, and infinitely more menacing as it raced ahead of him along the beach to the east, the way he would have to ride.

Scrambling over the dunes, he set off up the beach at a run, thinking of lurid tales he had heard of the encroaching tide catching people unawares. Local folk knew better than to go out alone. More fool he for not heeding the warnings. Halfway up the sand, he saw his horse, still tethered where he left him by the pine trees. Joshua slowed his pace to catch his breath, and looked around to find his top clothes.

Then he saw them, in the hands of a peasant woman standing beside the horse. There was nothing for it, but to walk boldly on and claim his property. At least he was partly clad. It was not much covering, but infinitely better than a month ago when he went swimming with the other lads. His courage failed, a few yards from his objective, and he stood waiting for the woman to speak.

"I found your clothes halfway down the beach, and then this handsome fellow all alone," she said, draping the garments over the saddle, before giving the horse her full attention.

In his haste he dressed without order. His long-tailed shirt came first to hand, but he fumbled with the buttons, and slipped his bare feet into his boots, forgetting his socks, then she turned back before he could find his breeches. At least he achieved a modicum of decency. His waistcoat, neckcloth and frock-coat could wait until he was alone.

There were too many distractions. Her soft drawl sent a shiver down his spine. Quite why he could not tell, for she was not a beauty. Her sand-coloured hair and weathered face gave her a comely air, but her gentle brown eyes were alive with humour. It made him want to smile as well.

She turned to look at him. "You must be one of the young gentlemen working at the Hall." Her matter-of-fact voice was soothing. "I've seen you down here before, when I've been out collecting wood along the shore."

He wondered what else she had seen. It was difficult to know what to say, but the woman solved the problem.

"I'm Tess Dereham," she said, extending a hand in greeting, much as a man would have done.

"Joshua Norbery, at your service, ma'am," he said, feeling the strong grip of a hand roughened by a lifetime of work. Honest hands, not scented and smooth, like so-called ladies he had known in the past.

It seemed incongruous, to be leading his horse along the shoreline, clad in his boots and shirttails, accompanied by a woman he did not know, but in Tess's company, he did not feel the slightest urge to scramble into his clothes and dash away. He felt safe.

Maybe it was the fact that she said, "There's no cause for you to be embarrassed at being seen by someone of my age. I'm probably a dozen years older, and married for the second time."

He followed her through the tree line and along the path until they reached a wooden shack he had not known existed.

When she stepped through the door, it seemed natural for him to follow.

"You'd better get those clothes off, and I will find you some of my first husband's to wear. Those women in the Holkham laundry won't thank you for putting sand in their water." She seemed amused at the prospect.

Sandy clothes? Then he realised she was right about the grouchy laundry workers. He waited as she went into a back room, reappearing immediately with a neatly folded pile of linen.

"Here you are," she said. "Try those for size. You can change in there." She nodded towards the back room.

Joshua stopped at the door, realising it was a bedroom. "Oh, but…"

"It's all right," she said matter-of-factly. "There isn't anywhere else."

Nowhere else, she said…apart from the room through which he entered the dwelling. A room stripped bare of all but necessities. He cringed, seeing rushes on the earthen floor, but no curtains at the windows.

In the centre, he saw two wooden chairs, their seats worn with age, one on either side of a well-scrubbed table, and on the top, a couple of rough platters and tankards. The sizeable barrel of ale in the corner, and small shaving mirror on a shelf seemed almost a luxury.

Tess seemed unconcerned, but he felt an intruder. It did not seem right to walk half-dressed into a room she shared with her husband. A space dominated by a cabin-type bed along the wall opposite a small-paned window that did not open. There was room for storage underneath. Not in cupboards, but screened by a strip of gathered cloth to match the faded bedspread. Despite the frayed edges touching the floor, the many-times washed linen was clean.

He looked around for a chair on which to sit. Not finding one, he sat on the bed to remove his boots, and pull his shirt over his head. As he stood up again, his coat slid to the floor, and a pencil rolled from the inner pocket, out of reach.

Annoyed, he swept back the curtain, and peered under the bed. It took but a second to retrieve the pencil, and a few more to see the wax-covered bundles stored beside a couple of wooden barrels. Then he looked away.

Aware of his indiscretion, he replaced the screen as he had found it, then stood up and reached for the dry underclothes. Try as he might, they did not fit. He almost laughed aloud. The previous owner was evidently a man with a larger girth. No matter what he did to hold the coarse long drawers in place, they slid unimpeded down to his knees.

The drab coloured undershirt looked no smaller, so he set it aside, and replaced his linen shirt, donned his buckskin breeches, and buttoned up his waistcoat and jacket. Finally, he added his stockings and boots.

Standing with neckcloth in hand, he noticed for the first time a rough wooden wardrobe in the corner, and in the tarnished reflection of the long mirror, he met the appraising gaze of the woman standing beyond the open door. How long she had been there, he did not know.

As he walked back through to the other room, with his underwear, Tess held her hand out expectantly, and he relinquished them to her care.

"The others are too large, I'm afraid," he said, "I've left them on the bed."

"Yes," she said, with a smile. "I should have known you were too slender."

"Thank you for allowing me to use your…room," he said. "I'm much obliged."

Ignoring his embarrassment, she gave her attention to his discarded underclothes.

"Mmm," she said appreciatively. "This is quality linen, not like the rough cloth I gave you. There is no need to worry I will spoil it. I was a laundress up at the Hall before I married my first husband." Having started to reflect, she said, "We were walking out together for seven years before we wed, and within a year of the wedding, he was taken with lung fever."

Joshua started to speak, but she continued almost conversationally.

"The next time, I married a fisherman, like my father, but he's out on the boats most nights, and when he's not, the pair of them go to the ale house down by the harbour."

Her words were a sad reflection of the lonely life she lived. Then, as if fearful she might have revealed too much, she said in a brisk tone, "Enough of that. If you come back next week, I promise your linen will be washed as well as they do it at the laundry."

Riding back up the drive, Joshua realised he had forgotten to ask about charges. When he returned the following week, he found Tess alone as before.

"I hope your husband won't object to my presence, Mrs Dereham," he said, not knowing how else to enquire the man's whereabouts.

"Don't worry," she said, with a wry smile. "He's not here and I don't expect him to be home for hours yet – if he bothers to come."

It was said from the heart and Joshua was glad when she turned her attention to his linen. In that, Tess was as good as her word and the standard of cleanliness was everything she had promised. He took a coin from his pocket, hoping that she would enlighten him. "Will this be enough to cover the cost?"

"That's far too much." Tess seemed surprised he took a guinea so lightly.

"Please take it," he said. "I have nothing less with me."

It was not quite the truth, but she had so little, and Joshua wanted to give something extra to repay her kindness. He felt a sense of relief when Tess accepted the coin and placed it on the table, then watched in surprise as she took hold of his hand and turned it over.

"These are too soft to be working hands," she said in a husky voice.

He felt a tingling sense of anticipation, as she stroked his palm and raised it to her lips, and then slid his hand inside her warm bodice.

"I have nothing else to offer you," she said, "but you are most welcome to it, and I would be happy to serve you."

Joshua blinked to shut out recollections of the last time his hands touched a breast, and then opened his eyes, knowing he could not avoid making a choice. To refuse and turn away as if in disgust would humiliate the woman; but to accept an offer she felt compelled to make was to take advantage of her.

Seeing the look of entreaty in her eyes, he reached out to stroke her cheek. She gave a little shiver of ecstasy as he trickled his fingers down her neck, past her shoulder to the curve of her breast, and then asked quietly, "Are you sure you want this?"

In silent response, Tess unlaced her bodice and let her skirt fall unhindered to the floor. She stood before him in mute agreement, and smiled. It was for him to take or leave and Joshua realised this gentle soul was everything he desired.

Who would have thought the drab clothes she wore hid the kind of lush curves the artist Rubens would have worshiped on canvas? Only a fool would leave her at home, unattended and unappreciated.

Warm, giving and responsive to his touch, Tess instinctively knew how to please. By so doing, she helped Joshua to shed the pent-up frustrations he had endured for months, and with it, his fear of being impotent. With a feeling of utter contentment, he slept in her comforting arms.

In a brief moment of waking, he listened to the sound of her breathing, and felt at peace. Outside, he heard the freshening wind rattling the window frame, and wondered if it might portend a storm. He knew he ought to go back to the Hall, but the realisation that Tess was lying awake watching him with anticipation, tempted him to stay. The sky was still light, so what difference would half an hour make? He had nothing better to do with his time.

When Joshua woke again he was alone, and knew by the gathering shadows in the room that more than an hour had passed. Hearing a voice outside the house, he leapt from the bed, and then realised with relief that it was Tess talking to the horse. He watched her through the window as he hastily dressed. She looked somehow different today, almost younger. Last week, he thought her hair was sand coloured. Now it looked the shade of ripening corn. Not only that, but she had softened her work-hardened hands.

One thought followed another. The fresh-smelling sheets on which they lay made him wonder if she anticipated this – or whether she normally changed the bed linen on a Saturday. He supposed that he would never know; and might never see her again.

After the intimacy they had shared, their parting was strangely formal.

Tess led the roan horse forward for Joshua to mount, before hurrying into the house and reappearing with his clean laundry. "You'd better not leave this behind, sir," she said, "especially after coming to collect it."

"Thank you," he said softly, slipping one of each item of clothing into the deep inner pockets of his coat, "for everything."

She gave a rueful smile and nodded acknowledgment. He left her standing amongst the trees her hand raised in farewell, but when he looked back she was gone.

In a daze, Joshua set off to ride his horse up the drive towards the stable block, oblivious of the gathering storm clouds and drizzling rain. Many times he and the other lads had covered the distance in ten minutes at a canter, but in his mellow mood and dawdling pace it took half an hour.

A sudden fork of lightning across the park brought Joshua to a sense of his surroundings. He urged the horse to a canter, but as he approached the stables there was a clap of thunder nearby and the deluge began in earnest. In seconds, he was drenched.

As he leapt down from the saddle, the stable clock started to strike the hour of six, and Ben Waters dashed out of the stables to take the horse under cover.

"Thank God you're back, Joshua. We were getting worried about you in case you were down at the harbour. It's due to be a high tide, and will be one hell of a night."

"Sorry, Ben, I forgot the time," Joshua said, preferring to let them think he'd been to the tavern than admit he'd spent the afternoon with another man's wife. Not that he regretted it for a minute. He was sated. He had never felt so satisfied by a woman. Whatever was lacking before, Tess had cured him. All he wanted was to sleep.

CHAPTER 34

For the last week of August, storms kept Joshua from the shore, but when he rode down to the beach on the first dry evening after he finished work, the thought of meeting Tess's husband prevented him from approaching the house amongst the trees. Everything looked quiet, but he had no idea of the working hours that would ensure the fisherman's absence, or how to explain his presence if the man was at home.

I've come to see your wife, Mr Dereham… to ask if she would oblige me again… No, that wasn't such a good idea, even if it was the truth. If he did that, he might be dragged off across the North Sea in a fishing boat and dropped overboard with no one at Holkham being any wiser. Joshua Norbery would simply disappear. He shivered at the thought and let a few more days go by.

Half-way through the following week, Ben Waters brought an invitation from his mother, asking if Joshua would like to share their Sunday tea.

With no valid reason to refuse, he accepted with grateful thanks and met Ben at the appointed time to walk the mile down the back drive to the cottage where they lived in the village. The groom would have saddled Joshua's horse but he felt that it would be churlish to ride while another man walked at his side. Fortunately the Sunday afternoon weather was kind to both of them.

The food on the table was simply presented but delicious. Home-made scones that melted in his mouth, thinly sliced bread and butter lavishly spread with the new season's preserves made from strawberries and raspberries grown by Ben's father and grandfather in the walled garden.

Joshua wished that he could have given his hostess something in return, but she expected nothing, and was pleased when he praised the seed cake that he learned she had made especially for his visit.

It was one of Ben's favourites, so she thought he might like it too. She sent him away with a chunky slice wrapped in a cotton serviette that he slipped into his pocket, and he wondered who would otherwise have enjoyed it had he not been there.

Amongst the family present, he recognised Ben's younger sister, Mary, who was in service at the agent's house. He had seen her earlier in the day when he sat down to eat his Sunday roast mutton with Mr and Mrs Blakeney. There were two siblings missing from the family group, but he met Ellie and Florence, the twins who were ten and little Tom, aged six, as well as Ben's grandparents who lived in the adjoining red-bricked cottage. Being part of a family made the day one of the most hospitable he had enjoyed.

It was the following Wednesday evening when Joshua finally made up his mind to visit the shoreline again, slipping away the moment he finished work, without waiting to take his supper.

He had a strange sense of foreboding when he followed the path across the saltmarshes and a hollow feeling in his gut that vied with an aching need for information. As he approached the little house amongst the trees, he was conscious of an eerie silence. It looked strangely lost in the twilight.

When he knocked, the door opened at his touch and he stepped inside the shadowy room that he entered with Tess, but she wasn't there now even if the kitchen furniture looked much as it did on the first occasion. He walked through an open door into the room where he had changed his clothes. The bed was neatly made as before, but the air was stale and the house had an unused feeling.

Curious, he stooped and swept back the curtain to look under the bed for the barrels that had probably contained "blue ruin", and the wax-covered packages of what might have been tobacco. As he suspected, they had gone.

He had heard the grooms saying that large bales and barrels of contraband went inland to the towns, but smaller ones could be sold to local ale-houses or individual buyers. He wondered if any of them had ever found their way to Holkham. Surely not, for Mr Coke was a magistrate.

Dismissing the thought, Joshua slammed the outer door shut, and stood gazing across the expanse of beach at the rapidly approaching tide, all the while hoping that Tess wasn't out in the gathering darkness.

Passing back through the village, he stopped at the Ostrich Inn to enquire her whereabouts. He only had to mention her name to gain a response.

"Mrs Dereham…?" the innkeeper's wife said when he asked. "Oh, you mean the poor woman that lost her husband as well as her father and two brothers in that dreadful storm last month. The house is empty now, sir, for she's gone back to live with her mother in one of the cottages near the harbour in the next village along the coast. The old lady was in a sorry state, by what I've heard. Half out of her mind with grief, from losing so many of her family. And worry too, I daresay, without the income they brought in."

It was reason enough for the two women to be together.

Thinking back, Joshua realised that the storm to which she referred was during the night that followed the blissful time he had spent with Tess, so she might already have been a widow without knowing it when he left her.

"One of the crew from the Revenue Cutter reported seeing them heading towards the open sea, at a time when they'd have been expected to come back to shore. There's no telling what took them out there with a storm forecast, but nobody saw them alive again."

That was all the information that Joshua could glean, and he made his way back up the drive to the Hall to seek bread, cheese and a tankard of ale for his supper, but it was hard to swallow and sat for an unconscionably long time in his belly.

Poor Tess…he kept thinking.

It was two more weeks before the sea finally gave up the bloated bodies of the lost men. Accompanied by Mr Coke and his fellow workers, Joshua attended the sombre funerals, and heard whispers amongst the mourners of the sad consolation that Ned Dereham's widow was carrying his child.

Joshua started in surprise, realising that it was Tess to whom they referred. He thought again of the wax-covered packages hidden under the bed in the cottage, and wondered if Ned Dereham and his fellow fishermen had set out under cover of darkness to collect more contraband on the night they died.

He wondered if the storm had really sunk the fishing boat or an encounter with the Revenue Cutter from Yarmouth, after the gruesome discovery of the missing riding officers in the salt marshes. Did the Preventives retaliate by sinking the fishermen's boat out at sea, and let the tide bring the bodies back to land? If they could blame it on nature, there would be no questions asked.

Over and over again, Joshua mulled the stark facts around in his mind, as he pondered the problem. In the end, there seemed to be only one course of action. At the earliest opportunity, he set out to offer condolences to the widows.

Finding the cottages by the harbour was easy, but when he looked at five black doors in a terrace, he realised that he did not know Tess's mother's name. The landlady at the Ostrich had thought she lived at the middle dwelling, but couldn't be sure. As he approached, a curtain twitched at windows on either side.

Joshua tapped gently on the door, knowing he was under scrutiny. And then, assuming an air of nonchalance he did not feel, looked over the harbour wall at the boats caught in the channel with the tide out.

He turned back, hearing the door open and saw Tess's look of shock as she realised who stood there. "I've only just heard," he said. "I looked for you at the cottage along the beach…"

"You shouldn't have come here," she said in a whisper, looking distraught. "People will see you… and talk…"

Tess seemed to have aged ten years since he last saw her, for the dark-coloured clothes she wore did not suit her. Her eyes were bleak, cheeks chalky pale and her sand-coloured hair that had flowed freely across a pillow was confined under a white mobcap, with only a few lank strands escaping the regimented frill. All the life seemed to have drained out of her.

Joshua suddenly realised her predicament. Tess had few possessions when he met her wandering on the wide-open expanse of the beach, but she had the freedom to walk where she liked, and do as she pleased in her husband's absence. Confined here in her mother's home she was subject to the restrictions of neighbours seeing everything that went on and making judgements about things of which they knew nothing.

And yet, knowing the nefarious activities that her late husband had combined with fishing, she was safer here, though whether she appreciated the fact he couldn't say. Filial duty was expected of a woman and it was the price she paid for respectability.

"I'm sorry," he said, realising that he had caused her embarrassment. "I didn't mean to intrude."

She shrugged her shoulders in acceptance of his words.

"Who's that, Tess?" a frail-sounding voice came from inside the cottage.

"It's all right, Mother. It's just someone from the Hall," Tess called loudly through the doorway, her voice calmer now.

Before he could move, the older woman said, "Don't keep the gentleman standing on the doorstep, Tess. Bring him indoors."

Tess gave a despairing sigh and stood aside to allow Joshua to enter.

"You'd better come in, sir," she said, and added as an afterthought, "mind your head on the beam."

Thankful for the warning, Joshua stooped, just in time to avoid the doorframe as he entered the dark hallway. Another step and he was inside a little parlour, lit by the flickering flame of an oil lamp and such light as passed through a small paned window to the front. From what he could see, the furnishings were sparse, but the beeswax and lavender scent was a testament to the attention lavished on what was there.

While his eyes grew accustomed to the light, he sensed, more than saw a sad little figure cloaked in the black clothes of mourning, huddled over a few glowing embers in the grate. He did not know how to explain his presence, so instead of simply uttering words of sympathy, he claimed to come as Mr Coke's representative to offer pecuniary assistance.

For a moment, Tess seemed ready to decline the charity, but her mother was mortified, so she had no choice but accept.

"Whatever will the gentleman think of you, Tess, wanting to refuse a gift from Mr Coke? I beg your pardon, sir. I hope you won't tell the squire of this."

Joshua reassured them, knowing the fewer people who knew of his visit the better. He left the house, well pleased with his action; little realising news of his contribution would travel fast, and directly back to its alleged source.

Summoned to Mr Coke's study, Joshua imagined it must relate to a message from Linmore, but to his chagrin found himself having to answer for his actions.

"It seems I am in your debt, young man." Mr Coke looked perplexed at being in such a situation. "I met with Widow Dereham today, and she thanked me for the generous offering you saw fit to give to her mother and herself on my behalf. I was at a loss to know how such a thing slipped my memory. Perhaps you can tell me how much I owe you."

"Five guineas, sir," Joshua said, his face burning with embarrassment. "It was all I had with me at the time."

"Yes, that was sufficient to help them for a month or two, but I think I could arrange for a more practical solution by providing the younger woman with some work. I believe she was employed at Holkham in the past, so it should not present a difficulty." Mr Coke was obviously familiar with the case in hand.

"But she is with child, sir," Joshua said, and then stopped under his benefactor's incredulous gaze.

"So it would appear, but hardly surprising, considering she is only recently a widow. However, as the delivery is not imminent I think something could be done until that time." The all-seeing grey eyes swept away pretence. "I wonder what precipitated your act of generosity. It is rare for young men to be so perceptive in these situations."

Joshua struggled to explain. "On my arrival, Mrs Dereham rendered me a service… with some laundry."

A puzzled expression crossed Mr Coke's face. "Laundry?" he said. "I thought we had very good facilities at Holkham. It seems there must be a deficiency in the service for you to take your washing elsewhere. If you could tell me in what way we have failed your high standards, Mr Norbery, it will be remedied."

"I'm sorry, sir. I did not intend to cause offence."

"No," Mr Coke said in a crisp tone. "I accept that, but I think, young man, you would be advised to make better use of the remaining time you have at Holkham, and leave me to deal with providing financial assistance to people on my estate. Bear in mind that, one day, you will have responsibility for your own estate, but at Holkham the responsibility is mine."

The interview terminated with a nod, but before Joshua could escape the penetrating gaze, he heard the final words.

"There is one last thing I have to say, Joshua. In the absence of your father, I will tell you that I do not expect you to visit Mrs Dereham again, and neither will she expect your call. Is that quite clear?"

In the absence of your father…

The words pounded in Joshua's head, until it ached. He was mortified that he had caused embarrassment to his host, making claims to be something he was not. Worse still, he had let his father down – again.

The Sunday morning weather matched his mood. Dark clouds gathered overhead, threatening to shed their load. Irrespective of that, he felt the need to go to church. The night hours brought little relief, so a walk across the park might turn his gloomy thoughts in another direction.

Joshua buttoned his greatcoat with the shoulder capes, pulled on his wide-brimmed hat and set off at a brisk pace, striding past the end of the walled garden and up the long slope towards the church at the top of the hill. The distance was less than a mile but it felt considerably more battling against an inshore wind that seemed determined to test his resolve not to slacken his pace. He reached the gates to the churchyard about twenty minutes later, and was forced to take a breath ready to ascend the even steeper path that wound its way up to the church door.

When he entered, worshippers filled most of the front pews in the centre row where he usually sat, so he slipped into an unoccupied seat opposite the door. He bowed his head trying to follow the service, but so wrapped in his thoughts was he that he missed many of the acknowledgements.

While others were singing hymns, he looked around the church and wondered how many people stood there acknowledging their mistakes and praying for guidance, or maybe for a miracle to happen.

When the sermon began, he intended to absorb the text, but other things took precedence. The sun came out as he walked down the slope to the stables, and the view across the lake to the Hall was a worthy memory to take home.

Contrary to his expectations, there was no reserve when he sat down to dine with the agent's family. It was quite the reverse. Mrs Blakeney had roasted the most succulent leg of mutton he had ever tasted. It was his favourite meal, but he could not enjoy it, knowing it might be the last time he sat there.

Soon after, he made the excuse that he wanted to write a letter to his aunt, and returned to his room. *Dear Aunt Jane, I wish I could talk with you…*

There the letter ended. He sat looking at the sheet of paper, knowing he was wasting his time, looking for excuses that did not exist. How crass to think his liaison with Tess entitled him to impose his notions of beneficence on two grieving widows. He meant well, but worse he could not say. It was no excuse for his deplorable lack of good manners in disturbing their privacy.

Then he realised there would be no time to write if Mr Coke sent him home. If it happened, he would never have another chance to see the local scenery he had come to know and love.

Within minutes, Joshua was riding his horse across the parkland towards the sea. He sat gazing at the expanse of beach with a line of water in the distance, wondering how far he could ride before the tide turned.

Then he was off, galloping into the wind from the west, feeling the sea breeze clear the cobwebs from his mind. Mile after mile he rode, past the salt marshes with their migrating birds, and out as far as the headland. He sat there, looking out to sea, letting his mind ebb and flow with the turning tide.

He thought back to his first sight of the House Rules, and about how Jack and Harry ridiculed the notion that Mr Coke wrote them. If they had felt the whiplash of Mr Coke's words in the study, they would not have doubted his involvement. Joshua had read the words, but not appreciated the implications. Now he did, and would do anything to have a second chance to prove his worth.

Eventually, the fidgeting horse drew his attention to the advancing tide, so he set the animal galloping back the way he came. By the time he reached the marshes, the tide was running too fast to continue on the beach, so he headed along the coastal path, and from there, took his horse through the woods towards Holkham. Tomorrow, he would begin again.

To his amazement, Mr Blakeney made no mention of his lapse, but his workload increased almost three-fold. If this was his miracle, he accepted it as such and was grateful.

When his future at Holkham was in doubt, Joshua sorted through his belongings and found a dirty smock-frock hidden under his bed. After the confrontation with a grumpy laundry worker, he had tucked it away and forgot its existence. Now the problem needed to be resolved.

He broached the subject of laundry with Mr Blakeney, and received an incisive response. "Mary-Anne doesn't complain about anything, so I would advise you to see her. Tell her I sent you."

Who was Mary-Anne, and how was he supposed to identify her? All the laundrywomen looked the same in their mobcaps and aprons, and since his meeting with Mr Coke, he avoided talking to women in case it was misconstrued.

Eventually, he made his way to the laundry door and spoke to the first person he saw. "Are you Mary-Anne?"

The woman shook her head, and then called inside the building. A few minutes later, a tall woman of comfortable proportions appeared at the door and looked around. On seeing Joshua, she bobbed her knees respectfully, and said,

"I am Mary-Anne, sir. I beg your pardon for keeping you waiting. How can I help you?" Her slow voice had a strangely familiar sound.

In a lowered tone, Joshua explained his problem and said Mr Blakeney suggested she might be able to help. He made a point of saying he did not want to cause any bother, and would pay for any extra work it incurred.

He was fascinated when Mary-Anne laughed. Her whole face lit up, eyes creased with merriment, and a grin spread across her face.

"Lor' bless me, sir. A bit of sheep dirt never hurt anyone. Mind you, there are some folk who moan about anything, but I'm not one of them, nor was my sister when she worked here."

"Your sister…?"

"Of course," she said. "I was forgetting you would not know Tess, my little sister, because she left here before your time. Mind you, she still does a bit of work here on the odd occasion. That was due to Mr Coke's kindness, after her husband died in the fishing boat accident. I expect you heard about it. My father and two brothers were lost as well as Ned Dereham and his brother."

A dark cloud passed over Mary-Anne's sunny smile.

Joshua murmured condolences, and let the woman go back to her work. The news that Tess might be working in the laundry stunned him. How was he to avoid meeting her? He started to walk away, but the woman called him back.

"I don't like to ask, sir, but as you want this work doing special-like, would you mind if I got Tess to do it for you, so she can earn a bit of extra money?"

He waited as Mary-Anne sidled closer.

"I save bundles of washing for her, because Mr Coke said she wasn't to come here too often until she's had the baby, and I'm afraid she might miss out on things."

Joshua readily agreed, stumbling over the words in his haste.

"Yes, of course, but I insist you take the money now."

A few meagre pence exchanged hands, and the woman returned to her work. Joshua smiled ruefully at his woeful lack of knowledge about the cost of everyday things, and remembered the last time he paid for washing to be done.

CHAPTER 35

I n mid-September, Holkham celebrated the bounty of harvest with a thanksgiving service and a supper for the workers on the estate. Joshua added a prayer of thanks for his continuing stay at Holkham and for Tess's absence from the church. No doubt, she would have been there if she still lived near the beach, rather than three miles away sharing her mother's home.

Two days later, he had news of impending change. It was the Tuesday after the harvest supper, when the agent called him to the estate office, and waved him to a chair.

"We have new students arriving tomorrow, Mr Norbery," he said. "I'd like you to show them round."

"Will they be staying in the Hall, as I did?" he asked.

"There's no need to spoil them, when there are beds in the stable block."

Joshua had settled into a routine, working and living on his own. Now he would have to interact with other people again. He wondered what they would be like. Jack and Harry had been settled when he appeared, and made him welcome.

"Will that be all, sir?" Joshua said, preparing to rise.

The agent raised his brows in surprise. "Are you not interested to know more about them, Mr Norbery?"

He sat down again. "I thought you would tell me when they arrive, sir."

"No, I thought an advance warning was appropriate. At sixteen, they are two years younger than you are, and less mature. I look to you to give them support, and ensure they do not go astray. I trust I do not need to elaborate."

This was Mr Blakeney's only reference to Joshua's lapse.

"No, sir," he said, flushing to the roots of his hair.

"They will, of course, receive the same advice that you were given. Nothing happens on the estate that I do not know, and I was well aware of the previous students' predilection for frequenting alehouses."

No doubt, he knew about the wenching as well.

"Mr Coke has assured Sir John and Lady Gransden, as well as Colonel and Mrs Inglethorpe, that their sons will not be led into temptation at Holkham. There will be no gambling on horses, drunkenness, or debauchery."

How the deuce was Joshua going to prevent them if they were that way inclined? What he needed was a Sergeant Percival to help him.

"So I am to be their nursemaid, sir?" It slipped out without thinking.

The agent gave him a hard look. "No, Mr Coke hoped you would be more of a mentor."

"Mr Coke said that…?"

"Yes, Mr Norbery," said the agent, with a wry smile. "He specifically asked it of you – but not to the detriment of your work."

When Joshua entered the agent's office the following afternoon, he stopped short at the sight of Mr Blakeney's bemused expression. Forewarned though he was, he did not expect to see new students, clad in the most flamboyant attire. Over-starched shirt-points, coats with exaggerated shoulder pads, teamed with pale lemon pantaloons and highly polished Hessian boots. Only with difficulty did he stop himself laughing.

On introduction, he learned that Michael Gransden had travelled with his valet and groom from Kings Lynn, and James Inglethorpe brought a servant from Bury St Edmunds. Although short in stature, Michael's loud manner demanded attention. Being quiet, he assumed James would follow.

"Mr Norbery will show you the accommodation."

When the agent said that, Joshua knew his peace at Holkham was over.

Opening the office door, he saw three gigs parked outside; each one with an inordinate amount of luggage. When the grooms looked for instructions, he mounted his horse and said, "Follow me around the lake to the stable block."

Michael Gransden stood by the office door, looking aghast.

"What do you mean? I am not staying in any stable block, nor is James," he said, intent on gathering support around him.

Joshua gathered up the reins in his left hand and repeated, "If you care to follow me."

James clambered into his gig and the Gransden valet and groom did the same, which left Michael to follow. Not willingly, or with good grace, but he did.

On reaching the stables, Joshua dismounted and waited for the others to arrive. James followed close behind, but Michael made a great pretence of stopping to look at the Hall as he drove past, then the end of the lake to point out the icehouse, as if there was all the time in the world.

"I'll find one of the stable lads to attend your horses and gig," Joshua told James. "They'll help to move your baggage as well."

"I didn't know what to expect," the other boy said. "This seemed the best way to travel from home."

"It's all right," said Joshua. "You'll soon learn. We all do."

When Michael finally arrived in front of the stables, Ben Waters was in the process of carrying James's box to the door.

"Where shall I put this, Joshua?"

"Leave it in the sitting room while they choose their rooms."

"What is this place?" Michael demanded to know.

Joshua took a deep breath and spoke slowly. "It is where we, the students at Holkham, live and sleep. If you follow me, I will show you. Best be quick, or James will have choice of the two rooms."

He wondered what Michael would say when it came to the work.

"This is not what I expected." Michael grumbled his way up the staircase. "Are you quite sure this is right? I thought I would be staying in the Hall."

"There is no mistake," said Joshua. "We all sleep here, and the washing facilities are in this room." He opened a door.

"Where am I going to accommodate my groom and valet? They must have somewhere to sleep," Michael said, looking at Joshua with suspicion. "What do you do about servants?"

Controlling the urge to laugh, Joshua said, "I have no need of assistance. I'm here to work."

It was not a good start. Joshua might say he didn't need help, but he hadn't mastered the way of keeping his boots and leather breeches clean, whereas Michael's clothes were immaculate.

Confronted with something beyond his comprehension, Michael ignored him, and Joshua realised he was relegated to the level of the lower orders, particularly as he was on first name terms with the grooms.

In the event, the servants found somewhere to sleep, but after a few days, the two grooms took the spare gigs home, and Kegworth, the valet, remained.

Two weeks in a row, Joshua came into his room to find it unusually clean and tidy. Instead of finding his crumpled clothes draped over a chair back, his neatly sponged and pressed jackets hung with his clean breeches in the wall cupboard. Everything smelled fresh and it was obvious that a practised hand had polished his boots.

He said nothing to Michael, but guessed Kegworth was responsible for the improvement in his appearance. He bided his time until he could speak with the man alone. They met as Joshua climbed the staircase to the upper level, but before he could utter a word, the valet sought to justify his actions.

"I know what you're going to say, sir, and I beg your pardon for entering your room without permission. I had no right to do that, but with time on my hands, I thought to make myself useful."

"Thank you, Kegworth; I am obliged to you for your assistance." Joshua took a coin from his pocket.

"No, sir," said the valet. "There's no need for that. Mr Michael said as how it's all right for me to help the other young gentleman, so I'd be grateful if you would allow me to assist you."

"It looks as if you have remedied the deficiencies already. My leathers and boots haven't looked so clean since I arrived."

The valet had also aired the contents of the clothes chest his father brought from Linmore in July.

"Well, I noticed you didn't have a manservant, and I can see your notion of work is different to the other young gentlemen. From what I hear, you seem to mix with the workers."

Joshua drew himself up. "What of it?" It was not for a servant to question his actions.

"No offence intended, sir. What I meant to say was that I reckon Mr Michael's reason for coming to Holkham wasn't the same as for you."

"We are all here to learn, Kegworth," Joshua said in a quiet voice.

"Exactly, sir, but some folks know how to do and others don't. I'm only saying what Lady Gransden said before we came here, and she's real quality, like you."

Joshua wondered what Kegworth thought he was. Michael Gransden obviously viewed him as the poor relation of the group, but servants always knew what was going on, and Weston's label in his coat told its own story.

Michael and James were soon firm friends, and they travelled to church by gig around the road, leaving Joshua to ride his horse across the park. This continued for several weeks, but when they attended the group meeting at the end of the first month, Michael broached a subject Joshua had wondered about but never asked.

"Why is the church so far from the village, sir?" Michael always took the lead to ask questions, and James was content to let him be the mouthpiece. "It seems a dashed silly place to put it when the village is a mile away."

Mr Blakeney was ready to enlighten them.

"The original village was moved to its present location when Mr Coke's ancestor, the Earl of Leicester, extended the lake."

Joshua had heard of landowners moving villages in parts of Shropshire, but his Norbery ancestors did the opposite. They extended the drive from the village and built the new Linmore Hall on the far side of the fishponds.

Several times in the succeeding weeks, James expressed quiet anxieties aside, and Joshua assured him that he had felt the same a few short months before. Michael did not admit to anything.

He did not want them to compound his errors, so he stressed the need to listen to what Mr Blakeney said. He emphasised the significance of the picture hanging on the wall behind the agent's desk, but Michael did not conform to rules, and in his company, James inevitably followed suit.

With so many places out of bounds, Joshua was relieved to know that at weekends, Michael and James preferred to drive their gig through the surrounding villages, dazzling the locals with their magnificent attire, and taking the tugging of forelocks by estate workers as due deference, whereas Joshua, riding alongside, soberly dressed in his black coat, recognised amusement. People knew there was no harm in them. They were young men, away from home for the first time, revelling in the attention they drew. It made him feel old, in experience, by comparison.

When he was going to work, a uniform, dark brown coat, tan waistcoat and fawn breeches with top boots suited Joshua well; but being a student who asked the how and why of everything, he had quickly acquired practical over-clothes for each placement.

While Michael and James delighted in their inclusion to a shooting party, Joshua occupied himself on another part of the estate – from choice. No one seeing him there would recognise the tall figure in a smock, leather waistcoat and sturdy boots as anything other than a woodsman,

When he returned to the stables, few traces of his activities remained, except dried mud on his boots and breeches. In the intervening hours, he revelled in the physical work, clearing undergrowth from established woodland, pruning hazel coppices, and splitting wood for wattle fencing.

It was part of woodland management. A process in which thousands of trees started life in the walled garden every year, and thousands more saplings from other years were transplanted. He was fascinated to learn that the holm oak originated in Italy, the acorns of which were found in the packing cases of statues brought back by the first Earl of Leicester, from his Grand Tour.

Joshua could not stand by and watch. He tried his hand at all kinds of work. His curiosity even led him to learn about pleaching hedges in the enclosures, which strengthened the base for better growth.

Every day, he set out, determined to learn new skills, and returned to the stables feeling weary but satisfied. It was backbreaking work for someone unaccustomed to such things, but he never complained, for it gave him a better understanding of the countryside.

He liked the honesty of the estate labourers. They might laugh when he did things wrong, but it was without malice and they showed him how to do it right. Then they shared their food with him. Bread and cheese tasted better in a forest, especially with a mug of local cider for which he had acquired a taste.

Some evenings, he felt almost too tired to ride back across the park. At such times, he thought he never wanted to see another acorn or horse chestnut. The next day, he gathered a dozen of each kind to take home to Linmore. If they grew well, he would have his own special piece of Holkham to remember.

That was what it was all about, but it separated Joshua from the other students. He forgot about everything but the job in hand, until he returned to the stables and found the other lads waiting for him.

"Why are you late?" said James. "We thought you must have had an accident."

"What do you mean?"

"Look at the state of your clothes."

Joshua realised what they meant, but he was not going to apologise for doing his work. "I've been planting saplings," he said, "hundreds of them."

The ensuing silence filled the room.

"Don't wait for me," he said, stripping off his jacket. "I need to wash and change."

They took him at his word and disappeared down the stairs. Kegworth appeared immediately, asking, "Did you want some hot water, Mr Norbery?"

"How much is there?" Joshua asked.

"The cauldron over at the forge is full," the valet said. "There's plenty for you to take a dip in the grooms' tin tub."

Joshua grimaced as he stretched. "Make sure I don't fall asleep."

"Don't worry, sir. You have plenty of time. Mr Michael never hurries anywhere."

By the time Joshua reached the dining room by the servants' hall; the other students were heading back to the stables. He found them later playing cards in the sitting room. They glanced up from their game, but neither said a word.

It did not matter. Joshua was tired, but still had things to do. He pulled up a wooden chair to the table and prepared to record the daily events in his workbook. He propped his chin in his hand and closed his eyes.

The light was dim when he awoke. Michael and James had exchanged their card playing for a tankard of ale, and Kegworth was setting the table to rights. It was eleven o'clock and all Joshua had written were three words on the page of his diary.

"Did you want me to get you a drink, sir?" Kegworth asked.

"No, thank you," he said, stifling a yawn. "It's time I was in bed."

This became the nightly pattern of behaviour. Joshua knew he should make an effort to talk, but he missed the easy camaraderie with Harry and Jack. With them, even silence could be companionable. He did not expect friendship, only a degree of civility. James was usually polite, but when Michael spoke, his manner was invariably condescending.

"I don't suppose you've done any travelling, Norbery? Unless it was to Wales, or wherever this border is that you live near. I mean, it's not likely your parents would think it necessary."

Joshua clenched his teeth, determined not to lose his temper.

"Actually, I did the Grand Tour a couple of years ago," he said, with cutting civility. "Have you travelled anywhere?"

Michael's face was a picture of envy. "Well, no," he said. "My parents don't seem to understand it is essential, and they won't see reason. The trouble is my mother is concerned about my safety. I am the only son and heir to the estate."

Joshua suddenly understood their problem. They wanted to appear grown up, whereas at their age, he was already travelling.

"Your parents are right," he said. "With the war on, Europe is not a safe place to be. Hardly anyone goes there nowadays."

"Will you tell us about your travels?" There was no hint of condescension in Michael's tone now.

That night, they sat until the lights were burning low while Joshua told them about the sea journey to Naples, and their close encounter with the French Naval brigantine. When they wished they had been there, he told them about the storms in the Bay of Biscay, and anxious times on the becalmed ship within sight of the Barbary Coast.

On the subject of travel, they thought he was the fount of all knowledge, and hastened to seek answers to questions they could not ask anyone else.

"Are Italian women as easy as they are reputed to be?" Michael waited eagerly for his reply.

"Easy… um…well…" Joshua tried to think of a comment he could make without committing himself.

Luckily, James had a question to ask. "Is it true they are available in Naples for a few shillings a day?"

Joshua could answer that without fear of telling a lie.

"I'm not the man to ask about such things," he said, with a rueful grin. "I never spent a farthing acquiring a woman abroad."

He did not elaborate further, knowing they would not believe money played little part when the women involved knew as much about the art of seduction as men – and more than he did at the time.

Seeing their disappointed looks, he digressed to a topic guaranteed to impress Michael – the process of inserting influential names in the conversation.

"We spent a lot of time with the British Ambassador's family in Athens, and met Admiral Nelson and his officers, when we were in Rome. They came to one of the Embassy functions."

"I must tell my mother of this," Michael said, his attention caught. "I am sure she and my sisters will want to meet you."

Joshua had no wish to meet them. Women invariably caused trouble.

"What about volcanoes?" said James. "Did any erupt while you were there?"

"No, Vesuvius was dormant," he said, "but we climbed to the top of the caldera. Then we visited Pompeii and Herculaneum."

They were awestruck.

"Oh, yes," he remembered. "We did a study course about the antiquities in Rome, which gave us a better understanding of the things we saw."

The mention of bookish occupation brought a glazed look to Michael's eyes. "I suppose your tutor insisted on that sort of thing."

Joshua nodded. "Our lessons in Greek, Latin and Italian continued unabated."

"Oh, languages aren't my forte," Michael said, sounding almost proud of the fact. "I can't get the hang of all those funny words foreigners use. You'd think they would speak English, when you've taken the trouble to visit their country."

Clearly, anything else was beyond his comprehension.

"How long were you there?" asked James.

Joshua considered the matter. "Almost a year and a half, most of which was spent between Athens and Rome. We were in Greece several months, but my tutor was ill in the mountains so we didn't see a great deal of the country."

He did not think they would want to know about the poverty he had seen.

"Did you bring back any art treasures?"

"Only the portrait we had painted, and that's hardly a treasure," he said, remembering the gift from Lady Kenchester.

"You didn't go on your own, did you?"

Joshua itemised the people. "No," he said. "There was Dr Hawley, the tutor, and a couple of servants from home. My father engaged a former soldier to act as guide, with some grooms as guards on the coaches, and…a…friend came with me."

Charlie was like a brother at the time, and far better than Joshua's sibling had ever been. Then they asked the inevitable question.

"Where is he now?"

Joshua had to prevaricate.

"He joined the army and I came here." That was all he knew, and the information came from Mr Coke. "We planned to join together, but my older brother died whilst we were in Italy, and I became heir to the estate."

Recounting the story left Joshua drained. He thought he had buried his feelings, but this touched a raw spot. It was lucky they thought the grief he showed related to a lost brother and asked no more questions. It did, but not the one they imagined.

CHAPTER 36

I t was still dark when Joshua awoke on a damp October morning. He glanced towards the window and listened, judging the hour to be almost time for birdsong to begin. It was strange how he noticed such things where once he was oblivious.

The rain that he heard in the night had stopped but there was a constant dripping of water outside. Most likely the oak tree, whose branches shaded his room in the summer, had shed its leaves and filled the guttering on the stable roof to overflowing.

He shivered and pulled the blanket higher over his shoulder, hoping for warmth, yet knowing there was little pleasure in lying abed with a coastal chill seeping into his bones. The rooms in the stables were clean, dry and functional, but not built for comfort unless one was a horse. Soon he must move and put some food in his belly, and to achieve this it was necessary to venture outside.

Joshua's introduction to gamekeeping involved studying the game books, which recorded the totals of pheasants, partridge, grouse, snipe and woodcock from the previous seasons, itemising the number and type of birds shot on a particular day, by members of the shooting parties. The ground game listed, he learned, referred to hares.

Order and method in everything, he thought with a wry smile.

Mr Blakeney must have read his mind, for he said, "This is an appropriate time to mention tenancy agreements, Mr Norbery, which permit the tenant farmer to shoot hare and rabbits on the land, except where the landowner reserves the sporting rights. I will find the relevant Game Laws for you to peruse, together with the appropriate certificate that anyone wishing to shoot game is obliged to obtain."

"Yes, sir," he said, without much enthusiasm.

"While you are studying the game books, you might find this one of interest," said Mr Blakeney, pointing to a book marked Deer Park. "It could be relevant to Linmore."

Joshua had seen the herds of red and fallow deer in the park but assumed that their breeding was left to nature. He should have known better.

"Not so", said Mr Blakeney. "Whilst a park of this size has the potential to sustain a herd in excess of five hundred head of deer, we do not retain that number. Stocks have to be carefully managed to ensure the total does not exceed the food supplies in the park for the coming winter season.

"In November, you will have the opportunity to assist with the annual deer count, which includes the fawns born in the summer. Each year we exchange some of the dominant young bucks with other deer herds to prevent interbreeding, which weakens the strain. After which there is a cull of the excess."

As he wrote the relevant details in his diary, Joshua realised that it was another form of stock breeding, with an end product of venison as opposed to beef or mutton.

The lecture over it was a relief to go outside to inspect the horse-drawn game-larder, which was an ingenious construction, built in sections with iron racks and hooks for various types of game, with an alabaster lining to provide cool storage.

Several days during the shooting season, he saw the vehicle empty in the morning, and again as the contents were stored in the large game-larder at the Hall. It was sufficient to illustrate the efficacy of the vehicle. To complete the study, he drew a couple of sketches in his workbook, intending to include them in a letter to Francis Weyborne.

Whilst adding new entries to the game book in the agent's office, Joshua's mind drifted back to the previous year, when he joined a shooting party at Linmore with his father and Charlie. That was why he declined the chance at Holkham, for it raised too many memories. A year ago, nothing had changed…

He sighed, trying to shake off his despondent mood.

"Are you bored with writing numbers in books, Mr Norbery?"

Joshua roused with a start, unaware of the agent's entry to the office until he spoke. "There's more to gamekeeping than shooting parties," said Mr Blakeney, waving a hand in the direction of the sound of gunfire. "They are the culmination of the gamekeeper's year. Preparation began many months ago, when the first pheasant and partridge chicks were hatched. Then they had to be reared and protected from vermin…of all kinds. A gamekeeper's life, Mr Norbery, is not an easy one, as you will discover. "

Joshua knew he was about to learn a new aspect of land management.

Mr Blakeney told him that vermin referred to anything that might endanger the young game.

"You would be surprised how many enemies these birds have. It is a wonder they survive, for predators steal many of the eggs before they hatch."

"What kind of predators?" he asked.

"Of the fur, feathered and scaly kind," the agent said cryptically. "Birds of prey take the chicks in the wild. Snakes eat the eggs, as do rats, which are particularly destructive. Then there are foxes, weasels, stoats, hedgehogs, or carrion, such as crows and magpies. Located as we are on the coast, seagulls are a menace.

"When they are fully grown, the young birds need protecting from their natural enemies – and man as well. This is the time of highest risk of poaching, and poachers, Mr Norbery, are an aberration. It cannot be condoned, because it is a case of unlawful people abusing the rights of the landowner on his land."

Having seen people in abject poverty, Joshua wondered what harm the loss of a few rabbits could do. He did not need to ask, for Mr Blakeney remedied his ignorance of the subject.

"I can see that you don't believe me, but if one allowed them the odd rabbit, where would it end? The Game Laws give the right of ownership to the landowner – your father amongst them. Magistrates have to judge the poachers who steal game for food against those who do it for profit, and take appropriate action against hardened offenders who stop at nothing to achieve their aims."

"You mean they offer violence against gamekeepers?" That put a different complexion on the matter.

"Gangs from towns outside the district come prepared to kill or maim; and the punishments are harsh. The penalty for such things is death. A lesser crime attracts a fine, a prison sentence or transportation to a penal colony. Bear in mind that one day, you might be the magistrate making such decisions."

That caught Joshua's imagination. Apathy and regret disappeared, and the need to know took precedence.

"What methods are used in poaching, sir?"

"There are many, but next week when the shoot is over, I will send you out with one of the senior gamekeepers. He can tell you what to look for."

A look was all Joshua intended when he set out to walk back to the stables from his evening meal at the Hall, an hour later than the other lads who were always ready before him. Then curiosity took over – a powerful incentive added to the recollection of what Dunbar, a gamekeeper with twenty years experience, told him.

He spent a week learning about the hatching and rearing of young pheasants and partridge. Three more days identifying vermin of the two or four-footed kind that Mr Blakeney had mentioned. Then he went out on the estate with Dunbar.

Accustomed to riding around the estate, Joshua found himself walking for miles and miles. With every step, the gamekeeper pointed out various things of significance. Abandoned nests in trees, repaired by carrion for their use, crows and such like, which attacked the young birds. Joshua's mind took in every detail.

"I notice that you didn't come on the shoot with the other young gentlemen," the keeper said.

"No," Joshua said. "Mr Blakeney said it was the end of your preparation."

"In a manner of speaking it is, but there again, it isn't, for when game stocks are high we are at our most watchful – for poachers. That applies to the deer as well."

"He mentioned need and greed," Joshua said.

The man nodded.

"Need is when a pothunter supplies his own table. Greed is for profit. Shopkeepers are supposed to have a certificate authorising them to sell game, but some folks aren't too particular about such things. They're the ones who pay a good price for game, and don't ask questions about where it comes from, or the sometimes violent means used to acquire it. The kind of thing we gamekeepers have to face. People can get killed."

That sounded like the running battles between the Revenue men and smugglers. As they walked, Dunbar pointed out places where pheasants might roost, citing a large patch of thorn trees in a wood, between the boughs of an oak tree, or in thick old ivy.

"Pheasants gather in numbers under oak trees when acorns are ripe. At night, the strength of the wind affects the height the birds will roost. We know what the birds do, and when to expect poachers."

"How?" said Joshua.

"They come when the moon is rising. Game is more plentiful during the first three quarters of the cycle. The last week and a half is poor."

"How can the moon affect it?"

"Take my word for it, but it does, and the experienced poachers know it. I've listened to a few in my time here, usually in the public houses."

"Bright moonlight, you mean?"

"No," said Dunbar. "The poachers need some cloud, with a light breeze to keep it moving. That way, it's light enough for them to see what they are doing, but not so bright we can see them."

He heard about snares, traps and of nets the width of a five-barred gate to catch rabbits, or set across grassland and quiet country lanes where hares spent time running up and down. Once caught in the net, the poachers quickly killed the animals, but Dunbar told him of finding abandoned nets when the gamekeepers disturbed poachers, and the difficulties of removing stiffened carcases.

That is why the poachers aimed to get their catch away from the area as quickly as might be achieved. Usually in a horse-drawn vehicle waiting nearby, for they could catch dozens, even a hundred or more hares in a night.

Joshua was still mulling over the details when he followed the drive alongside the lake. The reflection of the waxing moon in the water drew his attention to the clouds scudding across the sky and the freshening breeze that would soon sweep them away.

It was an entrancing sight. He felt the weariness of the previous hour evaporate, and in the brightness was tempted to take a walk across the park. Before he had taken two steps forward, he recalled his conversation with Dunbar.

"Do you go out at night after poachers?" he had asked the gamekeeper.

"We do, young sir," said the man, in a blunt voice, "but don't go thinking that you can do the same. We have enough to contend with, without looking for lost boys."

"What do you mean?" Joshua said in an indignant voice, wondering how Dunbar knew the idea had just occurred to him.

"We take guns, because they do, and in a park the size of this one, there's no way of telling a poacher from a gamekeeper. Mr Coke pays me to go out and risk being shot or hit over the head, but he'd take a dim view if anything like that happened to you, through your own stupidity."

Blunt words indeed, but they hit the mark. Joshua was feeling irked at the restrictions of playing nursemaid to the other two students, but he could not allow Dunbar to be blamed. He looked again at the poachers' moon, decided that he was too tired for adventures, and made his way back to the stables. Morning would come all too soon. Learning of the potential risks faced by gamekeepers was one aspect of game-keeping that Joshua would never forget, nor write about in his diary.

After that, Joshua confined his activities to working during the daytime. He wrote relevant facts in his diary and sent letters home to Aunt Jane and Francis Weyborne.

I will soon be starting my second round of placements. I have little time to write in detail, but record the daily happenings in the estate book the agent gave me for the purpose. It looks very grand, with the Holkham crest, an ostrich, emblazoned on the black leather cover.

My view of estate management is different to when I began, but the principle is easy to understand. The landlord maintains the buildings and the tenant has responsibility for the land, subject to the terms of the lease, planned by Mr Blakeney.

Of course, I can only equate this to Holkham by looking back to how Mr Coke replaced old farmhouses and buildings on the estate. His programme continued with labourers' cottages. The initial cost must have been prohibitively high, but over time, lower maintenance justified the expenditure.

Joshua reread the letter. The content looked all right on paper, but he could not make assumptions about what would happen when he returned to Linmore. He had never been in the position to consider cost before, but suspected that his late brother's debts were considerable. To what degree, he knew not.

When he accompanied Mr Weyborne and Francis on their daily rounds, he had seen buildings in need of repair, and some neglected land. At the time, he did not understand the significance. Now he did, and wanted to go home and play his part in the renewal of Linmore. If he were lucky, his father would let him have a say, but he had a further six months to acquire more knowledge.

To ensure he did not forget anything, Joshua strived to fill in the details before he went to sleep, and had done through all his placements, when he could remain awake. Some days he wrote half a page, but others managed only a couple of lines. He was sure Aunt Jane and his father would want to know what he had been doing.

October the twenty eighth. He recorded the date when the agent took the three students on a tour of the roads around the perimeter of the park. Other than the monthly meeting in the estate office, it was Mr Blakeney's way of bringing them together in their work, and always followed the same pattern.

They rode their horses two abreast. Michael and James preferred to ride together, so Joshua rode alongside the agent, who pointed out recent repairs to farm buildings, and new thatches to farm workers' cottages, using local reeds.

He had travelled this way many times before. When they approached the outer limits of the fishing village, they usually turned down a track onto the estate. Before that, they passed the local workhouse. At least, that was what the faded notice on the gate said it was.

The brick and flint building was surrounded by a high wall, in which were set a pair of sturdy wooden doors, chained together. There was little to see from the road, but riding a horse, Joshua could stand up in the stirrups and peer over the walls. All he could see was the tiled roof and narrow windows with many panes of dusty glass. It had a bleak, abandoned look, and not once in passing had he seen any signs of life.

He remembered seeing a similar building in Linmore Dale, and in other counties on his journey to Holkham. They were dark, gloomy places, overflowing with people, whereas this seemed empty. If not here, where were the poor of the district? Before he saw poverty on his travels, Joshua would not have been aware of such things, but now he was.

"Why are the doors locked, Mr Blakeney?" He felt silly asking the question, but wanted to know.

The agent brought his horse to a halt, and answered with another question. "Why do you think it might be closed?"

"I can only imagine that it wasn't large enough, and another has been built nearer the town," said Joshua.

"That's one option," the agent said, turning in the saddle. "Now, let me ask Mr Gransden what he thinks is the purpose of having such an institution?"

"To house the poor, of course, sir," Michael Gransden hastened to say, "but my father thinks they should be made to help themselves."

"Mmm, that is an interesting concept, young man. What would you do to assist the indigent in their endeavour?" Mr Blakeney's tone was quiet, but he accentuated the familiar burr.

Michael responded with the voice of youth and privilege. "If they aren't prepared to work then they should be left to starve."

The agent stroked his jaw before giving his response.

"Unfortunately," he said, "it is when families are starving that they are forced into the workhouse. These places are not for pleasure, gentlemen. They provide basic food and shelter. Conditions are harsh, and people only enter those doors as a last resort. The stigma is so great that some folk would rather die with their self-respect than ask for help. The majority would rather earn their living, even doing the meanest task than to be labelled thus."

For once, Michael Gransden was at a loss for words, and James was similarly afflicted, but Joshua's mind was teaming with thoughts.

"As this was your question, Joshua," the agent said, "I'll give you the answer. This building has been empty for well over a year, for the simple reason the people hereabouts have work to do. They maintain their dignity, which is an important factor."

The agent's words triggered a memory of something Sergeant Percival said about women trading services to young men in exchange for money, and Joshua realised the significance of Tess offering herself rather than accept his charity. She might have needed the money, but it did not make his misguided offer welcome. Her self-respect was all she had.

Mr Coke knew that and provided the means to earn her living – which added another dimension to his understanding of a landowner's responsibilities.

Contrary to Joshua's expectations, the second part of his apprenticeship did not follow the rigid lines of the first. Mr Blakeney offered him the chance to plan his timetable, which proved as confusing as the well-established routine at Holkham. He was not sure what he wanted to do.

"What type of soil do you have in Shropshire, Mr Norbery?"

Joshua was attending the November meeting of students in the agent's office. His mind was elsewhere, and Mr Blakeney had a habit of firing questions at people. Today, he was well and truly caught gathering dust.

"I…um…" Joshua frowned. What did he mean?

"Let me rephrase the question. What type is the local rock near your home?"

"It is limestone, sir," said Joshua, knowing there were quarries in the ridge across the one side of the valley, full of fossils.

The agent nodded. "That sounds about right, so you would need to deal with the soil in a different way to the light, sandy ground we have on the east coast. If there is a limestone escarpment, the chances are the soil in the valley is red clay, washed down from the higher land. Clay is a heavy soil, which holds the water and needs careful drainage, which means digging ditches and keeping them clear to avoid waterlogged fields or flooding the roads."

It started to make sense. Joshua had thought of this only in the context of Holkham, but if the type of soil was different, so too were the additives needed to make it fertile. Presumably, that was the reason the agent asked about the land at Linmore. Then he realised Mr Blakeney was still speaking.

"Can you stay behind after the meeting, Mr Norbery? There is a matter I need to discuss with you."

Within minutes, the agent dismissed the other students, giving them two hours' free time, and kept Joshua talking.

"I hope you realise the significance of my question about the soil."

Joshua nodded. "The acidity levels would be different at home, as would the types of fertilizer used."

The agent nodded.

"I drew your attention to the subject, because I am going to set you the task of planning your training programme for the next six months, based on the headings we used for the first. I want you to find out the practices used on your estate in Shropshire, then analyse what is good and what changes will be required when you return home. You will never be in a better position. If you bring your thoughts to me, we will formulate a plan to set before your father."

Joshua's mind was teeming with ideas.

"One more question. How many fertilizers can you name?"

Wondering if it was a trick question, Joshua said, "Marl, clay, manure… and… bonemeal, sir."

"Yes," said the agent. "I don't think you have encountered much bonemeal yet. There is a processing plant near here, so when we need another cartload, I will send you with the driver."

347

Joshua did not know what amused the agent. He was not a man to joke, but his mouth certainly twitched when he said that.

The next morning at seven o'clock, he returned to Mr Blakeney's office, armed with his diary and pencils sharpened.

"We'll begin with estate management. I want you to remember that Mr Coke started his restoration programme a quarter of a century ago, and it will probably take you as long. It is a costly process, and he didn't do it all at once – nor will you."

Joshua looked at the framed list of rules behind the desk. The agent caught his glance and responded.

"Yes," he said. "Time is a valuable commodity, Mr Norbery. It would be well to remember that in the years to come. Now, I will give you some basic advice about managing your buildings.

Joshua wrote in his diary. *It makes sense to maintain and improve the fabric of existing buildings. Replace only those too dilapidated for repair. That applies equally to tiled or thatched roofs. Clear the rot from the woodwork. Do not let a lack of mortar weaken the walls, and ensure drainage channels of stone floors are clear.*

If he could manage that, it would leave time to make other changes.

After the agent's questions in the office, Joshua started to look critically at farming practices on the Home Farm at Linmore. He did not pretend to be an expert, but the more he learned, the clearer it was that agriculture in Shropshire was decades behind Norfolk.

He wrote to Francis Weyborne, enlisting his support. Three weeks later, he received enthusiastic answers, which told him the trainee bailiff was prepared to work with him. That was the first hurdle overcome.

Joshua knew he must introduce change slowly, gain support and not allow doubters to deter him. The land at Holkham was in good heart, and he was determined to make Linmore its equal on a smaller scale.

Once he formulated his plan, his enthusiasm took over. Who would have thought such a mundane subject could be so fascinating? Certainly not he, but it was. If he thought the agent's schedule was strict, his motivation drove it harder. Unbeknown to his fellow students, he had another agenda, the details of which only Mr Blakeney was privy to know and give his permission.

His first task on discovering the winter ploughing was in progress was to watch the ploughmen go about their work. Clad in his wide-brimmed hat, smock and heavy boots, there was little to differentiate him from the labourers when he sat down to share their work break, supping a mug of cider and chewing a crust of bread spread with beef dripping. He did this for several days and came back well satisfied with what he learned.

Linmore was constantly in Joshua's mind. He knew fallow fields were a waste of land, but Francis hinted that his father, Jim Weyborne, was a believer in the old ways. He expected some opposition, but was prepared to justify his plan to increase the ploughing capacity by introducing teams of heavy horses, which could deal with almost twice as many acres in a day than oxen.

Deep down, Joshua knew that any changes he made would inevitably bring a degree of disruption. To labourers used to sowing seeds by hand, a seed drill might be revolutionary, but at a stroke, it would ensure a uniform depth and increase yield. It was essential to grow more root crops for winter fodder to improve the animal feeding regime, and produce better quality manure for the land the following year.

Joshua imagined his interest in the land passed unnoticed, but the subject arose when Mr Coke attended the December meeting in the agent's office.

Everyone was sitting around the desk. The landowner and his agent sat one side, with Joshua and the two other students opposite. They discussed many things and it was obvious Mr Coke's presence had a profound effect.

Michael was in his element, ready to volunteer opinions without letting James speak for himself. Joshua said little. He sat back and listened, with half an ear on the conversation. Then Mr Coke spoke.

"I hear you have been doing some ploughing, Joshua?"

There was a muffled snort of derision in the background from Michael.

"Yes, sir." Joshua could not deny the fact, but wondered where the news originated. As far as he was aware, only the ploughmen witnessed his efforts.

"What did you hope to learn?" said Mr Coke.

It was evident from the noise of scraping chair legs, and scuffing boots on the floor, that he had embarrassed his fellow students. They literally squirmed in their seats. Never mind. Maybe they would learn something.

"I spent hours watching the ploughmen set out work in the field, and plough a straight furrow. I wanted to do the same. They made it look easy, but it takes a lot of practice to manage a team of horses as well."

He received a nod of agreement from the agent, but it was Mr Coke who said, "That's true, but when you followed the plough, you gained a better understanding of the work involved, and how much land could be covered in a day. Moreover, you earned the respect of the ploughman. Old Tom told me of your determination to succeed, and he's not easily impressed."

To hear Mr Coke say that made everything worthwhile.

CHAPTER 37

Christmas at Holkham was the first for many years that Joshua would spend without Charlie for company. Linmore had never been a very social place, due to his mother's various maladies; but his father and Aunt Jane always ensured there were opportunities for the younger family members to socialize with neighbours. Now he was away from it all.

Three days before Christmas, he waved farewell to Michael Gransden going home to Kings Lynn, and James Inglethorpe to Bury St Edmunds.

Joshua told himself he did not care for grand social events, or wearing fancy clothes. All he needed was a decent meal to set him up for the season.

Mr Blakeney had other ideas. In the two days leading up to Christmas, Joshua experienced the bounty of the landlord, when he joined the agent on a tour of the estate to dispense presents of well-hung game with flagons of cider and ale to the workers' families.

At midnight on Christmas Eve, the sound of carol singing rang out from the church on the hill overlooking Holkham Park. A chill wind blew outside, but not a seat in the building remained empty.

Mr Coke and his daughters sat in the front pew by the pulpit, and the Holkham workers, from the highest to the lowest person on the estate, filled every other pew. The agent, his wife and children; ploughmen with their families, gardeners, foresters, stable lads, shepherds, cowmen, laundry workers, servants from the Hall and Joshua Norbery from Linmore.

It was the first time he felt he truly belonged, and in that joyful moment of singing Christmas Carols, he felt close to Linmore.

Of course, his mother would not go to church, but Aunt Jane would sit in the front pew beside his father, sing the same tunes and make responses to the prayers. It was as if he was there with them.

Christmas Day dawned, bright and crisp underfoot. Joshua exchanged his brown working coat for bottle green superfine and spent the time with the agent making merry with his relations, many of whom he knew from working on the estate. It was a jolly family occasion unlike any he had experienced before.

Mrs Blakeney organised a veritable feast. There was poultry and game, a haunch of venison, as well as fish, fresh from the sea, with a multitude of vegetable side dishes, followed by a selection of tasty puddings, sweet desserts and ices. The servants brought in tankards of ale and cider for the menfolk, and glasses of homemade wine and lemonade for the women.

The Blakeney family laughed, talked and sang songs. Someone played the fiddle while others danced. Then they handed out the presents. Joshua received a new work diary from the agent. He wished he had a gift to give in return, but none was expected.

When supper was over, Joshua said his thanks and donned his greatcoat in preparation to ride his horse back across the park to the stables. Ben Waters, the groom, joined him by the back door, similarly muffled against the weather.

"Come on, Joshua," he said. "You had better come with me in the gig. The horse might find his way, but you wouldn't make it on your own."

Joshua laughed, thinking the groom referred to the ale they had consumed earlier in the day, but realised his mistake when he looked outside.

He could see the path leading to the stable yard, but the drive and familiar landmarks beyond the gateposts had disappeared under a blanket of snow. There was no alternative but to accept the offer, which he did gratefully.

Joshua shivered, wrapped his woollen scarf around his neck, pulled up the collar of his greatcoat around his ears, and huddled down into the capes around his shoulders. With any luck, the mulled wine he drank before leaving the agent's house would keep the worst of the chill at bay, but he would be glad to be between the sheets tonight.

The night air was cold after the glowing warmth of the house, and the hazy light of the rising moon bathed the park in an eerie whiteness. It was so bright in the open, but a multitude of shadows lurked amongst the trees.

All was quiet, apart from the muffled hoof beats and turning of wheels. Lanterns hung on either side of the gig, flickered behind glass cases, attempting to light the way. The screech of an owl broke the silence, and Joshua saw a ghostly shape winging its way across the parkland. The sound came as a relief to break the monotony.

A coppice ahead indicated the direction they should take, but when clouds obscured the moon, the groom struggled to keep the gig on the road. Joshua knew if he had been holding the reins, the snow would have erased his sense of direction. Of one thing he was certain: rising moon or not, there would be no poachers abroad on a night like this.

Another block of trees on either side of the road formed a windbreak, and then they were in the open, feeling the force of the keen wind blowing across the park. By the look of the sky, it would snow again before morning.

Their pace seemed interminably slow. A mile and a half felt like three, and the quarter of an hour it normally took to cover the distance stretched to four times the amount.

"Not long now," Ben said. "We'll soon be there."

The groom had said the words three times already, yet minutes later, Joshua saw the stable block appear behind the next group of oak trees, and beyond the lake, the familiar outline of Holkham Hall. It was good to be home.

On Boxing Day, he swapped his green coat for one in burgundy as he joined the servants' hall celebrations. Mr Coke carved the roast goose, Mr Blakeney a sirloin of beef, and Joshua placed flagons of ale and cider on the tables. Then he sat down and ate his fill. When the dining was finished, the servants cleared the room and the country dancing began. He could not have enjoyed himself more, had he been a guest of the king.

The only problem he encountered was the mistletoe bunches hanging in every doorway, which attracted maidservants like wasps to a jam pot. Whichever way he turned, there was one waiting, and so he passed it off in grand style, bowing low and kissing their hands as he would a lady. It was a source of great amusement for the menfolk and kept the women at arm's length. Even the housekeeper could not resist the temptation to walk by at an opportune moment, and went away smiling.

Snowflakes were falling again when he trudged back to the stables in the company of the grooms. It was too cold to waste time, but the camaraderie kept him warm, and stopped him feeling sad. The weather continued thus until the year's end. Apart from a few lights in the windows, Holkham Hall seemed to be gently sleeping under a blanket of snow.

When he listened to the church bells ringing in the New Year, Joshua wondered what the year would hold. Eight months had passed since his arrival, which meant he would be going home a few weeks after Easter.

Michael and James returned before Twelfth Night, suitably refreshed by their family celebrations, and work began all over again.

Soon afterwards, the family at the Hall set out for London. Parliament was in session, and they would see little of Mr Coke for several months. Joshua expected his father was similarly in transit from Linmore, and within another month, the London social season would begin.

The thought triggered a memory of when he was in Rome, and of Lady Kenchester's ideas about him and Lady Rosie. Much had happened since then, and he wondered if she still remembered him.

The lambing snows came before the first covering melted. The shepherds were out in the days and the darkest of nights, gathering up the lambs, saving them from the cold and wet, and the ever-present danger of foxes and carrion.

Immersed in the second placement of stockbreeding, Joshua had no time to feel lonely. Perversely, while his fellow students slept, he was out by the Great Barn with the shepherds, keeping the promise he made to go back, even if only for one night.

In truth, it was for several nights and the reality was different to how he imagined. The hours were long and eerily quiet, apart from the occasional hoot of an owl, or call of a dog fox to its vixen.

He followed the shepherds around the fields, holding a lantern while they carried the newborn lambs to shelter. When they gave him one to carry back to the barn, he slipped it inside his coat to keep it warm.

Bittersweet memories caught him unawares. Thoughts of happier times flooded back as he remembered a night at Linmore when he, Charlie and Sophie sat in the stables, waiting for a foal to be born.

Together they shared the sense of awe at the birth, the wonder as the wobbly little creature struggled to stand and the tears of relief when it did. The part that touched him most was the maternal tenderness.

Charlie and Sophie had short but happy memories of their mother, which Joshua lacked. Thank goodness, Aunt Jane was there to cuddle him. Without her, he would have had no one.

He was thankful none of the shepherds made fun of him when he washed his smeary face in a handful of snow. The icy chill on his skin shocked him into wakefulness, and he cast aside his maudlin feelings of self-pity.

Back in the shepherds' hut, he shared a bite to eat and a drink around the log stove, but could not stay awake any longer. By the time he awoke several hours later, he was alone and the stove was burning low.

Outside, birds were singing, and the snow-covered landscape looked different with a chilly sun rising over the sea. The sound of a newborn lamb crying for its mother made him think of Tess, and he wondered who would support her when she delivered her baby.

Knowing he did not have the right to interfere, Joshua saddled his horse in the barn and took his leave of the shepherds.

"Will we see you tonight?" someone asked.

"You will," he said, fully intending to be there.

It was time to ride back for breakfast at the Hall, and he was there with his shepherd's hat in hand before the other students left their beds. The servants in the breakfast room smiled, but no one made fun of his eccentricity. Afterwards, he stumbled back to the stables and fell into bed for a dreamless sleep. It seemed only minutes later he heard the door of his room open.

"Come on, Norbery, you'll miss breakfast." Michael Gransden's voice came through the mists of sleep.

"I've had mine," Joshua mumbled and buried his head under the pillow.

"Please yourself, but don't forget the agent's meeting is at eleven o'clock." Michael's voice receded down the stairs.

"Come on, James. Some of us have to show the agent we are ready to do some work. I do not know what's happened to Joshua these last few days; dashed if I ever saw such a lazy fellow for sticking to his bed."

A few minutes later, Kegworth looked in to close the door, which Michael had left open. "It's all right, Mr Norbery," he said. "My young master doesn't know the world goes on while he sleeps. I heard you come in at about half past five. What time do you want me to give you a call?"

Joshua opened one bleary eye and yawned. "What time is it now?"

"Five minutes after seven o'clock. How would it be if I brew up some tea, and bring some hot water for washing and shaving at about nine?"

"Mmm…"

While the agent nodded approval to Joshua's requests, his fellow students found his interest in delivering animals as inexplicable as his predilection for working with the lower orders. They could not understand it.

In their opinion, a gentleman paid others to do such work. It raised questions in their minds about his origins, and his motives for learning. Had they possibly misunderstood that his father was a tenant farmer?

"Surely, Joshua, there's no need to get your hands dirty, or tramp across the estate wearing the clothes of a labourer?" Michael was the most vocal.

"What do you mean?" he said. "Mr Coke doesn't consider it beneath his dignity to wear a smock-frock and gaiters when he works on the estate, and he learned about agriculture by asking the people who knew."

They chose to ignore that aspect.

"Your father is a gentleman, isn't he? I mean… he's not a tenant farmer?" Doubt crept into James's voice.

That was outside of enough. Joshua had never before heard his father's status questioned, and his scathing tone lashed them.

"Of course my father is a landowner," he said. "The Norbery family have been at Linmore for at least seven generations."

The younger lad was profuse in his apologies. Joshua waved them aside and stalked away, but his anger evaporated before he reached the door. He stopped, turned and extended his hand.

"I'm sorry," he said. "That was ill-mannered of me."

James was almost pathetically grateful for the gesture, and Michael looked equally chastened. Neither of them, they assured him, intended any offence.

Joshua felt ashamed of his ill humour. His paternal grandfather reputedly had a fiery temper, and haughty demeanour, but his father was a gentle soul. He much preferred to resemble him.

He supposed he could have told them of the barony, which lapsed when his grandfather inherited the estate from a cousin, but it would have been no different to Michael's boasts of his father being a baronet.

Joshua gave the appearance of interest, knowing his father declined the offer of a title for reasons that concerned no one outside Linmore.

He could never reveal the reason for his determination. It was more than being heir to the estate. He had to prove himself a worthy custodian of Linmore. Sophie Cobarne had gone, but the stigma attached to his name remained. Only when it was resolved could he face the future, and one day seek a wife. That ultimately was his goal, but unlike his father, he wanted to marry a woman he could trust, and love.

As February merged into March, Joshua reviewed his workbook. He had not realised how war with France affected farming practice. It was not simply a matter of landowners producing cereal crops and meat for profit. There were strict war regulations governing the supply of food, with an ever-increasing demand to feed workers of munitions factories in the industrial towns. It was as simple as that. Good quality food earned results, and money to reinvest in the land.

That justified the animal sheds in the Great Barn, used for wintering stock cattle, fattening them with hay, root crops and oilcake. He could see how crop rotation and stockbreeding complemented each other. Well-fed animals gained more weight, and produced better manure to nurture the land the following year. Well-manured land produced a higher yield of cereal, root crops and hay. Maybe it was time for Linmore to invest in some wintering sheds.

Joshua drew a line under his writing and pondered what to do next. He knew if he asked he could play cards with Michael and James. Since their disagreement, the other students had offered many times. Usually he declined, saying he was not much of a card player. It was not strictly true.

There was a time when he could play with the best. He and Charlie spent many hours playing cards with the former soldiers in the wilds of Macedonia, when Doctor Hawley's life hung by a thread, and again in the villa gardens of Athens and Rome. He could probably have beaten both the lads without effort, but could not afford a repetition of the Fakenham overspend if he lost.

Usually, he wrote letters, or went downstairs to talk with the grooms, and often found Kegworth there ahead of him.

Tonight, he was at a loss to know what to do. His diary was up to date, and he had finished the letters to Aunt Jane and Francis Weyborne, so he started to write a letter to Lady Rosie, as a friend. By the time he had written two lines, he was opening his heart. Words failed him when he attempted to relate the trouble with Charlie, so he moved on to other news.

Of course, he would not send it. He did not know where she lived, but it helped to lighten his mood. Any communication between them would have to be in person when he went to London.

He smiled as he wrote, telling her about his stay at Holkham. There were several omissions, but he decided they did not matter. The lines flowed from the pen, on and on. He did not realise the others had stopped playing cards and were watching him, until Michael Gransden started to speak.

"You seem engrossed in your writing, Norbery."

Joshua glanced up and looked to the opposite end of the wooden table.

"Yes," he said, and continued writing.

"It can't be any of the agent's lessons to command such enthusiasm."

"No." Joshua resumed his writing, well pleased with his tactics. He was enjoying himself.

"It must be to a friend," Michael persisted.

"Yes," he said, deciding he could afford to smile. "One I met in Athens."

"Aha," said Michael, as if he said something original. "I think, James, our friend is writing to a lady."

"Oh, yes," said Joshua, with a grin. "She is definitely a lady."

"I thought you said you didn't have any *affaires* on the tour?" Michael sounded decidedly aggrieved.

"No," said Joshua. "What I actually said was I didn't pay a farthing for a woman. There is a vast difference."

Michael Gransden's expression was a picture to behold.

Having decided it was time to end the letter, Joshua sealed it with a wafer. He wrote the name *Lady Rosemary Chervil* on the front, and slipped it inside his diary. It served its purpose, and he felt better, but there were too many pages to send it through the postal service. Not that he really intended to do so. Even supposing he had Rosie's address, he couldn't take the chance of under-paying the postage for a billet-doux, and expecting her to pay the difference. That would never do.

CHAPTER 38

April 1802

"I say, Norbery; in my last letter home, I told my parents you hadn't been off the Holkham estate in almost a year. How would you like to come home to Lynn with me for a few days?" Michael Gransden was in one of his beneficent moods. Then he spoiled it by saying, "James is coming as well, so there is no need for you to feel out of place. We'll take my gig, so you and Kegworth can ride the horses."

Irritated by Michael's patronising manner, Joshua's first instinct was to decline. It would be no pleasure if all the Gransden family were pompous. Most likely they were not, though part of him wondered if he was equally inept with words at their age.

What reason could he give if he refused? It would only be for a few days, and he would have to re-enter the social world sometime. Why not here, where no one knew him?

"Thank you," he said. "I'd be glad to come."

It was just as well he did not consider it beneath his dignity to ride with the valet. How could he, when the man refused payment for maintaining his clothes, and promised to repair any deficits in supply when they reached Lynn?

Having gained leave of absence from Mr Blakeney, they set off from Holkham on a Friday morning. The weather was dry, but there was a fresh onshore wind, and most years, the month of April was notoriously showery.

When the agent forewarned of rain, Michael laughed at the notion, but Joshua donned his wide-brimmed hat, and the greatcoat with waterproof shoulder capes. It was better to be prepared.

Standing beside Michael and James, wearing their fashionable driving coats and high-crowned beaver hats, Joshua knew he looked countrified. Any doubts about his practical clothing vanished when Kegworth emerged from the stables, similarly clad for the journey of almost thirty miles to the Gransdens' home at Hopstone Court, a short distance from Kings Lynn.

Michael set a good pace with the gig, leaving Joshua and the valet to follow on horseback. They caught up with the pair at a country inn, where they were enjoying a tankard of ale.

"Have you watered your horses?" Joshua asked.

"Kegworth can sort them out," Michael said.

"I know, and so can we," said Joshua, as he went through the door and found Kegworth outside, attending the horses.

"It's all right, sir, you don't have to worry about this," the man said. "I was a groom before I took the job as valet."

"What made you change?"

"I broke me leg, and Lady Gransden offered me this work, thinking it was easier."

"Does it hurt to ride?"

"A bit, but not so you'd notice. I'll probably feel the effects tomorrow."

"Make sure you have a drink before we start."

"Thank you kindly, sir," said the man, pocketing the proffered coin.

When Joshua returned indoors, Michael said, "I was just telling James that my sister, Melissa, wants to meet you chaps. She is only just sixteen, so you will have to make allowances. She's a good sort really, for a girl, and much better than my older sisters."

As an afterthought, he said, "I daresay we'll have a few friends sharing dinner tonight; and with the three of us as well, there should be an even number. We might have a bit of dancing."

Irrespective of the reasons Michael enumerated, Joshua knew his presence was supposed to convince Sir John and Lady Gransden of the benefits their son would derive from European travel. The idea being that if a mere country squire considered it important for his son, then a baronet was under the same obligation. It did not matter what they decided; Michael was not going anywhere in Europe with the war on.

They arrived at Hopstone Court in good time to meet with the Gransden family, before changing their clothes.

When Joshua entered the guest bedchamber allocated to him, he found a servant preparing a bath for his use. Seeing the screened alcove set aside for the hipbath, and several other discreetly placed modern conveniences, it was easy to understand Michael's boast that his home was the envy of their neighbours.

Taking a bath at Holkham meant using the facilities in the servants' washrooms or a dip in an old tin tub in the stables. To have one prepared especially for him was sheer indulgence. He had not realised how much he missed that kind of thing, particularly after spending a day in the saddle.

Having washed himself, he leaned back to wallow in the depth of warm water. Then he closed his eyes and let his mind relax as memories of Thessalonica came flooding back. Mmm, that was just perfect…

It seemed only minutes later that he heard Kegworth's voice calling.

"Mr Norbery, it's half past five. Lady Gransden said I was to remind you we keep country hours here, and dinner will be served at precisely six o'clock."

The implications of being late for dinner exercised a powerful effect. Before the valet stopped speaking, Joshua was halfway out of the bath, reaching for the warmed towels. Damn, his hair was wet, and there was little time in which to dress and get it dry.

Luckily, the valet brought extra towels for just such a contingency: large sheets of thick cotton to wrap around his form and towel his shoulders dry. Kegworth anticipated his need for a shave and prepared to apply a razor. It was a blessing, for Joshua could not afford to cut his chin tonight.

Clean linen stood ready, with a selection of evening clothes from which to make a choice.

"Thank you, Kegworth; I'll wear the dark green tonight."

It was an easy choice with matching coat and knee breeches, teamed with a cream and gold embroidered waistcoat.

The valet gave a discreet nod of agreement.

"I can see you know what style suits you, sir. That will look a rare treat, if you don't mind me saying, and one that'll meet with Lady Gransden's approval."

That might help to obviate his faux pas in being late, but not completely excuse it. Joshua looked at the clock and saw it wanted fifteen minutes to the hour. It would be a close-run thing.

With time at a premium, he readily accepted the valet's deft hand tying his neckcloth, and said a silent prayer of thanks to Mary-Anne for achieving the right balance between crispness and comfort.

Thank the Lord, the first attempt succeeded, and the coat eased across his broad shoulders without a struggle.

By now, his hair was dry enough to tie back with a fine length of black ribbon. A quick dust of his shoes, then a final application with a clothes brush to his coat, and he was ready. The valet had performed a miracle with a minute to spare.

"I'll show you the way, sir," Kegworth said, opening the door to the corridor.

Joshua reached the top of the staircase as the butler sounded the dinner gong and saw the assembled guests join their partners and move forward towards the dining room. He ran lightly down the first flight and around the curve, hoping that he could slip unnoticed down the final set of fifteen treads that he had counted on the way up.

Too late, several of the guests sensed his presence, and turned their eyes in his direction, so he had to run the gauntlet. Resigned to the inevitability of being late, he stopped to take a breath. *Don't get flustered. Think about something else.*

The hum of voices resumed when he returned their scrutiny.

A gentleman never draws attention to his dress. The words came to mind as Joshua noted the vivid shades and flamboyant styles worn by Michael Gransden's circle of friends. They reminded him of gaudy peacocks vying for attention, and it made him glad he chose to wear a plain colour.

The knowledge he was well dressed helped him face the ordeal ahead. He could not avoid meeting these people, so he would have to pretend he was enjoying the experience. As he walked sedately down the staircase, he recited the names of the Gransden family he had met earlier.

Sir John Gransden was a bluff countryman, who looked as if he would be more at home on the hunting field than in a ballroom. Lady Gransden was tall and imperious, and reminded him of Aunt Winifred Pontesbury – not so much in looks as her disconcerting way of knowing everything that went on.

From what he gathered, Charlotte, the eldest daughter, was married. Harriet, the next oldest, living at home, seemed prim and studious, almost a blue stocking, whereas Melissa, if he remembered correctly, was nearest to Michael in age; and there were two younger girls in the schoolroom.

He reached the final step at the exact time that the last guest passed through the door that the butler held open in readiness. Then he noticed that waiting in the hallway was a young lady of medium height and tumbling curls in a rich tawny brown, reminiscent of Michael Gransden's colouring.

At the same time, the girl looked up and saw him watching. Then she smiled and moved to his side. "Hello, I'm Melissa," she said. "I hope you don't mind, but Mama said I was to go into dinner with you."

Mind…he was delighted to have her support?

She was a friendly little soul with unaffected manners, wearing a modestly styled gown in light blue muslin as befitted her age. In looks, she favoured her mother, but had not achieved the willowy build of her older sisters.

Joshua was more than happy to accept her company, because Michael and James were escorting two other girls of a giggly nature, who were, according to Melissa, daughters of the Gransdens' nearest neighbours.

Three other families sat down to dine with them; two neighbours with older children, with the local clergyman and his family to add leaven to the group.

The atmosphere in the dining hall was one of great pomposity, with a steady stream of uniformed servants scurrying hither and thither, loading the long mahogany table with a larger selection of food and wine than the twenty or so people had any hope of consuming.

Long before the meal was over, Joshua realised the pomp and ceremony was to support Sir John Gransden's notion of self-consequence. From what he could see, Michael's father appeared to be a man of many words and little sense. A tendency shared with his son and heir.

The image intensified every time the baronet interrupted his lady, mid-sentence, demanding to know something unrelated to what she was saying to the guests sitting on either side of her.

As Lady Gransden sat at the opposite end of the table to her husband, with Joshua on her left-hand side, and Melissa one seat to his left, this resulted in frequent interruptions. Other than adopting a pained expression, Lady Gransden showed little response to her husband's lapse of good manners, but when her son similarly raised his voice to gain attention, she quelled him with an awesome glance.

After one such break in conversation, Joshua turned to his hostess, and said in a lowered tone, "Lady Gransden, I must beg your pardon for my lateness."

He had not been precisely late, but etiquette demanded that he said something.

363

She fixed him with a penetrating stare, her lips pursed.

"I'm afraid I fell asleep in the bath."

He had learned from Lady Kenchester in Rome, that honesty was much preferred to excuses.

Whilst Melissa chuckled at his side, her mother asked, "Did you ride all the way from Holkham today?"

"Yes, ma'am," he said. "Kegworth can vouch for that as he rode with me."

She frowned at his words, and then smiled benignly as she touched his wrist. "I will forgive you on this occasion, Mr Norbery, but I think we can improve on the arrangements for your return journey."

Somehow, he sensed that would include the valet.

At the end of the meal, the gentlemen wasted little time over their port, before rejoining the ladies. The reason for this became clear when the older members made up two card tables in one room and the younger folk prepared to enjoy an evening of country dancing, to the accompaniment of the governess on the pianoforte.

It began that way, but as the evening progressed, the dancing turned into a romp, as Michael's friends made free use of the wine decanter, and then dashed out onto the terrace with their partners.

Melissa peered through the French doors. "Do you think we ought to go with them?" she said.

"No." Joshua did not wish to be churlish, but he had not forgotten the last time he ventured outside to remonstrate with a recalcitrant female. He was still dealing with the aftermath.

"Oh well," she said. "I expect they will come in when they are ready. What shall we do while we are waiting?"

The governess was still playing the pianoforte, seemingly unconcerned that the dancers had all but fled her charge.

Joshua saw nothing improper in sitting one end of a chaise longue, with Melissa several feet beyond at the other, but within minutes she was confiding a secret that she assured him was known to only a handful of people. An artless disclosure about her wish to groom her pony and the lengths her servants were prepared to go to help her achieve her wish.

It was an unremarkable tale until she admitted that it was done in the face of her father's opposition. Quite why she was reduced to stratagems that exposed her to the risk of scandal and the servants to instant dismissal if discovered, he was at a loss to know.

To Joshua, it was inexplicable. Surely a man of sense would ensure training in the care of the horse, when his daughters learned to ride, just as his father did at Linmore. Things were obviously different at Hopstone Court, and having met Melissa's father, he began to understand why.

As the story unfolded, Melissa inched closer across the seat, lowering her voice and peering around to see the governess was still engrossed in her music. What she didn't seem to realise was that her actions were likely to draw attention.

"When I asked Papa, he refused permission for he thinks it inappropriate for me to do menial work or confide in the servants," she said in an undertone. "Mama didn't agree but she said that one shouldn't argue with gentlemen because they like to think that they know best. At least I think that's what she meant."

Joshua sensed that Lady Gransden would allow her husband to think what he wished and do exactly what she felt inclined, while telling her daughters that she obeyed her marriage vows to the letter.

"I know that girls have a duty to obey their parents, but it seems unfair that we have no chance to form our opinions before being married off to a stranger who also tells us what to do."

Until then Joshua hadn't given the matter a great deal of thought, but when he considered it he realised why she had gone against her father's wishes. It was based on giving respect to her elders, and earning it for herself.

As a baronet, Sir John Gransden was not a man who impressed him. A phrase he had heard came to mind, about one of the occasions when Mr Coke had declined a title. "I'd rather be amongst the best of the ducks than the worst of the geese" – or words to that effect.

That placed Melissa's father fairly and squarely where he belonged, but irrespective of his lack of title, Mr Coke was a greater gentleman than Sir John Gransden would ever be.

Growing up at Linmore, Joshua hadn't been aware that girls were hemmed in by convention. But he knew that Michael Gransden would expect him to break a confidence about something in which he was now complicit. Such a notion revolted his sense of chivalry.

"Who else knows?" he said, sensing the web of intrigue spread further.

"Only Jenny, my maid, and Wilfred her brother; he's the groom who is teaching me," she said, "and it was Alfred who found me a pair of Michael's… unmentionables that Mama had given him, and the poor dear is in daily dread of me being discovered."

She turned aside to beam a glowing smile at the gangly footman standing to attention by the door. A move that brought a flush to the lad's cheeks; or maybe a warm feeling because Melissa had worn garments intended for him. Hmm!

"And now you…" she said, "but I suppose that you will feel obliged to tell Michael and Papa, for they would consider it was improper."

"Nothing of the kind," Joshua said, fully aware of how Michael would judge his concealment, and that Lady Gransden might not view his involvement with complacency. It was a thorny problem but not, he thought, insurmountable.

"That's why I wish I had been born a boy," she said, "then I could have worn the unmentionable garments with impunity. As it is I feel guilty."

All the frivolity of her brother's friends was as nothing compared to the image conjured in Joshua's mind. His mouth felt dry. The footman had reason to be scared for Sir John would surely dismiss him for witnessing the impropriety. In a former age he would probably have been transported.

"Does Lady Gransden know?" he said.

"Oh, no," she said, shocked.

But you embroil servants, however innocently, and they have no defence against your father's wrath when he discovers you have flouted his dictate.

"That's why I wish that I'd been born a boy," she repeated.

But you were not, he thought. You are a pretty girl, with a delightful smile that will be the downfall of many men before you settle to be the wife of a horse-mad country squire like your father.

Poor Melissa, he pitied her, but she would ruin all if her imprudence was discovered. Suddenly, Joshua knew that he must separate her from the breeches… but not in the way it sounded. Michael was the type, like Teddy Pontesbury, who would think nothing of pinching a housemaid's bottom, but would condemn a footman for looking at his sister. It seemed to be an instant brotherly reaction.

He said a silent prayer of thanks to whichever god promoted classical music, for the pianoforte-playing governess remained oblivious of the crisis being resolved a dozen paces across the drawing room. *Saint Cecilia, he thought...*

"Personally, Melissa," he said, striving to affect a drawl, "I think for you to be a boy would waste your...abilities,"

"Do you really think so?" she said, giving him a sideways look under her lashes. "Or are you trying to flirt with me?"

"Is that what you wish me to do?" he said, before realising that she was distracting him. "What I meant to say was that if you must groom the pony, it would be more decorous to wrap an apron around your skirt. Without the breeches," he could say it with impunity, "your mother might overlook the activity in the stable."

She looked at him with dawning understanding. "So you are saying that if I ask Jenny to return...*them*... no one will ever know?"

He shrugged his shoulders, feigning indifference. "Once out of sight... who can prove they were ever in your possession?"

She sighed with relief. "Thank you, Joshua; I'm so glad that I told you."

He sank deeper into the mire of complicity. "It might be prudent not to frequent the stables. After all, you've learned the process of grooming a horse, which was, I presume, the purpose of the exercise?"

He refused to compare her actions with those of Sophie Cobarne.

"How kind you are to advise me," she said. "I never believed, before today, that what Mama said about gentlemen being wiser than ladies was true. You've proved her right, and I am so grateful."

"I think that it's unnecessary to tell her how you reached that conclusion."

"Oh, yes," she said with a shy little smile and glowing eyes.

Joshua turned aside and met the glowering gaze of the young footman, and recognised it for what it was. *Dash it all, you dullard, he thought, do you imagine that you are the only one affected by her plight?*

He stopped, feeling a little hand touching his arm.

"I didn't answer your question, about whether I wished you to flirt with me."

He already knew the answer.

"Yes, please, if you don't mind," she said, "because Michael's friends think I'm a frightful nuisance, and they are the types that Papa will choose to be my husband. I think they are silly to prance around in garish colours, sounding like peacocks. Mama says that it is much more gentlemanly to wear plain colours as you do."

Feeling the ground wobble beneath his feet, Joshua said in a voice quite unlike his own, "I would predict that in a couple of years, when you go to London to be presented at Court, you will have a greater number of beaux from which to choose than the gentlemen from Kings Lynn."

"That's a pretty compliment," she said, "but two years is a long time."

"Believe me, it will quickly pass. Two years ago I was planning to join the army, but when my brother died I became heir to the estate. That's why I came to Holkham to learn about estate management."

It was only one of the reasons, but as Melissa had secrets, so did he.

"You don't live anywhere near Kings Lynn, do you?"

"No," he said, "My home is in Shropshire, near the Welsh border."

"I wish that I could go to Holkham," she said. "I'm sure that I could learn to do something useful, but Michael says that riding around the estate, doing inspections and observing the labourers is tedious. Do you find it so?"

"It may surprise you to know, but I don't," Joshua said. "I would, however, rather you didn't tell Michael for reasons that I prefer not to divulge."

"That sounds terribly mysterious," she said. "I won't say a word, as long as you promise not to tell anyone what I have said."

Halfway through the conversation, Joshua decided that Michael's friends must be blind not to see that Melissa had an engaging smile, but it was easy to say when he basked in its glow.

The footman was a fool to show his preference so readily, for if her father saw he would be ruthless. Even Lady Gransden's intervention would not save a minion. The recollection of Sir John set Joshua's teeth on edge, but he must be careful not to give any hint of his thoughts.

As an observer, he had seen that Sir John's apparent bonhomie hid a degree of selfishness unsurpassed by any except his son, and that Lady Gransden was hard pressed to veil her contempt for both. Michael and his father were cast in the same mould as Lord Cardington, with only a slightly lesser notion of their omnipotence.

Joshua wondered if this was how other families lived. Linmore had never been normal for they rarely entertained neighbours and never on this scale. His mother's unnamed malady had screened them from view for many years.

Melissa's voice broke through his reverie. "You will promise not to tell anyone, won't you…?" She sounded anxious.

For a moment, he couldn't remember what it was that was he supposed to have heard. "I'm sorry…" he said, trying to gather his thoughts together, whilst knowing that Alfred could have told him every word she had spoken.

"You don't approve, do you?" she said, disappointed. "I shocked you…"

He looked at her hand, inches away from his on the seat, and left it there, knowing that if he moved so much as a muscle, the governess, would be instantly alert and ready to cry wolf. As if he was stupid enough to touch a young girl in her home in full view of the servants.

"You have my assurance that not a word of this will pass my lips, Melissa," he said softly. "I will, however, remind you to ensure the same from your maid and her brother. A word out of place could still prove embarrassing."

It sounded pompous but was a safer train of thought.

"I shouldn't have worn them," she said, "they were too large around my waist, and not even the tightest belt stopped them from slipping."

At this point, Joshua felt the heat of the room closing in on him.

"I expect that your sister was the model of decorum," she said.

He nodded because words were beyond him. Caroline had been everything she should be, but he had grown up alongside a hoyden who regularly strutted around wearing her brother's breeches. As Charlie's sister, Sophie Cobarne had never aroused the slightest interest, and yet this young girl's naiveté stirred him in such a way that he had to curb the smile of appreciation.

Joshua was just thinking that the sooner he returned to Holkham the better, when the truants returned giggling from the garden.

"What," said Michael, "are you still talking to my little sister, Norbery? I thought she would have bored you to tears by now. You should have come outside with us. It was great fun, blowing a cloud. Even the girls tried it, but it made them feel sick."

"I wasn't bored in the least," said Joshua, glad that he hadn't been forced to listen to any more of the inanities he had heard over dinner.

"No, I suppose not, but you're a bit slower than the rest of us chaps with socialising, aren't you?" Michael said, before adding, "No offense intended."

"None taken," said Joshua, viewing him with disdain and wondering how soon he could plead tiredness and retire.

"Michael," interrupted his sister, "you are so rude to your guest."

"Oh, Joshua won't mind. We do it all the time at Holkham."

Melissa looked at Joshua and rolled her eyes in disbelief.

He was tempted to laugh but knowing that he would have to explain what provoked the outburst to Michael prevented him. Some things were better left unsaid.

CHAPTER 39

H aving decided they had had a truly wonderful time, Michael and his group of friends begged their parents to allow them to visit the Assembly Rooms in Lynn the following evening.

On the Saturday morning, Joshua rode his horse whilst Michael drove his father's curricle around the surrounding countryside, stopping at frequent intervals to introduce his friends and tell anyone who would listen of their plans for the evening. It was evident that when the Gransdens did things, everyone knew in advance.

Halfway around the local village, they met up with Michael's two sisters, who were on horseback, accompanied by a groom.

Melissa greeted Joshua with a smile and promptly turned her mount alongside the horse he rode, whereas her older sister recalled a visit she wished to make and set off, the groom dutifully remaining with her.

Immediately, the topic of conversation changed to horseflesh. For Joshua, the young woman's appearance was a welcome relief from the brash young men who sought his opinion on travel. Despite his cool response to such questions at Holkham, nobody believed he could have travelled so far without at least one illicit foreign liaison.

In preparation for the evening, Joshua elected to wear the coat of midnight blue, teamed with dove-grey knee breeches, and a silver-white embroidered waistcoat he wore to the ball at the Villa Borghese, in Rome.

He could not explain why he chose that, when the evening in question was full of drama. Maybe it was simply the knowledge that his outfit was acceptable in aristocratic circles, so the local gentry in Kings Lynn had no reason to complain.

This was his first public dance since Rome, and it was time he regained his confidence in such things. Next year, he determined to accompany his family when they visited London in the season. He might see Lady Rosie again, and who knew what the outcome might be.

This was an excellent way to complete his social visit. Tomorrow afternoon, he would leave Hopstone Court. On Monday, work would begin on the final weeks of his farming apprenticeship, and by the middle of May, he would return home.

"By the way, sir," said Kegworth, applying the clothes brush one last time. "I found this in the inner pocket of your coat."

"The blue coat?" said Joshua, viewing with astonishment the fine length of gold coloured rope in the valet's hand.

"Yes, Mr Norbery." The valet's voice was devoid of expression.

Joshua absently ran the silky threads through his fingers, recalling that on the night of the Ball at the Villa Borghese, the Contessa wore it as a belt around her shimmering toga. Later she used it to bind his wrists, when they were in the marble chamber – a few minutes before the interruption…

He remembered the moment in the courtyard when Lady Rosie discovered his bonds.

"The evil witch," she had said in a furious tone, struggling to untie the silken strands. "How dare she do this to you?"

Then, her tone changed to one of curiosity as the Contessa's intention of tying him to the bed dawned.

"How novel," she said, in a teasing voice. "May I keep this one?"

Joshua flushed to the roots of his hair, realising the significance of Rosie's question; but after her rescue, how could he refuse? She had slipped the memento into her reticule, and he stuffed the second strand in his inner pocket.

Seeing it again he thought differently.

"You were wrong, Contessa," Joshua muttered under his breath, as he recalled the Italian diplomat's wife who had sought to entrap him. "I have no use for such tawdry things, for I will never be a slave to the likes of you."

Thus said, he tossed the relic from the past into the fire and watched it burn. Then he nodded thanks to Kegworth and walked towards the door.

When he entered the dining hall, Joshua found that more guests were present for introduction. Lady Gransden's married sister was visiting, while her husband was on military duties in the town, as well as her oldest daughter, Charlotte, and her spouse.

Lady Gransden gave him a long appraising look, followed by a distinct nod of approval, and adjured her son to study Mr Norbery's style of dress, which, she claimed, would recommend itself to people.

372

"But Mama," said Michael. "Joshua has the advantage of having travelled to Italy."

His mother's only comment: "Well, that accounts for it."

Michael's older sisters said nothing, but Melissa declared, "Mama is right. You do look very fine. May I be permitted to hope you might dance with me?" She looked sideways at him and smiled.

Her father viewed her with an indulgent eye. "It is not quite the thing, little miss, to ask a gentleman to dance, but I am sure Mr Norbery will find a moment to sign your card."

Joshua tactfully requested the pleasure of a dance with all the ladies, including Lady Gransden's sister, Mrs Eccleshall, which accounted for most of the evening. Michael and James did the same.

When the time came to set off for the assembly rooms, the party climbed into two large coaches. Sir John Gransden, his wife and her sister, accompanied by their two older daughters, sat in one, while Melissa chatted happily to her brother and his friends in another.

Michael Gransden's party arrived first, but rather than stand outside in the chill air, went into the vestibule to wait for his parents. He moved forward to sign the visitors' book and introduce his guests, while Joshua stood to the rear of the group awaiting his turn.

Feeling a sudden blast of cold air, he looked around and saw a group of six or seven soldiers, dressed in smart regimentals, coming through the open door, one more loquacious than his fellow officers.

He heard one say, "You're too bosky to be in here, Lieutenant."

Another, with a hint of the Irish replied, "A trifle disguised I will allow, but 'tis a sad reflection if a man can't celebrate his sister's safe delivery from childbirth."

Joshua would have recognised the voice anywhere, but it was the content of the conversation that froze his blood. Charlie Cobarne's talk of childbirth could only relate to one sister…

His mind stopped mid-calculation of the months since their last meeting. It must be nearly a year since he left Linmore, but he could not recall how close. He was transfixed. If Sophie Cobarne had delivered a child, to whom did it belong? Suddenly, he felt sick.

A hand caught his arm. "It's your turn to sign the book, Joshua," Melissa said, standing at his side.

Her clear sweet voice carried to the new arrivals. Charlie looked him

373

straight in the eye, and for a brief second, the old flame of friendship glowed. Then an icy glaze of enmity extinguished it.

It was hard to keep a steady hand to write his name in the visitors' book. However much Joshua wished otherwise, the prospect of a confrontation seemed inevitable. He glanced over his shoulder, beyond the soldiers to the outer door, hoping for deliverance, but it remained obstinately closed. Where was Lady Gransden?

"Who the devil let you in here amongst decent people?"

Joshua met the other man's gaze, willing him to say no more, but this was not Charlie as he had known him. It was a harsh-faced stranger in uniform, unsteady on his feet and hell-bent on humiliating him.

"What's the matter, Norbery?" Charlie Cobarne taunted, his potations putting words in his mouth. "Does the cat have your tongue, or are you afraid I will tell these people about how the heir to Linmore Hall preys on innocent women? I'll do that readily enough, and give you a thrashing you'll never forget."

The soldier's words sent a horrified gasp echoing around the vestibule. People shrank back from Joshua, leaving him standing alone in the middle of the room. He faced Charlie with outward calm, but underneath he was in turmoil.

"Say what you like, Charlie; you let yourself down as well. I will not fight you. There is not, and never has been a valid reason."

Joshua's apparent calm seemed to inflame the other man.

"Sophie said there was…" Charlie insisted, bunching his fists.

His fellow officers tried to hold him back. "You can't cause a mill in here, Lieutenant Cobarne. Jolly bad form."

Michael Gransden stepped haughtily forward. "What's all this about, Norbery?"

Dear God; what was it all about? "It was a disagreement… from… our schooldays." Joshua said the first thing that came to mind.

"Schooldays, be damned," Charlie slurred. "You, sir," he pointed at Michael, "should have a care about the company in which you entrust your sister."

"My sister…?" Michael Gransden's haughty demeanour heightened. "What the deuce do you mean, sir?"

His hand snaked out and caught Melissa's arm, pulling her away from Joshua's side.

Charlie Cobarne was more than ready to enlighten him.

"What I mean, my fine buck, is that you should take care not to let a rake like this… creature, anywhere near her."

There were murmurs of dissention. "Here, I say, steady on, there's no need for that kind of talk in here with ladies present."

Others in the group moved to intercede. Door attendants came forward.

"Well, Norbery, are you going to admit it? Did you, or did you not ravish my sister?"

The former friends stood glowering at each other. The taller was pale-faced and rigid as a marble statue. The other, with a flushed, wild-eyed look, was increasingly unsteady on his feet. They had the attention of everyone in the assembly rooms vestibule. Not a soul dared move for fear of missing the next word.

"Irrespective of what she told you, I…did…not," Joshua said through gritted teeth.

"Lying scum." Charlie spat on the ground. "I should have killed you for it at the time, and I would have, but for…"

"My father's appearance on the scene," Joshua said quietly. "Isn't that what you were going to say? Are you satisfied now you have tarnished my family name for no good cause?"

"Wasn't my sister's honour reason enough?"

"If what she said was true, then maybe; but what harm did my father ever do to you, or her, to deserve having his name bandied about? Where would either of you have been if he hadn't cared enough to give you a home, when nobody else wanted you?"

They were verbally fencing now with the foil off the blades. Joshua's words caused Charlie's guard to waver. He struggled to make a recovery, but was too late for Joshua attacked without mercy and thrust the point home to the heart.

"And don't forget Ed Salter…" he hissed, "without whose help neither you nor your sister would have learned to ride, Lieutenant Cobarne of the Dragoons."

For a brief moment, Charlie stared at him uncomprehendingly, then his eyes clouded with tears, and he stood with head bowed and shoulders sagging in defeat.

Joshua's control similarly reached its limit. He knew he must leave before it snapped. He turned to his companions.

"Please make my apologies to your mother, Michael. I think it would be better for everyone if I return to Holkham tonight. I'd be obliged if you'd ask Kegworth to bring my bag when you come back."

Michael rounded on him, saying in a furious undertone, "No, I'm dashed if I will. If you leave, then you admit he is right. You have to stay, otherwise it reflects badly on my family, and I will not have that."

With no other choice, Joshua said, "I will stay, but if your sister wants to change her mind about dancing with me…"

"It's up to her what she decides," Michael growled. "That fellow is in his cups. Everyone can see that."

The bonhomie had gone; but almost immediately, an icy draught swept Lady Gransden forward from the outer doors.

"What is the meaning of this unseemly obstruction, Michael?" she said in an imperious tone. "It is preventing Colonel Eccleshall from entering the assembly rooms."

At the mention of their commanding officer, all military heads snapped to attention. Shoulders went back, feet clicked in unison, and within seconds, they melted away before anyone challenged their presence. Some dashed towards the card room. Others bolted through side doors, dragging Charlie Cobarne with them.

Hardly had they disappeared, than Lady Gransden said in a voice that would brook no refusal, "Mr Norbery, would you care to take a turn with me around the ballroom?"

Joshua offered his arm. "I'd be honoured, ma'am."

"Michael," she turned to her son. "Attend your sister, and James, escort Harriet, if you please."

No one dared refuse.

Footmen sprang to open the inner double doors, as the matriarch swept through the opening on Joshua's arm. The sound of orchestral music filled the air, and the assembly rooms glowed with the candlelight reflecting on the crystal chandeliers running the length of the room, with more fittings around the walls.

Joshua breathed in, wondering the purpose of the exercise. It almost seemed as if the lady wished to be seen with him, for she bestowed gracious smiles on the worthy and deigned not to see anyone beneath her notice. As they promenaded the length of the room, she said in a quiet tone, "I hope you will not think ill of me if I offer a word of advice, the sort that I might give to my son. It is better in these situations to affect not to notice such people, and then no one gives credence to their ramblings."

He breathed out again, wondering how much she heard.

"A look of disdain can be most effective," she said, and suited the word to the deed towards anyone with the temerity to approach.

Having completed the circuit, they stopped whilst the lady selected a seat that gave her the best vantage point of the ballroom, and waited for her family to join them.

"Now, if you care to leave me, you may safely return to your friends. My husband will attend me."

"I am obliged to you for the advice, ma'am," Joshua felt compelled to say.

"This show of unity has not been simply for your benefit, young man, as my own. I live amongst these people, and know their propensity to gossip. I have no way of judging the validity of that person's scurrilous claim. It is between you, and him; but what I will say is if Mr Coke deems you worthy to go to Holkham, who am I to cavil?"

Joshua bowed over her hand as the family approached them. Michael was looking stormy, but he dared not speak out for fear of attracting his mother's ire. James Inglethorpe arrived with Harriet Gransden on his arm, and Melissa with her father.

What was he supposed to do now? After the altercation in the entrance lobby, he did not know if anyone would dance with him.

He stood on the outer rim of the family circle, wishing he had stayed at Holkham, until Michael and James gravitated to his side.

"We'd better make an effort to find a partner before the master of ceremonies finds one for us," Michael said, and James nodded agreement. They slid away, leaving Joshua to make his own move.

He sensed a movement at his side, and looked down as a hand touched his arm. Melissa Gransden stood looking at him.

"Would it be very forward of me to ask you to dance now?" she said. "You're the only person who doesn't tread on my feet, and I was so looking forward to it." Her quaint little face had a determined look.

"Thank you, Miss Melissa," he said. "I'd be honoured to dance with you."

She pouted. "Only if you call me by my name, Joshua; the other thing makes me sound as old as Harriet, and she's ancient."

That was her older sister who was all of twenty years of age.

It was agreed. They went through a set of country-dances, and then she said, "That was lovely. I do hope we can repeat it later."

James came to interrupt. "I think this is my dance, Melissa."

"Is it?" she said, peering at her dance card. "No, there's nothing written here. Oh, I see, Michael sent you…" She wrinkled her nose.

Joshua thanked her for the dance and moved away. Clearly, Michael thought his sister was too much in his company. The last thing he was going to do was harm a friendly little soul like Melissa. Still she could not be too careful.

They met for another dance, followed by refreshments. Melissa was in her element, piling up her plate with lobster patties and sweet cakes. Joshua counted three of each type, and realised that the excitement of the moment had made her feel hungry.

"Do you know," she said in a low voice. "I've never met a rake before. You are not quite what I imagined, but I suppose there are all sorts."

Joshua almost choked on his drink of fruit punch. "I'm sorry to disappoint you, Melissa, but I… am… not… a… rake." He mouthed the words.

"No, of course you're not," she said, soothingly, "but I hope you don't mind if I pretend when I go back to school. Nothing exciting ever happens to me, whereas everyone knows you have been on the Grand Tour to Italy."

It was obvious that lack of excitement was the real reason why Melissa disobeyed her father and wore breeches to groom her horse. It was lucky for everyone that she wasn't caught out. Maybe girls weren't so different after all.

Outwardly, people gave the impression of having forgotten the incident, but Joshua knew it was already circulating as the latest on-dit. He hoped the news would not reach Holkham. That was the last thing he needed.

Who would have thought he would meet Charlie Cobarne on a visit to Kings Lynn? Where could he go to avoid him?

CHAPTER 40

The visit to a bone mill at Narborough was the perfect antidote for the disastrous weekend at Lynn. It started well, with Michael Gransden driving James in his gig, and Joshua riding his horse. Michael's parents welcomed them into the family circle, and the bonhomie continued until they visited the local assembly rooms. Then it went horribly wrong, and once again, a woman rescued Joshua. If he were not careful, it would become a habit.

The vile stench of boiling bones that assailed his nostrils was nothing to the accusation of having ravished a young woman. Joshua would have accepted the charge had it been true, or the female in question been anyone but Sophie Cobarne. The only thing for which she qualified was being young, but a lady she certainly was not.

Joshua stood watching the process of skimming fat from the boiling liquid.

"What will that be used for?" he asked.

"Grease for coaches and cartwheels," came the reply.

"So nothing is wasted," he said. "What happens to the bones now?"

"They be chopped up and then ground down smaller and milled into dust." The whole process sounded so simple.

The same man told him that when whaleboats came into Lynn, there was a constant supply of barges loaded with bones, on the River Nar between the blubber factory at Lynn and the Narborough bone mill.

Having watched the process, Joshua moved on to the Narborough bone shed to collect a cartload of bonemeal in bags for the Home Farm at Holkham.

He rode his horse back at the pace of the rambling cart, with his mind turning to the sound of cartwheels. When it was dry, his thoughts reflected the spring weather, with happy memories of his stay at Holkham.

Luckily, the rain held off until they were halfway home. Joshua's waterproof coat seemed too warm to wear. Then the April storms came from nowhere, sharp, sudden and drenching, and his clothes were wet before he could find sufficient shelter to don his cape.

The driver carried on regardless. He was well prepared with a broad brimmed hat, waterproof cape, and the cartload covered with sheeting.

After that, Joshua pressed his hat firmly on his head and endured the discomfort of the over-garment, for no sooner did he think to remove the coat than he needed it again. Underneath it all, his jacket and shirt were damp, but he was hot, so they would probably steam dry by the time he returned home, and smell abominably.

He rode on, cursing the fact that in Norfolk the rain fell sideways. He felt miserably uncomfortable, and his thoughts turned sour, trying to find an apt description to fit Sophie Cobarne's behaviour.

She was a *harlot, baggage, strumpet and wanton.* His mind continued its search – *trollop, hussy, slut, whore…* There were not enough words in the Lexicon, and it did not make him feel any better.

Whatever precipitated her action, Joshua knew he had not encouraged her to think it was welcome. Now, he was in the devil's own coil. According to her brother, she had delivered a child. It was obvious Charlie blamed him for her condition, whereas Joshua knew that it was not his, but to whom else might it belong? That was the unknown factor.

Things were not the same after the visit to Lynn. Although Joshua met his fellow students, there was an edge to Michael Gransden's civility, and he spoke only when it was necessary.

Joshua could not blame him. Charlie had poisoned their minds. He tried not to let it bother him. In a few more weeks, he would be going home to Linmore. First, he must ascertain the date of departure and make travel arrangements.

The visit to Egmere farm could not have come at a better time. Mr Danby was a tenant farmer, with the reputation of running the best four-course-rotation on the estate. Although Egmere was only a few miles from Holkham, Joshua lived for three weeks in the farmhouse with the farmer and his family. It was a welcome relief.

On the first weekend, he rode his horse to the nearest fishing village. He took care to avoid the cottages by the harbour, and set off to walk across the mile-long sea wall, built by the Holkham estate when they reclaimed the salt marshes from the sea.

Everything must have looked different then. There would have been no pasture meadows within the wall, and the harbour would have been on the sea front, instead of being a mile inland along a well-dredged channel, dependent on the tides. An effect caused by the silted bay.

At the beginning of May, he travelled to Holkham to join what he anticipated would be his last group meeting in the estate office. Michael and James were civil to him in Mr Blakeney's presence, but the atmosphere was strained when the agent asked him to discuss his findings at Egmere.

Joshua did so with pleasure. He had spent many hours exchanging viewpoints with the workers of an enlightened tenant farmer, and came away enriched by the experience. He did not need the approval of his colleagues. The agent understood his reasons for so doing, and on a previous occasion, Mr Coke told them of the time when he joined the workers in the woodland, and learned a great deal about the woodsman's lot. That was all the endorsement he needed.

As the meeting ended, Mr Blakeney turned to Joshua.

"I have received a letter from Mr Coke, telling me that he has agreed with your father for you to remain here until July. Mr Norbery will be coming to the sheep shearings, so it seems an appropriate time for you to complete your studies."

"Thank you, sir." Joshua could see the looks of astonishment darting between his fellow students. So apparently could the agent.

"Does your father know Mr Coke socially?" Michael could not forbear to ask.

Before Joshua could speak, the agent interceded. "Yes, indeed. Mr Thomas Norbery is a parliamentary representative for the county of Shropshire."

Michael Gransden's eyes widened as the implication dawned.

"Oh, I didn't know – nor did James. That's excellent news, Joshua," he babbled. "I mean, it will be splendid having you here for longer. I must tell my father. He is sure to be coming in July, and will want to meet him."

It seemed strange that a few days ago, Joshua was virtually a pariah, and now, because of his father's political connections, he was socially acceptable.

"Yes," he said with a wry smile. "I'll be sure to introduce them."

In June, they heard news that obscured everything else. There was joy and celebration in the air. Church bells rang out, announcing the war in Europe was over, and everyone knew of the signing of the Peace Treaty at Amiens.

The discovery of Joshua's connections so changed Michael Gransden's demeanour, he could not wait to issue the next invitation.

"Let me know when you next come to the shearings, Joshua. You must stay with us at Lynn, and I'll travel to Holkham with you."

It was one thing for Joshua to be the son of an obscure country squire, but for Mr Coke to acknowledge his father was another. Life was indeed strange.

"You made quite an impression on the ladies," Michael said. "Mother would be very happy to see you again, and Melissa hasn't stopped talking about you either. She's apparently told her friends, and they all want to meet you."

Joshua returned a non-committal answer. He could imagine Melissa's reason for the invitation, particularly after their previous conversation. The trouble with visiting Kings Lynn was that he ran the risk of seeing Charlie Cobarne again.

Lady Gransden's enthusiasm was something else. His life was complicated enough without being included in plans for her daughter's future. Melissa was a nice girl, but she was too young to think of marriage. Joshua was glad that he confined his response to her tale of woe, to advice not action; otherwise he might have found himself leg-shackled to the entire family. He couldn't imagine having a worse father-in-law than Sir John Gransden. His interference would be intolerable.

Holkham – July 1802

"Sir John's here, Norbery, where's your father?" Michael Gransden shouted as he climbed the stables staircase.

It was the final day of preparation before the opening that marked the Holkham sheep shearings. Sir John Gransden had travelled, as Michael took care to tell Joshua, *all the way from Kings Lynn*. What was a mere thirty miles compared to the distance from London that his father had to travel?

Joshua took an exasperated breath, choosing his words. "I showed you the note from Mr Coke last week, which said that my father would be here by tonight, Michael, and I've heard nothing to the contrary," he said, hoping that there would be no more delays. If there were, he didn't know how he would return to Linmore with his belongings, but that was his problem to solve.

"Just make sure that he's here by the morning. Sir John is staying at the Ostrich, and is not best pleased at being kept waiting."

And no doubt he was driving the landlord crazy with his incessant demands.

All the pent-up dislike that Joshua had felt about Michael Gransden's father came welling to the surface and almost overflowed into anger. He stopped himself in time, knowing that in three days he need not see either Michael or his bombastic baronet of a father ever again. He felt sorry for Melissa with such relations, but they were not his concern. Nor would they ever be.

He took a deeper breath knowing it was anxiety he felt. The message he received, saying that the delay related to family business, was vague, so he assumed it must concern Aunt Winifred, his father's sister.

It was lucky that Mr Blakeney kept him well occupied and out of Michael Gransden's way, for the other boy's usefulness, such as it was, ended when Sir John's coach came trundling up the front drive to Holkham. And there was little to show for his presence before.

After a lone supper, Joshua saddled his horse and rode down to the beach for what he assumed would be the last time. It seemed like months since he had last been there, but the sight of the breakers rolling across the sand helped soothe his frayed nerves.

Ebb and flow…ebb and flow…ebb and flow… in a never-ending rhythm.

He was sorely tempted to kick off his boots and paddle in the water, but time was against him. Even in the hour since he left the stables his father might have arrived. At the thought he turned the horse, and sent it galloping up the drive.

The first groom that Joshua saw on reaching the stables was Ben Waters. "Is there any news?" he said as he threw himself out of the saddle.

"Not yet, Joshua, but we'll let you know as soon as Mr Norbery arrives."

"Thank you, Ben," he said. "I'll be leaving Holkham in a few days, but I'll see you before I go."

It was twilight when Joshua dragged his feet upstairs, and lay on his bed fully clad. All was quiet in the students' end of the stable block but the grooms were busy dealing with all the extra horses and coaches belonging to the visitors staying at the Hall, one of which should have been his father.

He heard Michael and James come stamping up the wooden stairs just after the stable clock chimed eleven. Half an hour later, the sound of a coach and horses heralded the arrival of probably the last visitor of the day.

He stood up, ready to shed his clothes and get into bed, when there was a tap at the door and Kegworth's quiet voice called, "Sorry to disturb you, Mr Joshua, but Mr Coke sent a message to say that your father has arrived at the Hall and will see you after breakfast."

Joshua had hardly opened the door when Michael Gransden bellowed,

"What's going on, Kegworth, that needs you to disturb us in the middle of the night?"

"Mr Norbery's arrived, sir."

"About time too; Sir John is waiting to meet him."

Then he'll have to wait like the rest of us until morning.

The valet looked at Joshua and shook his head.

"Thank you, Kegworth," he said. "I'll see you in the morning."

"You can go to sleep now, sir," said the valet.

Sleep was but a dream. The knowledge of his father's arrival brought back a poignant memory from when Joshua was a lonely little boy, at the time he was bullied by his brother and his mother looked on laughing.

In those far-off days, Joshua had always known that he was safe when his father came home, but he hadn't realised until the loss of his only friend, how much he needed the comfort of his father's presence. He felt it now.

Determined not to waste a single moment of the day, Joshua rose with the dawn chorus just after four, and took advantage of the hot water for shaving that Kegworth brought upstairs. He strode out of the stables and across to Holkham Hall for breakfast before Michael Gransden opened his eyes. There was a glorious sunrise over the sea. The air was fresh and all was well in his world.

Having eaten his fill, Joshua hurried above stairs to the big dining room where the visitors and guests were taking breakfast. A room with much coming and going, of talking and laughter with servants refilling the heated trays on the sideboards, and too much noise for private conversation.

He hesitated just through the door, and a servant came forward to enquire his purpose. "I'm looking for Mr Norbery of Linmore," he said.

The name was repeated to Mr Coke, sitting at the head of the table. He looked up and nodded. "Come in, Joshua, and join us," he said, indicating to the servant that a space be found at the table.

384

"Thank you, sir, but I have taken breakfast," he said, "I'd be obliged if I could speak with my father."

Tom Norbery left the table to greet him, but there were too many eyes on them for more than a firm handshake, and a hasty greeting.

"I'll wait for you in the anteroom, sir." Joshua said, struggling to suppress a surge of emotion that the sight of his father brought to the surface. He concentrated instead on the need to warn of the impending meeting with Sir John Gransden, in case the gentleman mentioned the fracas with Charlie Cobarne in Kings Lynn. That would spoil everything.

He left the room and stood, affecting to study a marble statue in an alcove, and wishing that he had taken more time to eat his breakfast instead of gulping it down. Now he felt it sitting in his belly like a weight, reminding him of what must be said.

A few minutes later, he heard the sound of a door opening, and realised that Tom Norbery was watching him. Before he could speak he found himself engulfed in a hug, reminiscent of the ones he received as a child. It was all too brief before he was released, and they both sniffed, his father similarly reaching for a handkerchief and giving his nose a determined blow.

"I'm sorry to disturb you, sir," Joshua said, rushing to explain. "I was concerned last night in case… there was a reason for the delay."

"It was the sheer volume of coaches on the road," said his father, "many of which were coming to Holkham."

"Did you travel all the way from London yesterday?" It was over a hundred miles.

"Yes, I came on the Mailcoach to Cambridge and hired a vehicle from there. Daniel Salter is bringing the Linmore coach in easy stages and will be here for the return journey." Tom Norbery frowned as he stood back to survey his son. "You look anxious. What else is bothering you?"

"Oh, nothing untoward," Joshua said, striving for a casual tone. "I must warn you that Sir John Gransden is awaiting an introduction. His son, Michael, is a fellow student. They invited me to stay with the family in Kings Lynn at Eastertime."

He led the way outside to the courtyard where the estate office was situated.

"Yes, Mr Coke mentioned me that my presence was in great demand," his father said in a dry tone. "A persistent young man by all accounts."

"Extremely," said Joshua, wishing that he could find a quiet place to tell his father about the meeting with Charlie Cobarne. Although Lady Gransden had dealt firmly with the incident, he couldn't be sure that Sir John would not blurt it out for all to hear.

Before he could say more, Michael Gransden's petulant voice interrupted. "Ah, there you are, Norbery, hiding as usual."

"Hell and the devil confound it." Joshua almost said the words aloud. And then, resigned to the inevitable, he turned to face the newcomers.

"Well met, Michael," he said in an even tone and continued with a slight bow, "Good morning, Sir John, I trust that you had a good journey from Lynn." When that had been established, he said, "Permit me to introduce you to my father."

Joshua knew that as long as one mouthed the right platitudes, society was satisfied. He mentally compared the two men as they exchanged greetings. Much as he expected, the baronet was all bluff affability when his father said, "I must thank you for your hospitality to my son, Sir John."

Then he held his breath and waited for the inevitable response.

"Think nothing of it, Norbery. The ladies were delighted to have him visit. They had a splendid time, apart from a minor contretemps at the local assembly. Not his fault, of course, more a case of young army officer celebrating some family event too liberally. One doesn't expect a gentleman to cause embarrassment in public, particularly in the presence of ladies; but the army seems to allow anyone to take a commission these days." He beamed at Joshua and said aside, "My lady wife sent you this missive with her compliments, young man." He extracted a folded sheet of paper from his pocket.

"Contretemps…with the army?" said his father, frowning at Joshua.

"Please give my thanks to Lady Gransden," Joshua said, feigning deafness. He could feel everyone's eyes on him as he broke the seal and perused the contents, and could almost hear Lady Gransden's imperious voice speaking the words. *Mr Norbery, you will be pleased to know that the unfortunate episode was satisfactorily resolved. Colonel Eccleshall discovered the culprits and delivered a sharp scold about their social responsibilities to the regiment, before they were dispatched forthwith to the Low Countries for active service. I have no further knowledge of their fate.*

Joshua carefully refolded the letter and placed it in his pocket. So Charlie Cobarne was in the Netherlands. He took cold comfort from the thought, knowing that active service meant going into a battle in which Charlie might have fallen. And yet, he sensed that his old adversary was still alive, waiting to be faced on another occasion.

With difficulty, he forced a smile and repeated his thanks. "I am indebted to Lady Gransden for the information, sir."

All the time he could feel his father's gaze on him but nothing was said until the Gransdens' had moved away. "Would you care to enlighten me about the event, Joshua?"

He took a deep breath. "I saw Charlie Cobarne in Kings Lynn. I heard him say that he was celebrating his sister's safe delivery from childbirth."

"From your expression, I deduce that he did not keep his distance."

"No," said Joshua, unable to spare his father the pain that the knowledge would bring. "He took a savage delight in denouncing me as his sister's assailant and denigrating Linmore."

Tom Norbery frowned. "Did many people hear him say this?"

"There were a few newcomers signing the admission book in the assembly rooms vestibule, but Lady Gransden's entrance stopped the gossip, and the soldiers disappeared before their commanding officer entered the building. Colonel Eccleshall is married to Lady Gransden's sister. You may read her letter if you wish," he said, rummaging in his pocket.

Tom Norbery glanced at the paper. "This explains why Charlie was sent post-haste to Europe," he said, "and the reason his sister asked me to stand proxy as godfather for the child in his absence."

"Is she married?" Joshua said, reluctantly bringing Sophie to mind.

"Yes, to an older man in business," Tom Norbery said, and promptly changed the subject. "You'll be pleased to know that Ed Salter has made a good recovery."

That will keep her in order, Joshua thought sourly. Aloud he said, "I'd like to have Ed as my personal groom."

His father nodded. "That's an excellent idea. I think he is well suited to the post."

Joshua felt a huge wave of relief sweep over him, knowing that his father was aware of the truth. No doubt Aunt Winifred was instrumental in finding Sophie Cobarne a husband. It tied up some of the loose ends, but gave him no satisfaction, for he sensed that much was left unsaid.

There was, however, little time for further discussion on the subject.

For the next three days, Joshua threw himself into his work at the sheep-shearings. Talking, listening to visitors' queries and making other folk welcome. Having escaped from Michael Gransden, he met up with James Inglethorpe, whose father, a retired army colonel, was as dissimilar to Sir John Gransden as anyone could be. He came straight to the point.

"Mr Coke told me that you have acted as my son's mentor, Mr Joshua. I am obliged to you for not leading him astray, as can happen when young men are away from home for the first time."

Joshua smiled, and caught James's eye. "I did what I could to help him settle into the work, sir."

"He speaks well of you, young man; more so than the other frippery character."

Joshua acknowledged the compliment and moved on with his father, intending to make his way around the estate workers to whom he wished to say farewell.

On the second day, he renewed his acquaintance with Jack Syderstone and Harry Bircham, the young men who helped him to settle on his arrival at Holkham.

"Have you seen any ghostly apparitions recently?" Harry asked in a teasing tone aside, while their respective fathers were deep in conversation on agricultural matters.

"No, only that one occasion," Joshua said, with a rueful smile, "I never could find that particular tavern again." The excuse rolled off his tongue, but it was easier to imply that he'd tried and failed, than explain the reason why he hadn't ventured off the beaten track. Drinking alone made him maudlin, and to take Michael Gransden would have been more penance than pleasure.

"And have you…?" he said.

The anxious glance, which Harry cast in his father's direction, warned Joshua that wenching was not a good topic of conversation at the present time. Jack, standing beside them, lowered an eyelid and grinned. Joshua nodded his understanding and they parted company with a cheery wave.

On the final evening, he sat with his fellow students and heard Mr Coke describe them as fine young men and commend their unstinting dedication to their work.

"Tom Norbery's son, especially, has surpassed our expectations, and set the standard for future students. I have no doubt that, whatever Joshua does in the future, he will give of his best. Moreover, I hope he will come back to Holkham in future years to tell us what use he has made of his apprenticeship."

Joshua could have wept, seeing the look of pride on his father's face, and for knowing he had redeemed himself in Mr Coke's good opinion.

Then, in front of the assembled guests, Mr Coke said, "I thought it would be appropriate, considering we have given prizes for excellence in farming and stockbreeding, for an award to be given to Joshua Norbery, who will be leaving us tomorrow. I am sure you will all join me in wishing him luck for the future."

To the sound of applause, Mr Blakeney beckoned Joshua to go forward to receive a gift from Mr Coke. It was a brass capstan clock with barometer, and a framed copy of the set of rules from the agent's office, written in meticulously neat copperplate writing, dedicated to the memory of Mr Coke's late wife, Jane.

"I think Joshua deserves this, because he has learned the value of these better than anyone," Mr Coke said with a smile.

Indeed, he had.

CHAPTER 41

Morning came all too quickly, and there were still three things to do before Joshua was ready to leave. He went to see Kegworth first, to express his thanks, and bestow a generous remuneration for the many services the Gransden valet rendered him.

As they talked, the man said, "I don't reckon Mr Michael will keep me on as a valet once he's finished here, sir."

"Why not?" said Joshua. "You do the job well. I've been more than pleased with the work you did for me."

"Ah, yes, sir, but you're a different person to Mr Gransden. It's not just the cut of the clothes that makes a gentleman – it's in the blood, like a thoroughbred."

Joshua could scarcely poach a servant from the Gransden household, but he could show appreciation in a practical sense, so he gave written directions to contact him at Linmore Hall. "If ever you need a testimonial for another job, you can apply to me."

"Thank you, sir. I might just do that. My grandmother had some relations in Salop, so it could be that I'll visit your county."

Then he found Ben Waters, the young groom who made him welcome at the outset, but before he could open his purse, the groom said, "There's no need for that, Joshua; your father's seen to everything. He's a real gent like Mr Coke."

"Then please accept my thanks," he said, offering his hand, "for I am truly grateful for your support."

After that there was only one thing left to do. The recollection led his feet to the laundry in the hope of seeing the laundress, Mary-Anne. He could not leave without knowing what happened to Tess. Irrespective of whether the child belonged to her late husband, as Mr Coke averred, he wanted to know.

When Joshua entered the laundry building, various members of staff looked up from their work to wish him well. As he thanked the women for their good wishes, a voice chirped up from the back of the group. He recognised the girl who had scolded him about the dirty washing.

"Ooh… Look at him in his fine clothes," she said, nudging her friend. "If I'd known he were a gentleman when he came here with that dirty owd smock-frock, I'd have taken his clothes home to wash, special like. Nice young man like that."

"Never mind about the work clothes, Gertie," another woman said with a chuckle, "I'd have taken him home with me, for there's nobody like him within miles of here, saving Mr Coke."

The other women joined in the laughter. Joshua flushed, as he recalled how the girl's action affected his response to other things.

"That'll do, girls," a gentle voice interceded. "Go back to your work. You're embarrassing Mr Norbery."

When Mary-Anne spoke, the other workers cheerfully returned to their work areas. She moved forward to Joshua's side.

"I'm sorry about that, sir," she said. "They don't mean any harm. I think it was intended as a compliment."

In that moment, Mary-Anne's likeness to her sister was particularly marked, the sand-brown hair, hazel eyes, and quiet acceptance of life.

Joshua waited until the other women moved away, before he said, "Mary-Anne, may I speak with you, in private."

She made no demur, and they went outside the building, to a grassy area where washing lines of bedlinen dried in the breeze.

He stood for a moment, pondering how best to phrase the question to which he wanted an answer. In the end, the words just tumbled out.

"Has your sister delivered her baby?"

She looked surprised, and pleased. "It's kind of you to ask, sir. Tess had a fine little boy, about a couple of months ago."

Mary-Anne was brimming over with pride at her sister's achievement.

"There's not much of Ned Dereham to see in him yet, but Tess isn't worried. To be honest with you, he was an ugly sort of a chap. But I mustn't speak ill of the dead."

He hardly dared continue. "What has your sister named him?"

"Well, sir," Mary-Anne looked sideways at him, "that's the strange thing. I thought that having lost her husband, she would have named the child after him. But no, she picked up the Good Book, and found a name there."

391

"And what did she decide?"

"Joshua. I don't know what made her choose that name, when there were so many others," she said, shaking her head.

"My name is Joshua," he said, striving for a casual tone.

"Ah, then maybe I mentioned it to Tess in passing, and she likened it to the child. Yes, that must be it." The laundress seemed pleased with the conclusion she reached.

Joshua looked away, his heart singing. It did not matter now to whom the baby belonged; he knew Tess would remember him. He turned back to face Mary-Anne, knowing what he must do.

"I wonder if you would be good enough to do something for me. There's an old tradition in my home county of giving a purse of money to a newborn child, which is supposed to be lucky. I would like to give something to your sister for the baby. I hope she won't be offended."

"Oh, no, sir; Tess is not the kind to take offence." She stopped, as if deliberating about something, and then said, confidentially, "It's a good thing she did come back to work at the Hall, for it's almost a year since Ned Dereham died. This time she can marry a decent man with a cottage, who'll look after her and the baby."

He looked stunned. "Your sister is to remarry…?"

"Widows don't stay single long, sir. She knew Jim Dunbar years ago, and might have married him the first time, but father didn't approve of a gamekeeper, him being a bit of a poacher on the side, before he took up fishing."

Bemused, Joshua bestowed the promised gift and left her.

Having said his farewells, Joshua climbed into the Linmore coach, and as he sank back against the comfortable squabs of the seat, he breathed in the familiar smell of leather, feeling nostalgic. It made him anxious to see Aunt Jane and tell her all his adventures – well, not everything. Some things it was better not to divulge. He was glad he did not mention Tess in his letters, and there was no reason now. Mary Anne's news had surprised him, but he was glad that Tess would have a better life married to Jim Dunbar, than with her second husband. He did, however, wonder what Dunbar would think of her choice of the baby's name.

Meeting his father's gaze across the coach, Joshua decided that he wanted to explain more about the events at Kings Lynn. "I think that you

392

would have liked Lady Gransden," he said. "She reminded me of Aunt Winifred."

"I can't fault her on that," said his father, "but I noticed that her husband had similar mannerisms to Lord Cardington."

"That was my impression also, sir," Joshua said, glad to share his thoughts.

"I am curious to know how this formidable lady dealt with the situation."

Joshua could still visualise the scene, with amazing clarity.

"She swept into the vestibule scolding; saying that the crowd of onlookers was preventing Colonel Eccleshall from entering the building. The mention of his name was enough to vanquish even the boldest soldier. They all disappeared, dragging Charlie Cobarne with them." He revelled in the knowledge of their discomfiture.

"And then…?"

"She insisted that I escorted her around the periphery of the assembly rooms, and dared anyone to challenge her supremacy. It was a kindness I didn't expect from a stranger, but she implied that it was as much for her benefit as my own."

"So the evening went on as before?"

"I wasn't sure if anyone would want to dance with me, but Melissa, that's one of Michael's sisters, asked to bring our first dance forward. After that, no one refused to acknowledge me." He thought about her comments over supper and smiled to himself.

"Clearly she is her mother's daughter."

"More so than her father," Joshua said. "She's only about sixteen."

"Aunt Jane was that age when I first met her," his father said softly.

Joshua glanced out the window and tried to remember how many years had passed since he had travelled alone with his father. Far too many and there hadn't been a single time in his adult life without Charlie and Sophie Cobarne being with them. He hadn't thought like that at the time but he did now.

He looked back and found his father watching him. "I'm looking forward to going home," he said, feeling the need to say something. "Holkham is a wonderful place, but it's not the same as Linmore."

It wasn't what he wanted to say, so he closed his eyes, and then opened them again, anxious not to miss anything. As they drove past the end of the lake, he gazed towards the icehouse atop the grassy slope, and the next thing he knew, they were trotting up the rise towards the obelisk, built in direct line with the Hall.

"Can we stop for a few minutes, please?"

The coachman slowed as soon as his father hammered on the roof with his cane. Joshua climbed outside, wanting to take a final look down the long sweep of the drive towards the Hall.

He stood for a long moment, committing everything to memory. Holkham was a perfect example of the Palladian design, with the trees and lake stretching into the distance through the park. Then there was the stable block, out towards the walled garden and the church on the hill. He felt a rush of emotion, knowing he would miss this place. It was as familiar now as Linmore.

Realising it was time to move on. Joshua climbed back into his seat. He felt the coach sway as it gathered pace down the long slope, past the turn to the great barn, until it slowed again on the approach to the south lodge.

His last glimpse of Holkham was the view back to the obelisk as the coach turned through the archway; a poignant moment, when he closed his eyes and let the memories wash over him…

Tom Norbery felt inordinately proud – and relieved that Joshua had justified Mr Coke's trust in his ability. When he left for Holkham, Tom did not know how it would end, whereas Jane, knowing Joshua so well, never lost faith.

Last year, he felt devastated by the break-up of the family. He knew Charlie felt betrayed, and Joshua similarly shocked by Sophie's behaviour.

If only he, Tom, had warned Joshua of her obsession in advance, maybe they could have avoided the disaster that culminated with Ed Salter's injury. Thankfully, it was not fatal, but it might well have been.

It never occurred to anyone that she would precipitate a crisis of such magnitude. Seeing her in London, Tom knew she realised what she had done, but was helpless to change the outcome. Their talk before her marriage proved that.

Poor Sophie; it was the first time he had known her to rush her fences. How mortifying for a rider with her accomplishments to take a fall.

Considering the uproar at the time, Tom was pleased everything worked out so well. Millie was safely married, so there was no need to mention her new addition.

Looking at Joshua, facing him on the opposite side of the coach, Tom saw sadness in his face at leaving Holkham. More than that, it showed a new maturity and determination around the mouth. The sorrowful boy who left home had gone, and the man he would be emerged.

Similarly, his build had changed. The black coat he wore fitted snugly across the shoulders, evidence of muscular strength acquired doing physical work. He felt gratified, hearing of Joshua's determination to gain practical skills, which ensured he would be a landowner with the knowledge to do things the right way. With him in charge, Linmore's future was safe.

His mind drifted to other things. Who could have foreseen a meeting between Joshua and Charlie Cobarne in Kings Lynn? Tom had seen him at Sophie's wedding, and once in uniform after Christmas, when he was in London, accompanying his sister and her husband to a social function. Their meeting was rigidly formal, partly, he suspected, because of Charlie's scarcely concealed embarrassment.

He was glad Sophie greeted him with undisguised friendship, her pregnant state carefully disguised in the folds of her flowing robe. In the spring, he received a hastily scrawled letter, telling of her safe delivery of a daughter; and recently a request for him to stand proxy for Charlie at the baptism, which his military duties prevented him attending.

Tom was happy to oblige, and gained the reassurance he needed, that Linmore played no part in the procreation of Sophie's child. There were too many months between. Equally, its healthy size did not fit the dates of her marriage, so whoever fathered the child must have known her in the biblical sense whilst she lived at Cavendish Square. Winifred was right in her assertion, but who was it?

He sat, alternating between reading Joshua's work diary, watching his son in repose, and marvelling at how like Jane he was. One day soon, they must tell him, but it was too complicated to give a hasty explanation, and Jane would want to be with them. Their son needed her reassurance he was not the one born out of wedlock – that they had done things the way they had to protect Caroline. Now she was married, things were different.

Across the coach, Joshua roused from sleep and looked around.

"Where are we?" he said. "This looks like the road to Fakenham."

Tom nodded, and as they passed through the village, he said, "I trust you've not had any more financial embarrassments?"

"No, sir," Joshua hastened to reassure. "Michael and James, the other students, were keen card players, but I felt it best to refrain. I spent the time completing my work book, or writing the occasional letter."

"Mm, yes, so I see," said Tom.

A look of dismay crossed Joshua's face as a folded sheet of paper floated to the floor from the front cover piece of his diary. He lunged forward to intercept, but Tom swooped down and scooped it up in his hand. His eye caught the name.

"Lady Rosemary Chervil?" he said. "Is she one of the Kenchester-Chervils?"

From Joshua's look of embarrassment, Tom realised he had strayed into uncharted territory. His manner was different to when he spoke of Melissa Gransden, to whose mother Tom intended writing a letter of thanks on his son's behalf.

"Yes, sir," he said. "I… um… we met Lady Rosie, with her grandmother, the Dowager Lady Kenchester at the Embassy in Athens. They were en route from India, and travelled with us to Rome."

Lady Rosie? Tom's brows raised in surprise. "I had not realised you moved in such august circles. The Kenchester ladies are reputed to be notoriously select in their choice of company."

Joshua's explanation became increasingly confused.

"Lady Kenchester was a nervous traveller, and Lady Rosie was grateful to Sergeant Percival for helping her grandmother board the ship to Rome. We failed on two occasions, and might have been forced to remain in Athens for the winter."

Tom felt a bubble of mirth rising inside. If Joshua was on such terms of familiarity to call the lady by what would be a pet name, then this was more than a mere flirtation. Maybe, a word with Percival would elicit more information.

The amusement in his voice deepened.

"I am delighted Percival was able to be of service to the lady. A formidable matriarch, if her son is to be believed."

"You know Lord Kenchester, sir?" Joshua looked aghast.

"Of course, Joshua, I am acquainted with any number of peers in the House of Lords. Lady Rosemary must be his…"

"His eldest daughter, I believe, sir, but she lives with her grandmother."

Tom nodded, knowing that Winifred had mentioned her name in connection with Gus Pontesbury.

"Yes, I recall hearing of her before. I think she was betrothed, but left her bridegroom-to-be almost at the altar steps. It caused quite an upset to the family at the time. That must have been when her grandmother took her into care."

"I see," Joshua said.

"If I had known of your prior acquaintance with the lady, I could have introduced you to her father at Holkham, when we took breakfast together. He would have answered your questions. If you wish, I can frank this and send it to Lord Kenchester's home, requesting him to forward it to his daughter?

"No… Thank you, sir." Joshua thrust his hand out to retrieve the letter.

Tom smiled as he replaced the letter in the diary, and handed it to Joshua. He had teased him enough.

Clutching the book in his hands, Joshua closed his eyes and then opened them again. "Where are we going?" he said. "This isn't the road to Peterborough?"

"No, it's the one to Thetford, where we will stay tonight," said Tom. "Tomorrow, we will head towards London and from there to France. Aunt Winifred has taken the lease on a house in Paris, and invited us to spend a few weeks with the family."

"Paris?" said Joshua. "But I thought…"

"The city is open to visitors again," said Tom. "Everyone has been flocking there since the Peace Treaty was signed. My colleague, Charles Fox, assured me that he was going. I expect we will see him at the embassy functions."

Seeing Joshua's look of bemusement, he elaborated further. "I always intended you to see more of Europe, but the war curtailed it. This visit is by way of compensation. You must have some incentive for when you take over management of the estate."

Joshua stared. "What do you mean… take over?"

"In the light of your experiences at Holkham, I have little doubt there will be changes you will want to introduce. It will be your responsibility to see they work. When you were saying farewell to your friends, Mr Coke advised me to let you put your stamp on Linmore, and that is what I intend. Does it meet with your approval?"

"Yes, thank you, sir," Joshua said. "In fact, Mr Blakeney helped me to develop a plan for the estate, which you might like to consider."

"You can tell me about it en route to the Channel coast."

After a few minutes' thought, Joshua continued. "What about the peace? Do you think it will hold?"

"One must hope so, although there are dissenters who feel we gave too many concessions. Only time will tell."

"What happens about the army at such times? Do they go home?"

Having read Lady Gransden's letter, Tom guessed that Joshua was wondering about Charlie's whereabouts in Europe and the likelihood of them meeting.

"Sergeant Percival will know," he said. "We'll ask him when we see him in London. He awaits us at Cavendish Square, and will accompany us to Paris."

"How is he?" said Joshua. "It will be good to see him again."

"He is extremely well since his marriage and becoming the father of a daughter."

Joshua looked astounded. "But when did he marry – and to whom?

"It was about the time that you went to Holkham. He had lodged in the village for several months, next door to Dr Hawley, and came to an understanding with Miss Belinda, who is now Mrs Percival. Her brother gave them his blessing."

"I'm glad for them," said Joshua, "Gilbert told us about their previous connection and the reason for the rift between them. He said that Percival was a base-born son of Lord Chetton, of Neathwood."

"Don't despise Percival for that," said Tom, "for every family has a bastard in it somewhere. We certainly did at Linmore, though not of my making."

"Matthew said that I was a misbegotten brat," Joshua said in a tight voice, "but Fred Cardington told me that it was my brother who was the cuckoo in the nest."

"Frederick was right," said Tom, "but you need to understand how I came to be married to Kate." There seemed little point in calling her his wife.

"I returned from my Grand Tour in the summer of 'seventy five. A few months prior to that, Aunt Jane's father died, leaving his wife and family in debt. My father purchased the Hillend Estate to help the widow.

"I became aware of the situation, when I accompanied my father and brother to visit the bereaved ladies, but had little idea that he, who had been

398

widowed a dozen years, considered marrying the lady. I learned of this when she died, within the bereavement year, and left three daughters without a female relation to act as chaperone. That meant my father couldn't give them a home, so he ordered me to marry one of them."

"Did you know Aunt Jane before that?" said Joshua.

"Yes, but she was still in the schoolroom when Jack and I went away on our travels. Seeing her again, the choice was easy, but as we were both under age, I was compelled to wed another. Marriage to Jane would have served the family as well, but Elias Stretton, who purported to be guardian to the Littlemore sisters, refused permission. The reason became apparent when Matthew was born six-months later. Kate had needed a husband, and I, as the heir to Linmore, was the sacrificial lamb."

"What did your father… my grandfather say when he knew?" said Joshua.

"Rather than admit his complicity in foisting a bastard on Linmore, he tried to make me own Matthew as my son. When I refused, he blustered about annulment, but did nothing because of the scandal it would cause." Tom said in disgust, recalling the acrimony of an estrangement that had never been resolved.

After a few moments silence, in which he composed himself, Tom resumed the conversation in a different tone. "We were, however, speaking of Sergeant Percival and the old Lord Chetton, who died shortly after you returned from Italy."

"Did Percy know of this?" said Joshua.

"Yes," Tom said. "Jim Percival visited the sixth Viscount at Neathwood, a few days before he died, whilst the Honourable Robert Chetton was in London, gambling away what remained of his inheritance. One might say that the old gentleman had been waiting for such a visit, for it is said he died happy. I'm not privy to the details, but I understand that he gave Percival sufficient means to be independent of work although he continues to assist me at Linmore. That was why he could afford to marry. And now, his half-brother, the new Viscount, has also married."

"There must be something in the Linmore air," Joshua said.

"Robert Chetton had little choice in the matter, but I will tell you more of this over dinner. I think that we are on the approaches to Thetford."

The discussion gave Tom pause for thought. In the space of a few hours, he had told Joshua some of the Linmore family secrets, and learned of two different ladies of his son's acquaintance. One was a baronet's daughter, scarcely out of the schoolroom, and Lady Rosemary Chervil, whose connection with Joshua was infinitely more intriguing.

It was quite common for a young man to form a tendre for an older woman, but Lord Kenchester's daughter was not a member of the muslin company, which put a different complexion on the matter. Joshua was too young at present to think of marriage, but as the last of the Norbery line, it could not be long delayed.

There were aspects about Joshua's tour that Tom had overlooked in the aftermath of Matthew's death. Things he should have discussed with Sergeant Percival. Now he must tentatively raise the subject with his son without obviously prying.

Whereas, Miss Gransden's name had aroused no great response, the mention of Lady Rosemary brought an immediate reaction that suggested his son's feelings were involved. Why else would he have written her a letter, even if he was shy of sending it?

Unfamiliar with the Thetford hostelries, Tom would not have been surprised to have difficulty in acquiring rooms, but the mention of Mr Coke's name opened many doors and he had the feeling that other travellers might be incommoded. All he and Joshua required was a room each for the night and a tasty meal.

Instead he was given the best accommodation on offer, with a truckle bed for Jack Kilcot, who acted as valet, while Daniel Salter, the coachman, slept over the stables to look after the horses. Their presence reminded him of a journey to Ireland about which he could not speak with Joshua, for fear of breaking the spell.

A well-cooked dinner with courses of brown trout, capons and apple pie, followed by local cheeses and coffee took precedence over small talk, but sitting in a mellow atmosphere, induced by a particularly fine brandy, no doubt illicitly acquired from Gascony, Tom decided to return to the interrupted conversation about marriage.

There was no better time to discover Joshua's opinion on the subject, but it was his son who pre-empted the discussion.

"Were you aware that Sophie Cobarne was intimate with Robert Chetton?" said Joshua, making the words sound like an insult.

Tom chose to ignore the inference and guided the conversation the way he intended that it should go. "I expect that they had much in common on the hunting field," he said. "If you recall, he was another of the neck-or-nothing riders that she used to challenge over the hedges. His wife is a similarly accomplished horsewoman."

Eliciting only a grunt from his son in response, Tom plunged into the details.

"Robert Chetton married an heiress from Ireland. Her guardian, who was his godfather, left his fortune and racing stud to her, absolutely, on condition that she accepted the arranged marriage. She would have been a foolish lady to have declined, and risked losing her inheritance."

Tom had Joshua's full attention now. The brandy glass sat on the table untouched.

"Is that what happens in such cases?" He was clearly appalled by the notion.

"Yes," said Tom.

"What did Chetton have to say? He always seemed a care-for-nobody."

"It seems that they have a mutual interest in breeding horses. Had he refused, he would have lost Neathwood Park, which was mortgaged to the hilt. Her money saved it, and in return she has a title."

"So," said Joshua, "an arranged marriage was to his liking?"

Hearing the distaste, Tom said, "In our circles, Joshua, such arrangements are commonplace. Or at least, they were in my day."

"I'm not sure that would suit me," his son said, shaking his head.

Seeing his opportunity, Tom said, "If you discover that you have a preference for a lady – and I do speak of someone of our class – then I hope that you will feel able to tell me." He waited, seeing the secret smile playing on Joshua's lips.

"You speak of a lady, sir…?"

Tom smiled his understanding. "I think we both know that none of the working classes would enhance the position of Mrs Norbery of Linmore."

"Let us say of the gentry…or aristocracy?" Joshua persisted.

"If a lady of elevated birth was happy to live with you at Linmore – yes."

"But I can make my own choice?"

"Of course," said Tom. "You are well aware of the reason why I would never seek to influence your decision."

"It's unlikely to be for a year or two yet," said Joshua, "for I have a great deal to organise on the estate, but I'd like to explore the options in my own way."

"You may not choose to look locally for a bride. Go to London in the season and study the debutantes of the Marriage Mart."

Joshua shuddered. "You mean Almack's and all that sort of thing? I remember Caroline's season and it was ghastly," he said, "although it does have possibilities, for not all the ladies are straight out of the schoolroom. I mean, there are some who don't *take* at the first or second season…"

"So I believe," said Tom, reading between the lines, "and with you being young, maybe someone slightly older and wiser in the ways of the world would suit you better."

"Mmm," said Joshua, thoughtfully sipping his brandy. "Quite possibly…"

Tom went to bed happy, knowing that in having mooted the idea of marriage, he could see that Joshua was ready to give it his consideration. It was something to tell Jane on his return to Linmore.

He felt a deep sense of release in letting go the bitterness that he had carried for half his life. And the heartfelt joy of watching the dawning sense of understanding when Joshua realised that he was the legitimate heir to Linmore – and always had been.

There was more to tell his son, but it could wait until Jane was with them, for she was their strength and the reason for living. *Whereas he had been forced to accept a marriage of convenience, Tom knew that Jane would never allow it to happen to Joshua.*

Acknowledgements

I could not have written this work of fiction without the patience of my family and friends who have shared the time I have spent in Linmore Dale, giving me support and reading endless drafts. My thanks, also, to Doug, my editor and mentor, who has likewise guided my efforts – but is not responsible for any errors.

Lightning Source UK Ltd.
Milton Keynes UK
UKOW06f0317090915

258310UK00022B/332/P